Joy Martin was born in Limerick and is a descendant of the O'Brien family. She trained as a journalist and worked on Dublin's *Evening Press* – then moved to writing news for the Zambia Broadcasting Corporation and the BBC Home and External Services. She has also broadcast on radio in Ireland, Zambia and South Africa, and on British local radio stations. Now she lives in London and works as a freelance journalist.

Joy Martin is the author of *Twelve Shades of Black*, a study of the lives of the people of the townships around Johannesburg. *A Wrong to Sweeten* is her first novel.

JOY MARTIN

A Wrong to Sweeten

PARRAGON

First published in Great Britain by
George Weidenfeld & Nicolson Ltd 1987
Published by Grafton Books 1989

This edition published 1993 by
Diamond Books
77-85 Fulham Palace Road
Hammersmith, London, W6 8JB

Printed and bound in Great Britain by
BPCC Hazells Ltd
Member of BPCC Ltd

Excerpts from 'Oisin', and 'To Ireland in the Coming Times'
from *The Collected Poems of W. B. Yeats* reprinted by
permission of A. P. Watt Ltd on behalf of Michael B. Yeats and
Macmillan London Ltd.

Excerpts from *The Midnight Court* by Brian Merriman
translated by David Marcus, published by The Dolmen Press,
reproduced by permission.

Excerpts reproduced from *The Collected Letters of W. B. Yeats
Volume I 1865–1895* edited by John Kelly and Eric Donville
published by Oxford University Press, (1985).

For my husband, John

Acknowledgements

Research by the following writers proved invaluable to me in writing this book: Mainchin Seoighe, Olive Sharkey, Patrick Logan, Padraic O'Farrell and J. D. Williams.

J.M.

Know, that I would accounted be
True brother of a company
That sang, to sweeten Ireland's wrong,
Ballad and story, rann and song.

W. B. Yeats

1

Before he was fully awake, Dermot O'Brien was conscious of being happy, although he did not immediately realize precisely why. It was not, in any case, a frenzied exaltation, the kind of fervent euphoria that impelled him to leap out of bed and announce its advent to all and sundry, even if he was inclined to such excesses, but a quiet, restrained contentment, which hung around him like a heat haze and permitted his thin, inexorable lips to relax into a charming, ingenuous smile.

He yawned luxuriantly and stretched, so that the brass bedstead stridulated protestingly under his thin, fit body. He was just on six feet tall, with a head of thick, straight, dark-brown hair, astute blue eyes, and a fine-boned, aesthetic face that was very nearly handsome. At twenty-one, he was two years younger than his brother, Tom, the man responsible for his current state of serenity.

If Dermot had said to his mother, Fiona, or to either of his sisters, Mary and Carmel, that he was happy simply because he and Tom were planning to go riding, they would have wanted to know where the wonder lay in that, since the brothers rode over the fields of Crag Liath at some stage every day of their lives.

'But not *together* – that's the difference,' Dermot could have said to them. 'Most of the time, as ever, Tom is off with his friends, cavorting around the country, leaving me to the company of Tim-Pat Tierney in the stables and the three of you at the house.'

Most of the time, but fortunately not always. There were occasions, like last evening, when Tom, as it were, remembered the existence of his brother and made a benevolent gesture to him, suggesting a ride or a trip into Limerick or maybe a day at the races together.

'That will be fine with me,' Dermot would tell him then, because, of course, it *was* fine – and a great deal more. To be in Tom's company was to become a besotted and unresentful idolator, paying homage to and feeding off a gargantuan love of life, a contagious optimism and an unfailing *bonhomie*.

Sometimes Dermot likened him to an unbroken colt, inferring, correctly, that he was also wild, irresponsible and resistant to control. The phraseology was typical of the O'Briens, for they were obsessed with horses and hunting, having been taught to ride as soon as they could walk, and to assess a thoroughbred's potential before they had learnt to read and write, and it was characteristic of Dermot to make the criticism since Tom's carelessness offended his own meticulous nature. This perception of his brother's faults ran parallel to his need for Tom, diminishing it not at all. Others, less clear-sighted, just as needy, saw Tom as omnipotent and divine.

Well, thought Dermot, his own feet were firmly on the ground, even if he was still lying down this Saturday morning in May 1881.

His bedroom was small and sparsely furnished with a tallboy and wardrobe for his clothes, two tables and a dark, heavy rug making a half-hearted attempt to cover the floorboards. On the bigger table were his shaving mirror and safety razor, along with black plaister for cuts, carbolic tooth-powder, a pin for his scarf, a buttonhook, a shoehorn and his brushes and combs, all laid out in equidistant order, which made Tom hoot with derisive laughter. The scorn might hurt but it did not affect Dermot's propensity for the schematic. Harmony made him feel safe, a state that had never appealed to his brother.

Reaching out to the table beside his bed, he felt for his watch and, grimacing, consulted it: ten to seven and the sun calling him into the day. What was he doing, lingering under the bedclothes? He pushed them aside, and strode agilely across the room to thrust his head between the white lace curtains and fling open the window.

> Red sky at night, a shepherd's delight.
> Red sky in the morning, a shepherd's warning.

It had been red enough last evening, but now it was as blue as the Atlantic when a good mood was on it, and the air he was breathing was nectar itself. And it would raise the spirits of any man to look out on the splendour of glorious Crag Liath. Fifteen hundred acres of Ireland's richest land strewn out for the pleasure of his family at O'Brien's Bridge, in County Clare, eight miles from the city of Limerick. Land that made the O'Briens the envy of two counties, as they had been since their ancestors ruled as princes of Thomond, an area embracing the whole of County Clare, and large portions of the counties of Limerick, Tipperary and Waterford, from the tenth to the sixteenth century.

Of course, the O'Briens went back further than that – back, in fact, to Milesius, King of Spain, one of the princes who conquered and ruled over Ireland in 504 B.C. From Milesius was descended Brian Boru, King of Munster and later High King – *Ard Ria* – of all Ireland, who had perished while defeating the incumbent Danes in battle in the eleventh century. An ancestor to revere – a man well ahead of his time, who had constructed monasteries to promote learning in Ireland, and roads to help countrywide communication. He had understood the weaknesses of provincialism, and knew that the Danes would have power in Ireland as long as the country was divided into petty kingdoms and not united together against them.

Though Brian's death was the signal for ambitious chieftains to destroy with their rivalry and greed all hopes of true Irish nationalism, the powerful O'Briens continued to be influential throughout the centuries that followed, distinguishing themselves in battle, politics and the Church. And though some O'Briens became Protestants – William O'Brien, Earl of Inchiquin, and his successors formed part of the Protestant ascendancy that dominated Irish society for so many years – many more, and Dermot's branch of the family amongst them, stayed with the Catholic faith.

A unique family. A family destined to greatness. That was his conviction – and his creed.

For such a family, Crag Liath was an appropriate setting. It was two hundred and fifty years old and, naturally, it was named after an original O'Brien settlement, the one built by Lachtna, uncle of Brian, a few miles further on, along the road to Scariff. From his bedroom window Dermot could see the land, green and lustrous and splayed with the gold of marigolds and the white and gold of daisies. O'Brien land, all of it, and beyond it the blue-black hills of Clare.

From those hills you could see the house itself, nestled amongst trees. A sombre mansion, some said, but to Dermot, dignified and alluring – grey-stoned, flat-faced, with a superb oak front door that had its origins in the nearby woods on the Raheen estate where oak trees of much antiquity grew. The door boasted a smart Italian bronze knocker, in the shape of a man's head, and the big windows on either side of it were made of solid plate glass. When you were out in the garden, you thought that the heart of the house – warmer by far than its façade – looked out at you from those windows and made a request to you to come up the wide, low steps that ran from the vast sweep of the gardens.

Inside, Crag Liath *was* much more captivating, for the staircase hall had been painted an inimitable subdued orange, and it set off wonderfully the work of the landscape painter William Ashford of Birmingham, who had made Ireland his home. Over the staircase was a mural by an unknown artist – a depiction of a hunt, and who cared that the pink coats of the huntsmen clashed with the hue of the walls when the outcome was a blaze of vibrant colour?

The first owner of Crag Liath – another O'Brien – had seen to it that the drawing-room had a floor inlaid with satinwood and that the walls – traditionally painted rose – were further enhanced by Irish rococo plasterwork. The mantel, mainly of Italian marble, represented the Christ Child and angels, and there was a large gilt chandelier, which had been sent over from France.

The house was on a grand scale and there was even a secret passage, or so it was said, designed to help relieve past generations of O'Briens from the paying of excise duty on the French wines that were smuggled up to the house from the river, its entrance long since bricked-up but believed to have been in what was now the family boot cupboard. Two generations of footwear did not oust the mystique of what – possibly – lay behind rows of dingy shelves.

Up that passage, Tom insisted, a black sailor had once come in pursuit of one of the maids. Her own man had stabbed him to death on the stairs going down to the kitchen, so his ghost was in the house, even if no one had ever seen it.

And to think that, although he was an O'Brien through and through, Dermot had no rights to any of this glory! For he was deceiving himself when he maintained that the land was for the pleasure of himself and his family – it was not: it was for Tom's enrichment, and not a scrap for anyone else. It was Tom – not Dermot – who had inherited Crag Liath on the death of their father five years earlier. Tom was Master and it was his benevolence that permitted his younger brother to stay on at Crag Liath, and his mother and sisters, as well. Tom was rich while Dermot, by an accident of birth, was articled to a firm of solicitors in Limerick, and, by another mishap – that of being born into the Catholic branch of the family – was banned by Papal dictate from attending a university designed for his Protestant peers. One day – in the not-too-distant future, at that – it would be Tom's children, not Dermot's, that played in the apple orchard, whose ponies were stabled where his mounts had been, who would boast of the blood of Milesius running in their veins and have the land and the mansion to back up their claim. Tom's inheritance. While Dermot, humbled, was only second best . . .

He would not – could not – afford to think this way. Not today, with the sun beckoning and beguiling and the horses waiting and Tom himself on for a chat.

But was Tom even awake? It was unlikely. He had no sooner made last night's offer to Dermot than he had been out of the door, off to see his friend, Jamie Keegan, over at Killaloe, on who knew what kind of nefarious expedition. Jamie was a qualified vet, a good few years older than Tom, and a Protestant into the bargain. Bad company for Tom, according to their mother. She never said so to his face, for they were all under Tom's spell, frightened lest their criticism and concern result in loss of favour, in magic-deprivation. Not only that but, maybe, homelessness.

(But I will not think of that.)

No more dark thoughts. Discipline yourself. Get dressed. Unearth Tom from his bedclothes and his sunny soul will do the rest.

Fifteen minutes later, in breeches and boots, with the neck of his shirt left open, Dermot tiptoed along the landing, intent on waking Tom but no one else. The doors to his sisters' bedrooms were shut, although he could hear Carmel talking in her sleep, flirting, in a kind of way, with Andy Leahy, the man she was planning to marry.

The door to his mother's room, on the other hand, was wide open.

She called out, 'Who is it? Tom?' adding disappointedly, 'Oh, it's you, Dermot,' when he stopped in the doorway.

'I'm sorry, Mother. I didn't mean to wake you.'

'You did not. I have not been asleep.'

She sounded sorry for herself, the way she often did since his father had gone. She was a stout, handsome woman with Dermot's own hair gone grey. She had never been frail, always capable, bossy and confident, and self-pity did not suit her at all.

'You had a bad night then?'

'I did.'

Before she could expand upon this, Dermot, eager to be gone, intervened.

'I'm late waking Tom. We have a plan to go riding.'

'A plan to go riding with Tom!' she said caustically. 'You've little hope of that, I'd say, since his bed has not been slept in.'

'He didn't come home?'

Her announcement had wrung the happiness out of the morning, spreading her self-pity on to him. With it came a blast of the old, familiar disappointment that all too often followed arrangements made by Tom. As a boy, Dermot had cried his heart out every time his brother had let him down. As an adult, he had mastered the art of concealment, but the setback seemed no less.

'Maybe he's down in the stables.'

'Maybe he is,' said his mother, sounding as if he was not.

She was sitting on the edge of her bed with the bedspread round her shoulders like a shawl, obviously not having had a wink of sleep for worry.

'Go back to bed, Mother, and catch up on your sleep. I'll have a lookout for Tom.'

'Will you let me know if you find him?'

She had no intention of sleeping until Tom returned – that was obvious. He sighed, cursing his brother inwardly.

'I will. Don't worry. He'll be back all right.'

Brooding, he retraced his steps. What was it with

Tom that made him so indifferent to other people's feelings? It was not callousness; Tom was tender enough. He just seemed to float along from sensation to sensation on a cloud of happy-go-lucky spirits, oblivious of dull, inhibiting factors like work and duty and time. He paid scant attention to Crag Liath so that the estate seemed to more or less run itself. Worry that it did not do so effectively, that Tom would run it down or allow it to happen, plagued Dermot continually, but when he raised the subject, hinting that Crag Liath was nowhere near fulfilling its true potential, he found himself fobbed off with 'It's going on fine, just like it did when Father was alive.'

'*He* wasn't much of a one for work,' Dermot had said ruefully, while Tom edged away as he always did when there was something unpleasant to discuss – something that required an effort unconnected with the serious business of simply having fun.

Whereas I take after our hardworking mother, Dermot's mind ran on. It's we, not Father and Tom, who should have had the chance to manage Crag Liath.

There was another way Tom took after his father, and that was in the love of a dangerous wager. The toss of a coin or the turn of a card was to both of them an excitant. Hardly a day went by but Tom did not have a flutter on the horses or the dogs or have a plan for a hand of poker, and it did not matter to him that, in this field, he seemed to lose much more than he won.

Turning down the stairs to the kitchen, Dermot encountered Mary Markham, once nursemaid to all the children, now housekeeper at Crag Liath, coming up with a trayful of tea for his mother.

'She could do with that, I would say.'

17

The inference did not escape Mary Markham.

'I take it Master Tom is missing again,' she said, raising her eyes in despair, knowing Tom but, like the rest of them, offering no criticism of his ways. 'Himself is looking for you.'

'Tim-Pat?'

'In the kitchen. Putting back a huge feed and full of the way he's after taming that *angishore*, Mount Royal.'

'He is, is he?'

This was good news. Mount Royal, Dermot's grey charger, had been posing a problem for some time. Gentle in other respects, the horse had developed a habit of kicking in his stable at night, as if to make up for his habituary quietude at other times, so that he could not be safely stabled with another hunter. Tim-Pat had proposed curing him by nailing pads of hay covered with canvas to the parts of the box the horse could reach with his feet. Hearing no noise when he kicked thereafter, the puzzled Mount Royal seemed to have stopped the habit. As a test of his good behaviour, the groom had allowed Hero, Carmel's sturdy chestnut, to share a loose box with him the night before. The experiment seemed to have worked.

The click of the latch alerted Tim-Pat and he swung around, his mouth three-quarters full of fresh soda bread and butter. It was amazing how much he ate, without ever putting on a pound, though his appetite was not in itself surprising. The Tierney family had been evicted and forced to live on the roadside owing to their failure to pay rent to their landlord. A combination of malnutrition and tuberculosis had killed the rest of them off. Tim-Pat was the same age as Dermot, but he had been working for the O'Brien family for nearly nine years, ever since, as a waif and an orphan, he had turned up to beg and been taken into the house.

He was a bachelor with a pale, freckled face, crinkly yellow-red hair and heavy eyebrows to match it. His mouth was wide and capable of curling upwards into laughter – an irony, since there was deep bitterness inside of him and a terrible hatred of the English, whom he held responsible to a man for the fact that his family had perished homeless.

'I hear we've pulled it off,' Dermot hailed him, inaccurately, since none of the scheme for taming Mount Royal had come from himself.

Tim-Pat swallowed massively and his mouth curved into an arc of pure joy.

'Yerra, we have, Master Dermot. We've seen an end to his wickedness all right. Ah, sure, you'll have no problems with that fella from this day on.'

His happiness lay as much in giving to Dermot as in the satisfaction of a good job well done. Tim-Pat had an extraordinary rapport with horses but his devotion to Dermot was every bit as great. From the beginning, Dermot had gone out of his way to obtain the other boy's devotion. Having been himself the recipient of perpetual instruction from a potent army of parents and older siblings, he realized, in his relationship with Tim-Pat, his own deep and – of necessity – hidden need for power. Taking Tim-Pat under his wing was only partly altruistic, but it had paid off in terms of the love and loyalty it incurred. Tom might play fly-by-night with him, in more ways than one, but Dermot could bank on the fact that the groom, at least, would never let him down, and, at the same time, would do all in his power to restore his battered psyche.

'Have you finished your breakfast?'

Tim-Pat's wistful green eyes rested briefly on the half-finished loaf, before looking up to meet his own.

'Are *you* not hungry?'

'I'd like to get down to the stables,' said Dermot, power-revelling. 'I have an arrangement with Tom.'

'I'm your man so,' said Tim-Pat.

Small and lithe as a monkey, he was up and out the door, his breakfast forgotten.

Behind the house, beyond the two yards, the stables, flanked by the hand-ball alley, masked the poultry runs out of which came enough eggs for the household. Next to them were the pens in which Tom's fighting cocks swaggered and menaced and ill-naturedly bided time, and beyond them the apple orchard, where soft fruits also grew, and the vegetable garden and haybarns and sheds. You could look between the buildings and see the fields and the hills and conclude that you were half-way to Heaven already. It was Heaven enough for the tenants, Dermot thought. The attitude of the family to them had been benign even before Tom took over the estate. As soon as he did, half of them stopped paying rent altogether, and there were so many hand-outs in the way of food and loans, that you would have thought St Nicolaus of Germany had moved in on a semi-permanent basis. Yet there were other times, when a member of the family needed money, when Tom could get a shifty look in his eye and you got the distinct impression that it was not exactly there for the asking.

'Have you mucked out then?'

'I have indeed,' said Tim-Pat, ready to show willing.

'I don't suppose my brother showed his face in here before you came into the house?'

'He did not.'

Tim-Pat frowned. Loving Dermot, he, too, worshipped Tom and would not speak against him.

'Isn't it Mr Keegan that does be keeping him out till all hours, Master Dermot. He's a right go-by-the-road, if ever there was one, and him out of Trinity College and full of them heathen Protestant ways. Drinking and gambling! He'll scratch a beggarman's back yet.'

Smiling to himself at this prejudice – Tom needed no one to lead him astray and, in terms of the influence he wielded over Jamie in this respect, was the bane of the latter's much-neglected wife – Dermot strode ahead. Out of the corner of his eye he could see Bernie Lenihan, who helped in the kitchen, wending her way over the fields to work.

They were waiting for him, his pride and joy – his horses. Tim-Pat had already moved Hero back to his own box, to facilitate mucking-out. Mount Royal was alone and looking for company. He arched his great head over the stable door and looked at Tim-Pat beseechingly.

'Take me out!' pleaded the liquid brown eyes.

'Just now,' Dermot responded.

He scratched Mount Royal's forelock and the big horse shuddered with pleasure.

'Did you hear they've arrested Mr Thomas Brennan?' Tim-Pat asked.

'Is that so?'

'It was bound to happen after the brave speech he made against the power of landlordism. Wasn't he calling on the people to show that English coercive measures have no terror for them and that we should not lose sight of the principle for which we are struggling?'

'It isn't the first arrest of members of the Land League.' Dermot crossed to the tack-room and stretched out for Mount Royal's bridle and saddle, noting with pleasure that the saddlery was well-polished and the brass shining.

'Or the last.'

But Dermot was not interested in talking about the land war. For the sake of harmony, he kept his opinions to himself. In fact, he thought the Land League a bunch of trouble-makers whose actions made it ever more difficult for a moderate prime minister to introduce legislation to the ultimate advantage of the Irish tenant farmer. Tom held a more passionate, more nationalistic viewpoint. It was strange the way two brothers could be educated in England – at Downside College – but only one of them end up appreciating the Gladstonian position.

None of it, anyway, was as interesting as horses. Or, for that matter, as girls.

Like that girl he had laid eyes on at the last meet of the Foxhounds before the season ended. Striking she was – not really pretty but with something about her – her big, deep-set eyes and the contrast between her pale, oval face and her dark hair (the tendrils creeping out from under her riding-hat) that made you look at her again. And that strange moment when he realized that, although she was a superb horsewoman who enjoyed the wild joy of the chase, her attitude changed into virtual mourning when it terminated in a kill.

'Strange indeed,' he said softly to Mount Royal and, pushing open the stable door, he led him into the yard.

'Be the Holy Man, but isn't that himself!'

Startled back to the present, Dermot's heart leapt like a hunter over a fence.

'Do you mean Tom?'

'I do. Do you see him there – on the other side of the meadow?'

Happiness flooded back. Tom, riding Sprightly, his six-year-old bay, was cantering easily towards them, returning to the fold, even if he was in no great hurry to do so. As he drew nearer, Tim-Pat's mouth curled demonically.

'Shall we give him a bit of his own back, Master Dermot?'

'How do you mean?'

But Tim-Pat only said, enigmatically, 'I'll make him scratch where he doesn't itch all right,' smiling his demonic smile.

The bay, with the curly-haired tousled rider, drew closer – was, now, within earshot, and Tim-Pat, pursing his lips, emitted a curious, long drawn-out whistle, piercing, painful.

Dermot flinched. The effect on Sprightly was dramatic. The bay halted so abruptly that Tom, jogging along unwarily, was very nearly thrown. Recovering his balance skilfully, he was in control again when Sprightly, seemingly spell-bound, reared and tossed his head.

'Well, I'll be hanged, Tim-Pat . . .'

But the groom was whistling again, a different note, shorter and not as sharp. Now the bay ceased rearing and responded to the rider's heels and hands.

'Where the hell did you rake that one out of?' asked Dermot.

'It's easy enough,' said Tim-Pat, his sly green eyes shining with mischief. 'You can do it with any horse if the feeling between you is right.'

'What else – ?'

'Tim-Pat – you bastard! Are you at the back of this?'

Tom, laughing, shouting admiration, was almost upon them. Bareheaded, his clothes in need of a good iron, he was still the epitome of energy and enthusiasm and fun.

How did he do it after a hectic night out, wondered Dermot. His brother's black curly hair was tangled like a blackberry bush, his deep, black-blue eyes were shining with life, and his bold, handsome face with its full, satisfied mouth was that of a young king acknowledging the acclaim that was his due.

Or perhaps the face was that of an older angel. There was something indestructible about Tom's beauty that made one wonder if there were exceptions to human mortality – an almost (but not quite) grown-up angel with a key to Heaven in his pocket, and God's permission to transgress every now and again because he was so special . . .

'Where the hell have you been?' Dermot demanded, as the angel-king reined in.

He tried hard to cover his feeling for Tom with displays of overt disapproval, which went largely over the latter's head.

'Guilty – guilty!' panted Tom, sounding anything but contrite.

Everyone let him get away with it – he did not know what it was like to be truly sorry.

'But, anyway, here I am – though Tim-Pat's trickery would have it otherwise – and I'm all set for a good ride with my brother.'

'How did you know what Tim-Pat did?'

'Hasn't he been showing me what he can do every so often?' Tom shrugged, smiling at Tim-Pat, who smiled

24

adoringly back. 'Now, listen, are we going off for a ride or what?'

'I'll just tell Mother you're back – she was worrying about you,' said Dermot, virtue itself.

He was piqued that Tom should be more privy to Tim-Pat's tricks than himself. Who was playing games with whom? Tom never minded this kind of carry-on, but it made Dermot feel apart and insecure.

'I sorted Mount Royal out all right,' volunteered Tim-Pat, when Dermot, dignity intact, was doing his duty in the house.

'You have? And how did you go about that?'

In fact, Tim-Pat had explained this plan to Tom already, although he had obviously forgotten doing so. Still, thought Tom, it gave a man a bit of pleasure in life to boast about his achievements. Let him go ahead.

As Tim-Pat launched into his recital, Tom's mind wandered off to the lecture he had received from Jamie Keegan's wife, Helen, when he had returned with Jamie. 'Find yourself a girlfriend, Tom O'Brien,' and, 'Husband and wife need a *bit* of time together.'

Oh, women were terrors, the way they could stop an innocent bit of fun. It was only drinking and gambling, as Helen knew well, neither of them being womanizers.

Wasn't Carmel the same – and his mother in the days when his father was alive?

'Are we off?'

Dermot was back, wearing his invisible halo.

'Is she all right?'

'She's fine now. You know how she worries.'

'Do I not!' said Tom ruefully. 'Shall we go down by the river towards Castleconnell?'

'Suits me. By the way, Tom, did I tell you I sorted out that problem with Mount Royal?'

Tom looked at him queerly.

'And how did you do that?'

'That old trick with pads of hay. It just came to me. One of us should have thought of it before.'

'We should indeed,' said Tom, and there was a hint of sadness in his voice. 'And wasn't that the terrible pity . . .'

They were down by the river, the pale, shy Shannon, which wound tentatively to the west as if it did not wish to be the widest river in Ireland, when Dermot, with no pleasure, remembered the Laurel Hill fête.

'You know what – it's Saturday the twenty-eighth!'

'So?'

'So this afternoon we've got that thing at the school with Mother and the girls.'

'Holy blazes!' Tom exclaimed, groaning. 'How did we get ourselves into that?'

'Remember Mother telling us it was for the poor of Limerick? And then you said it would be an afternoon out for Mother, and a chance to see her friends?'

'Oh well,' said Tom philosophically. 'And a chance for the girls to see theirs since all of them went to Laurel Hill. I hope some of them are pretty, that's all.'

'So do I,' said Dermot fervently.

But even the thought of pretty girls did not enhance the prospect of an afternoon in a convent, instead of here alone with Tom. Dermot wished that the two of them could go fishing instead. Maybe they could have ridden to Castleconnell, one of the loveliest bits of landscape in the country or, even better, stayed on the Crag Liath side of the river and gone to the Falls of Doonass where the Shannon took on a different aspect altogether, broadening out to some three hundred

26

yards and rushing and roaring for half a mile over huge boulders and rocks. There were woods to hide you and beautiful banks to sprawl on, and falls and whirlpools and hurrying rapids to intensify whatever good spirits you had brought with you, or cultivate them, if you had not.

The two young men turned their horses to circumvent the triangular marshy strip which, in their childhood, they had believed to be the habitat of fairies. Avoiding it then out of fear, they did so now for the horses' comfort.

'Now you've got Mount Royal under control would you say he has lost any of his spirit?'

'Not a bit of it,' said Dermot, defensively. 'No, I've just succeeded in getting him out of a bad habit, that's all.'

'So come on then – let's see what style of a match he is for Sprightly today. I'll race you back to the house.'

'You're on.' Dermot's eyes were sparkling. 'Ready?'

'Ready.'

And as quick as that they were off, dark-haired, blue-eyed wild geese flying low over the soft grass, past the first of the small, thatched cabins, where the workers lived, up, over a loose-laid stone wall, into the second green field. The slight wind slapped at their faces, bringing blood to their cheeks and excitement into their eyes.

Neck and neck – with nothing to choose between them. The chance of a win for Dermot.

And then, at first by a head and then by a length and more, Tom started drawing ahead.

'Come *on*,' Dermot urged the gentle but able Mount Royal. 'After him. *Faster!*'

Up again, over a boundary that was half grass-tuft,

half loose-stone, and down along the last straight, into the field that bordered the grounds of the house.

'Better.'

But Tom was way ahead, and there was no chance at all that Dermot would win.

'Better.'

He could never be better than Tom, no matter what he tried to do.

He galloped up to where Tom, laughing and gasping for breath, was waiting for him.

'You did well.' Tom, the king, was encouraging the prince who could not be heir.

'But not well enough.'

'Ah, sure, who cares?'

I care, Dermot answered, but silently. Even if he could bear to reveal his thoughts to Tom, his brother would never have an inkling of what it meant to be always second best.

No, in one respect, he *was* superior to Tom and that was in his potential ability to handle Crag Liath. He knew it – and sometimes he thought that Tom was aware of it, too.

He fretted away at Tom's attitude to his great inheritance and was filled with misery at the knowledge that the one to whom nature had given the qualification to run Crag Liath would never be able to do so.

2

Rosaleen O'Flynn would have given the next seventeen years of her young life to be free, like Dermot and Tom, to ride over the fields of a morning, the way she used to do before her father's death and her own incarceration at Laurel Hill Convent.

She was a small, dark-haired girl with a pale face that was not yet pretty, oval-shaped, with a small *retroussé* nose, a soft, full mouth and big, violet-blue eyes, which, emphasized by heavy dark lashes, were by far her best feature – expressive eyes, which sometimes flashed purple with anger, or paled with a mist of tears.

She sat in the back row of the sixth class that sunny morning, with those eyes ostensibly glued to page three hundred and fifty-three of her history book, the epitome of a serious scholar. But Rosaleen was not concentrating on the mitigating circumstances leading up to the violation of the Treaty of Limerick, as Mother Mary Gonzaga fondly supposed. Inside her history book was another, to her, much more interesting publication – the diary of Amhlaoibh O Suilleabhain, the scribe, written in the earlier part of the century, in the original Irish.

Mother Mary Gonzaga was also blissfully unaware that Rosaleen had nothing but scorn for what she regarded as the bowdlerized English version of Irish history, which was taught at the school and at all schools throughout the country under the British system of education. Pushed into a corner and forced ess her opinions, Rosaleen would have said ...oly that there could be no excuse for a scheme, implemented by evil King William and his disreputable parliament, that resulted in depriving Irish Roman Catholics of three-quarters of a million acres of land and from their participation in public life.

Three years ago, when her Grand-aunt Carrie had first put her into the convent, Rosaleen would have challenged Mother Mary Gonzaga's integrity on this and similar issues right in front of the class. Bitter experience had taught her that overt honesty and courage do not always pay, especially in a group setting. She had learnt to hold her tongue although she had found it difficult to veer from transparency to reticence, and to assume a mask in class. Unlike Dermot O'Brien, she was utterly, artlessly honest. An only child, she had been encouraged by her father to arrive at her opinions through a relentless form of logic, and to express them freely.

Michael O'Flynn, widowed after Rosaleen's birth, would have preferred a son, but he had made do with a daughter. Finding difficulty in giving love, he had compensated by instilling in his child not only the ability to think for herself, but a passion for her country. Spoken Irish was seldom heard in the 1880s, expect in isolated areas; printed Irish and its literary use were almost unknown, and Rosaleen, speaking the language fluently, was something of an oddity amongst the other girls at school.

This ability had not raised her standing with the nuns either, who were more pleased with her good progress in English and Italian and French. Mother Gonzaga, looking across the class from her dais, thought Rosaleen O'Flynn a precocious, sulky kind of child, on the one hand full of information about everything under the sun, and, on the other, so taciturn you could not but harbour doubts about her sincerity. Without quite knowing why, she found herself holding Rosaleen at arm's length, putting off asking her questions in class and far preferring her friend, Milliora Fitzgibbon, a nice-looking girl who was sitting in one of the favoured seats in front.

What Rosaleen O'Flynn and Milliora Fitzgibbon saw in each other was an enigma to everyone but themselves. Rosaleen was an intellectual; Milliora, although she was not stupid, was more interested in drawing and needlework than in more academic subjects, although she was good at French, as a matter of principle.

Milliora had Norman ancestry. But the Fitzgibbons, like the others of their kind who had settled in Ireland all those centuries ago, had long since married into the Celts, becoming 'more Irish than the Irish themselves', and their children no longer bore the stamp of France upon their features. Gone, too, was the Frenchman's honeyed skin: Milliora's complexion was very pale, a foil to her brilliant red-gold hair, so thick and luxuriant that, in a country where redheads abounded, she was always sure to stand out. With this went soft, hazel eyes, high cheekbones, a thin, pointed nose, and a slender face and figure. Only in her gestures – quick, nervous and impatient – did she betray her continental genes. In her wit, her apparent warmth and her occasional cruelties, she was every inch a Celt.

Intending to ask Milliora to paraphrase her earlier words, Mother Mary Gonzaga was troubled by her conscience. She could not continue to ignore the O'Flynn child forever, much as she would have liked to do so.

'Rosaleen O'Flynn, the Irish Commissioners were careless when they drafted the Articles for the Treaty. Would you enlarge on that, please?' she said, rather more loudly than she had intended.

But not, it seemed, loudly enough to attract the attention of the dark-haired girl in the back row. Rosaleen did not look up from her book. For the first time, Mother Mary Gonzaga's suspicions were aroused.

'Miss O'Flynn – what are you reading back there? Is it your history book at all?'

'Oh, my goodness, I've spilt the ink – and all over my dress, as well!'

Wide-eyed, hand to horrified mouth, Milliora had leapt to her feet.

Turning to look at her, Mother Mary Gonzaga said crossly, 'You clumsy girl! Quick, somebody, get a cloth. Don't step in it, Milliora – it's all over the floor, as well.'

'I'm so sorry. How silly of me,' said Milliora, engagingly, satisfactorily contrite.

She always charmed the nuns.

'Oh, well, never mind. Accidents will happen,' Mother Mary Gonzaga melted.

By the time a cloth had been fetched and Milliora and the floor desultorily mopped up, Rosaleen's crimes were forgotten. Only Milliora, the saviour, knew all that had happened, and she thought the ruination of a school dress a small price to pay for saving her friend. Rosaleen, reading of a starving people who did not want for spirit or courage, was the least informed of them all.

Most of the time, though, she *was* appreciative of the way Milliora took her under her wing. If it had not been for Milliora, she would have been desperately unhappy, placed in the custody of a grand-aunt more interested in spiritualism and table-tapping than in surrogate mothering, who had packed her charge off to the convent within a week of her father's death.

What Grand-aunt Carrie lacked as a mother, Milliora had in plenty. Much of her natural source of mother love she had already expended upon her younger sister, Francie, now in the fifth class, but she had an enormity over to offer to a girl who had been orphaned. Milliora had lost her own mother when she was only ten and she had a very good idea of how Rosaleen must be feeling. So she had cossetted, comforted and protected her friend, and advised her how to proceed, and if there were times when her bossy ways seemed insufferable the sum of the good always exceeded the bad.

Almost always . . . and sometimes, too, their dissimiliar attitudes made it difficult to be friends. Milliora had no interest whatsoever in Ireland's great literary traditions, or in the injustices perpetrated on the country over the years; if you brought up either of those subjects, she would look bored and yawn and sigh.

Milliora's complete indifference to the evils done out of the past was actually part of her attraction. She was incapable of hatred and if someone wronged her, she forgave them in no time. And although she had a domineering nature, underneath she had a softness and a heart that was easily moved.

All of this Rosaleen had thought many a time before and had at the back of her mind as she turned back to the words of the scribe. She did not hear when the bell rang for the end of the lesson and did not rise when the other girls got to their feet as a sign of respect to their teacher who, gathering her books together and with her Rosary beads rustling against her black habit, swiftly strode from the room.

As the door closed, the class erupted into chatter, each girl packing in as much talk as she could before the next lesson – religious knowledge – was due to commence.

'Rosaleen?'

She looked up, startled, to see Milliora standing in front of her desk, wedged behind the chair of the girl who was sitting a row in front.

'Hello, dreamer. Are you back on earth now?'

'I think so . . .'

'Good. Because after religious knowledge I want you to come down to my dormitory and help me try on my dress for the fête. I only finished it this morning and I must have someone tie it for me at the back.'

Rosaleen knew better than to point out that there were five other girls in Milliora's dormitory who could have carried out this task. Milliora did not like to ask favours of those who did not love her, and not everyone could take her bossy ways and her popularity with the nuns, partly due to the generous gifts her father made to the convent.

'All right. Are you pleased with the dress?'

'Mm . . .' said Milliora slowly, not altogether sure.

Uncritical of herself in other ways, she was a perfectionist when it came to sewing, and knew more about fashion than any other girl at Laurel Hill.

'In the name of the Father and of the Son and of the Holy Ghost.'

Mother Thecla was in the classroom, eyes shut, face fierce with reverent concentration, making the sign of the cross before the prayer that preceded every lesson. Swift and lithe as a red-masked fox, Milliora was back in her place at the front before they reached the Our Father.

'If only we had a mirror,' lamented Milliora, looking over her shoulder in a vain attempt to see her back.

'The nuns will never allow that,' Rosaleen laughed. 'What a sin if we saw ourselves.'

'Or saw ourselves with no clothes on,' Milliora said, wickedly. 'Can you imagine being allowed to have a bath without our shifts?'

'Or any of them doing it. Do you remember the night we climbed on the bed and peeped over the top of the partition . . . ?'

'And saw Mother Lawrence sitting in the bath – and with a cap, as well as a shift, when I was hoping we would see her head shaved. Have you done the back?'

'Wait – I must tie the tapes before you turn around. There, that's it. It's perfect.'

'How do I look?'

Suddenly, Milliora did not sound at all like her old self, but oddly vulnerable and uncertain. The lack of sophistication in her voice was contradicted completely by her appearance. Not only was she wearing a very grown-up dress, but her left hand had swept most of her lovely hair on to her head, and she was a truly different person – elegant, and, apart from the tone of her voice, absolutely composed.

'You look – beautiful,' said Rosaleen, slowly.

It was true.

The dress into which so much labour of love had gone was made of a pale blue silk embroidered with pale pink roses. From any point of view it was a complicated garment – difficult to make, requiring a perfect figure to wear and almost impossible to move in. It fell sheath-like to the ground, the front was tied back underneath by tapes to flatten it, and it was so pulled in that Milliora could barely move her feet six inches at a time. But the effect was worth all of the anguish. There would be no other dress to come anywhere near it in the whole of Laurel Hill, Rosaleen was sure of it, and, on top of that triumph, it suited its wearer down to the ground.

'Truly?'

'Truly. You know I would never lie to you.'

'Yes, I know that,' said Milliora and her voice was odd again. 'It's just that – I have this feeling that something important is going to happen to me today. I want to look perfectly splendid.'

'Of course,' said Rosaleen, seriously. 'Who knows who might be there.'

Instinctively, they both glanced towards the dormitory door, lest any of the nuns might be passing and take exception to so provocative a remark. Although it was taken for granted in the convent that most of the girls would, ultimately, marry, the subject of men was taboo. Confidences, generally, were discouraged and best friendships frowned upon, the nuns laying emphasis on the irrelevance of human affections, in comparison to the greater love a girl should have for God.

Despite all this, there were girls in the sixth class who professed to be in love already, and have men in love with them. And last year, in the fifth class, there had been a girl who had been expelled for doing something unmentionable in terms of love, although neither Rosaleen nor Milliora knew what it was. They were both extremely naïve and no one – least of all

Grand-aunt Carrie or Milliora's father – had any intention of telling them the facts of life.

'Don't you want to try *your* dress?' suggested Milliora, in her normal voice, gesturing to Rosaleen to help her get undressed.

'Maybe.'

The silk dress was smoothed, laid reverently on the iron bedstead, accompanied by a pink Gainsborough hat, which would crown the whole ensemble. Also on the bed, partly concealed by the pillow, was Milliora's treasured picture of her father, with her sister, Francie, beside him. The picture invariably made Rosaleen want to cry, partly because she had no photographic record of her father while Milliora, who did, was secure knowing that hers was still alive.

That thought led on inevitably to other sad reflections, bringing with them vivid memories of her childhood at Knockfierna – *Cnoc Firinne*, The Hill of Truth, so called, it was said, because you could forecast the weather after looking at it to see if it was covered in cloud or clearly visible.

Blinking, Rosaleen tried to focus on the other picture, the one of the Holy Family, pinned on the wall over Milliora's bed.

'What's the matter?'

'Nothing.'

But in spite of her efforts to control them, the tears were trickling down.

'Don't cry, Rosaleen. I'm here. I'll look after you.'

'Yes . . .'

The tears were coming faster now and she wiped them away irritably, shading her face with her hands.

'Please tell me why you're crying.'

That was not so easy. She could tell Milliora that she

was crying for the loss of her father and have her
explanation accepted. But it was not as simple as that.
She *did* miss her father, even after all this time. Their
relationship had been far more that of teacher and
pupil than loving father and daughter, but she had
responded to it amiably, being diligent by nature and,
in any case, knowing nothing else. Her father's austere
attitudes had prohibited visits from affectionate aunts
and cousins who might have taken her mother's place.
So the Aladdin's Cave of learning to which he had the
key – the introduction to poems and songs and prose
in Irish, as well as in English – was more than mere
instruction. It was the only form of parental love that
Rosaleen would know and, as such, valued highly.

That alone was complicated to explain but what was
impossible to interpret to someone who had been born
and reared in a city was the depth of her sorrow in
losing the house and, more important, the land at
Knockfierna.

The house had not been remarkable itself but standing three-quarters way up Knockfierna, one of Munster's most celebrated fairy hills, it commanded a view
of six counties and many mountain ranges, and on a
clear day you could see the estuary of the Shannon
river.

And yet it was more than that, far more. Knockfierna
was riddled with ancient mythologies and to reside
there was to be knitted into the pattern of archaic
Celtic tradition, mythical and integral and strange.

Like the stories surrounding the mysterious being
called Donn Firinne, Fairy King or Celtic god of Death.
A deep hole at Knockfierna called Poll na Bruine was
held to be the entrance to his palace under the hill. To
go there was 'to knock at the spirits' door': a ball of

38

thread thrown into it was said to have been thrown back, covered in blood. And there were those who maintained they had heard the Donn screaming in the wind, and seen him galloping in the clouds at night.

The famous warrior band, the Fianna – who had inspired the rebel Fenians of Rosaleen's own century – had hunted there under the command of their leader, Finn mac Cool, and his poet son, Oisin, and on Strickeen, the ridge that ran westwards from Knockfierna, there was a big ring fort, *Lios na bhFiann*, the Fort of the Fianna, where, twice a year, young girls left gifts to commemorate the Celtic feasts of Bealtaine and Samhain.

Knockfierna was the realm of the *Sioga*, the fairy people, and their magic had got into her heart and into her blood, and would be there for life.

But not all of their magic could circumvent the fate that had made Rosaleen leave Knockfierna after her father's death. The law made no provision for women and handed the property over to the cousin who was Michael O'Flynn's male next of kin. She had been sent away with her pony, Conan Maol, to Grand-aunt Carrie's house in Kilmallack, where she was approved only for being well able to ride and not for her studies at all. All that remained to her of Knockfierna was the library of books which no one else wanted.

'Rosaleen, talk to me. Tell me why you're sad.'

She was back again in the dormitory, with Milliora by her side.

'It's much too hard to explain,' she said. 'You wouldn't – I mean – '

'Then don't try to tell me,' said Milliora, practically. 'Look, I'll tell you something that will cheer you up.

39

Over in England they're planning to give up wearing corsets.'

'They're not!' exclaimed Rosaleen, diverted by such a revolutionary idea. 'Everyone?'

'Well, not quite everyone,' Milliora amended, 'but a lot of people are saying they're unhealthy and so are too many clothes, and padding and boning. And some people – intellectuals, you know – are going to wear shoes without heels and let their hair flow down naturally. Can you imagine that?'

'No,' said Rosaleen, truthfully, 'I can't.'

For months she and Milliora had been looking forward to the moment when they could put their hair up and graduate to being women, instead of simply girls. And now here was news of people – intelligent women – who had ambitions to do precisely the opposite.

'So when we leave school and become fashionable ladies we'll end up looking like we do now?'

'Not quite like we do now,' said Milliora, struggling back into her black serge uniform. It had a plain collar, made of muslin, with a narrow piece of lace on the edge and, although they both derided it, it suited Milliora very well. 'Anyway, it won't happen over here that quickly. After all, we're leaving school next month.'

'So we are.' Rosaleen frowned again.

Leaving school meant that she would be thrown into the company of Grand-aunt Carrie instead of seeing Milliora every day. For most of the summer she would be lonely, with only an occasional journey into the city to relieve the monotony, and in the winter she would, she knew, make her debut at a hunt ball, be launched into Limerick society, and married off as soon as possible to the most eligible man her aunt could lay hands on.

The prospect of a debut in a white frock, something to which all the other girls were looking forward with pleasure, filled her with horror. Because of her upbringing by her father, Rosaleen was at ease with people much older than herself, but she was shy with her own age group and did not feel at home in a competitive hurly-burly. Three years at the convent had done nothing to alter this.

'Don't look depressed again! We're going to wear beautiful clothes, and get married to the most handsome men in Limerick and live happily ever afterwards,' insisted Milliora, trying to cheer her up.

She really did believe this would happen, Rosaleen knew. And it probably would – to Milliora. She always got everything she wanted and saw no reason why others should not do the same.

She looked at her friend – red-haired and vibrant and confident – and wished devoutly that she could emulate her in every single way. She forgot that Milliora was not loved by everyone and it did not occur to her to consider that Milliora might have as much a need of Rosaleen, as Rosaleen did of her. She thought only that Milliora was like a fairy – dipped in magic and fated to be a success at everything she did, whereas she was more of a lost soul, cast out of her true environment and doomed to wander shyly on the perimeter of life.

But Milliora had put her arms around her and was staring concernedly into her face.

'Now, Rosaleen, we're going to have a lovely day,' she said firmly. 'Don't think about the past. There's nothing we can do about that.'

'No.'

Although, of course, Milliora, by the comfort and compassion she offered, did a great deal, every day, to make up for Rosaleen's woes. More than anyone had ever done – much more.

'Oh, Milly,' said Rosaleen, impulsively, 'you *are* good to me. Whatever happens to us, you'll always be my best friend.'

'Always,' Milliora vowed. 'We've got ten minutes before the bell goes for luncheon. Come on – let me see *your* dress.'

Rosaleen's dress was violet-blue, fashioned from silk, trimmed with lace at the wrists but otherwise free of decoration, and it had cost Grand-aunt Carrie an absolute fortune. Tight-waisted, the bodice ran down to a sharp point in front so that the skirt, emerging underneath, had the effect of making the waistline look smaller still. The neck was high and rather prim, the sleeves long and clinging, and the back kicked out, not into the trailing train of five years ago, but into a cheeky little bunch that contradicted the austerity of the front. With it came a parasol with a lace border and a handle of lacquered violet cane.

These treasures, wrapped in tissue paper, had been lying in Rosaleen's school trunk since the beginning of term.

She was not quite sure why she had not showed them off to Milliora before now, as they each always did when they acquired something new and exciting. Was it because Milliora would criticize her extravagance in allowing them to be bought for her, instead of buying material and making a gown herself? Milliora was thrifty. It was in her nature to save both money and time, although she did not have to do either. Her father, George Fitzgibbon, was a well-to-do wine merchant with premises in Roches Street, and both Milliora and Francie could have had expensive ready-made gowns from McBirney's Stores any time they elected. Neither of them did so. Milliora took pride in making her own clothes to her own designs and Francie, who was religious, had already declared her intention of becoming a nun, as soon as her schooldays were over, and was inclined to renounce the vagaries of the world as proof of her good intentions.

No, Rosaleen decided, her friend might economize herself, but she would have been happy to know that Rosaleen had received such a gift and would have refrained from comments about recklessness and thrift.

The truth was that the dress and parasol seemed, in some strange way, to demand privacy, to be so closely identified with herself that she did not want to show them to anyone, even her best friend. Or, at least, not until she was dressed up and ready to be seen at the school fête.

'Milly, we don't really have much time. We'll be late for luncheon. You can see the dress afterwards, when we're getting ready.'

'Don't worry about being late. If we are, I'll make it all right with Mother Veronica,' said Milliora, airily. 'We must have a dress rehearsal, Rosaleen, otherwise you won't feel confident at the fête. And, after all, I've shown you my dress.'

She opened the door to Rosaleen's dormitory and hussled her friend inside. The room, long and narrow, with three beds down either side, was separated by curtains so that the girls could dress and undress without causing offence to each other. Rosaleen's bed was at the far end with the trunk acting as a bedside table beside it.

Raising the lid and looking down at the dress and parasol, Rosaleen felt regretful. It was almost as if, by exhibiting them prematurely to Milliora, she was about to betray them.

Silly.

'Hurry up.'

There was no way out.

'Don't look until I'm dressed then.' Still, she played for time.

'All right,' said Milliora amiably, plomping down on someone else's bed.

There was no one else around – that was something. Milliora, with her eyes closed as agreed, began to hum lightly to herself.

Rosaleen scrambled out of her school dress and, much more gently, stepped into the violet-blue silk, holding her breath in until, by an effort of will, she had managed to lace the waist.

'Are you ready?' Milliora sounded impatient.

'Yes. You can look now.' Rosaleen waited for affirmation.

But Milliora, frowning, said nothing at all. Biting her bottom lip, her eyes half-closed, as if to see better, she was looking Rosaleen up and down as if she was an object, rather than a friend.

The eyes ran over the neckline, took in the shoulders, ran down over the bodice, assessed the skirt, the waistline – detached, dissenting.

'Do you like – '

Milliora was looking at the cuffs.

'Turn around,' she commanded, 'slowly, so I can get the whole effect. Oh . . .'

'We – Grand-aunt Carrie and I – thought the back was rather special.'

'It is. It's very nice. Much, much nicer than the front.'

'You don't like it?'

How could she fail to do so? It was such a lovely dress.

'Oh, I do,' said Milliora, too quickly. 'It's just that – well – '

She stopped, at a loss for words.

'Well what? Tell me, Milly. We're always honest with each other, aren't we?'

'It's just that we have different taste, that's all,' Milliora said, hastily. 'The colour is marvellous. It's perfect for your eyes, I will say that. But – '

'But *what*?'

'It's too plain, that's all. Too like our school dresses, I suppose. I would have liked more detail. But, as I said, the colour – '

But the damage was done. Now that Rosaleen was seeing the dress through Milliora's eyes, it suddenly seemed rather dull.

Even the colour, which Milliora was trying so desperately to praise, struck her as unexciting.

Violet-blue. The colour of concealment, of shrinking violets – of the shy, the unimportant, the seldom even seen.

Just like me, thought Rosaleen, desolately. And then she, who valued honesty so highly, wished that Milliora had seen fit to practise concealment.

She said, 'I'm sure I heard the bell ring for luncheon. We must be quick.'

She took off the violet-blue dress and splayed it out

45

on her bed, just as Milliora had done with hers. And did not look back at it before she left the dormitory.

Walking back along the corridor and down the stairs to the dining-hall, she, like Dermot O'Brien, was acutely conscious of feeling second best, of holding a monopoly on mediocrity.

She blamed Milliora for her discomfort. It was the first shadow on their friendship.

3

By the time the carriage carrying the O'Brien family had reached the lower end of Henry Street, *en route* for Laurel Hill, Tom was also feeling unsettled. Suffering from a delayed hangover, he was irritated by Carmel and Mary who, he decided, were at their very worst, squabbling non-stop all the way to town. Mary's voice was particularly high-pitched, so it felt as if one of her hat-pins was piercing his ears.

'Isn't the Franciscans a beautiful building?' she exclaimed as they went past the new church with its fine portico of perfectly proportioned Corinthian columns. 'And yet they're so poor, having to ring the bell for help every time they're starving.'

'Since when have they rung it?' Carmel demanded.

No, Tom thought, *she* was more irritating, being the more aggressive. His head, as well as his ears, began to throb. What had possessed him to have had so much to drink? If only he could go to bed and sleep it off, instead of trailing up to the convent.

'Isn't it sad that the hanging gardens have been neglected?' said his mother, as she always did when they passed by what remained of William Roche's dream of a fantastic garden, raised on a series of arches, part of it seventy feet above the ground.

Roche, a wealthy citizen who had lived in Limerick at the beginning of the century, had laid out his garden in terraces, with glasshouses heated by a system of flues, to grow grapes and oranges and pineapples, the like of which had never been seen in Ireland before – or since.

'Mother, isn't that where Bishop Knox lived – the one who discovered the famous opera singer who went around the world?' Mary wanted to know next, although, like himself, she had heard the story already.

What was the matter with his sister that she was such a compulsive talker, Tom wondered – and that in a country where talk was a national pastime, a veritable sport in itself?

In company with his brother, Dermot did not utter a word. He was the quiet one of the family, and you often wanted to know what was going on in his mind. Sometimes, he seemed as cool as ice on a flooded turf-bog, in command of the whole world. At other times – like this morning when he had told the lie about Mount Royal – you could see right through the ice to the murky depths below, and then you could cry for what there was in Dermot that made him act so sadly.

Look at him now, dressed up like a dandy, with his tight trousers and the new double-breasted reefer jacket that he said was so fashionable. Tom himself had no interest whatsoever in clothes and Dermot's attention to them seemed to him an unhealthy obsession, all right for women but suspect in men. Tom realized his brother was far more dolled up than either his mother or sisters, the former being in her usual black silk and Mary and Carmel – although they thought they looked marvellous – in muddy dark pink and grey dresses that did nothing at all for their complexions.

Looking at the O'Briens, people often remarked how unfair life was, in this case to the girls. Sure, all the good looks of the family had gone to their brothers.

Tom and Dermot's hair shone black and dark brown; Mary and Carmel's were mousy, and both of them were plump and not tall enough to carry their weight.

'Isn't it strange that Andy cannot find the time to join us?' Mary said.

Her tongue was acerbic, a fact Tom attributed to her having failed to find a man.

'There's nothing strange about it,' Carmel told her tartly. 'He's up to his eyes in work on the farm – he can't afford to go gallivanting.'

'And what about having time for you then?' Mary riposted, rather weakly.

Feeling like wringing their necks, Tom turned the carriage into Laurel Hill Avenue, and dropped the family inside the convent gates prior to seeing to the stabling. But even that did not go off easily. As they were late, O'Riordan's stables were full. He had to go all the way back down Henry Street to Hackett's to solve the problem, and walk back up the hill to the convent, along with his aching head.

The grounds, which swept down into a dip from the school buildings, were packed with ladies in elegant silks and matelasses and printed cottons, their hats resembling mobile flower gardens – and with men forced by their wives into frock-coats and well-behaved nun-greeting expressions. There were chattering schoolgirls all over the place and bustling nuns and towering over all of them a giant statue of Our Blessed Lady, with the palms of her hands outstretched in love.

Tea, he thought. Maybe that would restore him, it being unlikely that anything stronger would be on offer. Over to his left, refreshments were being served, but just as he was about to head in that direction he noticed that his mother and sisters had got there first, and were talking away to their cronies. He cast a regretful look at the big teapot held by one of the lay sisters, decided that he had taken enough of Mary and Carmel's nonsense, and moved away.

And then – quick as a flash – he forgot that his liver was angry. Out of the blue he saw an apparition that, although obviously not emanating from Heaven, was enough of a miracle for Tom.

A girl – a most gorgeous girl – was standing a few yards away, gazing fixedly at him. Who was she, to make her interest in him so apparent?

He was not surprised; he knew that women of all ages admired him and he thought it reasonable that they should. All his life, he had been adored and pampered by the feminine sex – above all, by his mother and sisters – and he assumed, innocently and without conceit, that this state of affairs would continue forever.

Some of the women he met inspired his affection but none, as yet, had touched the spring of his love. The girl in the garden did not exactly do that, but she captured his interest. Having arrived at the convent in a tangle of frustration and petty pain, he had the feeling that someone important had subtly freed him.

What would happen next was anybody's gamble. What card would the girl play? And how brave a player was she really?

'Tom?'

He did not hear Dermot calling to him or notice his brother's approach. All of his senses were engaged elsewhere, focused on his gorgeous apparition. Above all, his blue eyes were occupied, laughing at her, applauding her cheek – daring her to take part in the game.

Who the blazes was she?

In spite of her reservations about Milliora's conduct, Rosaleen had to admit that her friend was looking particularly pretty, with her hair tucked into a high chignon under the Gainsborough hat. Both girls were carrying baskets of pale pink roses which they had been selling, with gratifying success, in aid of the poor.

'How much have we made so far?'

'Five shillings and – ' Milliora calculated, but Rosaleen never heard the exact amount they had made for at that moment a young man caught her attention and her heart leapt with delight.

He was a good-looking, untidy young man in his early twenties, wearing a rather crumpled, sack-like suit made of thick, clumsy material, with a low, turned-down collar and a narrow necktie carelessly knotted but, to Rosaleen, he seemed like a god.

And, indeed, Tom O'Brien did resemble the classical figure on the mosaic cover of Grand-aunt Carrie's gold and enamel snuff box, with his rounded face, straight nose, slightly protruding chin, and undeniably sensuous mouth. But his eyes were blue, not – as in the mosaic – a kind of brown, and, instead of laurels all over his head, the god who so expediently materialized over by the statue of Our Blessed Lady that afternoon had a mop of black curly hair that could have done with a barber's prompt attention, a fact that she took in and just as soon forgot.

Rosaleen had seen the young man before and then, as now, had been captivated by him, caught like a pike on a fisherman's line, on the dangerous hook of his

51

beauty. That had been in the winter, at a meet of the County Limerick Foxhounds, at the end of a hard day, as the hunt rode back to the crossroads where they had gathered earlier and where, in the dusk, country boys and girls were getting together for a wayside dance. The fiddler was already striking up a traditional air and the dancers were flushed with an anticipation that was hardly comprehensible to the exhausted riders, thinking of hot tubs, and dinner, and bed.

And suddenly there he was – a young man with a hunting cap in his hand, his curls blowing free, and the joy of life in his eyes that dispelled her fatigue, and gave her back the dancer's elation.

But there the matter had ended. Friends had called to the young man and he had responded cheerfully, moving off in their direction, and Grand-aunt Carrie, who, at sixty-two, still had a good seat in the side-saddle, came up on Rosaleen's other side.

'Isn't that the two O'Brien brothers?' she had said loudly, and the god had caught this and acknowledged her with a wave.

Tom, his friends had called him, and now Rosaleen knew his second name and the fact that, although she had not seen him, he had a brother as well. His beauty and his contagious gaiety had stayed with her all evening, and, at night, Tom O'Brien crept cheekily into her dreams.

And here he was, in the convent garden! She felt light-headed, wanting to laugh with absurd and delicious delight. The best part was the difference between that time and this. Tom O'Brien had not seen her then – or she had not thought so – but now he was looking straight across the garden to where she and Milliora were standing as if he was mesmerized. The thought crossed her mind that maybe he had noticed her at the hunt, remembered her all this time, and was overjoyed at confrontation, and, at this, she could keep silent no longer.

'Milly,' she whispered. It was a moment to share with your friend. 'Milly, look. Do you see that young man over there, the one who's looking in this direction?'

(At me, she marvelled, at *me*.)

And she turned, to find that Milliora was already looking at Tom.

At the same time she realized that her friend was beyond reach, and had not heard her words.

Milliora – intrepid, sensible, down-to-earth Milliora, Miss Parsimony herself, the least reckless of people – no longer seemed to be standing on the ground. Beguiled and hypnotized, she looked as if she was in the Garden of Eden before the Fall rather than the grounds of Laurel Hill. Her cheeks, which had been flushed already with the excitement of the day, were even pinker, her hazel eyes were shining with unalloyed pleasure, and her always-pert mouth curved up like that of a satisfied Cheshire cat.

No, a marmalade cat. A gratified, confident cat contemplating the bowl of cream it was about to consume.

Except that Milliora was looking at a man. (Or at a god, who climbed into your dreams at night.)

At that moment, Rosaleen hated Milliora, hated her confidence and her smile and her strange euphoria, her beauty and her ability as a seamstress, and the effect she had created with that dress.

Because, just as Milliora was hypnotically contemplating Tom O'Brien, so Tom was looking at *her*.

There was no doubt of that, however Rosaleen might try to persuade herself that the young man was looking in the general direction of both girls, and could be interested in either of them. Don't I have a fifty-fifty chance? she tried.

But that was a foolish question. The answer was spelt out in front of her very eyes. It was as if an invisible cord had been thrown out, binding Tom to Milliora. And Rosaleen attempted to slash at the cord, to ruin Tom for Milliora, the way he had been ruined for her.

'Will you look at that stupid fellow over there, staring like a fool at us?' she said harshly.

The force of her words horrified her. She had not known that she was capable of such strong feeling, or of such malevolence. But although she had fired this missile with all her strength, predictably, it missed.

Milliora did speak, but not to answer Rosaleen. It was as if what she had said did not count at all.

Still looking at the young man (looking, in turn, at her), Milliora said, 'Do you see that man over there? That's the man I am going to marry.'

And then, as an afterthought, she added, 'I'm going to sell him a rose.'

Before Rosaleen could utter another word, Milliora had set off across the lawn, clutching her basket, her eyes always fixed on the god whose own eyes danced with the exquisite joy of life.

It all seemed rather like a dream. Milliora was quite ethereal. Hindered both by her state of enchantment and by the tapes that bound her gown, she wafted over the grass, taking out a rose from her basket, holding it out like an offering, deaf and blind to all but the curly-headed god. Several people, struck by her expression, watched curiously as she went.

Fiona O'Brien and the two girls also saw Milliora. They had finished their tea and they were looking around, not for Dermot, whom they could see already standing nearby, gazing into space, but, inevitably, for Tom, as all of them did so often. When a large lady in a gargantuan hat moved out of their way, they had a perfect view of Milliora's dreamlike promenade.

None of them liked the look of it. Tom was their treasure, their darling, and, more than that, all their bread and butter. The sight of him staring entranced at a pretty girl who was advancing upon him intently did nothing to reassure any of them, or hold back their latent fears.

They knew – they could not but know – that Tom was the catch of several counties and was chased wherever he went. But hitherto Tom had not been that easy to catch. He was so much a man's man that they had slipped into an optimistic presumption that he could be a bachelor all his life, the way a lot of Irishmen were.

This, of course, was to close the door on reality, but Fiona and Mary could not afford too many truths and Carmel was protective of her mother and sister, both of whom could be, literally, out in the cold if Tom married the wrong woman.

Mary and Carmel had actually been at school with Milliora but, being much older, had taken little heed of her at the time, and they did not connect the beautiful girl in the Gainsborough hat with the child that they had known.

She struck all three women as a threat. She was making such an open declaration of her interest in Tom that Fiona and the girls were shocked, as well as startled. If she could be that brazen in public, they concluded, who knew what she would be like if she were to become his wife?

They exchanged anxious glances, knowing, by experience, that it was unwise to attempt to interfere in Tom's life. In spite of his easy-going temperament, he had the hot temper of his race, and he could not bear being ordered about, particularly by a woman.

It did not occur to any of them that they could be witnessing the start of a flirtation, nothing more, or that it was odd that they should be getting themselves worked up about a girl walking across a garden, albeit with love in her eyes. But, in recognizing the validity of Milliora's feelings, and Tom's delighted response, they were, for once, admitting the truth. Tom and Milliora were falling in love at first sight.

All the same, Fiona and the girls felt that they should attempt to protect Tom from the intruder. Without hesitation, by unspoken agreement, they set off in his direction, a robust, three-woman army who could attack as well as they could defend.

Obsessed by their call to arms, they swept past Dermot, failing to acknowledge him or to observe that his attentions, too, were being engaged by a girl.

Rosaleen might not have caught sight of Dermot the day she saw Tom at the hunt, but he noticed her early on, in the first field.

Initially, he had merely been impressed by her competence in handling her obviously flighty mount, which was pulling at the reins and trying to back into the other horses long before the hounds gave tongue. He liked her patience, the way she reassured the horse, speaking to it gently, edging it in and curtailing its fidgety ways. That, and her apparent self-possession, something he fought for in himself, and so respected in others.

He noticed her a couple of other times when the hounds were in full cry but soon the hunt had all his attention, and his blood was on fire, as it always was when the fox was giving them good value. They had a good run in open country, slipping through woods and mud until grey shadows streaked the silver sky and they had all despaired of a kill.

In the end, it was his age, as much as the pack, that caught up with him. The body of what turned out to be an old hill fox was taken from the bloodthirsty hounds whimpering around the Master. Mask and tail were removed, the remains thrown back to the captors. In the traditional ceremony, the youngest follower up – a boy of five or six, for that day the hero of the chase – was blooded, face and hands covered with the rich red blood of the fox.

While that was going on, Dermot realized that the girl he had seen earlier was reining in near him. Close to, she looked a child herself, with her violet-blue eyes very open and her mouth beginning to tremble.

The contrasting images he saw at that moment stayed with him forever; two children – or so it seemed – one laughing in ecstasy, with the freshly-shed blood of the dead fox streaming down his face.

The other face was tear-washed. The girl-child's sad eyes looked from the boy to the remains of the fox, and the hounds feeding off them and, with surprise, he saw her shudder.

So she was sensitive. Although her response to the kill was alien to a man who had grown up with the hunt and found it only natural – the fox being a predator who made off with sheep and lambs when he could – oddly enough Dermot liked it. It meant that she, like him, could think, and be grieved by man's insensibility.

She looked no happier today at the fête, but he thought her just as attractive in her violet-blue gown as she had been in her riding habit. He approved the simplicity of the dress as much as he liked the look of its wearer.

For the second time, the girl failed to see him. Her eyes were focused on something, or someone, that was making her unhappy. What, or who, could it be?

He looked away from her, following her gaze until he spotted the familiar figure in the crumpled, sack-like suit. Dermot swore fluently under his breath.

Tom! He might have known it.

Then Milliora wafted past him and with amazement he registered the fact that it was *she*, not the girl in the violet-blue gown, who was the object of his brother's attention.

So, after all, there was hope for him – as there would not have been, he was sure, had Tom been looking elsewhere.

The Amazonian army swept past him, but he did not take note of its advance. For *his* girl was walking after the other.

He set off to intercept her before she reached Tom.

Reverend Mother had been bothered for some time by the condition of the convent roof. She had known for several weeks that it was in need of repair. There was a particularly bad leak over Sister Imelda's cell and a bucket had been used to catch the water.

Since the lay sisters came from poor backgrounds,

brought no dowry into the order and did all the menial work of the convent, they did not need to be further mortified by torrents of rain coming down on their heads, in her opinion.

Only this morning, Reverend Mother had noticed that crows were getting into the roof, nesting up there as though it were a hedge.

'Any minute now we'll think we're conducting a hedge-school at Laurel Hill,' she quipped to Mother Mary Gonzaga, referring to the eighteenth-century classes, run by poet-schoolmasters, who had attempted to preserve Gaelic classical learning in hidden country places in defiance of Penal Law.

Mother Mary Gonzaga failed to laugh at the joke.

Now, mingling with the girls' parents and keeping a general eye on what was going on at the fête, Reverend Mother wondered who best could be approached for a donation.

Mr Fitzgibbon, Milliora and Francie's father, was always a good bet, but, Saturday being a full working day for him, he had not put in an appearnce. And most people had already forked out today for the poor and would not be susceptible to further requests for money.

Rats, she thought. We'll have rats in there next, as well as crows. And, under her breath, she murmured a prayer to St Jude, the patron of lost causes.

The sight of Fiona O'Brien, scurrying along immediately afterwards, struck Reverend Mother as evidence of saintly intervention and, although she knew that, as a widow, Fiona would have no money of her own, she was also aware that her son and heir should have, and might respond to his mother's plea for aid for the convent.

Reverend Mother had been listening, with what

passed for all of her consciousness and compassion, to the point of view of Theresa O'Sullivan's mother, who thought her daughter's examination marks too low.

'. . . every bit as good as Geraldine Gleeson and *she* got ninety out of a hundred in her French.'

'Would you mind if I left you for a minute?' Reverend Mother stated, rather than requested, cutting this tirade short.

Hot-footing it across the garden, she halted the combatant phalanx and before Fiona, Mary and Carmel could disengage, Milliora got to Tom.

As Mary said afterwards, if it had not been for Reverend Mother, none of it would have happened, because once that one's claws were into Tom, he had no hope at all of escape.

Although Rosaleen thought of her as confident, Milliora was unusually nervous, palpitating inwardly, as she walked across the garden holding out her rose. Above all, she was a romantic, and the beautiful young man who (it seemed) was calling to her to come to him appeared to her to have stepped out of the pages of the kind of books that she read surreptitiously during the school holidays, having purloined them from the housekeeper's shelves.

Her maternal eye had taken in the fact that, although he looked heroic, the young man at Laurel Hill was not that tidy. But his eyes were roaming all over her person in the most impudent and fascinating manner and she soon forgot that his hair wanted cutting in the conviction that her fate was sealed, and that her future husband awaited.

Unaware of the burning gaze of Fiona and Mary and Carmel – who, although halted by Reverend Mother, continued to glare – she stood in front of him, and waited for him to speak.

He did not do so. Look up – look at me, willed his cheeky blue eyes. The lower half of Milliora's body began to tingle and, in her confusion she wondered if she was not being overpowered by the Devil.

She was certainly feeling weak, but it was a curiously pleasant sensation, striking in an unexpected place.

However, as she had so often been taught by the nuns, a lady should be able to cope in any situation . . .

Look up – look at me, willed Tom.

Milliora, in the way of heroines, acknowledged the challenge. In the way of ladies, she tried to find her breath.

'Excuse me,' she finally managed. 'Would you buy a rose?'

Bold as brass, thought the O'Brien sisters and their mother, giving up all pretext of listening to Reverend Mother and wishing they could hear precisely what that girl was saying to Tom.

Then Tom said, so everyone around could hear, 'I'll buy a rose from you all right but only on condition that *you* put it into my buttonhole,' at which Mary gave an equally audible gasp.

Milliora bent her head so that the Gainsborough hat might hide her hot cheeks.

Tom saw the blush and was charmed by it. Admiring both her appearance and her courage in taking up his challenge, he was captivated all the more by the sign of vulnerability in Milliora. Much as he approved of human fearlessness, when it came to women, he liked them soft and tender too.

He had been right: she *was* gorgeous. He wanted to

step forward and take her into his arms, in front of everyone.

Instead, she took a step towards him. Her head still lowered, she pinned the pink rose into the lapel of Tom's crumpled grey-green jacket. In touching him, or his apparel, all sensations seemed to her heightened, so that the smell of the roses was intensified, and so, too, the scent of the women's perfume. The sun felt warmer on her trembling hands and she could feel her own heart beating so loudly that she thought Tom must hear it.

She was oblivious of the hostility of Fiona and Mary and Carmel; she did not see Rosaleen had come up on one side of her; the ladies in their extraordinary hats, their bewhiskered men, could have vanished from the garden, leaving only Tom and herself, enchanted in the sun.

'What's your name?'

'Milliora Fitzgibbon. And you are –'

'Tom O'Brien. Could you be George Fitzgibbon's daughter?'

'Yes, I am,' she said. 'Do you know my father?'

'Well enough to call on his daughter,' said Tom, grabbing his chance.

Milliora, who had never broken a rule of etiquette in her life and who knew perfectly well that heroines, under such circumstances as hers, should not be too eager, proceeded to flout all the rules in the book.

'When were you thinking of calling?' she asked.

And Tom, just as eager, if not more so, announced his intentions to all and sundry: 'Tomorrow afternoon.'

'Tom!' called Mary, desperately. 'Mother isn't well.'

'In a week's time I'll be leaving school. It will have to wait until then,' Milliora said softly.

'A whole week?'

'*Tom!*'

'I'm coming,' he called, adding more quietly, 'Until next week, Miss Fitzgibbon.'

His eyes still twinkling, he left her, and in the débâcle that followed, Dermot had no opportunity to talk to Rosaleen. As Mary pleaded with Tom to hurry and fetch the carriage to take their mother home, so Dermot was packed off by Carmel to find a glass of water.

By the time he got back with it Fiona O'Brien was installed on a bench, shaking all over, like an old otter trapped in a drain by the dogs.

While Mary grabbed the glass from his hand and coaxed their mother to sip from it, Carmel said, 'If you'd spent more time with Tom, instead of wandering off on your own, Dermot, none of this would have happened.'

So they're worried about Tom and the girl, Dermot thought – and maybe they should be, at that.

But he was not interested in Tom and Milliora just then, or in Carmel's complaints. The girl with the voilet-blue eyes was at the forefront of his mind. She was standing with the other girl a few yards away, both of them looking serious, and he wanted to go up to her as he had intended and offer to purchase a rose.

'Where is Tom? Go and hurry him up,' commanded Carmel, putting paid to this idea in her usual sisterly way.

He would pay lip service to her for the sake of peace, and buy a rose on his way back.

But by the time he had searched in vain at O'Riordan's and finally located Tom coming back from Hackett's, both Milliora and Rosaleen had disappeared.

With his mother sick and his sisters hysterical he could hardly set out on a search.

I'll find her, he vowed. Tom's going to call on her friend; he can make some inquiries. If only Tom wasn't so unreliable . . .

Tom's unreliability was the one thing in which the O'Brien women trusted, as the carriage wound its way home. He had made an appointment with the girl, but Tom never kept appointments, they said to themselves, grasping that comforting thought like cold children snuggling under a quilt.

4

'Are you going into Limerick, Tom?' asked Fiona O'Brien in the deliberately casual tone with which she had put this question to her son every day since Saturday.

Having caught little of the exchange between Tom and Milliora, the O'Brien women knew only that a tryst had been arranged, but not exactly when.

'No – not today,' said Tom, equally casually, though in this case guilelessly, since he was unaware of the women's anxiety. 'Think I'll go for a swim.'

'You're not going to dive off the bridge?' his mother, openly concerned, wanted to know. 'Now, Tom, you know well that the river is full of rocks. It's treacherous, I'm telling you, even swimming, let alone doing the good man and diving in off the bridge.'

It was the nearest she would ever come to a rebuke, but it was too much for Tom.

'You're worrying about nothing,' he said. 'I can take care of myself,' and was out of her sight before she could try to stall him, leaving her shaking her head over the lamentable fact that so glorious a creature as Tom should take such pleasure in danger.

Tim-Pat Tierney, riding over O'Brien's Bridge and seeing Tom poised to dive, also marvelled at the beauty of the man, the whiteness of his skin, his sturdy back and tight buttocks, his suppleness and unselfconscious grace.

And now – according to the gossip being put about

in the kitchen – this perfect specimen of manhood was about to fall into the predatory hands of a woman.

Tom dived. There was a last glimpse of his arched body before the wall of the bridge concealed it – a splash as it hit the water.

Tim-Pat, another recruit to the inimical army ready to give battle to Milliora, rode on over the bridge.

Dermot, who knew roughly when Tom was calling on his lady, had kept this information to himself, being reluctant to stir the pot.

Looking for the appropriate time to get hold of his brother quietly and instil into him the importance of finding out from Milliora the name and whereabouts of her friend, he was pleased when he ran into Tom in Limerick, as Dermot was coming down the steps from the offices of William Dundon, the solicitor to whom he was articled.

Tom was riding up from the other end of affluent George Street.

Hailing his brother, Dermot thought that he looked preoccupied.

'Oh, hello,' Tom called. 'Are you on your way home, then?'

'I am. Wait for me. I'll be round to Hacketts for Mount Royal and back in no time.'

'Hold on a minute,' Tom said. 'You're not in a hurry, are you?'

'Not particularly.'

'Then we'll go into the Royal George for a drink.'

This unforeseen honour rendered Dermot temporarily speechless. The hotel Tom was referring to was a few yards down the street. Dermot waited on the steps, holding the work he was about to take home, while Tom rode Sprightly round to the stables.

Dermot told himself that he ought to be far too old to be flattered by the idea of being bought a drink by his big brother and he was half surprised when Tom materialized again a few minutes later.

More surprisingly, by the time they were settled in the Royal George, it was clear that Tom was on for a heart-to-heart talk, something Dermot could not remember having had with him before.

'What did you think of her?' Tom asked suddenly when their whiskies had been poured.

'Of who?' said Dermot, bewildered.

He was not used to being asked his opinion by any member of the family, let alone by Tom.

'Of Miss Fitzgibbon, of course – who else?' said Tom, as if no other woman in the world was of any possible significance. 'That beautiful girl I met at Laurel Hill.'

'She's beautiful all right,' agreed Dermot, diplomatically.

He hardly remembered Milliora, having had his eyes so much on her friend.

'I've just dropped a letter off at her house,' Tom went on, not even bothering to lift his glass to his lips. 'I'm told the Laurel Hill term finishes tomorrow so it will be waiting for her when she gets home.'

'Schools over here close too early in the summer. When we were at Downside, we were still at school in July.'

'Well, why put more effort into educating women anyway? When will they ever use it? Anyway, I've sent her a letter and I'll be going in to see her this Friday.'

'Good,' Dermot said, though he was beginning to wonder if it was.

Thinking about Rosaleen, he had not worried this last week about what would happen to the vulnerable members of the family if Tom were to take a wife. Waking up to this prospect, he tried to conjure up the face of Miss Fitzgibbon. It evaded him. He was left with a slim figure in a filmy gown, wearing a Gainsborough hat, and holding out a rose.

'Love is a funny business, isn't it?' said Tom, acting completely out of character.

It struck Dermot that his brother was confiding something which he thought of as a weakness – something he could never admit to the stalwart Jamie Keegan and his ilk. Seen that way, the confidence was hardly flattering, making a sissy out of himself.

But it was an important confidence. Tom had fallen in love and wanted to share his secret. Maybe from now on it would always be that way between the two of them. With Milliora in his life, Tom would veer away from Jamie and lean more and more on Dermot who would be able to influence his elder brother at last, and get him to run Crag Liath properly, for the good of everyone. With this sort of a start, he would soon be able to talk Tom out of his relationship with Milliora, if it really posed a threat to the family.

'Have *you* ever been in love?' Tom wanted to know.

The conversation was becoming so intimate that Dermot felt impelled to order another round. To him, it looked as though they were set for a long session, an exciting prospect, with the two of them together and on equal terms for the first time ever.

Dermot paid for the drinks and laughed nonchalantly, in the manner of a man of the world.

'Well, as a matter of fact – ' he started to say when another voice drowned out his words.

'Good evening to you, Mr Thomas O'Brien – Mr Dermot O'Brien.'

Both brothers looked up at the man passing by their table.

Tom, acknowledging the greeting, said, when the man was out of earshot, 'Baron Inchiquin, back again from London.'

'Alias our cousin, Edward Donough O'Brien,' Dermot said bitterly, 'Lord Lieutenant of Clare, and a peer in the House of Lords. The power of it! The Protestant line got the pickings. Look at him – set up for life in Dromoland Castle.'

'We didn't do so badly ourselves,' Tom reminded him easily. 'Even if our ancestors had to connive now and again to hold on to Crag Liath, paying out on the side, and being polite to the right people, at least we didn't compromise ourselves – we didn't lose our faith.'

'We haven't got the same *style* as the Protestants,' Dermot insisted, 'the kind that comes out of having confidence. We were robbed of that. Did you not feel it, over at Downside, the slur that was on us, being Irish Catholics?'

'Downside itself is a Catholic school.'

'With English pupils in it. English Catholics – Irish Protestants – they work out the same in the eyes of those who count. You'll always be looked down on, if you're Catholic and Irish.'

'Ah, you're talking nonsense,' said Tom, derisively. 'You want to get rid of that attitude altogether or you'll be a failure for the rest of your life.'

He downed his drink in one gulp and stood up from the table.

'Come on, let's go on home. I can't stand that kind of thinking.'

With a last wave to the Baron, over in a corner, he was out of the door and gone.

So was their intimate moment.

Riding home, neither of them spoke of love. Deterred by the dark expression on Tom's face, Dermot did not ask him to find out about Milliora's friend.

Milliora lived in George Street in a Georgian terraced house that had been ruined by over-decoration and the strident colours favoured by her late mother, Elene. Purple, crimson and bottle-green predominated. The wallpaper in the drawing-room, into which Tom was shown by the same housekeeper who had taken his letter and who, on both occasions, looked him up and down as if he was an undesirable pauper, was reminiscent of medieval Italian velvet, but very much less refined in design. The heavily patterned walls were also covered by pictures of all kinds, small watercolours, indistinct oils, engravings, silhouettes, and daguerrotypes of George and Elene in their youth. The floral Kidderminster carpet clashed with the wallpaper and there was too much furniture in the room.

Tom, reared on the soft colours, elegant decor and open spaces of Crag Liath, felt as though a phantasmagoric blanket was being held over his head with the object of smothering him. He felt thoroughly let down, both by the room and by Milliora's failure to be in it when he was shown in.

He waited for twenty-five minutes, longer by far than he had ever waited for anyone, though much less than most people had put in waiting for him, and by then he was fuming.

Where was Milliora? All the way into town he had been sustained by the sense that he was about to set foot in a magic land where almost anything could happen, like Oisin, in the legend, going off to live with the beautiful fairy maiden, Niamh of the Golden Hair, in Tir na nOg, the Land of Youth, a risky excursion and one which, by its very uncertainty, appealed to Tom immensely.

The stuffy, overcrowded room was certainly no fairy-land. What sort of enchantress lived in a house like this, he asked himself, not knowing that Milliora, too, hated the decor and tolerated it only as a shrine to her mother's memory.

'Ah, there you are,' said a voice that was not hers.

Tom blinked in the gloom. Her father – of course. They had met occasionally at race-meetings and George Fitzgibbon seemed to him a fine fellow, the spitting image of his elder daughter to look at, he now saw, although, in a man, the features were less successful, and his hair had now faded to yellow.

'Sit down, sit down,' said George affably, moving in from the doorway. 'No need to get up at all. There'll be tea along in a minute.'

Did that mean for the *three* of them? It was not how Tom had envisaged spending the afternoon.

'So how are things out at Crag Liath?' Milliora's father asked, settling himself down in an over-stuffed chair covered in ugly yellow brocade.

'Oh, coming along – coming along.'

'Not an easy place to run by any stretch of the imagination,' said George Fitzgibbon. 'Your father always used to say that to me. Many's the chat we used to have on the subject after a race was over.'

'I didn't realize you knew my father that well,' said Tom, warming to the man.

He missed his father – missed his manly attitude to life, his humour and his disregard for the nonsense that seemed to bog down half the world. All that talk Dermot went on with about Protestant style and Catholic lack of confidence would have made their father roar with laughter as well as with derision.

George Fitzgibbon did not appear to be a man who thought the way Dermot did about that. *His* family had converted over to Catholicism.

'A great character your father was,' said George. 'Not prudent – no, I couldn't say that about him, but a man with a generous nature and a great love of life. One night – I remember it well – he came into the shop in the middle of winter with no coat on. "Where's your coat?" I said. "Aren't you out of your mind to be going around like that, asking to catch your death of cold?" And he said to me, "George, I met a poor fellow over in William Street with only a shirt on his shoulders so I put my coat on him."'

'That would be like my father all right,' said Tom, moved by the story and by George Fitzgibbon's appreciation of the event.

In that moment he felt at home in the stuffy room. It was far from Tir na nOg and there was still no sign of Niamh but the man in the yellow chair was filling a gap in his life that had been there since his father's death.

'Ah, here's tea,' said George, getting up again as the fierce housekeeper, her pale lips sucked together in disapproval, came in with a tray.

72

As she bent to set it down on a small rosenut and walnut table Tom could hear her corsets creaking and he had to stop himself smirking in glee.

'I'll leave you to it,' said George Fitzgibbon, unexpectedly.

'Are you not staying?'

'I must get back to work. You know how it is.'

'Indeed – indeed,' said Tom, who did not know at all.

George Fitzgibbon disappeared into the gloom and the front door slammed.

'I'll pour the tea for you,' said the housekeeper coldly.

Where *was* Milliora? Five more minutes and if she's not here, I'm off, thought Tom before spotting his favourite Madeira cake on the tray. Mollified by that, he was depressed again by the frostiness of the house-keeper. Why didn't she like him?

'Thank you, that's very nice.'

''Tis no trouble,' said the housekeeper, looking as if it was.

So Tom O'Brien, who had never been rejected or let down by anyone, was thrown off balance by the time Milliora made her appearance. It was a spectacular appearance and no one, least of all Tom, could have guessed from her unconcerned countenance the amount of effort and forethought that had gone into it.

She was wearing a tea-gown of spotted muslin printed in mauve and green on a background of white silk. The sleeves puffed up from the shoulders and the Watteau back fell in a wide box pleat across the shoulderline so she seemed to float effortlessly into the room. Her red-gold hair was pinned up to the top of her head, but she had allowed little tendrils to escape so it softened the face below. It was a warm day and in her right hand she carried a fan of painted white gauze and Honiton lace, which had once belonged to her mother.

'Holy Saint Joseph!' said Tom to himself.

He was standing over by the tea-tray, about to help himself to a slice of chocolate sponge. Milliora, with a swift glance at the tray, noticed that he had already eaten two pieces of the Madeira cake.

She had eaten nothing all day and was sure she could never face food again. Or sleep, either, having not slept all night in anticipation of Tom's visit.

None of this showed on her face, only the bloom of youth and under it the lamina of love.

'Good afternoon, Mr O'Brien,' she managed with, Tom thought, incredible assurance. 'Please be seated and make yourself at home.'

Doing his best to ignore his conviction that Milliora's parents were watching him from the walls, he eased himself on to a massive carved mahogany-framed sofa, highly over-ornamented and upholstered in black, shiny, prickly horsehair, while Milliora took up a position on a small-waisted, rococo chair, her hand hovering over the teapot.

'Sugar, Mr O'Brien?'

'Yes – please. Two.'

'And is your mother feeling better now?'

'She's very well. Thank you.'

There was a wall of gentility between them. Milliora had not anticipated the difficulty of talking to Tom between now and the altar. Having cast him as a hero, she had had a vague idea that he would come to tea having learnt his lines beforehand.

But Tom had always shrugged off any form of

affectation and he had no reserve of small talk. Waiting for him to say more, Milliora noted that his nails were rather dirty and that there was a hole in one of his socks. None of this worried her.

More troubling was the fact that she was experiencing a strong resurgence of the tingling sensation that had attacked her at the fête. After she had handed Tom his tea, she slotted in a silent prayer to Our Lady, asking Her to send the Devil away.

'You live at O'Brien's Bridge, my father tells me. It must be nice to be close to the river,' she essayed, hoping Tom would take up this theme.

'It's grand,' Tom said – and said no more.

It was not how the heroes in books behaved. Still, Milliora was not easily deterred.

'The river is quite wide at that point – and deep, too, I hear,' she persisted.

There was a loud knock on the door.

'Come in.'

'You have a visitor, Miss Milliora,' said the horrible housekeeper, and someone else came into the room.

Rosaleen wished she could go back to the convent. Grand-aunt Carrie was willing to spend money on her but she did not enjoy having her in the house, a late sixteenth-century cut-stone showpiece set in charming grounds.

To keep out of Grand-aunt Carrie's way, Rosaleen had gone into Kilmallock that morning. A hiring fair was being held, with farmers viewing would-be employees who had come in from various parts of County Limerick in search of seasonal work. At the junction in the centre of town, men in torn breeches and women with worn-out shawls eyed her resentfully, adding to her sense of rejection.

She turned into Emmet Street, where Blossom Gate, the town's last surviving gate, spanned the roadway, and thought again about Milliora and Tom O'Brien. She should not have allowed envy and hate to get the better of her. Milliora was of inestimable value and she was already missing her desperately. No chasm must form in their relationship.

Milliora, of course, had no idea that there had been a threat of fissure, not being able to understand how anyone could put energy into enmity and vengeance when they could be using it more positively to their own ultimate good, so Rosaleen decided she could hardly write to her and apologize.

By then she had reached the ruins of the Abbey, a thirteenth-century Dominican priory. On one of the corbels there was the figure of a woman, her function, to support the arch. A woman with love in her heart and her arms outstretched to the world, reminiscent of Milliora.

Rosaleen would write anyway. The letter could simply assure Milliora of their life-long friendship and ask when they could meet – nothing more than that, but it would serve to heal the breach.

Thinking about it, Rosaleen felt much better. Hurrying home with the letter in mind, she saw Grand-aunt Carrie from the drawing-room door. The room was in some confusion, she could see, with her grand-aunt supervising the placing of an oval table in the middle of the floor.

'No, no – more to the left. Yes – no. Now a little more to the right,' she was saying to the maid and the housekeeper, who were raising their eyes in despair.

'Ah, Rosaleen,' said Grand-aunt Carrie, taking a step backwards and bumping into the girl. She sounded disappointed and this was borne out by her next remark. 'I had forgotten all about you. Of course, you're home from school.'

'Since yesterday,' Rosaleen reminded her. 'You were having dinner at Mr Desmond Fitzgerald's when I arrived.'

'So I was. And a very good dinner it was, too. So you're home for the holidays, are you?'

'I'm home for good, Aunt Carrie. Have you forgotten that I've left school?'

'So you have,' said her grand-aunt, without enthusiasm. 'We must do something about that. But I'm afraid you've chosen an inopportune time to arrive, most inopportune. I have a number of people coming around this afternoon for tea and you really can't be here.'

'I can't? Not anywhere in the house?'

'No. You're not a sensitive, dear, and your presence would affect the success of the seance. The correct atmosphere could not be conjured up if you were to stay in the house. You were not here during our previous meetings but I can assure you that the most extraordinary raps were produced – and they were not only confined to the table. We received them through that footstool over there, and on the back of the prie-dieu.'

'But how amazing. Couldn't I just watch?'

'No, dear. Mrs Everitt would not like that at all. She is here on a visit from England and she is *very* particular about who she admits. We were all so impressed by the rappings but I understand that table-moving is very much more spectacular. Apparently, the table not only rocks, but levitates into the air as well. Of course, the real purpose of it is to transmit messages from the dead. She assures me that genuine spirit messages may be obtained, including any sentiments of a distinctly religious character. So you see how important it is that the atmosphere be absolutely right.'

'I do – I do,' said Rosaleen, earnestly.

She was beginning to realize that the seance could be used to her own advantage.

'If it is essential that I be out of the house . . .'

'It is – quite essential.'

'Then perhaps I could take Matt Ryan and the carriage and go visiting in Limerick?'

'What an excellent idea,' said Grand-aunt Carrie, relieved. '*Not* there, Mrs Scanlon. I thought I said to the *left*.'

She had already lost interest in Rosaleen.

I will not bother with a letter, the girl thought. I can call on Milliora instead.

'You have a visitor, Miss Milliora,' said Mrs Woulfe, the housekeeper, and once again Rosaleen was looking at Tom O'Brien.

Who was not pleased to see her – that much was certain. He got to his feet, smiling like a stranger greeting another stranger into whose company he has been reluctantly drawn. To him, Rosaleen was painfully aware, this was their first encounter. He had never noticed her before.

For a very long moment nobody spoke. Then Milliora, wearing a social mask to hide *her* dismay at Rosaleen's intrusion, said, 'Rosaleen, how lovely to see you. Come in and meet Mr Tom O'Brien. Mr O'Brien – Miss O'Flynn.'

'How do you do?' said Tom, looking more godlike than ever.

'What a nice surprise! Did you come in all the way from Kilmallock specially to see me or were you in town anyway? Sit down and tell me what you think of my Madeira cake.'

'Did you make it yourself?' asked Tom, impressed. 'It's the best cake I've ever tasted.'

'I'm so glad you think so,' Milliora purred.

They beamed at each other approvingly. There might have been no one else in the room at all.

How boring I must seem to Tom O'Brien, in comparison to Milliora, Rosaleen thought, a suspicion borne out by the fact that shortly afterwards Tom said that he must leave.

'I suppose you never get time for a rest, running that big estate,' said Milliora, who had prised information about the O'Briens and Crag Liath out of her father. 'Your responsibilities must be legion.'

'They are indeed,' said Tom, whose only plan for that evening was a visit to Jamie Keegan. 'If it's all right with you, Miss Fitzgibbon, I would like to call on you again.'

'That would be very pleasant,' Milliora said demurely.

'Shall we say Tuesday at this time?'

'That would be quite suitable,' said Milliora and, with all the aplomb in the world, or so it seemed to Rosaleen, she got up and saw the blue-eyed god to the door.

'Isn't he handsome?' extolled Milliora, when Tom was well gone. 'It's so exciting, Rosaleen. I can't tell you

79

how much in love I am! You do like him, don't you? It would be dreadful if you didn't.'

She executed a pirouette around the room, holding out her slender arms, laughing and landing with a plonk on to the sofa vacated by Tom.

'Rosaleen, you're not saying anything. Aren't you impressed by my beautiful young man?'

'Yes, I am,' said Rosaleen truthfully, feeling dull, unattractive and unwanted.

'You must help me plan the wedding,' said Milliora, gaily. 'When I think about it, which I do all the time, I can see the two of us, you and I, walking up the aisle.'

'The two of us?' Rosaleen was startled out of her self-absorption.

'Well, naturally, you will be my chief bridesmaid,' Milliora said. 'You're my best friend. Francie isn't half as close to me as you are and, anyway, she wants to be a nun. I do wish bustles were still in fashion, don't you? Or crinolines. Think how I could sway – and maybe show my ankles! Did you know that boots with high heels came in for modesty's sake because crinolines swung backwards and forwards and showed off so much of your legs?'

'No, I didn't know.'

How could Milliora be so frivolous? Surely there were more important things in life than wedding-gowns and boots.

But Milliora had veered on from wedding ensembles to another, just-as-fascinating subject.

'Did you know that Tom O'Brien has a brother? Father asked me which of the O'Brien brothers was coming to call and when I told him he said there is another one called Dermot. Tom is twenty-two or three, Father says, and his brother is two years younger. Which means he's just right for you!'

'For me?'

'Yes. Wouldn't it be wonderful if you were to marry Tom's brother? Oh, it's got to happen like that! Even if you don't meet him in the meantime, you'll be paired off with him at the wedding because he'll be the best man and then – you'll see – it will happen naturally. I just know it will. And when I'm married to Tom, and you two are wed, you and I will be sisters, as well as friends for life. Goodness, I'm hot and excited, aren't you?'

She picked up the Honiton fan.

'Would you like a piece of Madeira cake, Rosaleen?'

'I don't think so, thank you,' Rosaleen said. 'I'm just not very hungry.'

5

Tom belonged to Milliora. The fact was confirmed by his twice-weekly visits to the house in George Street during that summer, and Rosaleen had no choice but to accept it.

Spending too much time alone, without access to people of her own age other than – on occasions – Milliora, her dream of Tom was all the diversion she had to feed off. Believing herself in love with him, she continued to suffer the pain of the unrequited.

The women of Crag Liath suffered, too, the flames of their anxiety fanned by the rumours about Tom and Milliora that filtered back to the estate from various contacts in Limerick. Kitty McCormac, who had been in Carmel's class at school, swore that the couple had been unchaperoned at least once, she having been driving down George Street one afternoon as Tom arrived and Mrs Woulfe went out, but Kitty was a notorious and unreliable gossip and the trio dismissed her report as highly suspect.

Kitty did succeed in jogging Carmel's memory of Milliora as a bossy little piece, full of herself, who specialized in making up to the nuns.

'They only liked her because her father was always making donations to the convent,' said Carmel to the others.

'And what is he, anyway, but a publican, for all that he calls himself a wine merchant?' Mary said derisively.

'Tom was talking about him the other day. He says he was a friend of Father's,' Carmel said, thoughtfully.

'A friend of your father's, was he?' Fiona O'Brien was mortally affronted.

Throughout her marriage, she had been forced to stay at home of an evening while 'friends' took her husband cavorting. George Fitzgibbon would have been her enemy, even if he had not fathered a daughter who was pursuing Tom.

Fiona was soon beset by additional worry. In July, a heat-wave shimmered over the crops. In August, the weather changed drastically. The corn was fit for the scythe and the mowing machine but the labourers, taken out each day to cut it, were forced to return with half-earnings and broken time because of torrential rain. Large quantities of barley were left lying on the ground without drying out. There were signs of blight in the potato fields.

Crag Liath reaped a lamentable harvest but, characteristically, Tom seemed undeterred.

Not so Dermot, groaning with frustration that in the running of Crag Liath his own hands should be tied. How could Tom maintain an adequate cash-flow in the immediate future? If only he would make an attempt to collect the long-overdue rents there could be a glimmer of hope but misguided altruism and natural carelessness prohibited him from doing so. Unable to communicate even at the best of times, Fiona and Dermot worried separately, seeing Tom ride out risking a massive fall.

That possibility was on Dermot's mind one morning in October as he walked out to the stables, leaving Tom asleep in bed.

'Tom's getting worse, rather than better,' he

observed to Tim-Pat, 'lazing in bed at this hour of the morning and the rest of us off to work!'

'Have you heard the news about Mr Parnell?' was Tim-Pat's rejoinder to this. 'Hasn't he been arrested and put in Kilmainham jail?'

'Is that so? Well, if politicians will pander to the hotheads in the Land League what else can they expect?' said Dermot, without sympathy. 'That speech he made the other day at Waterford calling Gladstone a masquerading knight errant was simply asking for trouble.'

Why a Protestant landowner like Charles Stewart Parnell should devote his whole life to the cause of the Irish peasant farmer, moving out of his natural habitat and mixing with the riff-raff in the process, was as inexplicable to Dermot as Tom's behaviour in lying in bed late this morning when there was work to supervise on the estate.

Still, Parnell's arrest gave his mother and two sisters something to talk about other than Tom and Milliora Fitzgibbon, Dermot decided at dinner.

'Apparently he was as cool and composed and courteous as ever as they led him away,' Mary said.

'We had warnings that bad times were coming,' said Fiona, sepulchrally. 'This terrible harvest, and poor Mr Garfield dying in America, and Pope Pius IX in Rome.'

'What have those things got to do with Parnell?' Tom wanted to know.

'They were warnings of the displeasure of God with the world,' his mother professed solemnly. 'Oh, the world is in a bad condition altogether!'

Tom reached out for the butter and spread it liberally over his boiled potatoes.

'Mother, I'd like to bring Miss Fitzgibbon out here to tea on Sunday,' he announced, and added horseradish to his over-piled plate. 'Would that be suitable for you?'

It was a statement rather than a question, and all of the family knew it.

'Who is Miss Fitzgibbon?' Fiona asked after a long pause.

Under the table, Mary and Carmel reached out for each other's hands and Dermot pretended to cough.

'Miss Milliora Fitzgibbon – George Fitzgibbon's daughter. I have been visiting her for some time.'

'Is that so? And why would you be bringing her here, Tom?'

If there was to be further bad news in the form of an impending engagement Fiona suddenly wanted to know at once. But Tom was not yet ready to talk about marriage, or so he told himself.

He gave the impression of being blasé about his relationship with Milliora but this was not the case. Milliora to him was a decorative and desirable object, a life-size Staffordshire figurine that he wanted to possess. The currency, of course, was marriage and for the last five months Tom had been debating whether this was not too high a price to pay, even for so valuable a treasure.

Jamie Keegan reckoned that it was, that Tom should enjoy his freedom for as long as possible. But the frustrating afternoons in the stuffy drawing-room were beginning to tell on Tom. His desire for Milliora was so strong that he could think of nothing else but what it would be like to touch the tempting mound of her young breasts or even slip a hand under her petticoat. Both of these acts would be mortal sin but, contrary to Kitty McCormac's report, Mrs Woulfe the housekeeper had intensified her self-imposed chaperonage of the two of them recently, and there was no likelihood of Tom ending up in Hell on that score.

So he found himself in two minds: on the one hand, proceeding with a traditional courtship, and on the other, leading a bachelor existence, carousing with Jamie, at which time he pushed marriage right out of his mind.

This indecision would have astonished and shocked Milliora had she known of it. She expected his proposal daily and when Tom invited her to tea at Crag Liath she fondly imagined that his family would be looking forward to meeting her every bit as she was to meeting them. All that concerned her was what to wear for this momentous occasion and how to dress her hair.

Until the day Milliora saw Crag Liath, her attention had been completely occupied by Tom, her young king who, she had discovered from reading about the O'Brien's, was descended from Brian Boru himself. But when Tim-Pat, who had gone into Limerick with the carriage to fetch her, brought her out to Crag Liath, her vision of Tom widened out like a river in flood to incorporate his kingdom as well.

As the carriage sped up the avenue and she caught glimpses of the estate, she realized for the first time what it meant to be an O'Brien.

All that land, stretching away to the hills – and all ruled by Tom! No wonder he sometimes seemed tired, with dark shadows under his beautiful blue eyes. It could not be easy (although very attractive) for a person to wield such power.

Slightly dazed, she breathed in the good country air, approving of Tom's kingdom and envisaging her future role as its queen. She wanted to acknowledge the stares of the labourers with a nod and to tilt her right hand outwards to them like Queen Victoria but she thought that it might be a little early in the day for that, which was just as well for her. Next year, when Tom and she were married, the labourers would expect her to behave in a regal manner and by that time she would know them all by name. As Mistress of Crag Liath she would have to deal with their domestic problems, make sure that they and their wives and children stayed in good health, to facilitate the smooth running of the estate.

In her daydreams she paid no heed to what Tom's mother might think of her taking over. Milliora was playing a role in a fairy-tale and Prince Charming was standing outside a big oak door to greet her when the carriage pulled up. Milliora decided at once that she loved the house. Its sombre veneer she converted into majestic. She would have been worried had Crag Liath not taken itself seriously, as befitted a royal abode.

Seeing herself at this stage as a princess, she waited for Prince Charming to rush forward to help her out of the carriage. When he did not budge she found herself in a quandary for the shawl-like sleeves of her green dolman limited the mobility of her arms to such an extent that she was virtually in deadlock.

'Tom,' she called out, put out by his lack of manners but trying not to show it, 'would you help me down, please?'

'Of course I will,' said Tom, doing just that.

Although his gallantry was sometimes slow in manifesting itself, it did exist. As he assisted Milliora from the carriage they were both on view to Mary and Carmel, watching from upstairs with the bedroom window open so they could hear what was going on.

'Look at the power she has over him already,' said Mary, her heart breaking because no man had ever looked at her the way her brother was looking at Milliora.

'We had better go down. Dermot's in the drawing-room with Mother already,' Carmel said, slamming the window shut.

They reached the hall just as Milliora was being led into the drawing-room by Tom who, on her instructions, had prised off her dolman and hung it up. Underneath was a walking costume in the same green, which aptly showed off her hair.

Feeling pleased with herself, Milliora was quite unprepared for the frosty reception waiting her when she confronted Tom's mother, perched like a large black crow on a lacquered rosewood chair. Standing to the left of her was a young man with straight, dark brown hair and blue eyes, whom she guessed was Tom's brother. She had no recollection of seeing him at the Laurel Hill fête, counting only Tom as important.

What appalled her was that neither Tom's mother nor his brother were smiling as she approached them. She registered that Tom's mother had the same deep blue eyes as his, but hers had no humour.

'So you're Miss Fitzgibbon?' Tom's mother said.

No one introduced her to Dermot, or to Mary and Carmel, who had come in behind her and were looking her up and down the way, she recalled, the same girls used to do a few years back at Laurel Hill. Then, as now, they had not been given to bestowing benevolent smiles.

Mary Markham, coming into the drawing-room with a loaded tea-tray, was much upset by what happened next. Only a few days before, Tom, back from a late night out with Jamie, had fallen over a tapestry chair and broken one of its legs. Mary had propped it up against the wall and warned the family not to sit on it.

And now Carmel, who knew full well what she was doing, stepped forward and said, 'Miss Fitzgibbon, do sit there,' gesturing to that very chair.

'Ho, the shame of it!' Mary Markham said to Mrs Cash, the washerwoman, over a cup of tea a few minutes later. 'That a member of this family should behave in such a way! That poor child, Miss Fitzgibbon, sits down in the broken chair in front of the lot of them with herself, as cranky as an old plough, looking her up and down. And then what do you think happened?'

'The chair fell down, I suppose, and the young lady along with it,' said Mrs Cash, unlocking the tea-caddy and stirring another spoonful into the pot.

She glanced quickly at the door as she did so, ready to hide the caddy if Fiona came in. Tea was expensive and Mrs O'Brien kept track of what they drank.

'That wasn't all that happened,' said Mary, divided between her pleasure in a good story and her sympathy for Milliora.

'Well, will you go on. I suppose you're going to tell me that she fell over and the whole lot of them could have a look at her drawers.'

'Indeed she did,' said Mary. 'That poor child – the point of a rush would take a drop of blood out of her cheek, the way she crimsoned up. And Master Dermot standing there, as well.'

'That fellow,' said Mrs Cash, grimacing. 'Wouldn't he steal the eye out of your head and come back for the eyelash, if you gave him half a chance. And Master Tom – was he not in the room at the time?'

'He was indeed,' said Mary.

She paused, smiling, and slowly refilled her cup. Sipping from it, she forced Mrs Cash to wait for the best part of the story.

'And what did *he* do, may I ask?'

Gratified that Mrs Cash had been compelled to press for further information, Mary Markham proceeded.

'Wasn't he down at her side in two shakes of a lamb's tail, getting her back on her feet and holding on to her arm to steady her. And all the while the two girls are sniggering and herself is as windy as the Sally Gap about what is going on. Master Tom took account of it all, I can tell you, and there was fire coming out of his eyes. For all that had been done to her, Miss Fitzgibbon had a straight back on her as if she was after swallowing a crowbar and not a peep out of her against them. Then Master Tom smiled at her and he squeezed her hand in front of them all, and then he turned round to look at the family. And do you know what he said?'

'I do not,' said Mrs Cash, leaning forward with her hand cupping her chin. 'Will you go on and tell me before one of them comes in and spoils it?'

'They've got too much on their minds to be coming in here at the moment,' Mary Markham said meaningfully. 'Master Tom has surprised them all right. I could see their faces while he was talking and they were the ones in a state.

'"*Wasn't that a thing to have happened,*" he said, "*the day I bring home the girl who's going to be my wife!*"'

Rosaleen's day, although very different from Milliora's, had also precipitated her from happy excitement into the realms of trauma.

Grand-aunt Carrie having finally agreed that Conan

90

Maol was too small for Rosaleen to ride, had despatched her the day before to the home of Owen Hogan, the Kilfinane horse-breeder, to conclude the purchase of a horse.

She had been woken early by the milkmaid's singing and by ten o'clock the deal had been struck. Cu Chulainn – named after the legendary hero – was coal black, with a waving mane, a rapid foot, and an arching neck. He was the perfect mount for a woman, more elegant than powerful, and she could not wait to be up on his back.

'I think I'll take him out for a while,' she said to Mr Hogan.

'Do as you like, my girl. He's all yours,' he said, and she set off, riding further round the hill country than she had at first intended, circling the busy market town, going past Kilfinane Moat where long-forgotten rulers once held sway. Milliora, who had been full of O'Brien history since meeting Tom, had told her that Brian Boru's brother, Mahon, King of Munster, had been touring his kingdom not far from here when he was set about and attacked by his rivals.

But Rosaleen decided not to think about the O'Briens today, which meant not thinking of Tom O'Brien, lest she remove the happiness out of the ride and replace it with sadness.

She was trespassing, although she did not know it, in the grounds of Lady Ashton's estate when she ran into the big crowd, some of them brandishing sticks and most of them shouting. There were police everywhere. Cu Chulainn snorted his disapproval but otherwise kept his head and she pulled up on the outskirts of the crowd to see what was going on.

The disturbance seemed to be centred on a small

cabin, which she caught sight of when an angry man moved to the left and hurled a stone at the police. At once, he was cornered by two of them and held to one side.

Rosaleen saw then that the door and the two little windows of the cabin had been blocked up with stones to prevent the police getting in. An eviction, with people out to prevent it.

'Is there someone inside the cabin?' she asked one of the shawly women standing nearby.

'There's a woman in there, and a number of children with her.'

'The poor things. Is there no hope they can stay on in the house?'

'What do you think yourself, miss?' the shawly woman wanted to know, pointing out armed soldiers forcing their way through the crowd.

The soldiers deployed into a line.

'Fix bayonets,' came the order and the crowd, pushed back so that a hollow square formed about the house, fell silent.

Into the square marched other figures – the sheriff of the area and his bailiffs, burly men with hard, set faces. Their advent broke the silence. A man in a dirty, double-breasted waistcoat that had seen better days began to hurl abuse and at the same time the rain began to fall.

'Bastards!'

'This is no place for you, miss,' the shawly woman said. 'Why don't you be off home out of the way?'

'If it's good enough for you, it's good enough for me,' said Rosaleen softly.

Deep inside her an anger was rising. The rent on a cabin like this was probably fourteen pounds a year –

nothing at all to the likes of Lady Ashton, who would pay that much, and more, just for a beautiful dress.

'Where's the man of the house gone?'

'They took him away before the proceedings started,' said the well-informed woman, wiping the rain off her face with her hand. 'Wasn't he cursing at the constabulary, using words that didn't please them! Will you look at that now, miss – they're going to try and break in at the door.'

'Bastards!' shouted the man in the cast-off waistcoat again.

Around him, several men were picking up stones.

'Move in there.'

The pathetic defence was rapidly breached. With a final blow of his sledge-hammer one of the bailiffs dislodged the stones at the door. Suddenly, he screamed, dropping the hammer and reeling backwards, his hands over his eyes.

'What is it?'

'A bucket of boiling water, miss. Isn't it all she has to defend herself with, for all the good it will do her.'

But the shawly woman's words were lost in the uproar from the crowd. Above it rose the screams of the threatened woman, still invisible inside the house. Mesmerized, Rosaleen watched the bailiffs move forward, saw the windows broken open and, finally, the thin, haggard woman and her seven scrawny children pushed out into the rain.

The anger was consuming her now, throbbing in her head, obsessing her so she was unaware of her tears and pain. Huddling the children to her, the evicted woman stood helplessly and watched as the bailiffs went into the house again and re-emerged with a broken table, two deal chairs and an iron bedstead with a torn straw mattress. With a few pertinent blows of the hammers, what had once been an excuse for furniture was reduced to fragments on the ground.

Rosaleen had no memory of leaving the place, only of somehow finding herself in Hogan's yard, with the rain pelting down on her head.

But all her life she would remember the vow she made there, to do all she could for Ireland. There was nothing she could do for the evicted woman and her children – she knew that only too well. Only this morning, Owen Hogan had said he had all the labour he needed and more, and he wished he could find a solution to the numbers of people going round on the roads without work. She had no money of her own to give to such people. The purchase of Cu Chulainn had already been completed – she could not renege on that.

Anyway, selling Cu Chulainn and giving the proceeds to the woman would bring Grand-aunt Carrie's wrath down on her head, and maybe see herself homeless. Nor would it assist the thousands of other unfortunates who were evicted every year and made their homes on the sides of the roads or even in the trees.

Rather, she would *use* Cu Chulainn in a bid to help them, riding around to see what money she could raise on their behalf. Just how she would achieve this was still a little hazy, but thinking of it, becoming resolute, brought colour into her pale cheeks.

Owen Hogan, leading out a young horse from a loose box, caught sight of her and looked surprised. He had thought her a mousy little thing when she arrived yesterday, shy and unsure of herself. Now, with her head thrown back and her face alive with an unknown passion, she was looking a different woman.

94

'Little Miss O'Flynn has the makings of a beauty,' he said to his wife when Rosaleen had gone.

Mrs Hogan, having failed to witness the transformation, could not imagine what he meant.

'Insipid', was her opinion. 'I can't imagine any man falling in love with *her*!'

Tom's soft heart had bled for Milliora, when he saw her lying in an undignified position on the floor, with his sisters sniggering at her. He wanted very badly to wallop the pair of them but, even more than that, he wanted to comfort Milliora.

And to make love to her. It was not only the erotic sight of her white drawers and her slender ankles that affected him (that was all he saw of her legs, for most of them were covered by frills) but also her vulnerable plight. That quality in a woman drew him just as spirit did, but it was tenderness that most made him want to make love.

Burning with anger and desire, Tom gave way to an impulse that would, at one fell swoop, defeat his sisters and, ultimately, give him access to Milliora. He knew by then that the family was nervous at the prospect of his marriage but he also thought they were ridiculous to feel like that since, surely, they knew that he would always see them right and that no woman would overrule him.

In the meantime, Carmel and Mary could stew in their own bitter juice while he showed them who was master.

He could see their suffering written all over their pudgy faces as soon as he made his announcement. Elated by this, and by the realization that he would soon possess Milliora, he felt wildly, crazily airborne.

Milliora, her dignity restored, was looking at him with stars in her eyes and suddenly he could not wait another moment to get her out of the house and have her to himself for a few minutes.

'Well now,' he said into the vacuum caused by his bombshell, 'you know – and you can all offer your congratulations later. I'm taking Milliora down to the stables to meet Tim-Pat. If you're going to become an O'Brien, Milly, one thing is certain – you must learn to ride a horse!'

And before she had time to reply he put both arms around her waist and, to the amazement of the family, virtually waltzed her out of the room.

'Tom!' she tried to protest in the hall, but he shook his finger at her.

'Ssh. Come on,' and, taking her hand, ran with her down the back stairs, past the boot cupboard that might or might not lead to a secret passage, into the kitchen where both Mary Markham and Mrs Cash leapt to their feet in surprise, and out into the yard.

Her first view of the rear of Crag Liath house was a conglomeration of scattered images: fussy, cackling hens scattering; a puzzled dairymaid with a pail on her head and her mouth falling open as the two of them sped past; apples trees; a hay-barn; sheds. By the time they reached the stables she was completely out of breath.

A small man with a half-moon mouth was grooming a big grey horse.

'Tim-Pat!' Tom hailed him. 'I've got someone to introduce to you. This is the girl who's going to be my wife.'

'That's great news entirely,' said the small man,

putting his scraper down on the ground and reaching for Tom's hand. 'Great news,' he repeated.

But he did not sound sincere. Milliora decided that he was probably no better than Tom's sisters whose behaviour in the drawing-room had shocked her to the core. That Carmel could have positioned her in a broken chair out of malice never crossed her mind – she thought her fall was a genuine accident – but the lack of gentility shown by the girls, their giggling and nudging, was unladylike and distasteful. And they were *O'Briens!* She could hardly believe such a thing could happen.

They had been too open, whereas the man Tom called Tim-Pat was not showing his true feelings – she was sure of it. An inscrutable kind of creature and far too familiar with Tom, shaking his hand as if they were equals.

'Tim-Pat is a great man with the horses,' Tom said to her.

'Better than you?' She had finally caught her breath.

'Oh, much better than me. We'll get him to give you riding lessons and you'll be an expert yourself in no time. Isn't that right, Tim-Pat?'

'We will. No doubt about it,' Tim-Pat prophesied, nodding his head as if he meant it.

'Come on.' Tom was still elated and looking for an outlet for fun. 'Show Miss Fitzgibbon what you can do with a horse.'

And that was how Milliora learnt of the tricks Tim-Pat was able to play.

The apple orchard would have been a romantic setting in spring, with the blossoms on the trees and maybe falling on her hair, but on a windy day in October it was not the best place to try to kiss a girl.

Tom's euphoria was such that he took it for granted that, wherever they were, Milliora would be bound to respond to his mood. Leading her into the orchard, it never occurred to him that she might be feeling cold without her dolman, or fussing about what the wind was doing to her hair.

Or that she might still be in a state of shock about what had happened in the drawing-room, or dazed by the series of varied sensations that she had been experiencing since her arrival at Crag Liath.

Having drawn her into the orchard on the pretext that she must see more of the grounds, Tom pulled her into his arms more roughly than he intended.

'Tom!'

It was the voice of outrage, rather than that of love. Subconsciously, he registered his dislike of it, but he was too excited to pay it heed. He could feel Milliora's breasts against his chest and although so much of her was firmly corseted, the contact gave him a better idea of what was inside her many garments than he had ever had before. His left hand was hard on the back of her neck, agitating her hair; his right moved fast and forcibly down to her waist, pulling her vigorously into him so that her body arched and her nipples prickled and swelled.

'Tom . . .'

His open mouth was on her soft one and his tongue, brutal only because of his pent-up longing, was trying to force its way inside. Almost at once it succeeded, threshing inside her dry mouth in search of a response. The hand that had been round her waist moved down in a vain attempt to pull up her green skirt and her hands – which, instead of being around his neck, had been lying in shock at her sides – automatically reached out to prevent him.

'No!'

Somehow she had twisted away from him and, although his arms were still around her, all he could see of her was the top of her red-gold head.

'Milly,' he whispered in concern because he thought he had heard a sob, 'look at me. It was only because I want you so much.'

There was no reply.

'Milly, please look up at me,' Tom pleaded. 'I love you. Don't you love me at all?'

At that she did look up under her eyelashes while, at the same time, placing one hand against his chest as if to ward him off.

'Have I offended you?' he persisted. 'I'm very, very sorry.'

'Are you?'

'Truly I am. Have I done a terrible wrong?'

'Yes, you have,' said Milliora, pulling herself free of him and trying not to mind because it was so cold. 'You see . . .'

'Yes?'

'You haven't proposed to me formally,' she said, to Tom's astonishment. 'You should have done that first and then talked to my father. *After* that was the time to kiss me, Tom, but it just wasn't proper before!'

It was Tom's turn to be shocked. She was concerned about *etiquette*, for heaven's sake, rather than about passion!

'So would you propose now, please,' Milliora went on, seriously, 'and then when I go home, perhaps you can talk to Father.'

As the wind, blowing through the orchard, lifted the autumn leaves and blew them far away, so her words deprived him of elation. As much as Milliora approved of formality so Tom, the free spirit, abhorred it. He still wanted her, still believed that he loved her, but what she said was an icy blast, blowing spontaneity away.

He proposed to her in the orchard. He even – at her request – got down on his knees on a pile of coagulated leaves to do so, and was graciously accepted.

He rode after the carriage taking her back to Limerick and, as she had asked, spoke that night to her father and was given the appropriate seal of approval.

But, like the autumn leaves, his elation did not return.

6

Face-saving would always be of paramount importance to Milliora. Thrust into her mother's role from the age of ten, she needed dignity as a prop and drew strength from consciousness of her own sense of responsibility. Regaling Rosaleen with the story of her visit to Crag Liath and Tom's subsequent proposal, she omitted to mention the hostility of the women and her humiliation at Carmel's hands.

'You're so lucky!' said Rosaleen, from the bottom of her heart, longing herself to be encompassed into a family. 'Not only do you get the most sought-after man in the whole of Munster, but a mother of your own again, and two sisters, as well.'

'Yes, I am lucky, aren't I?' Milliora agreed, trying not to think of Fiona's unfriendly face and the sniggers of Mary and Carmel. 'The best bit, naturally, was Tom's proposal. Did I tell you he went down on his knees to me, and begged me to marry him?'

'Yes, you did,' said Rosaleen, wincing. 'And that he kissed you afterwards . . .'

In Milliora's version of the story, the kiss had come *after* the proposal, rather than before, in the proper order. Rosaleen did not press for details of the kiss, which was all to the good since Milliora did not want to discuss it either. Although, when she was alone, the kiss tended to take priority over everything else that had happened at Crag Liath, the memory shocked her. It had not been in keeping with her preconception of what a kiss should be. That was tender but formal and lovers did not open their mouths. The actuality was much more difficult to cope with, and she was relieved when Rosaleen moved on to more practical issues.

'When are you planning to marry, Milly?'

'On the sixth of May.'

'May? Isn't that a very short engagement?'

'I don't think so,' said Milliora airily, back on safer ground. 'In fashionable society, long engagements are not usual. May is a good month for a wedding. The country will look so pretty then. I've already spoken to Monsignor McEnvoy at St Munchins and everything is arranged.'

'Am I still going to be your chief bridesmaid? After all, there are Tom's sisters to consider.'

'Never mind about them. This is *my* wedding and I'll have everything just the way I want it. I've been thinking about bonnets and hair. I can see you with the front of your hair done in little ringlets round the fringe and the rest rolled back – like this – look. And perched right on the top a chapeau in Belgian straw, trimmed with white gauze and wild flowers and a cascade in one of the flower colours over the chignon. Straw would be so right for a spring wedding. What do you think of my idea?'

'It sounds lovely,' said Rosaleen, eagerly.

'It will be. I promise you that. Now about the dresses themselves – why are you frowning?'

Rosaleen got up from the massive sofa and wandered over to the window, gazing out thoughtfully at George Street and the people going by.

'It's all going to cost a lot of money, isn't it – your wedding, I mean?'

'What of it?' Milliora shrugged. 'Father can afford it.'

'A lot of people out there can't afford to eat properly,' Rosaleen said soberly, 'while we . . . Oh, I'm sorry, Milly, I don't mean to spoil your plans for the wedding.'

'You couldn't, anyway,' Milliora said. 'I don't know why you worry so much about these things. There'll always be rich people and poor people. There's nothing we can do about it beyond feeding the beggars that come to the door and giving to the St Vincent de Paul. God made it like that.'

'Did He? I think we made it like that – or the rich on the big estates who take advantage of the tenants by demanding too-high rents.'

'Oh, Rosaleen,' said Milliora exasperatedly, 'big estates wouldn't be economical if landlords didn't get their rents. How would Tom be able to run Crag Liath, for instance? Have you been paying attention to what those agitators in the Land League are saying? Your Grand-aunt Carrie will kill you, if she finds out.'

'She probably will,' said Rosaleen.

She was thinking that she would never be able to confide in Milliora about the secret life she was leading, and what she was doing, in a very small way, to try to help the poor.

It was a simple enough campaign, riding on Cu Chulainn around the Kilmallock district, virtually begging door to door, in order to build up a collection, but since it necessitated daily battles with her own shyness, Rosaleen found it anything but easy.

Milliora was right: Grand-aunt Carrie would have been wild with anger had she known that a member of her household was doing anything so intrusive and – as she would see it – demeaning, but fortunately, the older woman was too detached, too occupied with her seances and her table-moving, to be aware of what was going on.

Early on in her campaign, Rosaleen discovered that it was easier to get money out of people if you said it was for the poor, rather than for tenants who could not pay their rents. Generally, the richer people were, the more they seemed to think that defaulting tenants were lazy and that it was their own fault if they were evicted. These rich people being landlords themselves, they could hardly be expected to sympathize with the principle behind Rosaleen's action.

On the other hand, confronted with a pretty, well-dressed young lady who arrived in the grounds on an expertly-handled horse in magnificent condition, butlers and housemaids paved the way to satisfactory encounters with their employers.

The fact that Rosaleen blushed when making her requests was all the more endearing. When she said, 'It's on behalf of St Vincent de Paul – for the poor', no one doubted that she was a representative of an approved society.

And now she had seventeen pounds collected and she was going to prevent an eviction! In theory, the most difficult part of this undertaking lay in finding out where one was due to take place. It was not as if evictions were advertised in the *Weekly News*, the way Holohan's Mineral Waters were, or the steamships offering passages from Derry and Glasgow and Liverpool, over to New York.

In time, Rosaleen thought, she would pluck up the courage to talk to the people in the cottages too, and in that way find out what was going on in the Kilmallock district, but all she could do now was wander around on Cu Chulainn until she saw a likely crowd gathering. Remembering that eviction she had witnessed at Kilfinane, she tried to convince herself that it should not be too onerous a task to walk up to the sheriff before the family was thrown out on the road and announce that she was intervening on its behalf.

She was riding in the blue shadow of the Ballahoura Mountains when she saw ahead of her a contingent of mounted police moving fast in the direction of Ardpatrick. Her first instinct was – shamingly – to turn back, not from fear of the police, but from the horror of making a public spectacle of herself, giving out money in front of a crowd.

Then – like a vision – the desperate, haggard face of the evicted Kilfinane woman swam before her, reinforcing her vow, giving her the courage to proceed.

She urged Cu Chulainn on so that by the time the contingent had opened a gate and, turning right, had moved into the small green patch in front of the white thatched cabin, she was hot on its heels.

It was then that she realized that she was too late to stop the actual eviction, and that she had followed a back-up force, called out to quell an angry mob.

There were people everywhere – young and old, many of them wielding sticks and stones and all of them shouting abuse at the tops of their strident voices. A bailiff, his face streaming blood and an ugly bruise on his forehead, was escorted past by two members of the constabulary, to the accompaniment of jeers and laughs. Rosaleen's ears rang with the hate of these people and the temptation to flee was very strong, telling her that she was too young, too frail, too feminine to attempt to intervene.

She nearly gave way to it. The pathetic memory of a haggard woman, of seven scrawny children cast homeless into the rain, countermanded the order of temptation.

'Go on,' insisted the Kilfinane woman. 'Do it for your people.'

She was dismounting, commanding Cu Chulainn to be still, to wait till she came back.

Closing her eyes to the stares and the nudges, and her ears to the conjectures of the crowd, she forced her way through it, clutching the money she had collected in her hand, shaking with fear as she went.

She saw the pile of smashed furniture on the ground before she caught sight of the woman and children and then she did not see any of them clearly, only as a blur of weeping figures which, as she grew close to them, smelt of sweat and dirt.

Revulsed by their squalor, she was tempted again to flee, to dismiss them as animals who were used to surviving out in the open and would do so perfectly well without any help from her.

'Do it,' hissed the Kilfinane woman and, this time, her voice was harsh and ruthless and hateful.

Rosaleen reached out her clean, pale hand that, in her grand-aunt's house, was not required to wash a cup or brush a shoe, and, seeing it tremble, she pushed the money into the evicted woman's foul fingers.

Nothing happened. They were all rooted to the spot. Then –

'God between us and all harm!' the evicted woman whispered, unbelieving.

She took a step forward, moved as if to touch

106

Rosaleen, perhaps to reassure herself that the benefactor was real, rather than an illusion.

But Rosaleen had reached the end of her tether. She stepped back, scarlet-faced, acutely conscious of the crowd's interest in what was going on. She felt no sense of triumph in having helped the family, only sadness that she should have arrived on the scene after the furniture had been smashed.

'Excuse me.'

The people parted, gazing at her in amazement, and let her pass through.

It never struck her that, in creating her own diversion, she had stilled the crowd and made it easier for the police to disperse them later on. She had one thought and that was to get back to Cu Chulainn and ride home out of sight of the curious eyes and away from the horrible smell.

'Young woman . . .'

A priest was standing in front of her, a fine-looking man with a long, thin face and a beautiful smile.

'Father?'

'You gave money to those people?'

'Yes.'

'How much did you give, my child?'

'Seventeen pounds.'

'Seventeen pounds,' he repeated. 'A lot of money. Out of your own pocket, I suppose.'

'No,' she said, 'I collected it. I have no money of my own. I went round the country and told people it was for the St Vincent de Paul Society.'

'You did what?'

He was laughing. News of her action was getting around to the perimeter of the crowd. People were turning to point at her. Again, she wanted to flee.

'And did you enjoy doing what you did just now?' the priest wanted to know.

'I hated every minute of it,' said Rosaleen.

'Well, now, and isn't that quite a thing!' said the priest, still chuckling.

He suddenly held out his hand to her.

'I'm Father Matt Ryan, the curate of Kilteely,' he said. 'I'm an active campaigner against evictions myself and I admire you for what you did today.'

Milliora's day could not have been more different. Summonsed to Crag Liath again – this time, to discuss initial wedding preparations with Tom's mother – she made up her mind that, on this visit, she would not be intimidated by the women of the family.

As she drove out from Limerick, barefoot children ran into the road or looked over the loose stone walls ringing their cabins to see the fine lady going by. She liked that. She thought their adulation was her due.

Further into the country, the hedges reached out over her head for each other like lovers and united to form a yellowing ceiling. She drove through a still lush tunnel, its walls striated with wide, sharp grass, thistles and nettles. There was scarcely any sight at all of the autumn sun except where the ugly skeleton of an old tree, with branches like a chicken's wishbone, poked a resolute stab at the sky. Hidden, too, were the low, blue-black hills which, in summer, would run yellow with the gorse people believed to be lucky, and the misty pink lakes and turloughs of the Shannon. The country through which she was travelling was quite flat, for the County of Clare took its name from the Irish, *an clar*, meaning a level plain.

Soon, this would be her county. She would be a

108

countrywoman, rather than a city girl. She considered this, without emotion. She might know nothing of country ways but she was determined to rectify that, in order to be a good wife to Tom. If he wanted her to learn to ride a horse, she would do so and do it properly even if the thought of being perched on a horse's back sent cold shivers up and down her spine at the moment.

She would learn about the running of the estate and about the crop-growing and harvesting and animals – and even watch cows being milked, if Tom deemed it necessary, for the sake of her marriage, into which she intended to pour every bit of herself, the way women ought to do. This was the formula for success, she was sure, and she intended her life with Tom to be sublimely successful.

It was an anti-climax, therefore, to arrive at Crag Liath and find that Tom was missing. Dermot, looking both sympathetic and apologetic, greeted her in the hall.

'Tom went over to the Bloodsmiths' place this morning after a brood-mare that they're selling,' he said to her. 'We expected him back long since. I can't think what's holding him up.'

His heart went out to Milliora. Her second visit to Crag Liath and already Tom was keeping her waiting. Not to mention the tongue-lashing she could expect from his mother, when the two of them were alone.

'I'm sure that the buying and selling of horses is a very serious matter that takes a great deal of time to complete,' said Milliora, hiding her disappointment under what she felt was an appropriate gravity.

'Indeed it is,' Dermot said.

109

Let her retain her illusions about Tom, he thought. They will not be with her forever.

On an impulse, he decided to protect her from his mother, gate-crashing their tea-party and standing ready to intervene on Milliora's behalf if the going got too rough.

In no time at all, just as he had predicted, Milliora was out of her depth.

'*Straw* hats!' exclaimed Fiona. 'Straw is born vulgar and will soon die of the disease. I'm surprised at you, Milliora, I really am. The next thing we hear you'll be dispensing with bridesmaids' bonnets altogether. I'm told that, over in America, young women won't wear them anymore, to show how emancipated they are.'

'Straw was just an idea,' Milliora said hastily. 'And you don't have to worry about my having emancipated thoughts. I'm not like that, one little bit.'

'When we've had our tea, would you like to walk round the estate?' Dermot said to her before his mother could complete the process of annihilation. 'Mother could have a nice rest and we might run into Tom, coming back with the brood-mare.'

And I could talk to you on your own, and find out about your friend, he thought. For once, Tom's absence looked like being beneficial to himself.

Milliora smiled at him gratefully.

'I would love to walk round the estate,' she said, missing the venomous look that the remark provoked from the old woman sitting beside the fire. 'And, as you say, we might meet Tom.'

The poor optimistic girl, thought Dermot. Vulnerable as he was himself in relation to his brother, he saw her then as a fellow traveller walking a perilous road.

'You must excuse my mother,' he said when he had

finally prised her free. 'She had not been the same since my father died.'

'It's hard on people of that age when they lose their partner,' Milliora agreed. 'My father is in the same position.'

'Of course, your father is a widower,' said Dermot, thinking how sympathetic she was.

And a good addition to the family, whatever the others might say – or fear.

He did not feel at all apprehensive of Milliora. She was far less preying on the mind than either of his sisters and he began to look forward to having her close at hand, as an ally against sibling attacks and a direct link with Tom.

As he walked her round the front of the house, pointing into the distance to show her where the river acted as a boundary to the land, he found himself confiding in her about the man his father had been.

'Not very interested in the estate, I'm afraid. After the famine, people with heads on their shoulders realized that there was an alternative to competing with European prices for corn and root crops and they moved – at least partly – from tillage to pasture. But Pa only made a half-hearted stab at it and he wouldn't have done even that if Mother hadn't nagged him about it. I can well remember them arguing on the subject. Our corn and root yields compare favourably with Europe. We manage well enough, he would say. We don't want to just manage, Mother would tell him, but he didn't want to listen. You see, in spite of being a woman she knew what was going on and she realized that price movements favoured livestock more than grain. I say to Tom quite often that it's not just cattle we should be concentrating on at Crag Liath, it's sheep and poultry as well.'

'So would you dispense with corn and root crops altogether?' Milliora asked.

'No, not necessarily. But we have the climate and the soil to move exceptionally easily between tillage and livestock. On the other hand, if you concentrate on livestock production, you can reduce your need for labour and cut your costs that way. I've been trying to get that into Tom's head for ages!'

'Is that so?' Milliora seemed thoughtful. 'And what does he say when you tell him?'

'He thinks we're doing all right as we are,' Dermot said disgustedly.

'I see.'

But did she? Could she really be interested in the science of farming? Tom had said that, under her frills and flounces, she had a practical streak, but it was a far step from sewing and baking to understanding price movements and profit margins in relation to the farm.

'I hope I'm not boring you?'

'It's very interesting,' she said. 'I want to know *all* about the estate. You couldn't possibly bore me.'

What a change this was from the approaches of his sisters! By the time they had reached the dairy, where the weekly task of butter-making was almost completed, Dermot felt that he and Milliora were soulmates if not actually blood relations.

He showed her the butter-pats and the special butter-stamp with the family emblem, and offered her a sip of buttermilk.

'It's bitter!'

'Bitter-sweet. You'll get used to it in due course.'

To please him, she took a second sip and he thought

112

that his future sister-in-law was only sweetness; there was nothing bitter in her.

'Why have you got a St Brigid's cross hung up in there? Do the dairymaids say prayers while they churn?'

Dermot laughed.

'It's to ward off the fairies,' he told her. 'What a lot you have to learn about country ways. If they get in here and cast charms the girls will spend hours churning in vain. Or so they believe! Just like they're sure that the milk from a red cow is better than that from any other. Come on, let's walk over the fields a bit in the direction of Bloodsmiths' place. We could meet my brother coming back.'

And I could have a quite word with you about your little friend, he planned.

Following him past the milk sheds, Milliora barely missed stepping into a cow dung pad and tried not to look distasteful. Approaching them, she saw to her displeasure, was the man Tom had called Tim-Pat. In spite of the sunshine she shivered with apprehension.

'Great weather for this time of year,' he greeted them innocuously. 'Master Dermot, I just wanted to talk to you for a minute.'

'What is it?'

Tim-Pat glanced at Milliora and cocked an eyebrow at Dermot.

''Tis private, like.'

'Very well,' said Dermot, reluctant to relinquish Milliora's company. 'If you will excuse me for a minute – ' he said to her.

'Of course.'

She wandered tactfully out of earshot, pretending to

113

inspect the haggard where the hayricks and cornstacks were stored.

''Tis sorry I am to interrupt you, Master Dermot, but Master Tom has put me in a bit of a spot.'

'What has he done now?'

'I lent him a bit of money the other evening when he was going to the greyhounds. To tell the truth I didn't have it myself so I borrowed it off Michael Lenihan. And now –'

'Lenihan wants it back?'

'He has a lot of people feeding off him, the poor creature,' Tim-Pat said apologetically, 'or else he wouldn't ask.'

'Why shouldn't he ask?' said Dermot, furiously.

Tom, he thought, was not safe to let out alone. Borrowing money off his own employees and failing to pay it back! To make matters worse, he would take a bet himself on the fact that the greyhound in question was still running, way back on the track.

'I'll give you the money,' he said to Tim-Pat. 'Be sure that Lenihan gets it before the day is out.'

His own allowance, of course, came from Tom in the first place, but he looked after his money a lot better than his elder brother did. Knowing that, why didn't Tom come to him for a loan instead of jeopardizing the family honour by bothering the people who worked for him?

But it was in Tom's impulsive nature to borrow from whoever was near to him at the time.

'This is always a bad time of year for money, with the threshing just done and the milling still to complete and then the corn to be sold,' Tim-Pat said, trying to find, as they all did, an excuse for Tom's reprehensible behaviour.

114

'Every month is bad for money, as far as my brother is concerned,' Dermot riposted, paying off Tom's debt.

Someone really must get it into Tom's head that the O'Briens had standards to maintain. If they had to borrow at all, it should never be from their social inferiors.

But maybe Milliora would see to that. She smiled at him and he felt his bad mood lifting. Enough of Tom and his nonsense. Instead of dwelling on that, he would talk to Milliora about her pretty friend.

'He's so keen on you, Rosaleen, I'll have to introduce you.' Milliora was all set to match-make. 'Surely you remember seeing him at the fête? Or even out hunting? He remembers you well.'

'Does he?'

'Don't sound so disinterested. I promised him I would invite the two of you to tea. Let's make a date now.'

'I'm very busy at the moment,' Rosaleen said, frowning.

She was not at all eager to meet Tom's brother. However nice – however handsome he might be (and Milliora said he was both) – she could not possibly envisage his being able to match up to Tom. On top of which, Milliora's insistence and manipulative approach was beginning to be an irritant. If you wanted to remain yourself, you had to fend her off.

'Busy at what?'

'Just busy,' said Rosaleen, digging her heels in. 'Don't look so stricken, Milly. I'll meet Dermot all in good time. At the wedding – the way you once said – maybe that would be the right occasion. Let's talk about that instead. I can't wait to wear my straw bonnet.'

'Actually, I've changed my mind about straw for the bonnets,' Milliora informed her. 'I think a traditional wedding without too many unusual aspects really would be best.'

7

The bonnets were of yellow velvet, to match dresses in pliable soft satin, flounced and laced down the back opening so that the girls had to do each other up.

But trying hers on a few days before the wedding, Rosaleen found her attention not entirely on clothes.

'Mr Parnell has been released from gaol,' she announced.

'Oh yes?' said Milliora, without interest.

'And the Viceroy and Chief Secretary have both resigned and Lord Frederick Cavendish – Gladstone's nephew by marriage – and Mr Thomas Burke are going to take their places. It's all part of the new conciliation, Milly. I wonder if it will work.'

'I wonder,' said Milliora, head on one side, assessing the newly-completed, striped visiting-dress that formed part of her trousseau. 'Rosaleen, don't you think I'm daring to have put a spotted collar on this gown?'

'Very daring. Lord Frederick and Mr Burke are going to be sworn in up in Dublin the day of your wedding and there's going to be a big party for them afterwards at the Lodge in Phoenix Park.'

'*Who's* having a party the day I'm getting married?'

'You're incorrigible, Milly!' Rosaleen laughed. 'You don't take one bit of interest in what is going on in the country.'

'Yes, I do. Or, at least, I take an interest in what is happening that is relevant to my life. I know that the

Land League is trying to prevent tenants from paying rent to the landlords.'

'You got that from Tom.'

'I did. He says Mr Gladstone is terrified that Ireland may be heading for revolution and will do all in his power to stop it. Michael Davitt and the Land League are terrible people, leading the country astray.'

'Milly, most of the tenants are too frightened of being evicted to get involved with the Land League – that's the sad thing. They're too worried about not being *able* to pay their rents. What concerns them is keeping a roof over their families' heads, not claiming the land as theirs. Not that they know that in England. But then they've never really known what is going on over here.'

'Rosaleen O'Flynn, will you stop talking politics! No man will want to marry you, or even fall in love with you, if you carry on like that, believe me. Come and have a look at my wedding-gown. It will get your mind thinking about the things that matter to a woman.'

It was the perfect wedding-gown, the bodice simple and prim, buttoning down from a tiny, lace-trimmed collar into a V below the waist, and the skirt detailed, in the front of it alternatively loose puffing and ruched, banded satin, and the back formed of puffs above a detachable train of pleated frills. By comparison, Milliora's waist and hands and feet seemed tiny and dainty. Around the hips were the pannier draperies that had become fashionable that year.

'You're a beautiful bride, Milly,' Francie said, the day of the wedding.

'Isn't she?' agreed Rosaleen, filling the void left by

118

Mary and Carmel who, to her surprise, said nothing about Milliora's appearance at all.

'Help me put on my veil,' said Milliora to the room in general.

Her headdress was trimmed with orange-blossom and mounted on small wire springs so that it would quiver as she walked up the aisle, giving her the modest and timorous appearance expected of a bride. It was – literally – the crowning glory of the whole ensemble.

But where was it?

'Milly, Milly!' cried Francie in consternation, both hands to her face, her image of how a nun gone by the wayside should behave. 'McBirney's have forgotten to put it in the box.'

'You could always send your Mrs Woulfe down in the carriage to fetch it,' said Carmel, her eyes signalling to Mary, really, what a fuss!

Which was unfair, because Milliora was quite calm.

'Mrs Woulfe doesn't know which headdress we selected,' she said, thinking quickly. 'In fact, the only one apart from myself who does know is Rosaleen because she was with me when I bought it. Put a cape over your dress, Rosaleen, and go down to McBirney's to fetch it.'

That was why Tom was forced to hang around at the church for three-quarters of an hour, in anticipation of his bride.

The church was decorated with golden narcissi and deeper golden daffodils, to match the bridesmaids' dresses, but after half-an-hour in the proximity of this happy blaze, the bridegroom, tense to begin with, was uncharacteristically out-of-spirits, fidgeting in his tight new shoes.

Dermot was his best man but Jamie Keegan was one

of the groomsmen and it was to Jamie that Tom hissed, 'If she's not here soon I'm going for a drink,' as the carriage carrying George Fitzgibbon and his bevy of golden girls turned down by the Shannon on the final stage of its journey to the church beside the famous Treaty Stone, signed at the end of the Jacobite–Williamite war and intended to guarantee civil and religious liberty for Irish Catholics.

Milliora was far less nervous than Tom and much better able to cope with what excitability she felt. She only wished that Mary and Carmel . . .

But, no, she would not think about them, sitting sulkily beside her, or about the way Tom's mother, already waiting in the church dressed in a new black silk, still behaved towards her. Not today. And, after all, once Tom and she were actually married, all that would fall into place.

And then, with the organ playing, taking her father's arm and with all the girls behind her, she was walking up the aisle to Tom, allowing her nerves to get just a little bit the better of her, so she shook like her veil and he, seeing that, got over his annoyance and turned soft towards her again.

Only Dermot, standing beside him, took particular notice of Rosaleen and no one at all knew that she would have given her soul to be in Milliora's dainty little shoes.

Yellow, thought Dermot – I like her in yellow. It takes her out of herself and makes her glow with life, as if candles were lit inside her. She *was* worth waiting for, although he had queried that during the winter months when she had been so disappointingly elusive.

But now he had the opportunity to approach her – or would have, once the wedding ceremony was over.

'Brethren, let women be subject to their husbands as to the Lord; for the husband is the head of the wife, as Christ is the head of the Church . . . As the Church is subject to Christ, so also let the wives be subject to their husbands in all things.'

The words of the Epistle rang out. Tom was over his irritation – Milliora was so lovely – and when they were married and his ring was on her finger – just after the priest had admonished them of their duties to God and to each other and sprinkled them with Holy Water – Dermot saw his brother wink at Milliora, right in the middle of the church. What could you expect – Tom was outrageous.

'*Ecce sic benedicetur omnis homo, qui timet Dominum; at videas filios filiorum tuorum; pax super Israel*,' Monsignor McEvoy intoned, and the bride and bridegroom took Holy Communion.

What a sensitive little thing Rosaleen was, Dermot thought tenderly. She was so carried away by the beauty of the ceremony that her violet-blue eyes were once more awash with tears.

The reception was held at Crag Liath, and after it, Milliora would be moving into the house for good. She rejected the idea of a honeymoon outright, having got it into her head that Tom would be too occupied with the estate to leave it more than a day at a time.

Dermot, placed beside Rosaleen at the wedding breakfast, was in his element. She was not the easiest person to talk to, he found – her shyness and insecurity put up their own barriers on her behalf – but he was well able to spell-bind as long as he had the stage to himself and an audience outside his family.

In a short time he managed to find out a great deal

about the girl sitting next to him, particularly about her political leanings, which he thought fanatical and nothing more than the idealism of a lonely, only child. She would grow out of her dreams, he decided – he would see to that. In the meantime, he had no intention of jeopardizing his position with her by disagreeing with what she said.

So he pandered to her attitudes and wove into her fantasies, telling her stories of the O'Briens, and for the first time, he saw her smile. It was a nice smile, too, and the voilet-blue eyes sparkled with it.

'Will you fill your glasses for the toast to the bride,' a voice called out and after that there was much drinking and the cutting of the cake.

All the time, Dermot stayed close to Rosaleen. She thought that it must be hard on him playing second fiddle to Tom, and not geting all the pickings. Maybe he and she did have something in common – being second best.

Still, he was an interesting and sympathetic companion and he was making it plain that he was genuinely interested in herself. And he agreed with her politics, saying that the Davittites were right in their actions and that Mr Parnell would lead everyone to Home Rule if only Mr Gladstone would give him a proper chance.

She looked up to the top of the table where Tom and Milliora were gazing into each other's eyes and where much ribaldry and teasing seemed to be going on and felt what was now getting to be a familiar twinge of envy. Luck Milliora, married to glorious Tom and destined for absolute happiness.

But she must stop being jealous of her best friend. And cease thinking of Tom.

She turned to Dermot.

'Tell me some more stories about Limerick,' she said, and let him have his head.

By late afternoon most of the party had moved into the drawing-room, which had been cleared for dancing. A fiddler had come in and Mary, the most musical of the O'Briens, was strumming away on the piano. Rosaleen was pleased to hear from Dermot that Tom and Milliora had invited the household staff and Tim-Pat, the groom, to the wedding, even if it all added up to more people than she could handle. On that basis alone, it was good to have Dermot at her side.

Milliora, she saw, was circulating freely amongst the guests, as was Tom, although they were not together. How poised she was, with the confidence to cope alone.

Rosaleen would have been amazed to hear that Milliora was envying her because of Dermot's allegiance. Having meandered off across the room in search of a refill over an hour before, Tom had not been back to her since. Instead, he was chatting with Jamie Keegan, and he had refilled his glass not once but several times. Attempting to talk to the many people from all over County Limerick and County Clare whom she had never met before, Milliora felt deprived by her husband's desertion. She could not even fall back on her father for support since he, tired out by the events of the day, had gone back to George Street taking Francie and Mrs Woulfe with him.

If only Rosaleen would come over and lend her normal support. But she was too tied up with Dermot. She signalled discreetly to Tom across the room, but her husband did not look up. Jamie Keegan was gone from his side, as was the awful groom, Tim-Pat, who should be kept in his place in the stables instead of infiltrating social gatherings way above his station, but Tom, ever congenial, was now over by the piano encouraging Mary's efforts and quite unaware of his wife's plight.

Then there was a muffled shout from the doorway and the people clustering at that end made way as nine figures rushed into the room. Milliora's first thought was that they were all about to be murdered by savages wearing horrible straw masks and probably hiding knives under their streely clothes.

All the girls screamed and made as if to flee although none of them actually did so. Priding herself in stifling her own cry by rigid self-control, Milliora failed to register the fact that these screams only simulated fear and that most of those present were, in fact, already laughing. There was no time to get anything into perspective for the head savage had leapt up in front of her, grabbed her round the waist and was whirling her into the semblance of a dance. She wanted to scream for help – for Tom to help her – but the fiddler and the pianist had stepped up their efforts, there was much shrill shrieking, and she told herself that Tom would not hear her screams above the noise.

'Put me down. How dare you!' she managed, but the savage held on firmly.

Disgusting – and so was the smell of his breath for he had, of course, been drinking, having stolen it, doubtless, out of the house.

'Let me *go*!'

And then the savage's straw mask fell on to the floor and she saw it was Jamie Keegan.

'Don't take it so seriously,' he said to her. 'It's only a joke.'

124

'It's a country custom,' expanded Carmel, appearing beside them from nowhere. 'We thought you'd have heard of the Claghera. The Strawboys, they're called. You must learn about the country, Milliora, now you're going to live here, and, after all, you were the one who said she favoured straw.'

The other savages were removing their masks. One of them, Milliora noticed, was the hideous Tim-Pat Tierney.

The arrival of the masquerading Claghera brought the wedding reception more or less to an end. Helen Keegan, heavily pregnant, nagged Jamie to take her home and, for once, got her way. Andy Leahy, like Jamie, was chastened by Milliora's reaction to the joke, decided enough was enough and carted Carmel away. Without the ringleaders, the party fizzled out.

Tom was back at his wife's side to see the last of the people off and not by the flicker of an eyelash did Milliora reveal that he had hurt her by leaving her on her own.

Fiona O'Brien had retreated to her bedroom hours before. Mary was to spend a week with Andy and Carmel to get out of Milliora's way. Barring the jaded household staff, the newly-weds were alone.

'Where's Dermot?'

'Don't you know? He's escorting your friend Rosaleen back into Limerick so she can meet her grand-aunt at their hotel.'

Milliora frowned. 'Tom, is that quite right? They're not chaperoned, after all.'

'Why do you worry so much about these things?' Tom said, sounding irritated. 'Dermot's riding behind the carriage and Rosaleen's groom is up in front. Why didn't her grand-aunt come to our wedding?'

'She was on the official list for an invitation,' said Milliora, easing one tired foot out of its shoe and wiggling it round under her petticoat, 'but Rosaleen said she had decided to have her fortune told with the Tarot cards instead. She's a funny woman, Tom. Rosaleen doesn't have a nice time living with her at all.'

'The poor girl,' agreed Tom, propping himself up against an amboyna wood tea-table that was never intended for this purpose. It creaked a plea for help. Ignoring it, Tom traced a line with his finger around one of its fretwork brackets.

Both Tom and Milliora were putting off the moment when they had to go upstairs. In spite of being married to Tom, Milliora still felt like a guest at Crag Liath and was waiting for his invitation to do so, and the attack of nerves Tom had experienced prior to the wedding had suddenly come back.

He was disgusted with himself for his cowardice and glad that none of his friends – Jamie, for instance – knew that he was scared.

Cross with himself, he frowned. Milliora's stock of confidence was much depleted but she drew on it yet again and told herself that Tom, having eaten and drunk more than was good for him, was suffering from indigestion.

'I think I'll have a bath,' he announced, heaving himself up from the tea-table and making for the stairs. 'I'll go and ask Mary Markham to put the water on to heat. Why don't you go up to the room and I'll see you there later on.'

Milliora looked at him as if he had taken leave of his senses and Mary Markham did the same when he put his request for hot water to her in the kitchen. All water used for bathing, cold as well as hot, had to be carried upstairs in pails to the large iron and enamelled bath and emptied back into them for disposal after it had been used. To ask for hot water in the evening was revolutionary. To do so after Mary had been doubling up as housekeeper and wedding guest all day and evening was to tax her patience to the limit.

'A bath is it?' she exclaimed.

Having removed her shoes and loosened her corset, she was sitting at the kitchen table, looking forward to dissecting the wedding with Mrs Cash, who had been recruited to help wash the enormous piles of dirty dishes that had been taken out from the dining-room in seemingly endless procession while the dancing was in progress.

'Didn't you have a bath this morning?' Mary said to Tom.

She was not at all in awe of him. Having smacked his childish bottom and wiped his runny nose, she still thought of him as a small boy, one who was taking his time about growing up and joining the adult world. Loving him much more than the other children, she had always ensured that he got the first piece of hot soda bread as it came out of the oven, or the biggest slice of cake, and in his manhood she pandered to his ways.

Tom knew it.

'I did. And I'd like another one, Mary, if it's not too much trouble. I'll help you carry the pails myself.'

'All right so,' said Mary, pretending to give in. 'But only because it's your wedding night, mind.'

In her bare feet, she got up and padded to the scullery for pails.

'You can go up,' she called to him. 'Mrs Cash will help with the carrying.'

But Tom did not want to go.

'Is there a cup of tea going?' he wanted to know, while the water got hot on the range.

And when he had drunk two cups of tea, he still vacillated, asking for more, and wandering into the pantry in search, he said, of food.

Eventually, the water was ready and he insisted on prolonging the exercise by carrying up the first two pails himself, and then returning to refill them.

'Did you ever see anything like him?' Mary said to Mrs Cash when they had finally got rid of him. 'What class of carrying-on is that, may I ask?'

'Isn't it obvious the poor boy's nerves are torn to shreds, wondering what's waiting for him up in the bedroom?' the washerwoman said.

Mary did not approve of the question. Mrs Cash, she thought, overstepped the mark all too often.

'Master Tom is well able to look after himself,' she said tartly. 'He wouldn't be a son of his father's otherwise. Are you settling down there for the night or what? We have a whole host of crystal glasses strewn around the house and needing washing.'

The minute Tom disappeared, Milliora followed Mary Markham's example by removing her other shoe. With both of them in one hand and her train in the other, she limped up the main staircase towards the room she now shared with Tom.

The house was very still. Fiona O'Brien had fallen into a deep sleep and although her door was ajar as always, she did not stir as Milliora tiptoed past.

Her trunks had been sent out to Crag Liath the day

128

before to be unpacked by Mary Markham. The contents – the walking-dresses and evening- and visiting-gowns over which she had laboured all winter – had been ironed and hung up on the padded hangers she had made herself, and put into the big Hungarian ash wardrobe that Fiona O'Brien had once picked up for a song at a local auction. The wardrobe was inlaid with purple wood, which set off the central mirror.

Apart from reflecting her own, by now, pale and weary visage, this mirror cloned the foot of the large and ornate mahogany four-poster bed in which Tom and she would sleep, with its brilliant patchwork cover. The bed was hung with brocade and velvet hangings in deep maroon, a colour she did not like but was now too tired to care about.

She had been in the room once before when Mary Markham was getting it ready and she knew that in the cupboard beneath one of the bedside tables was a chamber pot, made of milky golden-yellow Belleek china. Thinking of the pot made her blush, and all the more because there was a black and white under-glaze print of Mr Gladstone inside it, looking exceedingly disapproving in his high collar and black bow tie, with his dark side-whiskers bristling.

Much more pleasing – although, in fact, they matched the pot as part of a set – was the delicate wash-jug and basin on the marble-topped washstand, made in mahogany to match the bed.

And there was her own dressing-table with a long runner of Limerick lace on it and the oval tray, flanked by a pair of candlesticks which, with her pin boxes, her hair-tidies, her coloured glass scent bottles and her silver pillbox, had been sent out with her trunk. A table for Tom's toiletry needs had been set up, too, but the brushes and combs, the clothes-brush and glass pomade pot that a gentleman should use for his hair were all conspicuously missing. Tom, it seemed, used his fingers to dress his hair, a fact she had often suspected.

How long would his bath take, she wondered. Father's baths took an age. He said he did much of his thinking in them, and they were a subject for laughter at home.

Only now Crag Liath was home. It did not feel friendly though, no doubt, it would in time. It only seemed hostile because she was too tired. There was nothing wrong with the house – or with the people in it. Mrs Markham was such a kind lady. Tom himself was wonderful. And Dermot was going to be a real brother. And when he was married to Rosaleen . . .

Rosaleen. Milliora turned to the window heavily draped, like the bed, with maroon brocade and velvet, and looked out at the garden. From this vantage point, she could see the river in the distance winding like dark hair-ribbon to the sea. What was Rosaleen doing now – brushing her hair? Thinking of Dermot who had paid her court all day?

In spite of the splendour of being married to Tom, Milliora realized that she was missing Rosaleen badly. If only she had spent tonight at Crag Liath, instead of staying in Limerick, everything would have been perfect.

It was strange and unsettling being alone in the bedroom. Why, oh why, didn't Tom come out of the bath?

The water in the tub was already quite cold but Tom, having scrubbed himself from head to toe half an hour before, now proceeded to do so all over again. Even as he did so, he felt humiliated. Was he really such a coward at heart, he asked himself – Tom O'Brien, whose prowess on a horse had him admired all over three counties and who thought nothing of scaling a six-foot wall at a hunt?

He was making a fool of himself. If he sat there any longer contemplating the soap his bride would think so, too. With a great effort he heaved himself out of the bath and, having dried himself thoroughly, put on the long cambric nightshirt he had whisked out of his old bedroom earlier on. In a few minutes he would be with Milliora.

Why was it that, when he could not possess her, his body was on fire for her and his courage prodigious and yet, when not even Monsignor McEvoy could object to their union, when it was probably sinful *not* to make love, he had no interest in it whatever? Perhaps he never could? Maybe he would prove an impotent husband, a eunuch, a joke instead of a hero, and the people of Munster would laugh when they heard of his inability in bed.

Come on, he said to himself. Maybe you have never made love to a woman before but what does that prove except that you were deterred by Confessional warnings? When you see Milliora in her nightdress you will be apprehensive no longer.

He wrenched the bathroom door open, leaving the water still in the bath, and tramped along the corridor to the nuptial bedroom, waking his mother in the process and stubbing his big toe on a piece of loose board that leapt up maliciously at him along the way.

Opening their bedroom door, he saw Milliora standing by the window. She *had* changed and was herself

131

delighted with what she was wearing – the kind of nightgown which she fondly imagined made her look a fashionable bride.

Tom thought the nightgown was frightful. It was a perfect froth of white Limerick lace and it covered every inch of her slender figure so that she looked to him more like a superbly iced confection than a woman – and the icing hard at that. His desire for her, far from being re-activated by the sight of her ready for bed, was not in the least inflamed, though it might have kindled had he looked into the depths of his bride's warm hazel eyes, glistening with love and with relief because he was back.

'Hello,' he said, not looking, trying to be natural and casual. Because he supposed she expected it, he added, 'Is it about me that you're thinking?'

'Yes, of course,' said Milliora, trying to sound composed.

Where was her softness? Her reality? As well as being hard, she was looking artificial. Tom closed his eyes and a vision of himself in bed with his wife, mounting her like an animal, assaulted his unhappy mind. How could he reconcile that act with the figure at the window?

Milliora came towards him and touched him gently on the arm.

'Shall we go to bed?' she said.

He was rooted to the spot by the audacity of her question. His mouth half-open in surprise, he gazed at her and she stared innocently back.

'I'm very tired,' she said.

And it struck him that she was simply that. There were tiny smudges under her eyes and she yawned

132

compulsively, putting up her hand to her mouth as she did so, lest Tom see the yawn and think she was bored.

He noticed it anyway, and at the same time he saw Milliora as she really was – a nineteen-year-old girl trying hard to be a woman. And he thought that she had been forced to be a mother to her young sister when she was still a child herself, and that she had always taken her responsibilities too seriously.

He looked at her and confronted the reverence and trust in her eyes and his sentimental heart was moved, and flattered. Poor little thing. And Carmel had played that silly joke on her at the reception which must have upset her, though she said it had not.

'Let's go to bed,' he agreed and when they got there he waited, without making any move, for her to fall asleep.

In the night he woke relaxed and free of fear and, with no worries about mortal sin, slipped a daring hand under the lace nightgown. At once, he began to laugh, first quietly, then loud enough to wake Milliora from her sleep.

He could see her in the moonlight that streamed in from the window, for in their mutual fatigue they had forgotten to draw the curtains. She was blinking, probably wondering where she was and why she was not in bed alone.

Then her eyes opened wide.

'Why are you laughing at me?' she whispered.

She was not used to being the source of merriment, he could see that. Oh, she was affronted all right – no doubt about that, but his confidence was back and he knew that he was in full control of the situation.

And what a situation!

'You're laughing at *me*,' complained Milliora.

And why shouldn't he laugh?

'Milly – ' he began, and then stopped.

For how could he tell her that a married woman had no need to wear her drawers to bed?

Out of the laughter grew an immense tenderness and from that arousal. He pulled off his cambric nightshirt and, naked, drew her into his arms.

'Tom, what are you doing?'

With the tip of his tongue he caressed her lips. The lace nightgown quivered, the mouth responded by opening. His tongue probed further. At the same time, he was fumbling for the ties on the side of her drawers.

'Tom, you can't. Why are you taking off my clothes?'

The innocence of her question opened the most tender of his flood-gates.

'Milly, my darling, with your husband it is all right to remove your clothes.'

'Oh.'

But she no longer protested. She permitted the fumbling. The drawers were loosened and removed.

'And your nightgown. *And* your chemisette.'

It was very strange, she thought, to be lying under the starched white sheets without your garments. It was also quite delicious. The tingling sensations were back and stronger than ever and when Tom touched her ankle, caressed her calf, slowly but insistently moved his hand over her knee on to her bare thigh, they became hardly bearable, but she never thought of the Devil. She was mesmerized by Tom's hand, by its strength and its kindness. For a man who had not made love before and who was being overpowered by his need to do so, he was extraordinarily gentle. He had

134

compassion for almost everyone and in bed with Milliora he was both explorer and philanthropist.

How could he have thought her hard, he reproached himself. She was the softest creature in the world. His recognition of his wife's vulnerability combined with his own passion knife-edged him to the brink of tears.

'Tom – '

Touching, as he had longed to touch, one perfect breast, he felt the nipple harden – heard her catch her breath in wonder. His hand moved down, over the indent of her waist, in over her stomach. All the time his compassion held on to his desire until she was inside the soft seeping waterfall of love, and the waterfall was inside her body.

'Tom,' she called out. 'Tom – '

But he was carrying her forward through a forest of rain, tenderly and determinedly, and perhaps he could not see, as she could, through the clearing, to the silver-pink of the sky, and against it the misty silver-grey hill that, to her, would always be their glorious destination.

8

The day Tom and Milliora were married was destined to be remembered all over Ireland and England not because of its festive aspects but because, while the wedding guests were dancing in Limerick, up in Dublin a gang of assassins set upon Lord Frederick Cavendish and Mr Burke as they strolled through the Phoenix Park after their investiture, and savagely knifed them to death.

The newly-weds were still sleeping when news of the murders filtered through to Crag Liath, relayed by Tim-Pat Tierney.

''Tis cursed the day was,' Mrs Cash promptly announced, looking up from the wash-tub where she had been pounding one of Tom's shirts against the oak bittle. 'There can be no happiness for themselves, when something like this has happened.'

Mary Markham looked at her uneasily. Mrs Cash had gypsy blood in her and was thought to be clairvoyant.

'We'll have none of that talk here, if you please,' Mary said, all the more brusquely because she was afraid. 'What more did you hear at early Mass, Tim-Pat Tierney? Did they find the men that did it?'

'They did not,' said Tim-Pat with satisfaction. 'The whole lot of them got away and only one small boy saw it happen.'

'A small boy, is it? And what was he doing in the park on his own?'

'Looking for birds' nests. And didn't he think that the fellows below were only doing a bit of wrestling.'

His mouth curved up into a contented smile. He's delighted that another Englishman has been killed, Mary thought with fury. With people like him and Mrs Cash in the world, no wonder the place was crazy.

'I haven't got time to be talking to either of you,' she said haughtily. 'I have work to do, even if you have not.'

She glared at Mrs Cash. 'Cursed indeed! Maybe sometime when I've nothing to do – even if it's unlikely – you'll sit down and explain to me how God in Heaven can make a connection between Master Tom and his new bride and the men that were murdered in Dublin.'

Going back into the kitchen, she slammed the door behind her.

Rosaleen heard about the murders that afternoon when Dermot came out to Kilmallock. Having arranged to do so the evening before, he turned up at exactly the appointed time, wearing white socks and sporting a red silk handkerchief in his pocket.

He looked smart and pleasingly attractive, but his expression was serious and she knew from it that he had bad news to impart.

'The poor men,' Rosaleen said, 'and poor Ireland, too. They'll judge us all on the basis of this over in England.'

'They will, and are no doubt doing so already,' said Dermot. 'The sooner the brutes who did the killing are caught and hanged, the better for the reputation of the rest of us.'

'It's strange timing,' Rosaleen said thoughtfully. 'Mr Parnell is just out of prison and Michael Davitt, as well. Do you think it's a plot to discredit the two of them and what they stand for?'

'It could be.'

She had a cool, analytical mind under her idealistic trappings, he thought. He liked that. And she was not aggressive in putting forward her views. He saw no reason why she should not do that. Things were changing. From England came rumours of women demanding the right to vote, which was going too far in his opinion. But there was nothing wrong in a woman being objective enough to conduct an intelligent talk with her husband.

'You *are* an admirer of Mr Parnell's, aren't you?'

'He tempers the attitudes of the Land League – ' Dermot began and, remembering her political leanings, added hastily – 'who, of course, are admirable people. They will suffer because of the murders. I suppose you are aware Tom and I are cousins of Mr William Smith O'Brien, the great nationalist patriot?'

'Are you?'

That got her interest all right. William Smith O'Brien, although originally a Protestant and once a Conservative Member for Ennis, and for Limerick, had later become an ardent supporter of Catholic emancipation, being deported to Tasmania for his pains.

This cousin, long since dead, had been a second son like Dermot, his father being Sir Edward O'Brien, the fourth baronet, of Dromoland Castle. But Mr William Smith O'Brien had inherited his mother's family estate at Cahermoyle, had been educated at Harrow and Cambridge and had turned his back on these riches to support the Irish Arms Act of 1843; he might be a hero in the eyes of the common people, but to Dermot his arrest for seditious writing and speaking, not to mention the part he played in the rising at Ballingarry, made his cousin seem a fool.

A fool saved by his mother's money – by a woman's money. Right now, Tom was in a similar position. Milliora's generous dowry would tide his brother over nicely for the moment. Unless, of course, he went gambling . . .

His own girl did not have a wealthy father, more was the pity, or he could have pressed his suit at once, knowing that they could safely marry on her dowry while he established his career.

No rich father. But there *was* money in the offing, although, according to old Mr Dundon, Rosaleen did not know it. Dermot had no intention of telling her either.

It was sheer coincidence that Dundons should be Rosaleen's grand-aunt's solicitors and that he should thus have known about her will. An eccentric old lady, by all accounts, but he liked her before even making her acquaintance!

Grand-aunt Carrie was studying fourteen cards laid out on a small table and did not look up as Dermot and Rosaleen came into the room.

'The Cup is the image of the Passive or Feminine,' they heard her say to herself. 'The Sceptre is the Male.'

'Aunt Carrie, this is Mr Dermot O'Brien,' Rosaleen began with what Dermot decided was commendable bravery.

'Come in. Come in.' Her eyes still on the cards, she beckoned to them. 'Are you acquainted with the Tarot, Mr O'Brien?'

'I'm afraid not,' Dermot said politely.

Eccentrics did not worry him. At Dundons he

encountered his fair share of scatter-brained and doting clients who changed their will for no apparent reason. He was only concerned that Grand-aunt Carrie never varied hers.

'It is the gypsy Bible,' Grand-aunt Carrie informed him. 'Romany gypsies, I mean – not those layabouts who go round on our roads. Some people may think of it only as a means of amusement, for telling fortunes and enabling the gypsies to gamble, but I can assure you that it has formed the basis of the synthetic teachings of all the ancient nations.'

The lady was clearly too absorbed to suggest that he sit down so he did so unasked.

'Really? Can you tell my fortune with them?'

She looked up at him for the first time and he saw that she bore a slight resemblance to Rosaleen. The face was the same shape and there was a similarity about the nose and mouth. The eyes, though, were grey – not at all like Rosaleen's. But then no one had eyes like hers.

'Yes, I can tell your fortune,' she said. 'Would you like me to do that?'

'Very much,' he said. 'Is this an appropriate time?'

For answer, she swept up the cards and, dividing them into five packs, she set them out again in a pentalogy, face upward.

'You see,' she said seriously, 'the Higher Arcanes go into the middle and the Pentacles, Cup, Sceptres and Swords are set at the four corners.'

Darting a quick glance at Rosaleen, Dermot saw that all her attention was focused on the elderly, grey-haired woman sitting at the table. She did not return his glance and he loked back dutifully at the cards.

'What do they tell me?'

'Please explain the significance of the series to Mr O'Brien, Aunt Carrie,' Rosaleen said softly.

'The first card is the most important: the Queen of Pentacles, Mr O'Brien. A fair woman, inimical to you.'

He tried not to laugh aloud, thinking – at least, it is not Rosaleen if the lady is fair.

'And what do the Pentacles signify?'

'Money,' she said, 'money and development. Cups are for love. The Ace is the commencement of a love affair. Keep still, Rosaleen. Please do not fidget. The Sceptres concern enterprise and agriculture – creation.'

'The card is a six. What does that mean?'

'It is very confusing,' said Grand-aunt Carrie, crossly. 'Sometimes it means the realization of the opposition. But it can also mean the failure of the enterprise in the midst of its execution. The Swords, on the other hand, are very clear, especially in your case. They signify transformation, hatred and war.'

'But I've got another Ace,' protested Dermot, amused at her intensity.

What a strange lady Rosaleen lived with. She seemed to think of nothing but the Occult sciences and gypsy superstitions, and he was glad that she and his mother had not met. He intended to keep them as far apart as possible. His mother would regard Carrie O'Flynn as ungodly and dangerous, and her suspicions of Rosaleen would follow from that.

'It is the Ace of Swords,' Grand-aunt Carrie declared. 'In the Swords, the figures generally indicate opposition raised against the house. The Ace of Swords means commencement of enmity.'

'Aunt Carrie, Mr O'Brien had come out from Limerick with the most alarming news,' Rosaleen said, changing the subject. 'Please explain what has happened, Mr O'Brien, while I see about the tea.'

Once again, he recited the story of the murders in the Phoenix Park the night before. His listener snorted with fury as he finished, sweeping up the Tarot cards and putting them back into a delicate tortoiseshell box.

'Rabble!'

'I beg your pardon?'

'I said rabble, young man. Can you not hear? I am referring to the gaolbird Parnell and his cohorts, leading the country to ruin with their talk of Home Rule.'

'You do not approve of Mr Parnell?'

'I do not. Of course, he was instrumental in the murders.'

'Oh, I don't think – ' Dermot was lost for words.

'I can assure you I know what I am talking about,' his companion continued. 'I am well up on these things and I happen to know for a fact that one of his lieutenants, a Mr Tim Healy, I believe, gave away his intentions. He was overheard discussing the appointment of Lord Frederick. Shall I tell you what he said, Mr O'Brien?'

'By all means,' said Dermot faintly.

'He said – ' she paused for dramatic effect and then slightly raised her voice – 'He said, "We will tear him to pieces within a fortnight." That's what he *said*, Mr O'Brien, and that is precisely what the rabble did.'

Reeling under the shock of this verbiage, Dermot decided that Rosaleen's Grand-aunt Carrie was not to be dismissed too lightly, not because her opinions were credible – on the contrary, he thought, they were wildly off the mark – but because, should he displease her, she was strong enough to attempt to drive him away from her grand-niece forever.

And if he stood up to her, paying court to Rosaleen anyway, she might well alter her will and cut his loved one out.

Treading delicately, he said: 'Davitt, of course, is a dangerous man. The Land League itself is composed of extremists.'

She beamed at him.

'You strike me as a most intelligent young man, Mr O'Brien. I'm very pleased that you appear to be paying court to Rosaleen.'

Rosaleen had left the drawing-room door ajar to facilitate the entry of the tea-tray and, having given the order to the kitchen, she was coming along the passage when she heard her Grand-aunt's raised voice.

Pausing in trepidation, convinced that Dermot was about to be ejected in disgrace from the house, she held back, waiting for the next instalment in what promised to be an alarming series of events.

'Davitt . . . a dangerous man. Land League . . . composed of extremists.'

Dermot's voice, betraying everything in which she had been convinced he earnestly believed.

'You will exert good influence over her, I can see that.'

Her Grand-aunt again. Now, they were discussing herself. It was hardly credible.

'Do you know that she has actually expressed a wish to join the ladies branch of the Land League?' Grand-aunt Carrie said clearly. 'Have you ever heard such nonsense, Mr O'Brien? Apparently, Parnell's sister is high up in it, instead of looking after that beautiful estate they have at Avondale where I'm told that the ground is carpeted with bluebells and azaleas. I told

143

her to put the idea right out of her head. The Land League is an organization for peasants, run by peasants. And do you know what she said to me?'

'I can't imagine.'

Dermot's head was ringing. He silently thanked Heaven that Rosaleen was well out of earshot, seeing to their tea.

'She quoted the man Parnell to me: "Davitt would get stoned by the farmers only he talks Greek to them," he said. As if our farmers – they're *tenants*, not farmers at all – would know a word of Greek.'

'Indeed.'

'Excuse me, Miss Rosaleen.'

It was Mrs Scanlon with the tray of tea. Rosaleen made a point of coughing loudly before she opened the door and let the housekeeper pass before her into the room.

'You're very quiet all of a sudden,' Dermot observed when it was time to go and Rosaleen was commanded to see him out.

'There's a reason for that.'

'Please tell me,' he said with infinite charm. 'I would be very upset if I thought it was in any way my fault.'

'It *is* all your fault,' said Rosaleen and the eyes that he had only seen fill with sadness and laughter now flashed Hell's own fire. 'I heard what you said to my Grand-aunt when I was out of the room. I thought you were a true Irishman, Mr O'Brien – like your cousin Mr William Smith O'Brien.'

So that was it. She had been listening at the door. The little vixen, thought Dermot, struggling to retain his poise to hide his irritation. He managed a most disarming smile.

'You force me to wear my heart on my sleeve,' he said. 'I have fallen in love with you, Miss O'Flynn. You are very young and your Grand-aunt could stand in the way of my suit if she was so inclined. I can't afford to upset her. I can assure *you* that there is no question of my sincerity, either in regard to politics, or to yourself.'

He thought it was rather a good speech, especially when you took into consideration the inhibiting circumstances and the fact that he was forced to virtually whisper in Rosaleen's ear.

It succeeded brilliantly. Hell's fire faded out of the voilet-blue eyes and they softened once again. Rosaleen did not speak but speech was unnecessary since her delight was there in the eyes. She was glad to know he loved her; that was an excellent start.

'I may call on you again?' he queried, confident of the reply.

She nodded her head, smiling. He was half-way down the avenue before he allowed himself the luxury of an enormous sigh of relief.

Having just made it to the twelve o'clock Mass, Tom and Milliora learnt of the murders over luncheon.

'On my wedding day?' Milliora gasped in disbelief.

'Ah now, don't be worrying about things you can do nothing about,' Tom comforted her. 'It's a terrible thing to have happened but aren't the two of them up in Heaven now and not in any pain. What shall you and I do today?'

'I was going to bake you a cake,' Milliora said. 'Madeira cake – your favourite. I thought you'd like it for tea.'

Fiona O'Brien frowned.

145

'We usually let the range go out on Sunday afternoons,' she said. 'Isn't it meant to be a day of rest? Oh, by the way, Tom, another bad thing happened yesterday – we forgot to say the Rosary, the first time in thirty years that a member of this family did not take out the beads at night.'

She looked at Milliora as if to insinuate that her new daughter-in-law was the culprit.

'I'm sure They'll understand Up Above,' said Tom, drily. 'Milly, why don't you leave the house and the cooking to my mother and Mary Markham? You and I have another project to settle.'

'What's that?'

'Tomorrow we're going to buy you a present.'

'We are?'

Milliora was enchanted. What could Tom be planning to buy? A new gown? Or a piece of jewellery perhaps . . .

'And you'll have to help me choose it.'

Earrings, she thought. No, a brooch might be preferable.

'Are we going into Limerick to get it?' she asked, probing for a clue.

'Not at first,' said Tom mysteriously. 'We'll go in there afterwards. Milly, do you remember when I said that if you were going to become an O'Brien you must learn to ride a horse?'

'Ye-es.'

'Well, you're going to do that. And you and I are going over to the Bloodsmiths' place tomorrow and we're going to buy you a horse of your own.'

So that was to be her present. A horse – instead of a brooch or earrings. She swallowed, trying not to show her disappointment. A horse, she thought – and I'll have to learn to ride it. At the mere thought her stomach contracted in fright.

'The Bloodsmiths – aren't they the people from whom you bought the brood-mare?'

Tom nodded, pleased that she remembered.

'They're beautiful people who breed beautiful horses,' he said cheerfully, 'and when we've bought your horse the two of us *will* go into Limerick to get you a riding-habit. Then Tim-Pat will start giving you lessons. By the time winter comes you'll be ready to come out hunting.'

She smiled wanly. There was nothing else she could do.

Her kid shoes had been exchanged in the scullery for a pair of Mrs Bloodsmith's functional boots and the rain was beating down on her smart new hat and turning the ground over which they were walking into a veritable sea of mud. Milliora decided that the country could be very hostile, unlike the town where you could stay securely inside on a bad day without jeopardizing your appearance.

'Do I look a fright?' she asked Tom, only half-joking. She was sure she would look dreadful in no time if they did not move in from the rain.

Tom's mind, however, was on the horse they were going to buy and nowhere else.

'You're going to love this,' he said to her. 'Mr Bloodsmith here tells me he has a great little mare for you, three years old with a long, lean head on her.'

'Is she quiet?' Milliora asked faintly.

'She's a spirited little lady,' Mr Bloodsmith answered. 'You wouldn't want her to be too placid if you're going to hunt her next season. Would you bring out Bealtaine,' he called to a groom, 'and let Mr O'Brien here have a look at her?'

'There you are,' said Tom. 'Bealtaine – named after the month of May.'

'Our wedding month – ' Milliora started to say but Tom's eyes were on the black mare being led out of her stable.

At fifteen hands, Bealtaine was not large, but she looked it to Milliora. Her mane was fine, silky and rather scanty, her ears thin, delicate and pointed, and her eyes and nostrils wide.

To Milliora's surprise, Tom went up to the black horse and began to examine her teeth.

'Why are you doing that, Tom?'

'To check her age – it's routine. Come here and I'll show you. A few months before three years old, a horse will shed the two centre milk teeth and permanent ones will grow in and a year or so later the same process will be repeated with the next two milk teeth. You see? This lady isn't lying about her age, are you?'

Patting Bealtaine's rump affectionately, Tom's eyes ran down to her feet and he bent, checking the hooves for defects. Satisfied, he straightened.

'She's fine,' he said to Mr Bloodsmith, and then, to Milliora: 'Shall we see how she suits you, my girl? It's no good my buying her if the two of you don't get on.'

'You mean – you want me to *ride* her?' Milliora was almost in tears at the prospect.

'Just sit up on her and Mr Bloodsmith here will lead her round the paddock so I can have another look at her paces.'

'But – I haven't got a riding habit yet. We were going into Limerick to buy one.'

'My wife is the same size as yourself. She'll fix you up,' Mr Bloodsmith said, infuriatingly, and before she knew where she was Milliora was back in the paddock wearing someone else's clothes.

If only she had a block from which to mount. But Tom was insisting that a woman should always be able to mount from the ground without assistance and having told her to place her left foot in the stirrup, grasp the cantle with the right hand and spring from the right foot, he stood back to watch her.

'Pull yourself up with both arms, Milly – *throw* yourself into the saddle.'

Somehow or other, she made it, placing her right knee in the pommel and adjusting her skirt. Her smart hat was back at the Bloodsmiths' house, her head was bare and the rain was pelting down, and Tom was so busy talking about high withers and firm crests that he didn't even notice!

'It's a deal,' he said to Mr Bloodsmith. 'We'll take her,' and Milliora tried not to look at the ground lest she suffer from vertigo.

It seemed several years before the two men released her from torture and permitted her to dismount and even then they were more concerned about their ideas of a good-shaped horse, than the kind of shape she was in. She could not wait to get back to the house to change into her own clothes and make herself presentable.

In the scullery she stopped to take off the functional boots, slipping her feet into her own shoes.

'Oh!'

'What's the matter, Milly?'

'There's something – something horrible creeping inside my shoe!'

'Probably a black beetle,' Mr Bloodsmith said. 'They're everywhere, at this time of year.'

'A *beetle!*'

'Kick off your shoe, silly,' Tom said with remarkable lack of consideration. 'That's right – shake it out.'

'I can't . . .'

'Milly, look. It's only a little wood-louse. Nothing to be frightened of – '

'A *wood-louse?*'

'They prefer rotting dead wood to people,' Tom said unfeelingly. 'Here, put on your shoe and we'll go and complete the deal.'

The country was more than hostile, she decided – it was vicious and full of unsuspected terrors. How would she ever get used to country ways?

And how could she be a good wife to Tom if she failed to do so?

9

Getting used to country habits was not her only hurdle, Milliora soon discovered; she also had to grow accustomed to her husband's wandering ways.

This tendency in Tom did not surface for the first two weeks of their marriage. In that time, Tom was glorying in the novelty of having a wife beside him to whom he could make love more or less whenever he wanted, and Milliora was hell-bent on impressing him by the way that she conformed to her new life.

Bealtaine might terrify the daylights out of her, and Tim-Pat might give her the creeps, but she forced herself out to the stables every day and submitted to riding lessons. Riding side-saddle looked so elegant but that was poor consolation when Tim-Pat let slip the fact that it was actually much more dangerous than riding astride. Or had he said that deliberately, just to upset her? She suspected that he had, that he took a sadistic pleasure in watching her fear. Still, she gleaned that everything depended on a good seat, and that, in turn, depended on balance and correct position, both of which she mustered.

She was as stiff as a board, Tim-Pat concluded, watching her progess with narrowed eyes. Much good she would be at the hunt if her muscles did not relax and allow her to sway with the horse's gait, not only looking right, but saving herself and Bealtaine from unnecessary exertion.

Seeing Tom come into the paddock he called out

helpfully, 'Keep your right shoulder squarely in line, Mrs O'Brien, not forward nor down, and keep the left leg against the saddle.'

It was all so complicated, Milliora thought, much more difficult than baking a Christmas cake or making a hat. And to think that Tom expected her to be able to hunt this coming season.

The theory of hunting, as applied to women, had already been partially outlined to her and from it she extracted several alarming facts. The worst of them was that, in entering the hunting-field, she would be meeting men on their own terms. Tim-Pat had made it quite plain that there, at least, she would be entitled to none of the courtesy and deference to which she could look forward on other occasions. Field etiquette stipulated that if she were to lose her stirrup or her hat a man would not pick them up – or even pull back for her if the two of them went at the same fence. And when she asked if the hunt would stop if she took a tumble, Tim-Pat said callously, 'That depends how badly you're disabled.'

'You're doing well. Your hands are light enough,' Tom called her.

That was a real compliment, she now knew. After balance light hands were the most important attribute of a good rider.

'Thank you,' she said demurely, wondering what Tom would say if he knew that the only part of the whole exercise she had enjoyed was the acquisition of her breeches and skirt, which was entirely cut away on the side next to the horse so that, when she was mounted, her legs were in direct contact with the saddle.

For hunting she would also wear a smart postilion

coat, black, like her silk derby, and a white Ascot stock which tied in a most becoming bow. Her hair would be securely coiled and her corset worn loose, to give her body more freedom.

But before then she would have to learn to jump! Tom said Bealtaine would take her jumps in a steady stride when the time came but Milliora could not bear to even think about it.

'She's coming along, isn't she?' Tom said to Tim-Pat, meaning Milliora, not Bealtaine.

Tim-Pat shrugged. 'You can take the man out of the bog but you can't take the bog out of the man,' he said. 'She's a town woman, your wife, and that's about the size of it.'

He was damned if he was going to give her credit for light hands, he thought. She was a spoilt hussy from the City and, like the women of the house, he wished that she had not married Tom.

So Milliora's endeavours with Bealtaine won her credit from her husband, but even her determination could not stop the novelty wearing off. Tom was used to reaching out and taking what he wanted with no apologies to anyone, and after two weeks what he wanted was an evening out with Jamie and a bit of banter at the bar. He would not have looked for an opportunity to slip away from Milliora – he would simply have gone off – but one turned up uninvited when Helen Keegan gave birth to a son and there was cause for celebration.

Hearing this when he bumped into Jamie in Killaloe where he was buying milking-cans for the dairy, Tom took off with him on the spur of the moment and adjourned to the nearest pub. As Jamie said, it wasn't every day that a man heard he had a nine-and-a-half-pound baby son who was the spitting image of his father.

'Indeed it's not,' Tom agreed whole-heartedly, ordering another round.

He had been missing Jamie's company, he realized. After two weeks apart, they had a whole load of stories to catch up on. Eight o'clock came before they knew what had happened, and then nine, and at a quarter to ten they were still in the bar with a crowd of men around them, far too engrossed in the talk and the laughter to cast their wives a thought.

Helen Keegan was used to it. Milliora, yet to be initiated, was sick with worry when Tom did not turn up for dinner.

In the dining-room, she was facing her third hurdle, the animosity of Fiona and Mary. Although they would have done better to have made the best of a bad job and shown tolerance, if not friendship, to Milliora, they were by nature too emotional to think logically. In Tom's presence, the O'Brien women maintained a neutral face. In his absence, they relapsed into a cold war, ignoring Milliora and talking to each other as if she did not exist. Caught up in a passionate and romantic whirlwind, Milliora was still not thinking clearly and she was as bewildered by their hostility as she had been on her first visit to Crag Liath.

Dermot, her potential ally, was spending more and more time out of the house, either working late or visiting Kilmallock, and could not provide allegiance. This evening, she noticed wistfully, his place had not been set at table.

'Is Dermot not in tonight?' she ventured when Mary,

relaying details of a visit she had paid to Limerick that afternoon, finally drew breath.

'He's out making a will,' her mother-in-law said shortly. 'So Michael McInerney is to marry Kitty McCormac, is he? Does he know what he's letting himself in for with her family?'

'He's so stupid he can't see his own two feet,' Mary opined, not even commenting, to Milliora's surprise, that Tom was not at the table.

Where could he be? She began to tick off the possibilities that could have delayed him and one seemed worse than the other. He had been set upon by assassins, like Sir Frederick Cavendish and Mr Thomas Burke had been, and was lying somewhere in a pool of his own blood. Sprightly, living up to his name, had bolted and thrown him and he was staggering back, bruised and bleeding, in desperate need of comfort.

Or maybe he was dead! She looked down at the mackerel on her plate, grey and cold and untouched, and she wanted to be sick. When Bernie Lenihan brought the trifle in, she had to avert her eyes.

Why were Tom's mother and Mary not worried by his absence? How could they just sit there, talking about inconsequential things?

Indignant at this evidence of heartlessness, she demanded, with some of her customary hauteur: 'Why aren't you worried because Tom isn't home?'

Mary laughed shrilly. 'Why should we worry about that?' she replied. 'Aren't we used to his comings and goings? It would take a lot more than you, Milliora, to keep my brother at home!'

After that, she went on talking about Michael McInerney and Kitty McCormac and Milliora went to bed.

155

But not to sleep. She was wide awake at eleven-thirty when Tom, somewhat the worst for wear, came into the bedroom and, pulling off his clothes and throwing them on the floor, got into bed beside her.

'Hello,' he said cheerfully, and pulled her into his arms.

He had been drinking! He was reeking of liquor. And all the time she had been worrying herself to death.

'What kept you?'

He nibbled her ear, running his tongue inside it.

'Jamie Keegan has a baby son, Milly. We've been celebrating his arrival.'

'All this time?'

But she was already mollified, locked into his arms.

'It isn't every day a man has a nine-and-a-half-pound son,' said Tom, paraphrasing Jamie.

Well, that was true. As he bent over to kiss her mouth she thought, I would *love* to have a baby. And then: it was a special occasion. Tom won't do it again.

Rosaleen, meanwhile, was leading a double life. Every Saturday and Sunday, Dermot rode out to Kilmallock to see her. He was very circumspect. Having declared his love for Rosaleen early in the race, he was careful now not to rush his fences.

This deliberate regression was aided by the fact that the two of them were seldom alone for long. Acquiring Grand-aunt Carrie's trust, he discovered, was a two-edged sword. She made a point of being in for his visits and, since she had an insatiable interest in card-games of all kinds, he found himself drawn into them when he longed to be alone with Rosaleen.

'Ah, Mr O'Brien,' Grand-aunt Carrie hailed him on

a damp, depressing Sunday. 'A friend of mine, the wife of an army officer, has just returned from India and she has given me the most fascinating Indian cards. If you will look at these, you will notice that one of the court cards of each suit represents one of the ten Incarnations of Vishnu. Here he is on a white horse, and here on a piebald camel.'

'They are Hindu cards?'

'Naturally, but you know all about them, I take it. I don't have to explain.'

'It's not necessary,' he told her, catching Rosaleen's eye.

But it was five o'clock before she adjourned for a rest, leaving them mercifully together.

'How is Milly?' Rosaleen asked at once.

'Well enough, I suppose. She and Tom are in Limerick this evening. Her father isn't well.'

'I'm sorry. I have a letter for her. Will you give it to her?'

'Of course I will. She'll be pleased to hear from you. She misses you a lot.'

'I'm sure she doesn't have time to miss me,' Rosaleen said. 'She must be so busy in her new life with Tom, entertaining and going round and meeting people.'

'Tom was never one for entertaining at home. And when he goes out it's usually with his men friends. Marriage won't change him; he's already going back to his old ways.'

'But Milly does have your mother and sister for company, and I suppose your other sister comes over to visit.'

'They tend to stick to themselves,' Dermot said. 'Milly is in need of her friends, I assure you.'

'Well, I'm going to go and see her shortly,' said

Rosaleen, digesting Dermot's report on Milliora's life-style. 'That's what the letter is all about. And perhaps Tom will settle down in due course.'

Dermot picked up a gaily lacquered wooden card-box – as elaborately decorated as the cards, with pictures of the Incarnation on the sides and lid.

'In our family, Tom is the gay spark and I'm the hard worker,' he said. 'Sometimes, I envy him for that. He's concerned with having a good time; I have ambitions. As soon as possible after I qualify, I want to go into practice myself. Does that sound very dull and predictable to you?'

'Not at all. You sound – '

Like myself, she was going to say – a worker, not a queen bee like Milliora. But her head was buzzing with what Dermot had said about Tom's behaviour and she no longer felt so sure about her facts.

' – very interesting,' she added, rather lamely.

But Dermot was nervously dusting the Indian card-box with his sleeve, although it was shining clean already.

'*I* want a settled marriage,' he said. 'I don't want to go gallivanting. Though, for financial reasons, that won't be possible for the moment.'

'I suppose not,' Rosaleen nodded.

'Unless something unforeseen happens . . .' He stopped, and smiled at the improbability. 'But I don't think that's at all likely.'

Seeing him out, Rosaleen gave him the letter for Milliora.

'You seem very fond of her.'

'I am,' he said. 'We're friends.'

Out of the blue, he remembered the other cards that

had been laid out for him in this house that very first Sunday. He thought of the Queen of Pentacles.

'*Very* good friends,' he said defensively.

Riding home, he wondered why on earth he had found it necessary to emphasize that fact.

Rosaleen was becoming quite attached to Dermot. If you did not think of Tom O'Brien, any woman would rate him as handsome and he had a serious, dependable personality that appealed to her earnest self. She and he had a lot in common, including their political outlook. Yet she asked herself why, if she felt such compatibility with Dermot, she did not want to tell him about her other life, collecting for the evicted.

She decided she did not want to compromise Dermot by putting him in possession of the facts. Grand-aunt Carrie might probe for information if rumours of her activities got back to the house. Being a socialite, her grand-aunt was invited to parties around the county, and Rosaleen lived in continual fear that one of the hosts or hostesses would mention that she had been collecting for the poor.

Like the high-principled lady who had pressed the princely sum of three shillings into her hand and said how much she admired her charitable attitude, not knowing that the money would be in the pocket of the lady's agent, for return to her, before the day was out.

Procuring the money had been much easier than assuring the suspicious woman at the cabin door that hers was an altruistic role. The husband had been equally sceptical. By the time Rosaleen had convinced the two of them of her sincerity all their nerves were in shreds.

'Did Father Matt send you?' the woman wanted to

know, finally, when the man had gone off to pay the agent.

'Father Matt?'

'Father Matt Ryan from Kilteely. Isn't he risking arrest every day of his life, speaking out against the evictions.'

'I know who you mean,' said Rosaleen. 'We don't work together, but I've met him all right.'

Maybe I'll go over and see him at Kilteely, she thought. She could not get away forever with what she was doing now. Father Matt might be able to suggest some other, less exposed way she could go about helping the threatened people.

She did not mention that to Dermot, either, so that he, reaching the house at Kilmallock a couple of Sundays later, was startled to be met by Grand-aunt Carrie in a formidable rage. She wasted no time on politeness.

'My niece is in disgrace,' she greeted him. 'She's up in her room and there she will remain.'

'I see,' said Dermot, not seeing. 'What has she done to merit this?'

'She's joined the Fenians,' Grand-aunt Carrie said loudly. 'Can you imagine anything worse?'

'The *Fenians*? But they've been disbanded since the late sixties.'

'The Land League then. It's the same thing,' she said to him crossly. 'Come in – come in. It's pointless standing in the hall.'

In the drawing-room she said, 'Got herself mixed up with this dreadful priest Father Matt Ryan, who stands up on platforms and speaks out on behalf of the trouble-makers. I do not understand why the Pope doesn't have him deflowered.'

160

'Defrocked,' Dermott offered. Then, seeing her face, he added hastily, 'How did Rosaleen get herself mixed up with this man?'

'She was seen in his company on an occasion when the bailiffs were evicting some lazy peasants who had failed to pay their rent. I've had the details since yesterday and I had it out with my niece and do you know what she had the nerve to say to me? She says the landlords are profiteers, living off the people. Dangerous talk. She's referring to my own friends, Mr O'Brien. I said if I heard any more of it I'd put her out of the house.'

'I'm sure that won't be necessary,' said Dermot suavely. 'She's idealistic and impressionable, but she's still very young. Why don't you let me talk to her? I'll put some sense into her head in no time.'

She beamed at him.

'Of course, you will,' said Grand-aunt Carrie, more gently.

A blue-veined hand reached out for the bell and when Mrs Scanlon appeared she said, 'Bring Miss Rosaleen down here, would you? Tell her Mr Dermot O'Brien would like to have a word.'

'What on earth have you been up to?'

It had taken much of Dermot's charm to persuade Grand-aunt Carrie to let him talk to Rosaleen in the library alone.

She explained while he listened in amazement.

'My God! You could have been attacked by the crowd. You took a terrible risk,' he said when she had finished.

'I took no risk,' she said, wearily, 'except that of being found out by my Grand-aunt. She doesn't know

161

all I've done by a long straw. She just thinks I was present at an eviction in the company of Father Matt.'

'Then let's make sure she doesn't find out any more. You can't afford to displease her, Rosaleen – not for the moment. It will be different later on.'

'Later on?'

'After we are married. Then you will be free to do as you like. You will marry me, won't you? Please say you will.'

At that moment, Rosaleen honestly believed that she could love Dermot. She was almost sure that she loved him already, she was so grateful for his allegiance. And it was very pleasant to have an attractive admirer around – she had been feeling that for ages.

'Will you, Rosaleen – please.'

'Let me think for a while,' she said to him, but when he reached out to kiss her, she did not protest.

Trouble – Tom had his share of it. If only he had not had that big bet on the Two Thousand Guineas – or the other one on the Oaks. Major Boyd-Rochfort's Brave Boy had been almost a certainty for the Guineas, having won the Madrid Handicap over a mile at the Curragh in April, and Joe McGrath's Gold River had been generally expected to live up to part of his name.

He groaned, thinking about his debts. Milliora's dowry could have wiped them all out, and left the two of them solvent had not her father decided to dole it out, making a third available on marriage and the remainder only to be touched when she was twenty-five.

By that time he could be in the poor-house and the

whole family with him. His creditors had been generous for a long time but they could hardly wait forever.

He groaned, remembering that he was in debt to Jamie, too, though he was still convinced that if he had yielded to his impulse to bet heavily on Lord Talbot de Malahide's High Spirits in the Cesarewitch, instead of listening to Jamie and backing Colonel Blake's Brushwood Girl, he would have got on to a winning streak.

Meanwhile, what was he going to do?

Milliora did not help the situation, either.

'Dermot's proposed to Rosaleen,' she said. 'Isn't that lovely? He's just been confiding in me about it.'

'Oh yes?'

'It's so sad that they won't be able to afford to marry for so long. You know, Dermot was telling me that there was a time when land was subdivided between all the sons. In those days, he said, everyone got married much younger. We used to be one of the earliest marrying people in Europe, Tom, and now we're one of the latest.'

'So what do you expect me to do about it?' Tom sounded edgy. 'If you slice the land up to accommodate all the sons, there'd be no estate left. Would you want me to do that so Dermot and your friend can go off and get married?'

'No,' Milliora said, bewildered. 'Of course I wouldn't want you to slice up Crag Liath, though it would be marvellous if you were to lend Dermot the money to get married.'

She had expected generous Tom to react positively to this suggestion but he did nothing of the sort.

'Did Dermot ask you to approach me?'

'Not at all. It was just my idea – to help the two of them out.'

The conversation was not going the way she had planned it. Tom sounded suspicious and cross.

'It was just – Rosaleen is coming to tea today and I thought I might surprise her . . .'

'Well you know better now,' Tom said curtly.

She could not fathom what had got into him.

'Do you know that solicitors these days are making the best part of a thousand pounds a year?' he said, in a gentler voice. 'Dermot will be rich enough to marry soon enough.'

'I suppose so. When that happens I want Father to give Rosaleen away. We must talk about it today over tea.'

Tom seemed abstracted. 'Your father?' he said vaguely. Then: 'That's an idea. I must go and see him this afternoon.'

'You don't have to arrange the wedding today!' Milliora said. 'Aren't you staying to see Rosaleen?'

'What? She'll be here when I get back. I'd like to see how your father is getting along.'

He went off without remembering to kiss her goodbye. She was distinctly piqued at this cavalier behaviour. Fair enough, it was her father he was intending to visit but, in spite of his promise, Tom had been out with Jamie Keegan on a number of recent occasions, coming home late for dinner and once at eleven o'clock. She had been too tolerant about these relapses, she decided. Tom had bewitched her with his lovemaking – that was the trouble. She was going to have to lay the law down to him so that he would see she was not a doormat like that pathetic Helen Keegan.

By the time she had reasoned all this out, Milliora was at her most haughty and it was in that mood that Rosaleen found her when she arived at the house.

164

'I hear you and Dermot are going to get married,' Milliora said when they were sitting together in the rose-coloured drawing-room.

'I haven't given him his answer yet,' Rosaleen said, thinking it was just as Dermot said: no sign of the rest of the family and Tom must be out gallivanting. 'You two have obviously been discussing it.'

'We have. And about your problems with your Grand-aunt. Honestly, Rosaleen, you must be careful of the company you keep. Archbishop McCabe of Dublin has denounced the Ladies' Land League, you know. He says it's another area where the sense of deference wanes as lay power waxes and that his life has actually been threatened as a result of his opposition to it.'

'I haven't joined the Land League,' Rosaleen protested, 'although I would like to do so. Did Dermot tell you that I had? If he tells lies like that I'm certainly not going to marry him.'

Her eyes began to flash. Milliora was forced to climb down.

'He didn't actually say that,' she admitted. 'He just mentioned that your Grand-aunt was concerned about your involvement with those kind of people.'

'Did he?'

'He's supportive of you. You know that. *I* just think you should be careful. The Land League do awful things, Rosaleen – they cause lots of trouble on the land.'

'That was because of the Phoenix Park murders, and no one knows who's responsible for those,' Rosaleen said huffily.

Milliora was so aggressive and so opinionated! She felt much less sympathetic towards her.

A few minutes later she let slip the fact that her mother-in-law and Mary, knowing she would be entertaining an old friend, had gone out to give them privacy for an intimate chat.

And then Tom arrived in from Limerick all happy to see his bride.

'How's Father?' Milliora asked him after they had lovingly kissed.

'Not bad at all, I'd say,' Tom told her.

So he had been making a family visit, not gallivanting at all!

He still made her heart beat faster. Rosaleen found that, as usual, she was envying Milliora. And to think she had arrived ready to feel sorry for her!

'Everything's fine, as a matter of fact. Nothing to worry about at all. Milly, my love, is that Madeira cake I spy out of the corner of my eye?'

'It is,' said Milliora, returning his impudent smile.

'Cut me a nice big slice. Rosaleen, I hear you're planning to marry my hard-working brother?'

What had Dermot been on about, Rosaleen wondered. Tom was a devoted husband and Milliora was as sure of herself as ever. She neither looked nor behaved as if she was in dire need of friends.

Three weeks later, Mary Markham opened the front door to a messenger from Limerick with a letter in his hand.

'It's from Mrs Woulfe of George Street,' he said, 'and I have to bring a reply back with me.'

'What are you doing coming to the front door, instead of to the back?' Mary said, for the boy had a cheeky face.

She peered at the envelope. 'Mrs Tom O'Brien is

out at the stables having her riding lessons. You go round the back and wait there while I deliver this to her,' she commanded.

Waiting, he saw a beautiful red-haired lady rush into the house wiping tears out of her eyes.

'Was it bad news I brought?' he asked when Mary Markham came back.

'It was!' said Mary grimly. 'Mrs O'Brien's father has just died suddenly and the whole house is upset.'

And then another letter arrived at Crag Liath delivered by the postman. When Fonsie White gave it into Tom's hand he was sorry he had not had the chance to read it himself. He usually managed to peruse the more interesting letters before he delivered them, opening them carefully in front of the Widow Casey's boiling kettle. They both got a great kick out of keeping up with what was going on in the neighbourhood and she repaid him well for giving her access to the post with a good meal in the middle of the day.

But, that Monday, the Widow Casey was in bed with a cold and her daughter, a cross-eyed creature with not a hint of a welcome about her, had been far less forthcoming. Fonsie could not be bothered to go through the letters without his accomplice and it was only when he noticed that the one for young Mrs O'Brien was an official-looking kind of document, the kind of thing you might get from a solicitor maybe, that his old curiosity revived.

''Tis for herself, then, is it?' he said, lingering in the yard where he and Tom had met.

'It is,' said Tom, leaving it at that and not even opening the letter the way any husband would do.

Instead, he stuffed it into his pocket.

'So you'll give it to her then, will you?' Fonsie said to him.

Even he thought that this was a foolish kind of a thing to say, the minute he had said it. As if Tom O'Brien would not give his wife her letter.

But, in the event, Tom, in fact, did not.

Was it sorrow, Milliora wondered, that was making her so dizzy? She had felt peculiar at her father's funeral and the same at Mass this morning. Her body, too, seemed to be changing. Her periods had stopped altogether and her breasts were oddly swollen and continually sore.

Although she had learnt how to make love, she had no idea that there was a connection between this act and conception and it had not crossed Tom's mind to enlighten her further. She had a vague idea that babies grew in women's stomachs, and that God arranged it but, at the age of nineteen, she had no knowledge of the procedure or how they finally got out.

She was in the hall when dizziness overcame her and she put a hand out to steady herself. There was a curious buzzing in her ears and her vision was blurring. Like a blind woman, she tried to feel her way along the wall but the wall itself was no longer there and neither was the hall, only the ground rushing up to meet her and she sinking down into its blackness.

'You poor child,' said Mary Markham, concernedly. 'Can you try to sit up? Put your head over your knees – there's a good girl. Now we'll get you upstairs and into bed and you'll be as right as rain in no time.'

As she said afterwards to Mrs Cash, she knew from that moment that there was a baby on the way.

'Isn't that great news altogether?' she exclaimed,

168

carrying an enormous pile of dirty washing into the scullery and setting it down at the washerwoman's feet.

Mrs Cash scowled. 'Bad scran to you, Mary Markham! That's a terrible amount of work you're inflicting on me and I with enough on my hands as it is.'

'There'll be a sight more washing every week once the baby comes,' said Mary, cheerfully. 'Ah, you have no call to carry on like that, Mrs Cash. Would you listen to my story? You wouldn't expect her to be knowing about men, like – not until she was married,' she continued. 'But wouldn't you wish she could talk to old Mrs O'Brien instead of it having to come from myself. Not that there is much hope of them two ever talking!'

'You had to tell her then?'

'Everything!' said Mary, dramatically. 'She's only a child. I'm sorry for her, for all that she behaves as if she was the bee's knees and the spider's ankles, for she's not made welcome in this house.'

'Sure, the master's mad about her,' retorted Mrs Cash. 'What does she want? Isn't she laid out like an altar, with a fortune spent on her clothes?'

'Doesn't she make everything herself,' said Mary, quickly, leaping to Milliora's defence.

The women of the family should be ashamed of themselves, she thought, though it was easy to understand the reasons behind their behaviour.

'They give her a bad time,' she said to Mrs Cash, 'nudging and winking behind her back and calling her Miss Airs and Graces. And it isn't easy being married to Master Tom either, for he's as wild as a mountain goat, what with his socializing and his horses and his gambling.'

169

'That fellow would bet on two flies going up a wall,' observed Mrs Cash, sagely.

She began to sort out the washing, separating the white bed linen from the tangles of Tom and Dermot's socks.

'Still and all, he's pleased with the news,' Mary said. 'He's up there with her now, trying to choose names for the baby. "If it's a boy," says young Mrs O'Brien, "we should call him Murchad, after one of your ancestors. Murchad was the great grandson of Brian Boru."'

'And if it's a girl?'

'Vivienne. Brian Boru's mother was called Vivienne and so was one of his daughters, says she. It means "melodious lady".'

'There's nothing melodious about a new baby!' said Mrs Cash, 'unless you can count the squawling. 'Tis good news, though. Maybe a baby will make himself settle down.'

'Maybe it will,' agreed Mary.

Neither of them sounded convinced.

10

After that, the long and languid summer lulled them all into a false sense of security. In August no rain fell. Without hitch the hay, piled up into haycocks two months earlier, was drawn in on the undulating wooden hay-carts, and piled into the haggard.

That month Tom, chastened by the death of George Fitzgibbon, was a stay-at-home husband and Milliora believed him tamed.

But once the corn was in the rick he started getting restless. Relapses were followed by tears and promises and further relapses, but not by the laying down of the law: Milliora, too, was chastened by death and temporarily tamed by pregnancy.

But, in the meantime, there was the *meitheal*, the festival that signified the end of summer, a source of joy to Tom. He saw to it that barrels of porter and stout were brought in for the workmen, for there would be glorious feasting then, and music and dancing out at the back of the house.

One evening, Tom made his way up to the Lenihans' cabin and found young Liam Leniham there, washing his feet, and his sister Bernie boiling cleavers to make a tonic for her hair.

'Master Tom!' exclaimed Bernie, flustered at seeing him and hastily throwing a black drugget over something in the corner.

'What's that you're trying to hide from me?' Tom asked at once.

'Liam?' Bernie sought assistance. But Liam, who had a hearing problem, remained conveniently deaf.

'*Poitín* – I thought so!' said Tom triumphantly, peering under the drugget. 'That stuff is mighty potent. You'd better not let the constabulary get wind that you've got it or you'll have the lot of us locked up.'

He laughed, his blue eyes twinkling. Everything was adding up to a merry festival, the kind of occasion he most enjoyed when he and the men and women that worked for him had a chance to have fun on even terms.

On his way back from the Lenihans he went through to the poultry runs to inspect his fighting game-cocks, his Brown Reds and smutty Gypseys, with feathers round their heads like hoods. He reminded himself to get a man in to cauterize their combs; a dubbed cock, slashed at the head by the spurs of an opponent, stood less risk of being blinded by its own blood during a fight.

He thought that he must get some people around for a cockfight. A Sunday would be a good day. You could depend on most people to be free then – in the afternoon, anyway.

A law had been passed against cock-fighting but Tom, like many countrymen, blithely ignored it. It was a fine sport, he felt, a time when all classes were equal, and a great occasion for a bet. He was blind to its cruelty. Immensely kind to the people with whom he came into contact, he was far less sympathetic to the plight of animals and birds. It was not Tom's way to dissect and assess, but pressed to analyse his attitude, he might have said that the death, even the suffering of a bird or animal, was immaterial since, after all, they did not have souls – at which point he would have looked embarrassed about being drawn into so unmanly a discussion.

With so much fun in the offing he was in his element. On the evening of the *meitheal* he could not wait to be off for the *cuardiocht*, singing and dancing and drinking and having a bit of crack.

In the past, although Dermot had put in an obligatory appearance at the festival before retreating to bed, the women of the house had kept well out of the way. So it was a shock to Tom to find Milliora ready to accompany him, dressed up in a red skirt and a puffed-sleeved blouse with a bow at the neck and insertions of yellow lace. She did not look at all pregnant and under any other circumstances he would have thought her a fine sight for sore eyes.

'Will the party go on for a long time?' she asked him. 'Shall I be taken round and introduced to all the workmen beforehand?'

She seemed to think it was a party in honour of themselves, at which they would act the high and mighty.

'It's a bit of a hoolie,' he said. 'It could well go on all night. You must understand that it's not *our* party – it's for the country people in general to celebrate their prosperity. There'll be hundreds of people there.'

'I don't think I could stay up all night,' Milliora said. 'I'm a bit tired already.'

'Then you don't have to,' said Tom, not showing his relief. 'You let me know when you want to go to bed and that will be the end of it.'

It was not that he wanted to get rid of her, he told himself, only that there was a time and a place for wives.

By the time they got going, the festival was already

173

under way. A fiddler was playing an Irish reel, men were drinking and talking, and the excited faces of the girls were illuminated by the light of crusie-lamps suspended from the branches of trees.

'*Slainte*,' a man called to him, holding aloft a bottle of porter.

'Who is that?' Milliora asked.

'The fellow who does the thatching for us – the *tuiodoir*. Everyone's here, you'll see. That's Ned Hayes the blacksmith, and the fellow over there makes baskets. You're enjoying yourself, I see!' Tom shouted out to Tim-Pat Tierney who was eating a plate of food.

'It's but a daisy in a bull's mouth!' the groom called back and went on talking to the thin, mousy-haired youth Milliora recognized as Liam Lenihan.

'How are you doing?' Tom said to her, and gave her hand a squeeze.

She gazed back at him adoringly, catching the attention of Mary Markham sitting under a tree with Mrs Cash.

'Isn't that the picture of perfect happiness?' Mary said, sentimentally.

'Maybe it is,' said Mrs Cash, 'and maybe it is not.'

Mary frowned. 'Either it is,' she said, 'or it isn't. Make up your mind! What's ailing you to be so indecisive?'

But Mrs Cash did not rise to the bait. Instead of coming back with a snappy answer she raised her mug of porter to her lips and drank from it deeply, swallowing audibly. And then she did not reply.

'Have you lost your hearing or your tongue?' Mary asked her, 'or is there something else on your mind, other than the *meitheal*?'

Mrs Cash turned and looked her straight in the eye

and, although it was a warm night, Mary shivered. She did not like the expression she saw – did not like it at all. Or what she heard, either.

'There's something in the air that's troubling me,' Mrs Cash said. 'It isn't with me yet in its entirety but I'm getting a premonition.'

And suddenly Mary, too, was uneasy, and her throat was going dry.

'What kind of premonition?' she demanded. 'You'd better tell me. Does it concern one of us?'

That was when Mrs Cash glanced furtively at Tom and Milliora.

'I don't know for certain, Mary Markham,' she whispered, 'but it's connected with Master Tom.'

It was a very noisy party, Milliora decided, and there was a lot of uncalled-for drinking. Only a few yards from her the man who made baskets was singing loudly:

> Whiskey, you're the devil,
> You're leading me astray
> Over hills and mountains
> And to Amerikay.
> You're sweeter, stronger, decenter,
> You're spunkier nor tay . . .

'Tom,' she said, 'I'm tired now. Shall we go into the house?'

'Just now,' Tom said, not really listening but talking to the thatcher, not about making roofs, but about how a pig's bladder made the best kind of football.

Feeling slightly queasy as a result of this conversation Milliora sat down on a thrashing frame and leant her head back against a tree trunk.

'. . . Soil belongs to us . . . aristocratic locusts . . . eaten the verdure of our fields . . .'

'I can't hear you, Tim-Pat.'

The voice of Liam Lenihan, louder than the others.

'. . . Proclamation of . . . 1867,' Tim-Pat said, '. . . spirit of rebellion alive in our hearts . . .'

So, on top of everything else, Tim-Pat Tierney was a member of the Land League, was he? Full of seditious talk and anarchistic behaviour. She might have expected nothing less.

'Tom,' she said, getting up again and plucking her husband's sleeves. 'Tom, come – I want to talk to you.'

Tom sighed, catching the thatcher's sympathetic eye. The man nodded, melting back into the crowd.

'What is it, Milly?'

'Do you know that Tim-Pat Tierney is a member of the Land League? And he's trying to get others to join it. All right-thinking people know that Davitt and his rebels are out to break up the big estates and give the land to the workers. This man is trying to ruin Crag Liath!'

Tom burst out laughing.

'Tim-Pat? What nonsense you do talk, Milly!'

'But I *heard* him!'

He shook his head.

'Tim-Pat hates the English because of what happened to his parents, that's all. And even if he wanted to break up Crag Liath – which he doesn't – he wouldn't have a chance. Did you hear Davitt's own tale of what happened when he advocated the abolition of landlords up in Mayo? An old man said to him, "To who do we pay the rent, then, sir?" The workers are conservative – they don't want to change. You're tired,

176

that's your problem. I'll take you upstairs and tuck you into bed.'

But when they got upstairs, Tom, to Milliora's horror, announced that he was returning to the *meitheal*.

'You're not!'

'Just for a short while, my darling,' he said, cuddling her. 'They expect it of me. You saw yourself that Dermot only put his head round the door, as it were, and then took himself off to bed. They'd be offended if I were like that.'

'I suppose so,' said Milliora, mollified. 'You really won't be long?'

'I promise,' Tom said, reassuringly. 'You have a nice sleep and when you wake up I'll be asleep in bed beside you.'

In spite of his instruction she lay awake for some time, thinking about the *meitheal*. It was a good thing for the people to have a party after they had all worked so hard on the land – she agreed with that.

But – all that drinking? And the way Tom fraternized with the workers as if they were all the same, and he not Master of Crag Liath at all? They were different matters.

And as for Tim-Pat Tierney, no matter what Tom maintained, she thought him a dangerous man. If Tom would not keep a firm eye on him in future, she would, she vowed.

Then, with a sigh, she turned over on to her right side, facing the spot where Tom slept, looking forward to his return, and promptly fell asleep.

Tom did mean to keep his promise and return shortly. He had been drinking whiskey for which he had a good head and if he had only stuck to that and not been tempted by Ned Hayes to have a sip of *poitín*, he might not have been led astray. He danced a jig with Bernie Lenihan, who was wearing a new paisley gown, and had a long argument with Jamie, who turned up after the pubs had closed, on the pros and cons of dehorning cattle. He did not notice the hours flying by – no one did – and it took him completely by surprise when dawn began to break.

'Will you look at that?' he said to Jamie, in a slurred voice, pointing to what could only be the sun, or the very edge of it.

'The party's over,' said Jamie sombrely, though there were still enough people around to contest that statement.

'Can't have that happen,' said Tom. This seemed to him to take priority over everything else. 'Must go on,' he added, and Jamie agreed.

'Tell you what,' said Tom. 'We'll organize a cockfight! I was only thinking the other day that it was time we had a main at Crag Liath.'

'There's no one here has fighting-cocks,' said Jamie, sadly, 'no one but yourself.'

'Then we'll go and round up everyone who has,' Tom said, happy at solving the problem.

Straight away, they were on their feet – although not very steadily – and by the time the sun had taken another peek at the day, they were off on their horses to rouse the country for another bit of fun.

When Milliora woke and found Tom was not, as he had promised, sleeping beside her, she felt sad and apprehensive. He had already ridden off with Jamie by then, and the other revellers, seeing his departure, had trailed off home to their cabins. So by the time she had dressed and gone downstairs in search of him, all that was left of the *meitheal* were empty jars and bottles strewn around the grounds.

There was no sign of Mary Markham, who had the day off, or of anyone else and after a while Milliora wandered back upstairs again and stared mournfully out of the window.

It was clammy and warm and a thunderstorm was brewing, and there were passionate feelings fermenting inside her for Tom – love, but hate, too. In spite of the heat, there was a hint of autumn in the landscape. The white chrysanthemums were flowering and the leaves of the big plum tree were more maroon than green. The tree grew close by the bedroom window and when she looked higher into the branches she noticed that the top of it was already purple-red. Every so often, a plum fell with a splatter on to the bright green grass below, which looked as if it was wounded.

And, way in the distance, the river. Nothing could take from its majesty. From its source in the limestone cauldron called the Shannon Pot, in a mountain valley in Cavan, it was, at O'Brien's Bridge, nearing its long journey, and still it did not falter.

All the same, the dry summer had reduced its flow. She could see its ribbon, and small promontories in it that she had not seen before. Close up these would reveal themselves as weeds and rocks and floating grasses, tangled with the unprepossessing carcases of small animals but, from this distance, each one might be a diminutive fairy island and on it fairy hosts who had come up from the land called *Tir fo Thuinn* where they lived in style. In all the stories, spirit folk lived sophisticated lives. To be sure, some of their time was spent fighting, but a lot more went into feasting and hunting and making love to beautiful women.

Fairies would be out in force now, it being *Lughnasa*, the season of harvest-time. Or so she had once taught Francie, when her sister was little and gullible, and they had scattered flowers in a ring round the door in George Street afterwards, to keep the fairies out.

But now Francie knew the fairies were all *pisreoga*. She had her own life, so had Rosaleen, and neither of them cared that Tom O'Brien was missing and that she, Milliora, was lonely and bewildered and, suddenly, unable to cope.

And frightened. Because maybe Tom did not love her, after all, and didn't want to come home any more . . .

In the plum tree, an orange-breasted robin clucked, its brown beady eye sparkling like a jewel in its head. As Milliora watched, it turned away from her, melting into the foliage of the tree. She was more alone than ever.

And even more so when, at ten o'clock, Fiona and Mary came down from their bedrooms and she went to them out of desperation saying that Tom had gone missing.

'You'll have to get used to my son,' Fiona said coldly, and no one would have guessed that she too was worried at hearing the news. 'He's very independent. No woman could ever tie him down.'

'I'm sure he'll come back – sometime,' Mary said, more lethally. 'We're away to Carmel and Andy's for luncheon. Tell Tom I hope he enjoyed himself last night.'

'So where is he now?' Dermot asked, joining them.

Like his mother and sister, he was dressed to go out.

180

'I don't know,' said Milliora miserably. 'He came up to the bedroom with me last night and then he said – ' she paused, trying not to let tears overpower her – 'he said he wouldn't be long.'

At this, all three of the O'Briens burst into spontaneous laughter.

'I wouldn't worry about Tom,' said Dermot when this mirth had died down. 'I have to be off myself, I'm afraid. I'm expected at Kilmallock.'

He was expecting Rosaleen's answer to his proposal that day, and his mind was fully occupied with his own expectations.

So Milliora waited again, until midday, and one, and two, and three – and all the time anxiety and resentment, love and hate, turned and tumbled inside her, fermenting into another potent brew.

It was near to four o'clock when she heard horses' hooves coming along the avenue. She was back in her bedroom by then and she sped to the window, and craned out to see who was coming.

There were lots of horses – lots of men arriving at the house! What could be going on?

And then her heart seemed to turn over for there was Sprightly with Tom astride him coming after the others.

Thank God! she thought – he's safe. And two tears of relief eased themselves out of her eyes and fell down her flushed cheeks.

'Jamie!' she heard Tom shout and give – there was no doubt of it – a very drunken laugh.

So that was it: he had been out all night and all morning drinking while she had been worrying herself sick at home. And on top of all that, he was bringing a crowd of friends home with the purpose of, she imagined, continuing the party.

Well, she would stay in her room and ignore them and when Tom came up – as he doubtless would do, within the next few minutes – she would give him a piece of her mind.

That decided, Milliora sat down on the bed, smoothed out her skirt, and waited for the moment when she could express her pent-up feelings in words.

She was still sitting there half an hour later. Tom had not come into the house.

In that case, she had no alternative but to go out and join him. If she waited for one more moment she would, she was sure, go mad with frustration and curiosity and (though she no longer wanted to admit this, even to herself) thwarted love for Tom.

Having made up her mind to act, she got up and ran down the stairs, holding up her skirt and petticoat in one shaky hand, and out through the kitchen and scullery. Whatever was going on was happening at the back of the house, probably where the *meitheal* itself had been held.

Once in the yard, she slowed down, walking slowly, the better to play her role as mistress of the house. O'Briens, after all, had standards to maintain and an example to set to others, and she was now very much an O'Brien.

From the yard, she could hear noise – men's voices and laughter – coming from the back of the barn. Someone, mystifyingly, shouted 'Place your bets', and there were several cheers.

It was a relief to be out of the claustrophobic atmosphere of the bedroom. She tiptoed round the side of the barn, holding up her red skirt to reveal her shiny, buttoned boots, and saw that there was a motley assortment of men gathered round in a circle. A few were dressed in tailcoats and knee-breeches but many had not bothered to dress up at all; some were downright shabby and one or two were far from clean.

What could Tom be thinking of, inviting all these people out to Crag Liath? Hadn't he had enough riff-raff around at the *meitheal*?

She crept closer and saw, through a clearing in the crowd, two figures, each holding a black-hooded game-cock in his hands. A fight was about to commence.

'Place your bets!' shouted the voice she had heard before.

There was a flurry of activity as men jostled to hand the bookmaker their wagers. A second voice, more muffled, gave a direction to the men with the game-cocks. The hoods were removed from the birds' heads. The red-combed game-cocks – one brown-red, the other a birchen grey – confronted each other across the grass pit.

Intent on the fight, none of those present noticed Milliora reach the back of the line of men. The game-cocks had stepped warily towards each other and she saw that each wore tiny spurs, which were glinting in the light. She heard a weird, purposeful cry.

Suddenly, the birds moved so fast that her mesmerized eyes could hardly follow their furious race to engage. The waiting was over; the free-for-all had commenced.

She had thought their spurs merely decorative. Now, she realized that their purpose was to kill.

The brown-red game-cock cried out, its hatred deep and ancient and inexhaustible, slashing at the head of the silver birchen. Blood spurted freely on to feathers and grass.

Despite herself, Milliora was drawn into the primitive attraction of the cockfight, excited by the blood and its statement of death and victory. She was no longer certain of her own identity – could no longer say I am a lady and Mistress of Crag Liath.

'Kill!' an alien voice within herself was screaming, as weirdly as the brown-red game-cock screamed – and the clammy heat, the threat of thunder and the strange, poignant power of pregnancy combined with this voice, contributing to the sensation that she was in another, wilder, more ecstatic world.

At that moment, she saw Tom. He was far from sober, as she had suspected. Amiably waving a bottle (though not at her) he was quarter-way into the pit, on the other side. Behind him was Jamie Keegan.

An O'Brien, she thought – a descendant of Brian Boru, High King of Ireland – my beloved husband, mixing with this riff-raff, drinking from a bottle, and forgetting about me.

The whole thing was too much for her. The bizarre attraction of the cockfight, her pregnancy, the contrast between the intensity of the love she made with Tom and the way he deserted her whenever it suited him combined to unhinge her. Before she knew what she was doing, Milliora, the always-controlled, had torn through the line of startled men. She did not notice the brown-red game-cock's last concerted attack. She brushed against someone's shoulder as she ran and lost a hairpin so a lock of red-gold hair partly blocked her vision and gave her a wild and mad appearance.

She ran straight across the pit, so even the game-cocks, intent as they were, were momentarily diverted by her flight, up to where Tom was standing, brushing the loose hair aside in her impatience and shouting at the top of her voice.

'What are you *doing?*' she demanded angrily.

Tom blinked at her, uncomprehending. The crowd, equally stunned, was still, many of them wondering what the red-haired virago was contemplating next.

'Tell me!' she screamed.

He laughed foolishly. 'What am I doing? She's asking me what I'm doing,' he said to Jamie Keegan.

His words partly undid the gag that Milliora's action had put upon the crowd. Around him, the beginning of a murmur permeated from the men.

'She's as wild as a March hare,' someone said uneasily.

'Cross as a bag of cats,' agreed another.

Milliora caught some of these remarks and thought they lacked respect for her situation. She had not yet learnt to laugh at herself and she felt insecure without a modicum of veneration.

Tom, in his drunkenness, betrayed her. It had angered her that he had addressed his first words, not to herself, but to Jamie.

Now, he did much worse. He addressed them to the crowd.

'She asks me what I'm doing, but what is *she* doing, I ask you?' he called to them, hiccuping, appealing to his friends.

This proved the last straw for Milliora. People said that she shouted again at Tom, but she had no recollection of that, only of Tom's impudent face, stupid with drink, and of the huge, horrible, red wave of anger that came up from nowhere and engulfed her.

He had taken a step back from her. She stepped

forward and reached up. Then, with all her strength, she slapped the foolishness out of his face.

The crowd gasped its shock.

'Jesus Christ Almighty!' said a stunned voice from the back.

Tom said nothing. The mark of his wife's hand stood out on his face like a scarlet accusation. He gazed at her aghast. His blue eyes no longer sparkled with mischief; they burned with anger and with what she wrongly construed as hatred for herself.

Like his wife, Tom was not much good at hating. But he had his pride. He was convinced that a woman had no right to tell her husband what to do, especially in public.

Instead of hitting her back, as he was strongly tempted to do, he pushed her to one side, strode out of the pen, and disappeared from sight.

The murmur of the men rose to a babble.

'He'll never forgive her for nettling him like that in front of the county.'

'Why didn't he lambaste her?'

'Couldn't she hold on to her tongue? She's like a haggard of sparrows.'

With the spotlight of County Clare focused upon her, Milliora stood forlornly in the middle of the pit. At her feet was the inert body of the silver-birchen game-cock, soaked in its scarlet blood. She did not see it.

The men watching her were, on the whole, unsympathetic towards her, sharing Tom's view of her conduct, but when she began to cry, bending her head so the tears fell straight from her eyes on to the bloodied grass, many of them softened. They fidgeted awkwardly; their embarrassment over the scene she had

186

made prevented them from talking to her, or escorting her out of the pen. Still, they had nearly all forgiven her. They were used to hot speeches and hasty actions and, despite her intrusion, they were not going to bear any grudges – except for Tim-Pat Tierney, watching her with hatred in his eyes. He had wanted Tom to hit her back, and grieved when he did not. Her tears gave him a curious pleasure.

Milliora, who had always been so conscious of the need to keep face, was now blind to everything but her need to apologize to Tom. Having risen as high as she could on the red anger wave and been hurled by it on to the sad, pale, sadistic shore where she lay bruised and anguished, she wondered if he could ever love her again.

She remained rooted to the spot for several minutes, absently wiping her tears away with the back of her hand. Then, muzzy with reaction, she crept away through the men, who parted for her to pass, and back into the house.

When she had gone, the crowd, predictably, threw itself into a frenzy of analysis and conjecture. Comparable incidents were dredged up out of the past. Jamie Keegan, knowing of Milliora's condition from Tom, said, out of his own experience, that pregnant women, like pregnant mares and cows, needed careful handling. A man from Ennis recalled the way his cousin had threatened her husband with a cake-knife when he had drunk too much at a wedding and had had to be restrained.

'Women!' he said ruefully, and drank from his bottle.
Jamie Keegan agreed.

* * *

187

Milliora had expected Tom to be upstairs in the bedroom, although she had little hope that he would talk
to her when they met. But the room was empty. There
was no evidence to show that Tom had been and gone.

Maybe he was in the bathroom. She crept there to
check and found the bathroom door open.

And he was not downstairs – not in the drawing-
room or the library or anywhere in the house.

So he must still be out in the grounds, brooding
about her. She could not face the idea of going back
there after what had happened, not with all those men
around.

She would wait for him in the library, she thought,
and as soon as he came into the house she would beg
his forgiveness and plead for his love. From the library,
she could see into the yard and spot him as soon as he
appeared.

She settled herself down in a stout oak chair and
propped her elbows up on the window-sill.

She waited in vain. Fiona and Mary came home that
night and so, eventually, did Dermot. But Tom did not
return.

11

In contrast to this drama, Dermot and Rosaleen spent a quiet day at Kilmallock, although it was not altogether tension free. After a prolonged luncheon during which Grand-aunt Carrie spoke incessantly and they listened, trying not to look impatient, they were mercifully released and allowed to sit in peace in the garden while the old lady went to lie down.

Dermot came straight to the point as soon as they were alone. He wanted the structure of his life mapped out for him and although he appreciated that it might be years before he and Rosaleen could afford to marry, he was anxious that she commit herself at once.

To his disappointment, she did not.

'I'm *almost* sure I will marry you, Dermot,' she said. 'I'm just not altogether certain.'

'What makes you hesitate?' Dermot asked, more sympathetically than pushing. 'I hope you don't have another suitor that's causing this confusion!'

He managed a teasing laugh at this and Rosaleen joined in.

'No, I don't,' she said, and found she could not go further.

For how could you say to a man that you were not one hundred per cent convinced of his integrity? Especially when your suspicion was founded, not on logical facts so much as an inkling that he did not always speak his mind, that he was deeper than he would have you believe, that he had another, less acceptable side to him, buried under his charm?

'I understand,' Dermot said gently. 'I promise that I do. You must take your time.'

As soon as he said that, she felt that she *did* love him. He was so encouraging and so strengthening – so selfless in his love, that she, who was in need of reinforcement, could not fail to respond to his overtures.

'I'm sure I will marry you in the end,' she said. 'I can't imagine that I would not.'

And with that he had to be content.

Had he not been so preoccupied with this conversation, Dermot would have noticed that Mount Royal had a shoe loose before he left for Limerick. As it was, his mind drifted so that he was unaware of the white road and the green hedgerows and the muggy overcast weather.

Then Mount Royal stumbled, drawing attention to his plight. Having dismounted, Dermot inspected the horse's hooves, and found, to his shame, that the loose shoe must have been discarded several miles back. He thought of stopping the hoof with cowdung up to the level of the shoe so they could go on home and decided against it. Cowdung was more irritant than emollient, in spite of its softness, and Mount Royal could suffer all the more.

The nearest forge was three miles back but he had much farther ahead of him. He had no alternative but to turn. In deference to the unshod hoof, he walked Mount Royal all the way. It seemed to take an age, and when they finally got to the forge Dermot found, to his irritation, that it was deserted.

He had no alternative but to wait for the missing

blacksmith. He did so for nearly an hour before a small boy with a freckled face turned up to deliver a pail of milk.

'Are ye looking for himself? He's over at the Widow Dolan's,' said the child.

'Where would that be?'

'Up that road and round a corner. Ye can see the house from here.'

Located, the blacksmith was eased out of what Dermot thought was bound to be a Land League meeting – or a Fenian reincarnation, according to Rosaleen's aunt – and persuaded to return to the anvil.

''Tis a front shoe you're after?'

'That's it – the left.'

Dermot stood around while the shoe was fitted and was almost asleep in the saddle by the time he got home.

Virtually sleep-walking, he staggered up the stairs and into his room, threw himself on to his bed, and fell asleep without undressing, quite unaware of Milliora's anguish.

'Dermot,' his mother whispered in his ear, 'Tom hasn't come home.'

'Hmm?'

'Tom's not back. Wake up, Dermot – listen.'

Opening his eyes to her anxious face, he said crossly, 'For God's sake, Mother, what time is it?'

'It's nearly five. Dermot – '

'*Five!* Mother, Tom is a grown-up man,' he said, wondering how on earth he could get sense into her head. 'He has a wife to worry about him. Why don't you let *her* do it – and tell him off, at the same time?'

'You don't understand,' she said. 'This is the second

191

night in a row he hasn't been home. I haven't been sleeping much. I found Milliora downstairs in tears when we got back from Carmel's. She says they had a row.'

'So then he's at Jamie Keegan's – and you can't expect me to go over there at five in the morning, to check if he's in the guest-room. Be reasonable. Just think of the number of times he's done this to us before.'

'The number of times makes no difference,' his mother said.

Nevertheless, she retreated. Pulling the sheet over his head, Dermot heard her troubled footsteps creaking back to her room. A storm in a teacup, he said to himself, and trust Tom to stir it.

The extent of the damage done by the storm he only realized after his breakfast, when he ran into Tim-Pat in the yard.

'Any sign of Tom?' he asked hopefully.

He had a busy day ahead at Dundons. The last thing he wanted to do was go out looking for his irresponsible brother.

'He's not back so?' said the groom. 'After what happened, I thought that might be the way of it.'

'After *what* happened?'

There was a lot to recount and Tim-Pat, unlike Dermot, was not in a hurry.

'Holy St John!' said Dermot finally. 'What got into my sister-in-law to carry on like that? I suppose I *had* better go and find Tom, under the circumstances, otherwise, they'll be hysterical inside the house. Have you got Mount Royal saddled?'

'I have. Do you want me to go with you?'

As always, Tim-Pat was panting to be in his company. Now and again, it could give you a kick to take him up on his offers.

'You may as well.'

'I'll ride Sprightly for a change. I'll be with you in two shakes of an ass's tail.'

'Sprightly? But doesn't Tom have him out?'

When Tim-Pat shook his head Dermot felt for the first time that something was up.

Following the river into Killaloe they arrived at St Flannan's Cathedral, built by Donal Mor O'Brien, a twelfth-century King of Munster. The cathedral, with its magnificent Irish-Romanesque doorway, stood on the west bank of the river, just below the purple and yellow sandstone bridge. Above it, on the same side, was the Keegans' house.

And Tom was not there.

'Have you seen him at all since yesterday?'

'Not a sign of him,' Helen Keegan said. 'Jamie said that he went off in a huff. So he didn't come home all night?'

'No.'

'There's nothing unusual in that,' said Helen, in the cynical voice of experience.

'Yes. Well – my mother worries. You know how it is.'

'Oh, *I* know,' she said. 'But he didn't come here. I'm sure Jamie hasn't seen him. He could be at the Dooleys, or the MacNamaras maybe. Are you sure you won't come in?'

Dermot shook his head.

'I have to be going. I have work to do, even if Tom has not.'

At the end of the street, he turned to wave, but the door had closed behind her.

The Dooleys had not seen Tom, neither had the MacNamaras, nor any of the other half dozen families they went to in their search. Dermot was running out of ideas and, in spite of his basic conviction that worrying about Tom was a waste of time since he would inevitably turn up unscathed, the slight feeling of unease he had carried with him since discovering Tom had set off on foot was growing from a nudge into a more insistent agitation.

With this went the usual resentment he felt about his brother on these occasions. Tom was so inconsiderate, especially where their mother was concerned, and yet he got all the consideration in the world when he decided to go missing.

'Did you think of the possibility that he might be at home by now, having the laugh on us?'

Tim-Pat's laugh at his own question infuriated Dermot.

'I've had enough of this kind of nonsense,' he said. 'Come on – let's go home.'

The warning signs were plain enough for anyone to read. Tim-Pat allowed a distance to fall between the horses.

By the time they were within sight of O'Brien's Bridge they were riding side by side but, still, Tim-Pat was the first to comment that something seemed to be happening.

'Look at the crowd gathering at the bridge, Master Dermot.'

Crowds smacked of vulgarity. As a rule, Dermot

avoided them, if he could. So what instinct spurred him into a canter?

'Come on!'

They reached the bridge. The crowd, their eyes on the river – or on something that had been pulled out of it – did not look around.

Now, there was danger. He was numb with fear. All the same, he forced himself to try to behave normally, in a hazy way telling himself that he could thus avert the danger . . .

'What's going on here?'

'Yerra, they've pulled a body out of the river,' a man said.

Holding the horror out.

'*Whose* body?' he heard himself say and he was conscious that he had raised his voice and was attracting attention.

'Take it easy now.'

'Hold on.'

Then –

'How can he take it easy,' asked a woman, 'when 'tis his own brother that's been drowned?'

'Easy.'

The word went crazily round and round in his head. It was the only sane entity in a world gone suddenly mad.

'Easy.'

'Drink this.'

He swallowed and gagged. *Poitin*. He had tasted it before and marvelled that men's livers could actually survive it.

'Christ!'

'Easy.'

195

Tim-Pat's arm was around his shoulders. For a moment, he half-buried his head in the groom's thin chest.

'What happened?'

'You blacked out, Master Dermot. It was the shock.'

'I don't mean to myself. To Tom, for Christ's sake.'

'He must have dived off the bridge. He'd done it many a time before.'

'But Tom was a great swimmer. He couldn't – '

'He'd had a lot to drink, Master Dermot. And he was upset. He was in a sweat over that woman.'

The river was low. He must have misjudged it. His head was hit on the rocks . . .

'*No!*'

Tom is immortal, Dermot wanted to say, childishly. He cannot die.

'. . . body trapped by the rocks.'

He looked beyond Tim-Pat. To the men and women still gathered, blabbering . . . To the thing that lay on the bank.

'I must go to him.'

'There's no point in doing that,' Tim-Pat said gently. 'You can't help him now, Master Dermot. You keep your strengh. You'll need that, for when we get back to the house.'

He thought of his mother – and of Milliora.

His mother broke down completely, old and defeated and baffled by the injustice of it. Mary, screaming her pain, had to be slapped in the face. Telling them first, since they were first encountered, battered and crushed by the intensity of their reaction, contending with his own grief, Dermot could not imagine finding the strength within himself to tell Milliora too.

196

'Master Dermot, young Mrs O'Brien is up in her bedroom, worrying herself sick about Master Tom. Wondering if he's coming home to her . . .'

'I know,' he said, desperately, agony piling on agony. 'I'll have to tell her.'

'I'll tell her,' Mary Markham offered, weeping her own tears for Tom. 'You have enough on your plate.'

'Maybe that would be the best idea.' He was only about to say that when it struck him for the first time that all the responsibility was now his. He was heir to Crag Liath. His mother and Mary were looking to *him* for guidance as well as for consolation. Where once he had been the insubstantial second son, he was now head of the house and, as such, revered, his opinions sought and respected.

'No,' he said, 'I'll go up to her. You stay here with my mother.'

He braced himself for a wildly emotional outburst, a repetition on a more grandiose and more horrendous scale than what had gone on below.

Her door – hers, no longer Tom and hers – was closed and he tapped on it gently.

'It's Dermot. May I come in?'

'Yes,' she said at once. 'Yes. Come in.'

Stepping further into the nightmare, he obeyed. She was sitting by the window, as immaculately turned-out as ever. Waiting for Tom.

'Milly.'

He called her by the diminutive sometimes, as Rosaleen always did.

Her eyes – she had obviously been crying for hours – were red-rimmed and fuzzy with pain. She looked too fragile to be able to withstand the murderous blow he had no alternative but to inflict.

197

'Milly, I have something to tell you.'

'What is it?'

Her voice had a huskiness about it he had always thought attractive.

'You're going to have to be very brave.'

Trite words. Of no assistance.

'It's Tom,' she said. 'Something has happened to Tom.'

'Yes.'

She did not flinch. It was as if she had been expecting bad news and was only awaiting confirmation. Her hands, pretty pale hands with long slender fingers, remained clasped in her lap.

'He's – dead. Isn't he?'

He nodded mutely, struggling for the non-existent phrase that would substitute for the ugly reality. Drowned. Bloated. A body looks dreadful, taken from a river.

'He dived from the bridge. He must have hit his head on a rock.'

'I see,' she said, quite calmly, her eyes flickering away from him to the window.

'Milly?'

'You can see the river from here, on its way to the bridge. I watched it yesterday when I was waiting for Tom. It was my fault, you see. I shouted at him – hit him. It's my fault that he is dead.'

Her voice was devoid of emotion. In shock himself, he found he resented her reaction. The fact that she was sparing him a histrionic outburst suddenly seemed to him more offensive than if she had not.

'It's not good for you to sit up here alone,' he said, still proferring a kind of comfort. 'Come downstairs with me to the drawing-room.'

She shook her head.

'No, Dermot. You go down. I'll be all right.'

'She wants to be alone,' he said to Mary Markham. 'She said so.'

Shivering, he realized that there had been a dramatic drop in the temperature. Rain was teeming down outside. Andy and Carmel, running from their carriage into the house, were soaked to the skin.

In the enormity of their grieving that evening, the O'Briens almost forgot about Milliora. She did not appear and it was well over an hour before anyone mentioned her name.

Andy it was who said she must be in a terrible state.

It was not the time for enmity and Carmel did not feel it.

'Go on up and bring her down.'

'*I* can't go into her bedroom,' Andy protested, embarrassed.

'What harm could you do? I want to stay with Mother. Dermot, you go up.'

'She wants to be on her own,' Dermot said.

Even in mourning, Milliora and the family sat in separate rooms.

No one at Crag Liath slept for more than a few hours that night. Dermot, obsessed by the image of lively Tom lying cold and still in one of the empty bedrooms, lay in bed listening to the rain until he could bear being there no longer. For the second night in a row he had not undressed before getting into his bed. Eventually he was up and sneaking downstairs, and out into the garden.

It was just after two-thirty. In two hours the estate

would spring to life; men would be off to the fields, the cattle herded in for milking.

Meanwhile the rain was pelting down and since he had come out without a coat, he was wet through in minutes. In a curious kind of a way, this punishment had a healing quality, the physical discomfort distracting him from the emotional pain with which they were all scourged.

From the rose garden he climbed over the five-bar gate into the first of Crag Liath's many fields, and headed vaguely for the river. Sleepy cows, their stomachs full of the dandelions and marigolds that would dye their butter yellow-gold, blinked great brown eyes at him as he passed them. Beyond them was a stone wall overlaid with yellow-green moss and dark green ivy. He vaulted over it and wandered on aimlessly.

Much later, he found himself by a marshy strip, an elongated bit of grassland with a big hump in the middle. Infested by reeds, it was, according to local belief, not O'Brien property at all, but belonging to the fairies. As children, Tom and he had avoided it for that reason, as did the workers on the estate. Everyone knew that if you offended a fairy – built a house on one of their paths, or cut down one of their trees, or encroached upon their property – they would be likely to cause an outbreak of disease among your cattle, even though this would go against their own interest, for they were fond of milk and had a vested interest in the well-being of the cows. In spring, bunches of primroses and other flowers were tied on to the tails of the cattle to protect them from the fairies, and white-thorn or mountain ash branches were placed on the lids of milk-churns to ward off fairy thieves.

Another way was to place a clay imprint of a cow's foot over the door of the byre. There were several such imprints in the clay in front of him, a warning that a cow had strayed out of its regular pasture and was in danger of falling into the river.

He bent down and picked up one of the imprints, muddied by rain, and held it in his hand. Despite the superstition, it was Crag Liath soil all right and as such, had a magic of its own, for it was part of the land handed on by kings.

Handed on to himself! The massive advantage of his inheritance came home to him: the power he would wield; the speed with which he could wed; the money he would have.

But it was more than that – much more, although Tom had not been able either to understand or respect the full meaning. As heir to Crag Liath, he was being acknowledged as the holder of one of the oldest European pedigrees, going back not just to Brian Boru, but to Milesius, pre-Christian King of Spain, and beyond.

Tom had not cared about any of that. But he had not honoured his duty to Crag Liath, either – not sparing a thought about running it more effectively, while he, Dermot, had thought about that continually, pining to put his good ideas into practice.

It was almost as if God had recognized that Dermot was the more suitable brother to manage the place, and had intervened accordingly.

Could He really have done such a thing, *inter alia* causing the family such misery? He had no compunction about letting the most desperate prayers for the alleviation of pain go unheeded when it suited Him, so it was possible. God's ways are not our ways, his mother often counselled. There is a divine pattern in all things which we mere mortals with our less-than-satisfactory mentalities cannot comprehend.

The pattern of Crag Liath, though, was simple if you worked out that Tom had been given his big chance, and had failed to make the most of it. He had thus been relieved of his duties and a more able man put forward in his place.

Why had he not seen that earlier? Why had he not *foreseen* it? He had known that he was perfect for the job . . .

He looked down again at the muddied clay he held in his hand and marvelled at its significance.

He would not fail to honour his duty, either to Crag Liath, or to God, Who had chosen him for the task.

Milliora, too, thought that God had been instrumental in taking Tom away but she thought He had done so to punish her for failing to adhere to her wedding vows. She had promised to love, honour and obey her husband, but she had shouted at him and assaulted him instead. No wonder God was angry.

She, too, accepted His intervention and did not try to fight against it. As Tom had been struck and then become part of the flotsam of the river so she felt that she was drowning in a foetid stream of pain. There would be no end to this journey, she knew that, and thought that she deserved nothing less.

In that tormented night and the many others that followed it, Milliora never once contemplated the fact that she might not have been at fault. She did not pray for Tom because she felt in her heart that he was blameless and had therefore been taken straight to Heaven, with no further need to consider his welfare.

Tom was beyond pain, but she would live with it forever.

At the top of the stairs, Fiona O'Brien had placed a huge long-cased clock. Each tick was a blow in itself, a reminder of time as an instrument of pain. The hours went by, each one a year. Milliora lay awake, an open-eyed oblation to reprimand and vengeance.

By sunrise it had stopped raining and still she had not slept. There was only one change in her condition. Until then, her suffering had been emotional. As the sky grew red, presaging more rain, it was physical as well. By midday it was being whispered around Crag Liath that the young Mrs O'Brien had lost her baby, and was in danger herself.

12

It was inevitable that details of the row between Tom and Milliora would reach the ears of the O'Brien women. Sure enough they did, and their reaction added to the worries Dermot already had, coping with Requiem Mass and funeral arrangements.

'Your mother wants you, Master Dermot,' said Mary Markham, buttonholing him on the landing. 'She's in the drawing-room. I'm afraid Mrs Cash has been talking to her – a woman who makes it her business to know everything, and who has not the ability to keep a civil tongue in her head.'

'What has she said to my mother?'

The place was an immense hive with a multiplicity of bees buzzing with news and speculation.

'She told her what happened at the cockfight, Master Dermot – the way young Mrs O'Brien slapped poor Master Tom across the face, God rest his soul. Not that I blame the poor girl for doing it. Don't we all know she put up with a lot, with himself coming and going. But your mother is poorly herself and the story has destroyed her completely.'

'God in Heaven!'

What next, he thought wearily. Still, what could he expect – all their nerves were on edge.

'I'll go and talk to her,' he said. 'You go on up to attend to my sister-in-law and keep out of the thing entirely.'

* * *

'She drove Tom to his death,' said Fiona O'Brien, not for the first time. 'I might have expected it. It was written from the beginning.'

'By all accounts Milliora is near to death herself, Mother,' Dermot said, mildly reproving.

'Let her die then,' she said, 'though death is too good for her after what she has done.'

She was wild with grief and there was no reasoning with her. Dermot decided that he would talk to Carmel after the funeral about having herself and Mary to stay until the dust had settled – if it ever did. Even that suggestion would require tactful presentation since his mother was quite capable of leaping to the conclusion that he wanted her out of the house for good.

Thinking that they would improve with Milliora *in situ* was, to say the least, foolishly optimistic. If she lived, she could not stay on at Crag Liath, Dermot concluded.

In which case, what was to become of her? Her father was dead, her sister was now in the convent, she had no close relations and he did not know whether she had been left money by her father or whether George Fitzgibbon, thinking she was set up with Tom for life, had given way to an altruistic impulse and made Laurel Hill Convent the main beneficiary of his will. If that was the case it would be necessary to find a little house for her somewhere and provide her with a living allowance.

In the aftermath of death, more and more crises and problems seemed to loom at his door. People said that the organization of a funeral was a necessary distraction from grief but Dermot felt he had enough distractions to keep him going for years.

'I have to go to Killaloe,' he said to his mother, not

telling her that this excursion was in connection with the funeral. 'You stay with Carmel and Mary and try not to think too much while I'm gone.'

As he went out of the room he heard her say again: 'Let her die.'

Thinking that she might, he found himself pitying Milliora once more. Near to death, she was supremely vulnerable and easy to pity. He did not think of Tom anymore, only of the clinical necessity of arranging his funeral.

And once the funeral was over Dermot detached his thoughts from that, occupying himself with his new responsibilities, talking to the men of Crag Liath about the threshing and the winnowing and all the time making plans for improving the estate. It was several days before he had a chance to go into Limerick. By that time, Fiona and Mary had been packed off to Andy and Carmel's for an indefinite stay and Milliora was out of danger, although still confined to bed.

He still had work to do at Dundon's and a visit there was top of the list of his priorities, even if there was also the vitally important business of buying a new threshing-mill and a winnowing riddle. He owed loyalty to Dundon's – it had to come first, in spite of the fact that he would soon be cutting his ties with the firm forever. The heir to Crag Liath could not concurrently pursue a career in the law.

Old Mr Dundon shook Dermot's hand and commiserated, and said that he was pleased to have him back.

'There have been a few rumours flying about the town about your brother,' he said. 'A few problems there, it appears.'

'Yes, his wife and himself did have a bit of an

argument,' Dermot said, keen to gloss this matter over. 'A young couple – you know how it is.'

'That wasn't – Ah, well, leave it there,' said old Mr Dundon, abstrusely. 'You have a lot on your shoulders, Dermot.'

'I have indeed.'

Just how much, he found out within the hour when the first of a new set of demands turned up, literally, on the doorstep.

'I didn't like to come to the house,' said Jamie Keegan. 'I'm told that Milliora has lost the child.'

'That's right.'

Dermot had never felt at ease with Jamie, who was too much a part of the gregarious, hard-drinking, hail-fellow-well-met milieu in which Tom had thrived, to appeal to his brother.

'How is she?'

'Getting over it, I'm told. I haven't seen her myself.'

'And your mother?'

'In a bad way. But that was to be expected.'

'It was,' said Jamie, and added: 'She was always mad about Tom.'

What did he want at Dundon's, Dermot wondered. He wished Jamie would get to the point and then be on his way.

Finally, when they had exhausted the family grief as a topic, the visitor came out with the real reason for his call.

'I take it you're seeing to Tom's affairs, Dermot?'

'Since I've inherited, naturally – '

'That was why I came – feeling that I should bring it to your attention. When Tom was alive I wouldn't press but – '

'What are you talking about?' Dermot asked bluntly.

Jamie looked embarrassed.

'Tom owed me money,' he said at last, 'a lot of money. As I said, up to now I had hoped he would be able to pay me back in due course and I would have let him have his head till then. But I thought if you were sorting things out – '

'How much?'

'Just under six hundred pounds.'

'*Six hundred pounds?* That's a lot of money. Are you sure he owed you as much as that?'

'Yes. Of course, I haven't got proof of the debt. Tom was my friend. I trusted him. He was reckless all right, but he was never dishonest. I had no need to draw up a bill.'

'How was the debt incurred?'

'It was a gradual thing – a bit here and there. You know – like all Tom's debts.'

All Tom's debts?

'How many more did he have?'

'I don't know,' said Jamie, not looking at Dermot. 'I mean, Tom was in trouble, Dermot. He had been for some time. He had a whole year of bad luck with the horses and . . . Surely *you* know?'

I do not, raged Dermot silently, hating Jamie and his lot for leading Tom astray in the first place. But there was no point in voicing his thoughts for the moment, ranting at his unhappy visitor. Much more relevant was the need to extract from Jamie some idea of how much Tom owed around the country. There was no question of ignoring these debts. The honour of the family demanded that they be paid. Or paid in due course. How bad had that whole year of bad luck been?

'You'd better tell me the whole story,' he said to Jamie. 'There's no point now in trying to shield Tom.'

208

So Jamie told him what he knew and that was a lot. When he had finished talking there was only one conclusion to draw: Tom had not only been a gambler with an unlucky streak, he had held a bad hand every time and had lost continually.

'You'll get your money back,' Dermot said. 'And so will the rest of them, but it may take time. I'll have to go into the whole thing thoroughly.'

'That's all right. I can wait. I just thought I might as well mention it now, as later.'

And be first up in the creditors' queue, Dermot thought.

'You did the right thing,' he told Jamie. 'I'll be in touch with you shortly. You have my word.'

He had hoped for a week or so to catch up with his work at Dundon's before dealing explicitly with Tom's affairs. Now his plans would be upset.

It would all have been easier had Tom done as he had asked and transferred his affairs over to Dundon's, but his brother had resisted that move, saying that as O'Malleys had handled their father's business, what was the need for change?

Or was it that Tom had not wanted Dermot nosing around, finding out about his problems? Happy-go-lucky he might have been, but he had still been conscious of being the older brother, and had never risked impairing his dignity in front of Dermot.

He tapped on old Mr Dundon's door and was invited in.

'It looks as if I'll have to set some time aside for my brother's affairs before I finalize things here,' he said. 'I should be in again tomorrow.'

'Of course – of course,' old Mr Dundon said. 'Take your time, Dermot. Don't feel you've got to come in tomorrow. What you need to do may take longer than an afternoon. Yes, Miss Purcell – what is it?'

'There's a man called Mangan that's called to see Mr O'Brien.'

The man called Mangan turned out to be a pleasant fellow, even if his mission was unpleasant.

'Your brother owed me a few bob,' he began.

It was to be a familiar refrain.

And yet, if only it had stopped with Tom's immediate debts . . .

Hoping to see Mr O'Malley senior at once, Dermot went across to the other solicitors' offices. The clerk inside the counter recognized him but, unlike those who had attended Tom's funeral, he did not pay him particular respect.

'Mr O'Malley isn't free this afternoon.'

No 'sir' or 'Mr O'Brien'.

'Then how about ten o'clock in the morning?'

'He's not free then, either,' said the clerk, pleased about that.

'Well, would you like to tell me when he *is* free?' said Dermot sarcastically, and managed to make an appointment for the following day at three.

Turning up to keep it, he made a point of snubbing the clerk, ignoring his command to wait when the door to the inner sanctum opened and the previous client came out.

'Mr O'Malley, good afternoon to you.'

'It's Dermot, isn't it?'

No 'Mr O'Brien' here, either. Still Mr O'Malley was old enough to be his grandfather and had probably called Tom by his Christian name as well.

'Sit down,' the old man said. 'What was it you wanted to see me about?'

Even odder, this. Had he not heard that Tom was dead and concluded that, with only two sons in the family, the next in line would want to put his claim to Crag Liath on the Register of Lands and officially take over affairs?

'I should have thought it was obvious,' Dermot said, just managing to keep the scorn out of his voice.

'It's not obvious at all,' said Mr O'Malley, perfectly polite, puzzled and apparently in total command of his senses.

'But – I've come to see the title deeds to Crag Liath, of course.'

Mr O'Malley's puzzled expression did not change.

'What's that got to do with O'Malleys?' he asked, just as politely as before.

Dermot could hardly believe his ears.

'You're my solicitors. You acted for my father, and for Tom, and now you're acting on my behalf.'

'In what matter, Dermot?'

'I *told* you – in the matter of my claim to Crag Liath.'

'We're at loggerheads here,' said Mr O'Malley. 'Let me clarify this. You say *your* claim to Crag Liath. You did say that, didn't you?'

'Of course, I did,' said Dermot irascibly. 'My brother is dead. I'm the only other son. Crag Liath is mine.'

But this assertion seemed only to flummox Mr O'Malley. Pulling at his side-whiskers, he leant back in his chair.

'You mean to say – ' he began – 'but, no. Surely that isn't possible!'

'*What* isn't possible?'

His heart was beginning to pound too quickly. Something was dreadfully wrong. But what? It was not

211

possible for Tom to have played a hopeless hand in the matter of his brother's claim to Crag Liath.

Or was it?

The answer was unequivocally – yes. Mr O'Malley could not have been kinder in the telling but no one could have erased the brutality from what he had to say.

Tom, hopelessly in debt, had mortgaged Crag Liath in a desperate bid for a life-line. He had not repaid the debt and the creditor had foreclosed.

'*Foreclosed!* Who was his creditor?'

'His father-in-law, Mr George Fitzgibbon.'

'*George Fitzgibbon?*'

Milliora's father? But –

'George Fitzgibbon is himself dead.'

'We know that, Dermot,' said Mr O'Malley, humouring him. 'We passed everything over to his solicitors some time ago, but we knew that he had died. I can't imagine how your brother managed to conceal all this from the family. If it had just concerned himself . . . Still, I suppose she saw no need to reveal that the estate had passed from one of them to the other.'

She?

'She was saving face, I suppose – his face. After all, it's a most unusual situation – a woman inheriting a property like Crag Liath.'

She?

'Her father had a good sum tucked away, I believe. That's hers as well, from what I hear.'

Milliora – not himself – the heir to Crag Liath?

'It doesn't seem possible that you were kept in the dark about it. I'm sorry for you, Dermot. It's terrible

212

luck. A strange thing, though, the way she didn't tell you.'

Reeling past the clerk he had intended to impress, Dermot virtually fell into Glentworth Street. Force of habit got him round to Hackett's and on to Mount Royal's back, had him head for home.

Or what he had naïvely believed to be home until less than half an hour before. But the sombre, grey-stone mansion and the rich land that went with it was home no longer. He could not shirk from that fact, although the realization scourged like a whiplash, seering into his body, it seemed, as well as into his soul.

Crag Liath had been taken from him – the house, the land, the horses and the livestock, the apple orchard and the flower gardens. The Italian mantel, the landscapes and the staircase mural. The large gilt chandelier.

He knew then – had perhaps always known – that he loved Crag Liath more than he had or would love any woman – more than he loved Rosaleen, although he was certain of his feelings for her, too. But Crag Liath was much more bewitching – had seduced and enslaved him long before Rosaleen had come into his life, and his love affair with the estate would be subject to no fluctuation or lessening of passion on his side as the years went by.

Yet, he had been cuckolded in that love affair – worse, had lost out, so that he had become an impotent lover and, as such, an object of derision.

That was a birch-blow, too, bitter and abasing, yet bad as it was, not the ultimate. That was the loss of his own identity.

Only a few days before he had held the soil of Crag Liath in his hands and paid tribute to its sorcery – part of the land handed on to him by powerful pre-Christian kings. He had marvelled at its significance, vowed not to fail in honouring his duty to it, unlike Tom, who had lamentably failed in honouring his. And a pattern – a divine pattern – appeared to have emerged. He had believed himself selected by God to play a very special role.

He laughed aloud at the irony in that. He was out of the city now, riding past the Sweeps' Cross, near Long Pavement Station, where the Ennis train made a last stop before puffing into Limerick. There was no one on the road, no one to laugh at him or nudge his neighbour, winking. That would follow in time. At this very moment, Mr O'Malley would be talking about him, reporting back to his son and junior partner the way Dermot O'Brien had been taken for a ride. In the morning the story would be all over Limerick and the world and his wife would be laughing their heads off at the way he had been deceived.

At this, Dermot's proud face blushed an ugly, angry red. To think that *he* had believed in divine intervention. Far from that being the case, God had let him walk right up the garden path without putting a finger out to stop him.

The first wave of hate hit him and he was almost drowned by its magnitude. God was against him. He could see that only too clearly.

He had never been as devout a Catholic as his mother and sisters – even as Tom had been – not because he quarrelled with or questioned the Faith but because his admiration for the style of the Protestants outpaced his interest in his own religion, but he

214

believed implicitly in the concept of a godhead. God had not only let him down, He had given clear proof that He was ranged against him.

Then the hatred was mutual. Who could be on the side of a God who could betray with such facility?

Tom had once shocked him by repeating a story he had heard of a man who had also felt betrayed by God, and who, as a measure of his hate, had persuaded a prostitute to accompany him to an empty church, and to copulate with him on consecrated ground.

'Can you imagine any man doing a thing like that?' Tom had asked, equally shocked.

'No,' Dermot had said then. Now he could say: 'Yes.'

However he might hate God, he could never have the satisfaction of watching Him being hurt, whereas . . .

'Sorry for you, Dermot . . . terrible luck . . . a most unusual situation . . . a woman, inheriting a property like that.'

Let her die, his mother had said – though death is too good for her after what she has done.

He began to examine his hatred for Milliora and found that it was just as great as that other hatred festering inside him.

The lying slut. Simpering and hanging on his every word. Listening to his ideas for Crag Liath. How she had deceived him – and deceived Tom, too, no doubt.

Poor, foolish Tom. Running up debts, mortgaging Crag Liath to her father, playing into her grasping little hands. And going to his death. (Or being sent to it.)

Well, she would pay for all of it, since God could pay for none. He would see to that.

Dermot was nearly back at Crag Liath now and his

mind was bloated with hate so when he rode up the long avenue to the house he did not look with his usual love at the green land stretching away to the blue-black hills.

He dismounted in the yard and with a curt call to Tim-Pat to see to Mount Royal he walked into the house with what Mrs Cash described as a right puss on his face, acknowledging none of the staff.

'Isn't he as black as the ace of spades?' she said to Mary Markham. 'As sure as there's a bill on a crow something is going on.'

For answer, Mary abandoned her cooking and tip-toed after him up the stairs. Dermot's expression had given her the willies, she said afterwards. He had murder written all over his face and the certainty that someone was about to suffer for whatever had occurred. And not himself, either, she said.

Mary did not exactly reason that Dermot was after Milliora's blood but, as she said, she loved young Mrs O'Brien like her own child by then. So she went after Dermot in the instinctive manner of the female animal protecting her threatened young.

When he got to the landing she was hot on his heels, though keeping out of sight, and she saw him stride to Milliora's bedroom door and, with no regard at all for propriety, virtually wrenched it open.

Mary's eyes, she said, stood out on two sticks. She could not imagine what young Mrs O'Brien could be thinking when Dermot appeared in her room with that look on his face.

For her part, Mary stood on sentinel duty on the landing, ready to intervene at the drop of a hat if the matter got out of control.

216

13

Milliora's cheeks were hollow. There were dark circles under the hazel eyes and no colour in her cheeks.

She had, too, an odd, shocked expression. She did not react when Dermot came into the room. She appeared not to be aware of his presence.

Her vulnerability, which, in the past, would have endeared her to him, now had precisely the opposite effect. Like the foxhound sensing the ultimate weakness of the fox, so Dermot's blood-lust was exacerbated by her condition. Knowing he could not kill her, he came in, all the same, for the kill.

'You bitch!'

Her expression did not change. She lay completely still, her pale face contrasting with the brilliant patchwork quilt that covered the rest of her body.

'Slut!' he said, wanting to reach out and throttle her so that some sound, even a cry for help, was wrung out of her throat. 'Sucking up to me. Pretending to be interested in my ideas. All the time, *knowing . . .*'

Nothing. Her quiescence was disturbing. It was not only that she was speechless – she did not even seem to breathe. The eyes stared back at him, uncomprehending, dazed. Wondering for a moment if she *was* dead, he went closer to her to check.

She was alive all right – or half-alive. Good, he thought – I want you alive so that I can punish you, make every day a living torment so your life will become a protracted Calvary, with every second intensifying the agony of the thorns and nails and taunts. Like *my* life . . .

'Where are the title deeds?' he said to the inert figure under the brilliant patchwork.

Predictably, this did not elicit a response. Impelled by a masochistic whim to witness his own damnation, he began to look about the room for the deeds, at her dressing-table, at the table set up for Tom's toiletry needs and on which only a tray of rejected food was standing.

'Where have you hidden them? In the wardrobe maybe?'

Opening the wardrobe he saw only a tightly-packed row of gowns, on pretty, padded hangers.

'What pretty dresses,' he said to the woman on the bed. 'What a lot of time you must have spent sewing them before you married Tom,' reaching out for three of them, wrenching them from their hangers, pretending to examine the intricacy of the stitching. 'How industrious. It's almost a tragedy that I – have to destroy them!'

He dropped two of the dresses on to a chair and held out the third to her.

'*Very* pretty. Pale blue silk embroidered with pale pink roses. What a lot of time you must have spent on the embroidery, Milliora. What a great shame it is to tear it into pieces!'

Watching her face, he began to shred the silk, pulling off the tapes that used to pull back the front, wrenching the sleeves, tearing the bodice and skirt apart at the seams.

'See?' Smiling, he threw the pieces on to the floor and turned back to the chair. 'And what have we here? A wedding-dress, no less! What a delight to rip off this

218

little lace collar – and the train of pleated frills. Yet – when I think of the day you wore this gown – it almost moves my heart!'

Why the hell did he not get a reaction to his actions, he thought, looking at her in frustration. How could she just lie there watching what he did without as much as a murmur of protest? The urge to throttle her was very strong. Instead, he picked up the third garment – or garments, he realized, looking at a red skirt and a long-sleeved blouse with an insertion of yellow lace, and began to attack them in the same way, holding up each remnant for the benefit of the figure on the bed.

Nothing. No reaction whatsoever.

'Damn you!' he shouted at her, finally. 'Damn you, Milliora! I'm going to make you pay for what you have done.'

In his frustration, he swung away from the wardrobe to the window hung, like the bed, with maroon brocade and velvet. As he had wrenched at the dresses so, in his fury, he tore at the curtains, pulling at them with all his strength until they fell, like great birds that have been dropped in a shoot, fold on fold to the floor.

'Master Dermot.'

Mary Markham was standing in the doorway, her anger as obvious as his, although she did not raise her voice.

'You have no right to be in this room,' she said icily. 'Go out.'

Advancing, she pointed to the door.

'Out, Master Dermot. Before I'm forced to go for help.'

'There's no need for that. I'm going.'

She said no more to him, but her words followed him all along the landing. No right . . . no right . . . no right . . .

He was left with the tiny satisfaction of the shredded dresses, not knowing that this was denied him. Milliora was too far gone in shock to have understood either his words or his actions, and she would remember nothing of what happened that day.

In his own bedroom, Dermot slumped on the bed, his anger not abated but contained, and took stock of his situation.

He would have to leave Crag Liath as soon as possible. If he lingered, Milliora would rally and take retaliatory action against him. But where to go – and what to do?

He found the answer to his second question almost at once: he would have to return to his original idea of becoming a solicitor. He had no alternative and old Mr Dundon, having hardly got used to the idea of doing without him, would be pleased to have him back.

For accommodation he could stay with Andy and Carmel for a few days but after that he would be outstaying his welcome, he knew. Their house was already overcrowded with his mother and Mary in it and they, too, posed the problem of where to go in the end.

If only he had money of his own instead of always having to rely on handouts from the estate. His face reddened in anger. The burden he had to bear was intolerable. He could not – *would* not carry it without at least attempting to relieve himself of the load.

Something had to be done. Putting his hand to his forehead he found that he had pins and needles in his arm, something he had not even noticed. To relieve the sensation he stretched out, accidentally knocking over the silver candlestick that stood on his bedside table.

And then it came to him. The silver. He would steal some of the silver.

Like most historical houses, Crag Liath had its share of valuable items which various ancestors had added to over the years. His mother had no great interest in the silver, much of which was not on display, but tucked up in the sideboard in the dining-room. He would not take the most valuable pieces – unlike his mother and certainly unlike Tom, he knew which fell into this category – but he could easily get away with some of the lesser items, particularly if he took them from the back of the sideboard, without anyone ever noticing they were gone.

What would his mother say if she were to hear of this escapade, he wondered. That he had scored just a little over Milliora?

She would disapprove and would plague the life out of him to make a clean breast of it in Confession, after which he would be bound to put the silver back.

He would not tell her – or anyone. But his mother would benefit from his actions once the silver had been pawned at Pashie Browne's. That was a job for Tim-Pat. An O'Brien could hardly be seen at Pashie's, along with women pawning their blankets and shawls, even their children's boots, to get money for food: Limerick, which would be buzzing with conjecture about his bad luck, would seize on this new development with relish. No, Tim-Pat could go along to Broad Street in the morning taking the silver and an explanatory letter from himself.

It was already quite dark. He would just have to force himself to stay awake until he was quite sure that everyone else in the house was sleeping soundly. After what had happened earlier on, all he needed was to run into Mary Markham or Bernie Lenihan, both of whom had volunteered to stay near Milliora at all hours of the day or night.

So once more Dermot crept downstairs in the middle of the night with one of the sheets from his bed in his hand to carry off his booty.

His mission was accomplished with the utmost efficiency. He passed over an inverted pear-shaped teapot complete with stand, which he knew had been made by Nicholas Sprimont of London, as being too near the front of the sideboard. And a rococo tureen, its bombé form and decoration concentrated in the fruit and foliage of finial, handles and feet, he decided against for the same reason, although it was very tempting.

But there was an oval milk jug with four small feet that he felt would not be easily missed, and a pair of lyre-shaped candlesticks on spool pedestals. He put them on to his sheet.

There was so much silver packed into the sideboard that you could hardly tell any had been taken out. He could go on adding to his collection in safety.

Half an hour later, having re-adjusted several pieces so no gaps remained in the sideboard, he tied the ends of the sheet together and slipped out of the house. Again, no one saw him go. Carrying the silver, he went down the avenue almost to the road and hid his loot in the high grass under one of the beech trees. Then, with what might have passed for a smile, he retraced his steps back to the house.

He was still in agony but he did not expect relief from his pain. All that mattered was that he had done something constructive about his situation.

To his surprise, he slept soundly. Waking, he confronted the terrible thought that today he would have to leave Crag Liath forever.

'It can't be true,' Tim-Pat kept saying. 'She can't have done this to you. God Himself would not allow it.'

'Well, He has. Look, I have a job for you. I'm going to send you in to Pashie Browne's this morning – '

'Pashie Browne's!' cried Tim-Pat, hoarsely. He had often been to the pawnbroker's on Tom's behalf, but he never expected to go for Dermot.

'I wrote a letter for him this morning. Come down the avenue with me. I've something to show you. You'd better take the carriage to town. You won't be able to carry what I have to show you on a horse!'

'God knows it's hard to dance with the devil on your back, but you managed it so!' Tim-Pat said admiringly, a few minutes later.

'So,' Dermot repeated, his mind on other matters. 'You'd better come up and see me at Dundon's afterwards and give me a report on what went on.'

'I will indeed. Master Dermot?'

'Yes?'

'Where will you be spending the night?'

'I don't know. I had thought of going to the Leahys but then again I don't want to upset mother any more. I may try to find lodgings. I'll look into that later this morning. Go up to my bedroom before you go and get my belongings. You'll find them packed and on the bed.'

'God love us,' wailed Tim-Pat, ''tis a wicked thing that has happened and a bad woman that's at the back of it, sending Master Tom to his death and yourself out of the house.'

223

'Yes – yes,' Dermot said.

He nodded to Tim-Pat and, scowling, rode on into town.

'You sorted things out yesterday then, did you?' inquired old Mr Dundon. 'That was very quick.'

'One side of the matter took very little time,' Dermot said bitterly.

'And the other?'

The other – catching up with Tom's creditors, assuring them that they would be paid in time – was no longer his responsibility. He could no longer leap into the breach as a hero and save the family name.

'In a sense, that has nothing to do with me anymore,' said Dermot. 'A lot of things have happened. I wonder if I could talk to you about staying on?'

'I see,' said old Mr Dundon, looking into the distance. 'Come in to my office, will you? It's early in the morning but I think a little drink would not come amiss. You look as if you could do with it.'

'I suppose I do,' Dermot admitted cautiously.

Commanded to sit down, he watched old Mr Dundon produce a green glass whiskey decanter encased in silver from behind a pile of files and with it two matching glasses, which he laid carefully on his desk.

'A good strong tot,' the old man said to no one in particular and proceeded to half-fill Dermot's glass with neat John Jameson. 'Get that inside you,' he added, before giving himself the same.

'Thank you.'

'It seems to me, Dermot, that you could do with a bit of help. Naturally, I would like you to stay on here. But I have another suggestion. I have a house on the

Ennis Road that I was going to rent. It's empty at the moment. Would you like to move into it?'

'I – yes. Yes, I think I would.'

'I thought you might. Things have been getting back to me, you see. That would deal with the accommodation problem. Then, of course, you'd be wanting something to live on. I gather that your mother and sister would be wanting to stay with you, as well?'

'In the end, yes.'

'Oh, yes – they're at Andy Leahy's place at the moment, aren't they?'

I did not tell him that, Dermot thought. He knows the lot. Another one, ahead of me, familiar with my business.

Before the stab of resentment fully hit him, old Mr Dundon went on: 'I'd like to make you a loan. You can repay it when you qualify. I have faith in your ability you see. You'll go straight to the top all right. In the meantime, I suggest you have enough money in your pocket to maintain yourself and the women.'

'Thank you. Thank you very much indeed.'

'Finish your drink,' old Mr Dundon said. 'Then you and I can work out an appropriate sum and I'll let you know my terms.'

And then Tim-Pat came back from Broad Street with the news that Pashie Browne would extend his pledge so that the silver need not be lost to the O'Brien family if Dermot's affairs went well.

All of a sudden, there was money to burn, although it was on loan.

To hell with Limerick and its gossips, Dermot thought. He would show them his strength tonight by booking into the Royal George Hotel.

'Tomorrow I'm moving into a rented house on the

Ennis Road,' he said to Tim-Pat, not admitting that he would not be paying rent.

The groom's face broke into his customary curly smile.

'And I'll be joining you, Master Dermot. You can forget about my wages. Where you go, I go. And one day the two of us together will get her back for what she's done.'

At the end of the day Dermot wrote a letter to Rosaleen:

I know that Milly was your friend so it hurts me to tell you that I hold her wholly responsible for my brother's death. And now she has played a dirty trick on me . . .

He left the good news to the end. In that way, Rosaleen could trace the progress of his suffering and see how he had ultimately triumphed over the evil that had been done.

Mr Dundon tells me that he does not want to lose my services once my articles are completed. He needs young blood in the firm. He has offered me a partnership. I'm sure you will be pleased.

The future, which had seemed so dark only this morning, was reasonably bright.

Reasonably.

But nothing could relieve the torment of losing Crag Liath. As clear as the Clare hills on a sunny morning, the image of Milliora's haggard face swam before his eyes.

'You bitch,' he said to it. 'You damned bitch. If I have to wait for fifty years to do it, I will pay you back.'

14

Amongst the bad and good things that happened to Dermot and Rosaleen over the next five years there were also some surprises.

It was bad when Fiona O'Brien slipped and broke her hip while staying at the Leahys' so that she was forced to lie flat on her back, developing painful bed sores. There was no question of moving her to Dermot's new home on the Ennis Road and Mary stayed with her to assist Carmel with the nursing. In the end, their efforts proved futile. A woman with more of a will to live might have recovered completely, but, as Mary Markham and Mrs Cash agreed, old Mrs O'Brien had lost that when Tom died and by the following March she, too, was dead.

Dermot, faced with the necessity to do the decent thing and offer Mary a home for life, was pleasantly surprised when his unattractive sister announced that she was going to marry Andy's widowed uncle, a Samaritan in shirt-sleeves with four grown-up children and money in the bank. Hardly able to credit his luck, Dermot gave her away.

He was finishing his articles by then and on the verge of being independent, with the prospect of riches, as he was at pains to explain to Rosaleen.

She smiled. 'You don't have to impress me with money, Dermot. That's not what I'm seeking in a husband.'

'But you will marry me when I'm made a partner? You did agree that you would.'

'Yes, I'll marry you,' she said, 'but not so I can become a wealthy woman!'

Going on to talk of other things, they avoided mention of Milliora. Dermot's feelings in this connection were simple enough: he hated Milliora – that had never changed.

Rosaleen's emotions were very much more complex. Horrified by Tom's death and by Dermot's descriptions of Milliora as a vicious, bad-tempered wife who had driven his brother to suicide, she was equally repulsed by the Machiavellian role Milliora had appeared to play in laying hands on Crag Liath.

She wondered if she had ever really known Milliora and she was flooded with compassion and loyalty for poor, able, hard-working Dermot who had been so vilely tricked. In this mood of commiseration she wondered why she had hesitated about marrying him and promptly agreed to do so.

Honest as she was, she failed to face the fact that, for a long time, she had nurtured a secret wish to punish Milliora for always being so successful, or that, in accepting without question Dermot's version of the tragedy and its aftermath, she was seizing on an opportunity to do so. Most of the time, she dodged thinking about Milliora but there were times when she could not, when she knew, deep down, that there was also guilt added to her pot-pourri of feelings.

She did not get in touch with Milliora and Milliora did not contact her – the relationship lay in limbo and Dermot became his fiancée's best friend. Nothing wrong in that – it was a situation most women would envy. So why, then, were there times when she thought nostalgically of Laurel Hill and Milliora, and found it difficult to refrain from sending a conciliatory letter to Crag Liath?

These thoughts were further submerged when, quite unexpectedly, Grand-aunt Carrie died in her sleep and Dundon's, the solicitors, sent word that Rosaleen was the main beneficiary in the old lady's will. Having told Dermot that she had no particular interest in money, she found herself a wealthy woman.

It was an astonishing revelation and another strange aspect of it was the fact that, after all, Grand-aunt Carrie must have had affection for the grand-niece she so frequently ignored.

Assimilating her altered situation, mulling over a revised image of her Grand-aunt, Rosaleen took time to realize that, as Dundon's had drawn up the will, it was almost a certainty that Dermot had known all along about what it contained.

Another of those periodic and disquieting circumstances that made her query her fiancé's integrity . . .

'Why didn't you tell me?' she confronted him. 'I can't believe that you – a junior partner – didn't know.'

'I did know,' Dermot said, not turning a hair at being put through an inquisition. 'It just goes without saying that I am honour bound to protect our clients' privacy in these matters – and all the more so, when the beneficiary is the woman I'm going to marry.'

That sounded honourable enough. But –

'All that talk about riches – when you knew I would be rich myself!'

Dermot took her by the hands and gazed steadily into her eyes, his blue ones pleading with her to accept him at his word.

'I want my wife to be wealthy because of *me* – not

because she has inherited money from anyone else,' he declared. 'I'm not the sort of man who likes to take advantage of women.'

All the same, when they were quietly married, he did not object to Rosaleen selling the house at Kilmallock and using the money to buy the one he had been renting from old Mr Dundon along the Ennis Road, a typical dark red-brick Victorian Gothic on three floors, set in two acres of overcrowded garden.

Rosaleen said that she had been itching to get her hands on the house for ages. In its original state, evergreen shrubs and an excess of privet hedge and laurel bushes blocked off light from the house itself and gave the grounds an air of damp, shiny gloom. The hall was narrow and dark, and the drawing-room in chaos, with a grand piano, a horsehair sofa, innumerable small tables, chairs, stools and china cabinets, vying for space with wax fruit and flowers under glass, and bottles of all shapes and sizes.

Setting out to effect a metamorphosis, Rosaleen cut back over-abundant shrubs and bushes so that light streamed through the windows, introduced gayer and crisper colour schemes and prettier furniture. The heavy, brown lincrusta paper that had previously covered the walls was ripped off and replaced with wallpaper in floral designs and pale colours. The woodwork was painted white and the original fitted carpets removed, being considered unhygienic, and smaller carpets set on the polished floors, echoing the pattern of the new wallpaper.

Dermot liked the dining room best because, in it, the O'Briens' deep involvement with horses and hunting was deliberately played up. Rosaleen lined the walls with coaching and hunting prints, and displayed the silver cups Dermot had won in point-to-points on the great oak sideboard.

He had been trying for a long time to arouse in her a deeper interest in hunting. After all, it was Ireland's oldest sport, the fame of Ireland as a hunting ground being known to writers of the first millennium A.D. and Irish hounds had been sought after by the Romans, he said.

Rosaleen's reply was not to enthuse but to work a tapestry screen for the drawing-room, depicting a horse and rider, to stack Dermot's hunting books in the library and to line up foxes' masks – the legacy of kills with the County Limerick Foxhounds – on either side of the white marble chimney-piece that she had had installed in the extended hall.

The house was very much Rosaleen's creation but Dermot had one say in its transformation and that was in renaming it Kincora, after the castle on the River Shannon once owned by Brian Boru.

The house had changed and so had its owners. Dermot had filled out so he looked more man than boy and his hair was cut shorter than Rosaleen liked it in deference to convention, although to please her, he was clean-shaven, unlike most of his contemporaries.

Time, too, had effected subtle alterations to Rosaleen's features, padding the pale cheeks, maturing the soft, full mouth so that, in her new, slightly remote beauty, there was more than a hint of an Ingres Odalisque, questioning yet wary of the reply she might receive.

In terms of her looks, Mrs Dermot O'Brien might have come into her own; in terms of her whole self she had not, although anyone in Limerick who knew the set-up would have wondered what was up with her, with her husband doting on her and her Grand-aunt's money secure in the bank.

Rosaleen would have had an answer to this though she would have kept it to herself. Although Dermot loved her and she tried very hard to return that love, in the end she could not do so.

She did not love Dermot because she discovered quite early in their marriage that her suspicions of him were correct, and that her husband could not be trusted. When she heard him talking to Andy Leahy, who idolized Parnell and supported Michael Davitt and the Land League, and found that Dermot loathed all that they stood for – that far from sharing her own political ideals, he actually opposed them vehemently – she despised him for his lie while acknowledging that he had told it to gain access to her love.

And in due course she was also repelled by Dermot's obsessive hatred for Milliora and disturbed by his continuing references to the loss of Crag Liath. At first she counteracted his anger by pointing out how affluent the two of them were now, not only because of Grand-aunt Carrie's money, but by Dermot's own success at Dundon's. Wasn't that enough?

Dermot gave her a look that was beginning to annoy her – patronizing and slightly weary.

'How could it be enough? How many times have I tried to explain to you – Crag Liath was mine by *right*?'

After a while she learnt not to pursue the subject.

But when Dermot attempted to pressurize her into altering her political views on the basis that they were unconventional for a woman in her position, Rosaleen had plenty to say and she said it vehemently. Then Dermot, too, learnt to change the subject.

232

In this way, in a kind of truce, they were able to live together. At first, much of Rosaleen's energies went into the renovation of the house but when that was completed she grew restless, and began to wonder again how she could live a more productive and satisfying life and still stay married to Dermot. That was the time when she was also uncertain about her ability to conceive. While most couples had their first child within a year of being married, she and Dermot had been married for two years already and still she was not pregnant.

And then, to her surprise and Dermot's delight, she found she was going to have a baby. She had expected to be ecstatically happy and was disappointed when she discovered that she actually hated being pregnant. She riled against nausea, the fainting and the restrictions that the condition placed upon her body, for she had never liked having her freedom curtailed.

'It will be different when you feel the baby move,' Carmel, who had two babies already and another one on the way, tried to reassure her.

In Rosaleen's opinion, it was not at all different. The bony ripples across her swollen stomach did not endear her to the parasite dwelling inside it. And how could you feel for a bone which, having pressed painfully on some invisible nerve at an inappropriate moment, vanished before you had the chance to define it as a hand or foot or knee?

She felt guilty about her lack of compassion for the mysterious thing she was carrying inside her (she could not think of it as a baby, let alone as her own child), and bewildered that, having believed herself a humanitarian, she should be transformed by pregnancy into a virtual ogress.

When she learnt that she was expecting not just one baby but two, she waited in vain for the information to excite her, and lost more faith in herself when it did not.

That was towards the end of March. On the evening of 6 April 1887 Dermot arrived home from Dundon's to find that Rosaleen had been seized by a strange desire to walk barefooted through the meadow that ran behind the house.

Announcing this, she had flung herself into his arms at the front door, brushing aside the new maid, Bridie Flanagan, and generally behaving wildly.

'What's all this? It's raining cats and dogs out there,' Dermot said in amazement.

The sky was as black as a coal bucket, and raindrops as big as berries were falling out of it and being thrown about by the wind.

'Oh, nonsense,' said Rosaleen, tossing her head impatiently. 'What does the rain matter? Anyway, I want to feel it on my face. I *have* to walk, Dermot. Don't you understand?'

Of course, he did not. She did not understand the compulsion herself. She felt charged with energy, capable not only of walking through the wet meadow, but of running through the tangled spring grasses and pungent meadowsweet, all the way to the curve of the river, with Dermot – now seeming to her more like he had been in the beginning of their relationship – running along beside her.

Dermot looked at her nonplussed. Women were supposed to have unusual cravings when their time was near, he knew, but Carmel had only asked for stewed apples and oatmeal porridge with cream, or so Andy reported, and had expressed no desire to commune with nature on a dark, wet evening. Trust Rosaleen to be out of the ordinary, he thought, and at the end of a tiring day at that.

She smiled at him and he softened. It was good to see her full of life instead of apathetic.

'All right then,' he told her. 'I'll take you down to the meadow. But only for a short time, mind,' marvelling at his own foolishness in giving in to her whim. 'What if you catch pneumonia and die?'

His wife dismissed this notion as further nonsense. 'It's spring,' she said, as if the time of year made any difference to whether or not rain would fall in Ireland. 'It may be a little damp but it's as warm as a hot oven. I can't wait to be going.'

All her life, Rosaleen would remember that evening – the intensely green grass beneath her feet, the sad, low, dark hills lurking under the malevolent sky, the shivering Shannon River.

As she stood in the meadow, raising her face so the rain could slap and tease it, a hare leapt up ecstatically and gambolled only a few feet away from her, its Titian pelt contrasting with the emerald lush of the pastures. A thrill ran through her. She wanted to leap and frisk and frolic with the pure joy, and amazing luck, of simply being alive. She felt outside her overweight body, released, energized and possessed by a primitive force that impelled her to run free over the tufts of green grass, calling out to the hills and to the silver river that she was one with them.

Instead, she tore the hairpins that bound her dark hair and shook it loose, so it tumbled over her shoulders and down her back, sure at last that her imprisonment was ending.

Eighteen hours later, she gave birth to baby boys

and soon afterwards Dermot told her of the plan he had been mulling over in his mind that might – just possibly – restore Crag Liath to its rightful owners.

It was a very simple plan and, although not in any way foolproof, it was the only real chance that existed to ensure that justice was ultimately done, said Dermot.

'Yes, but what *is* it?' Rosaleen asked, wishing her husband would get to the point rather than bogging himself down in the inevitable mire of how he had been tricked out of inheriting Crag Liath.

She was finding it very difficult to concentrate on anything but the twins – Daniel and Eugene, as they were to be named. She found them utterly irresistible and quite remarkably handsome although – since their faces were still a bit crumpled – anyone else might have said that they looked more like a couple of wily old sages than two tiny Adonises.

'You're not listening to me,' complained Dermot. 'I'm trying to tell you my plan.'

'I am – I am,' Rosaleen said hastily.

'We're going to ask Milliora to be godmother to the twins.'

'*Milly?* But we haven't spoken to Milly in years.' Rosaleen was astonished. 'You hate Milly. So why do you want her near Daniel and Eugene, for Heaven's sake?'

Dermot smiled. 'Rosaleen, I want you to take a sensible view of what I'm going to say. I know I hate Milly and who can blame me for that? But a few weeks ago, Tim-Pat bumped into Mrs Cash outside McBirney's and she told him a few interesting things about Milly that got my mind working.'

'What sort of things?' Rosaleen asked suspiciously. 'You know how I hate intrigue, Dermot.'

'I do. But this isn't just gossip. It's information relevant to the future of Daniel and Eugene. Mrs Cash says Milly virtually lost her mind after Tom's death and couldn't remember anything of that time when she was normal again . . .'

'Really? But I don't see –'

'That's beside the point. When she pulled herself together she set about getting the estate back on its feet. Mrs Cash says she sees Crag Liath as a kind of shrine to Tom's memory and she's built her life around it. Apparently she minds terribly the way the rest of us have rejected her and would give anything to be taken back into the fold.'

'That's easily rectifiable.'

'Yes, it is – isn't it? Mrs Cash said something else, too. She says Milliora is mad about children. Apparently the Keegan children go over there quite often since their mother died and she's all over them.'

'Is that so? Well, that's a good thing – maybe she'll marry Jamie.'

'She won't,' Dermot said confidently. 'She's told Mary Markham that she could never marry again after loving Tom so much and, anyway, Jamie Keegan is a Protestant. Milliora wouldn't consider a mixed marriage – or not from the reports about how holy she is these days.'

'I still don't see what all this has to do with Daniel and Eugene.'

'But it's simple: Milliora wants to be in the O'Brien circle; she's mad about children, so she acts as godmother to the twins and, not having children of her own, who does she leave Crag Liath to but the two fellows fast asleep upstairs.'

He paused, looking at her, waiting for her reaction.

Rosaleen sighed. 'It's not – honest,' she said, slowly, 'pretending to be friendly with Milly – inviting her to be godmother. And what will Carmel and Mary say? They're probably wondering at this minute why you haven't approached them before about one of them being godmother.'

Dermot looked at her. They were talking in bed and Rosaleen was sitting bolt upright with her dark hair streaming down her shoulders. If only his wife wasn't such a romantic. She had no appreciation of the strategies most people had to employ in the everyday battles of life. To tell her that it was, on occasion, necessary to bend the truth a little, tell even the whitest of white lies, was to court disaster. Then the purple eyes would blaze with scorn and before people knew what had happened, a wave of red-hot fury would be breaking over their heads, hurling them on to the scalding sands of Rosaleen's contempt and condemnation. She was an idealist who would fight to the death for what she believed in, and she was always ready to challenge what she saw as evil without a thought for her own safety or expediency. Those kind of people were not easy to live with – or to negotiate with, either.

But where Crag Liath was concerned Dermot had no intention of listening to Rosaleen for, much as he loved her, his love for the family estate, as always, was greater still. He was determined to do his best to see it revert back to the O'Briens.

'Leave Carmel and Mary to me,' he said quietly. 'I can deal with them. Just think what it would mean to Daniel and Eugene to be heirs to Crag Liath. You really have no right to try to step in the way of their happiness.'

That impressed her.

'I suppose I don't,' she agreed, 'but, Dermot, Milly is only twenty-four years old. She's unlikely to die for years – maybe not till she's seventy or eighty. The twins could be into their fifties then. It's a long time to wait.'

'For Crag Liath it's worth the waiting,' Dermot said, more to himself than to her. He took her hand. 'Think of the twins, Rosaleen,' he said again, 'and then tell me if I shouldn't write to Milliora and ask her to be godmother. Come on – do you agree?'

'Very well,' said Rosaleen, 'though I'm not happy about it.'

But it was enough to content Dermot.

Oh, the joy of knowing that Milliora had lost her memory in the days after Tom's death and would have no recollection of his own behaviour to her that dreadful evening in the bedroom. It made the letter so easy to write.

'. . . We all regret the misunderstandings of the past and now we want you to share the happiness of the present with us . . . Would you consider being godmother to the boys . . .?'

He paused, then grinning, added: 'Although not identical, they both look the image of Tom.'

That should do it, he thought. Tim-Pat could ride out to Crag Liath with the letter this very minute. Sealing the envelope, he took it out to the stables. It was always good going out there. When a man needed a bit of solace, the stables were the perfect oubliette.

Mount Royal was waiting there for him, as was

Grian, his other hunter, friend to Dubhfoilean, the jet-black she-cat now curled up in the iron manger.

There were four loose boxes, the others stabling Rosaleen's Cu Chulainn and the carriage mare.

. . . freedom sits throned on each proud spirit there.
Down the hills twining, their blessed steel shining,
Like rivers of beauty that flow from each glen;
From mountain and valley,
'Tis liberty's rally –
Out and make way for the bold Fenian men.

'Tim-Pat!' Dermot shouted above this refrain. 'I have a letter for you to deliver.'

The groom's head appeared over the half-door of Cu Chulainn's loose box and suddenly Dermot knew that he needed to tell Tim-Pat of his plan to regain control of Crag Liath, or, at least, for his children to do so. He badly needed reinforcement – someone to say 'Yes, of course, you are right and you will win through in the end', instead of 'Isn't it underhand, Dermot?'

'Come on out,' he said. 'I have something to tell you,' as he had done many a time as a boy, and Tim-Pat knew that the words prefaced a revelation of the greatest possible interest.

'Holy Mother!' he gasped when Dermot had finished, so loudly that in Grian's stable Dubhfoilean started nervously, her claws tensing. 'But 'tis a brilliant scheme!'

'You think so?' said Dermot, gratified at last.

He leant back against the stable door and felt Cu Chulainn's breath hot on his neck. When he reached a hand back, the black horse nuzzled into it. With Cu Chulainn you were always safe. He had never been a biter.

The smell of the stables was strong in his nostrils. They had been mucked out already but the odour of fresh dung, mixed with the smell of the leather saddles, the fodder and the horses' coats, was evocative, as was Tim-Pat's supportive voice, of spring mornings in those other stables which, by mischance, were his no longer . . .

'Who knows?' Tim-Pat said suddenly. 'God is good – she might die young . . .'

At the thought, Dermot shivered with pleasure.

Rosaleen, holding both babies in her arms, was thinking that she was glad they were not identical twins for, in that sense, they were individuals already. Daniel had his mother's beautiful violet-blue eyes, hair that seemed surprisingly red and rather sallow skin, while Eugene, the younger by a mere ten and a half minutes, had deep blue eyes, a mass of black curly hair already, and his skin was pale and creamy.

The whole of Limerick would marvel at their beauty, their mother decided. What a shame that her father – or mother, or Grand-aunt Carrie – could not see them. At the thought that they could not, Rosaleen's eyes clouded with tears. Unable to wipe them away with her hands, because of the babies, she determinedly shook them out.

One fell on Daniel's cheek and he blinked his astonishment. How sweet he was. And how wrong of her to shed tears on him. Dermot was right – she must never do anything to stand in the way of the babies' happiness, even if the plan he had devised to ensure – he hoped – that they inherited Crag Liath offended her own principles.

She decided not to think about the plan at all and to

concentrate instead on her babies. The love she felt for them was almost too much to bear, an unsuspected fountain that had gushed out of her from the first moment the twins were placed in her arms. Interspersed with love was relief. She was not, after all, a cold, insensitive woman, indifferent to the children she had carried. In place of her pre-birth resentment there was now the vivid consciousness of having humbly joined the unending stream of women who, in giving birth, accepted the terrible joy of motherhood.

'Mrs O'Brien, I think I should be taking the young men from you so you can be getting some extra rest.' Mrs Galvin, the midwife who had delivered the babies, was standing by the bed, with a determined expression on her homely face.

'Not yet,' pleaded Rosaleen, holding on to Daniel and Eugene.

She loved the feel of them in her arms. Feeding them, on the other hand, was a strange experience, warm and comforting to all three of them and infinitely moving, but painful, too. Daniel, in particular, had tugged hard at her nipple.

'Mrs O'Brien, you need all the sleep you can get and it's time you had a nap.'

In spite of their mother's protests, the babies were taken out of her arms.

'Sleep well, my little darlings.'

'And see you do the same, Mrs O'Brien,' said Mrs Galvin, trying to look severe. 'I'll pull the curtains so the light doesn't come into the room.'

'No – no – leave them. I love the light.'

When the midwife had gone Rosaleen jubilantly ran her hands over her stomach and up under her rib-cage, and her soft, rosy lips curved into a smile.

242

All the same, it was good to be free. And good for the boys to be so. Although, already, she could feel that feral need to protect them, she vowed she would not be one of those mothers who molly-coddled their children and tried to restrict their freedom in order to hold on to their love. She would encourage them to be real individuals, she thought, who used their freedom wisely.

Dermot, being delighted with his sons, was talking about the great men they were going to be when they grew up, as well as all the things he planned for them before they were adult. The most important – apart from the ponies he was proposing to buy for them – was the school they would attend, and therein lay the foundation of a massive future argument between Rosaleen and himself.

Dermot wanted them to go to Downside, as he and Tom had done, to have an English education, while she felt very strongly that the boys should go to school in their own country, like their mother, so that they would remain truly Irish and not be influenced by English mores. At the same time, she wanted them to learn to speak their own language. In this she would have to help them, for they would not be taught in the medium of Irish, even in an Irish school.

It was so *wrong* that Irish children should be instructed solely in English. Ireland was a remarkably literate society, with nearly eighty per cent of the population able to read and write and vast numbers of newspapers and periodicals being printed. But all of them, and the books, were in English. In five-sixths of Ireland, it was as if the Irish language simply did not exist. If any new literature in Irish was being produced, in the tradition of the great eighteenth-century Irish

243

poets to whom Rosaleen's father had introduced her, the Irish people did not know about it.

It was not all the fault of the government in England, either. It was also the fault of the Irish for having lost pride in their nationality, Rosaleen decided. The Irish language had survived seven centuries of conflict and five of hostile legislation but now the people themselves had no active interest in retaining it anymore. It had declined during the famine, said the voice of reason inside her. Do you really expect hungry people to care about anything else but food?

'Anyway, my children will grow up speaking their own language, and that's that,' she said to the empty room.

It was an exciting thought. Daniel and Eugene would be proud to be Irish – she would see to that. And they would teach others to be proud of it, too, instead of cowed down and ashamed.

She snuggled down under the bedclothes, telling herself that it was more pleasant to consider the twins' future in a comfortable prone position, when, unbidden, into her mind crept the thought of Milly.

Would she agree to be godmother to the twins? If so, they were fated to meet within the next few days. Would Milly have changed in five years? And would anything at all be left of their friendship?

15

Milliora had certainly changed in five years and at that precise moment Liam Lenihan, for one, would have testified that it was not altogether for the better.

Anything that interfered with the smooth running of Crag Liath infuriated young Mrs O'Brien, and Liam – having brought news that Bawnie Kinsella, groom and coachman, would not be at work for the next two weeks – was visibly apprehensive.

'What do you mean he's in Barrington's Hospital suffering a compound fracture to his hip? How could such a thing have happened?' she demanded loudly, giving him no opportunity to pretend he could not hear.

Liam hesitated. Bawnie, at a time when he should have been collecting the new wheel plough his employer had ordered several months before, had followed the Mary Street Fife and Drum Band as it played in George Street in honour of the football victory obtained by Garryowen over the Galway team. There, in the excitement, he had been trampled on by a half-bred mare in the uneasy care of a man who was later arrested for his neglect.

This explanation was not likely to go down well with Mrs O'Brien and Liam, flustered at the best of times in her presence, could not think of an acceptable alternative.

'Where is my plough?' Mrs O'Brien went on, getting to the crux of the matter. 'Though why I'm bothering about it at all I don't know. It's already so late in the season.'

'I could go in to Limerick and get it,' Liam offered.

But Mrs O'Brien only snorted in disgust. 'Much good you are in an emergency!' she said scornfully. 'When the roan filly was trapped between the carriage shafts, swollen with colic, you had no solution. It was I that had to force a good wallop of whiskey into the animal's throat, to get rid of the gas from the stomach. If Bawnie Kinsella can end up in hospital looking for the plough, what could happen to you?'

She was a holy terror, Liam said later in the kitchen, provoking the wrath of Mary Markham.

'That may be your opinion,' she said, 'but I'll thank you to keep it to yourself, Liam Lenihan, and you living off the fat of the land that Mrs O'Brien has salvaged. If it wasn't for her, wouldn't you and Bernie be sitting in the poorhouse this day instead of moping around like a stray ass getting under my feet in the kitchen. Look at the way this place is run in comparison to when Master Tom – God love him – was in charge.'

'The yard is full of hens and ducks and turkeys,' Liam said, 'and geese. You can't hear yourself think for the clucking and cackling.'

'For all the thinking you ever do, Liam Lenihan, you can't be so affected,' said Mary promptly. 'Look at the eggs we're selling – and the live poultry for the pot.'

'Queer kind of hens that have baggy trousers on their legs!' Liam said. 'And white ganders hissing at you, and black turkeys strutting around as if they owned the farmyard.'

'The hens you're referring to are cochins – ' Mary was starting to say when Tim-Pat Tierney, followed by

Mrs Cash, walked straight into the kitchen as if he had never been away.

There was a letter in his hand, and a knowing look on his face and instead of Mary telling Liam what a miracle it was that young Mrs O'Brien, a city girl born and bred, should have turned into a hard-working, efficient woman well-versed in country ways, she lost track of the conversation.

'What are you doing here?' she managed to say, not that pleased to see Dermot's ally arriving at Crag Liath.

'I have a letter from Master Dermot for herself,' he said, as bold as brass. 'Is she at home today?'

'Where else would a woman who works hard as she be at this hour of the morning?' Mary said. 'Give me the letter. Mrs Cash here can make you a cup of tea, since the two of you seem so friendly and she has more time to spare for gossiping than myself!'

Not pleased with the way the morning was going, she sought out Milliora. Mary, too, felt apprehensive, not because she was in any way frightened of young Mrs O'Brien, but because the mistress of Crag Liath was soon located out at the back, calmly watching Mr Keegan removing a ring of cartilage from the nose of the big black bull – the one that was known to be dangerous – with a view to inserting a copper nosering so the creature could be more easily led by a rope.

Mary ventured to within ten feet of this group before losing courage completely, flapping the letter to draw Mrs O'Brien's attention – not daring to call lest the bull be excited by her shouting.

But it was Mrs O'Brien who was excited once she had opened the envelope and laid eyes on what was inside it. Excited and happy – smiling the way she used to smile when Master Tom was alive.

Mary could not imagine what Master Dermot could have written to produce such a reaction and Mrs O'Brien did not enlighten her just then. But it all gave Mary a bit of a turn. She took a wander round the apple orchard in order to get over it and when she got back to the house, Tim-Pat Tierney was gone.

And good riddance.

'Did you give her the letter?' asked Mrs Cash, appearing unexpectedly with a pile of freshly laundered linen.

Mary glowered at her. 'What is wrong with you creeping up on me like that?' she said darkly. 'Of course, I gave her the letter – what do you expect?'

'There's something quare about the whole thing – you mark my words,' said the washerwoman. 'Wasn't Master Dermot a schemer from the day he was born? And what is he doing now for a living, I ask, but scheming? Writing her letters! Oh, I can feel the *miadh* on this house, Mary Markham. There's trouble in store – you mark my words.'

'Look at the cut of that sheet you're planning to put away in the linen press!' Mary said, with the object of putting Mrs Cash back in her place.

The Devil's curse on the house, indeed! You had to remind yourself that Mrs Cash was connected with the tinkers. And what but nonsense could you expect from a crowd that claimed a tinker stole one of the four nails prepared to crucify Holy Jesus?

'Extraordinary!' Milliora said aloud, as soon as she was alone, and she wondered if that single word would prick a bubble of somnambulism and precipitate her rudely from a most enjoyable dream into unsatisfactory reality.

When this did not happen, she laughed happily and resisted an urge to get up and dance for joy.

The O'Briens wanted her to be one of them. Dermot and Rosaleen had twin sons to be christened Daniel and Eugene who looked the image of Tom. And she was to be their godmother. Each of these happenings was a wonder in itself and she was having a certain amount of difficulty in working out which was the most splendid.

Dear Dermot, she thought, he always was a good, supportive friend as well as a fine brother-in-law, and now he has used the arrival of his twin sons to persuade the rest of the family to accept me back.

That they should have rejected her in the first place she saw as perfectly reasonable after the unspeakable thing that she had done to Tom. The only surprising aspect was that any of them should be ready to forgive and forget.

And Rosaleen – who had no option but to side with the family five years ago – she would see Rosaleen again. Losing Rosaleen's friendship had been part of the terrible punishment that had been inflicted upon her at the time – she had always accepted that – but, she hoped, that too was going to be restored since Dermot, in his letter, emphasized that both of them were dying to see her.

To think that neither was sure that she would take up their offer to be godmother – as if she would refuse! She would write a letter immediately assuring them of her acceptance and her excitement and Liam Lenihan could take it into Limerick and deliver it by hand.

But when the letter was written she decided that she, too, would drive into the city. Christening mugs, she thought – I must order them and have them engraved and Liam Lenihan is hardly capable of doing a thing like that. At the same time, I can pick up the wheel-plough.

Oh, it was going to be good telling Dermot and Rosaleen all about the changes she had effected at Crag Liath. Dermot, in particular, would be pleased to hear that she had followed the good advice he used to give to Tom about moving from pasture into livestock. Not just cattle and poultry, of course, but also sheep. Milliora had introduced new breeds to suit the land, and bred her cattle for milk or beef. It only remained to see whether or not she should move into pig-farming as a supplementary venture and import fleshy Large Whites from Yorkshire.

Thinking all this, she went from the library up to her bedroom and started to change for town. A few minutes later she was dressed in her black sateen corset which was narrower and straighter than her old spoon-shaped one, and made walking and breathing much more difficult, her silk and muslin combinations with wide full legs, and a red satin petticoat with flounces at the hem.

She reached into her wardrobe to take out a grey-green day dress and wondered, as she often had before, whether her stolen wedding-gown had ever been worn by another bride. She knew it had been stolen because Mary Markham had told her so, explaining that the dress had fallen off its hanger during her illness and been taken down to the kitchen for ironing, along with two of her other outfits, before being packed away in a box.

'Mrs O'Brien?'

'Yes, Mrs Markham?'

'Mr Keegan is wanting a word with you before he goes home. Shall I tell him to wait or what?'

'Yes, tell him to wait,' Milliora said, putting on her jewellery – the hair ring with the silver filigree surround, which she always wore in memory of Tom, the single cut garnet on a delicate hinge which opened to reveal a tiny lock of his hair beneath the glass, and a mourning bracelet, with silver lilies of the valley set into black enamel.

There were other monuments to Tom at Crag Liath, notably the pale pink roses in the garden, commemorating the day they had met. But then all of Crag Liath, in a sense, was a monument to Tom, and her own reason for living.

After his death, there had been those who had dared to be critical of Tom O'Brien, and to point out that he had neglected the estate and run up terrible debts. There had been others who maintained that he owed them money and demanded to be paid back. The critics had been silenced by the sharp end of her tongue and the creditors reimbursed; Tom's name, and that of the O'Briens, had long since been cleared. There was no blame attaching to Tom, in her opinion, beyond a youthful exuberance that she had once tragically failed to understand.

She had been immature and selfish and silly then, but at least she had been ultimately able to face her faults and make a minuscule compensation – like in her relationship with Jamie Keegan, once a man she had seen as a threat. And how wrong she had been about him, too, as she had discovered the day he turned up at the house, asking what he could do to help her. His expertise with animals had proved invaluable over the last five years and it was hard to imagine how she could ever have coped without him. All that first year, he had not breathed a word about the money Tom owed him, he was so keen to see her getting back on her feet, and the matter had only come to light after a heart-to-heart chat between herself and his wife when she had gone to visit the children.

She slid her feet into black kid walking shoes, laced over the instep, the toe-caps emphasizing the sharp points, and her hands into matching black kid gloves, frilled with lace at the wrists. Her hair was pulled up under her grey-green hat, invisible, except for a curly fringe and two tiny ringlets. She was both elegant and beautiful, Jamie Keegan thought, as she came into the drawing-room to talk to him, and it was a sad thing that she had no man in her life to remind her of that fact.

'No trouble with the bull?' she asked him.

'None at all. He's back in the end field. I was taking a look at the brood-mare. She *has* got glanders.'

'Any fever?'

'Not to any noticeable extent. We'll keep her isolated and I'll be over once a day to inspect her nostrils and glands. But you've nothing to worry about.'

'You're not just saying that to reassure me?' said Milliora, anxiously.

She treated the horses like children, Jamie thought. You would never think that, five years back, she had been a city girl.

He grinned when – seeing her down to the waiting carriage a few minutes later – he saw her inspect the sturdy lancewood shafts and the satinwood panels to make sure that they had been polished. It was as well for the man with the reins in his hands that, on this occasion, he seemed to have done his duty. He waved her off, still smiling. Her head was held high and her chin stuck out and she sat bolt upright in the carriage so that her new corsets would not assault her. She had behaved like a queen when she was married to Tom and, in the matter of her dignity at least, there had been no alterations over the last five years.

But although Milliora looked as haughty as ever as the carriage wound down the long avenue between the birch trees and turned right on to the Limerick road, her thoughts were somewhat sentimental. She was thinking about the twins and herself in relationship to the babies, considering the wonderful toys she would buy for them when they were older. And she decided she would make a nursery out of one of the bedrooms for the time when the boys would come and stay at Crag Liath.

What a time they would have then, the three of them together. And at that moment she actually forgot that they had a mother of their own, more entitled than she to proprietorial rights over them.

The babies, the babies, she thought as the hedgerows parted exposing the carriage and its occupants to the white-flecked blue-grey sky and some curious stares from the cabins. The road dipped and swung so the low hills rotated round to confront them. They reached a crossroads.

In her imagination, Milliora was holding one of the twins, charmed by his magical likeness to Tom. The tinkers were over by the carriage before she had time to notice that they were even on the road. There was a sly-looking woman with sharp features and a dirty face, holding a snotty-nosed toddler by one hand while the other caressed the swollen mound of her stomach, a few older children around her.

'Missus, could you spare us something? I need money for the child that is coming.'

Milliora opened her handbag and felt in it for her purse. She began to count out the shillings – one – two . . .

Unexpectedly, Liam Lenihan intervened.

"Tis a pillow she has in there, Mrs O'Brien. 'Tis not a baby at all.'

'It's not true, missus,' protested the tinker woman, angrily. 'It's a pack of lies he's telling. Aren't I the one that is having the child?'

'I know that one well from Limerick,' said Liam. 'I've seen her many a time, going around the town with her stories.'

'Drive on!' said Milliora angrily.

Her hazel eyes were scornful and the pity that had been in them was gone.

She's pretending to be pregnant, she thought, while I would give half my life to be in that condition. She demeans motherhood, makes a mockery out of it, while I –

But then she thought – they marry so young, these tinker women, and by the time they are in their twenties their lives are almost finished. Many die in childbirth or of disease. Rumour had it that there was not a tinker of either sex alive over the age of forty.

I should have given her the money. She must have had need of it, to have to lie and beg. I'll find her on my way back from town and give it to her then.

A little later they reached the first of the bridges that they would have to cross to get into the city of Limerick. Bawnie Kinsella would have known that, by the time they got to the Athlunkard toll bridge, Mrs O'Brien's throat would be dry and her hands, inside her smart kid gloves, would be shaking with the fear, for he was a sensitive man, in spite of his unreliable streak, and, like Mary Markham, he had the measure of his mistress.

Bawnie would have urged the mare to go faster for he knew that every time Mrs O'Brien went anywhere near a bridge the agony of what had happened to Master Tom came flooding back to engulf her. He would have been well aware that panic was surging up inside her like a dark, bloated animal, so big, so powerful, so resolute that she raised an involuntary hand to parry its attack and a passer-by thought that she was waving to him, and raised his hand in return.

But Bawnie was in Barrington's Hospital, in temporary disgrace, and Liam Lenihan was never in a hurry.

At Mathew Bridge – named in honour of Father Mathew, the temperance reformer who had tried so hard to persuade the men of Ireland to desist from drinking – they were close to the hospital and Milliora reluctantly thought of Bawnie, and went on doing so as she was carried past the grand, eighteenth-century Custom House. Country women, wrapped in shawls, walked barefooted over the cobbles, carrying their boots, in order to save the soles and heels. Beyond the turning they would put them on, making sure they looked stylish enough for the city.

'Liam Lenihan!' Milliora called and, leaning forward, she tapped him with her handbag.

'Mrs O'Brien?'

'While I'm shopping you will be taking my letter to Master Dermot's house. On the way back you will stop and purchase a pound of chocolates from the sweet shop and a new blanket from McBirney's. Take them up to Barrington's Hospital for Bawnie Kinsella. You never know, but they might not have him warm enough. Is that clear?'

'Yes, Mrs O'Brien.'

'I hope it is,' said Milliora.

After that, she studiously ignored Liam. Arrogant she is, he thought – with her nose stuck up in the air.

He would have been shocked out of his mind to learn of her hidden fears and regrets and longings. But, like a lot of people, Liam did not see through her hauteur.

So, when Milliora went to Kincora a few days later to act as godmother to the twins, only Mary Markham at Crag Liath and Bawnie Kinsella in Barrington's knew full well that she set out on her journey with happiness, excitement – and a lot of trepidation. After all, it was one thing for Dermot to intimate that she was forgiven and to make grand conciliatory gestures, she thought, but the family might feel quite different about her, when they were face-to-face.

16

On the morning of the christening, Cathal O'Mahoney was also on his way into Limerick and he too was deep in thought about what was in store for him over the next few hours.

He was twenty-five years old, thin and tall, with a long, angular face, deep-set blue eyes under dark, worried brows, light brown hair worn long at the nape of his neck, and a thick moustache to match it.

Cathal was riding into town from his father's farm at Meelick, having had a row over breakfast with his elder brother, Seamus, over opposing political views.

Seamus said that Cathal was a dreamer for idolizing their cousin, Colonel John O'Mahoney, who, with James Stephens of Kilkenny, had founded the revolutionary Fenian Brotherhood thirty years before. True Cousin John – an intellectual and a Gaelic scholar like Cathal himself – had gone to America and formed there a huge Fenian movement, intended to take Ireland by storm, while Stephens stayed in Ireland.

But it was equally true, Seamus said, that the Fenian invasion had failed and was now a thing of the past which could not be resuscitated.

Cathal said that it could be. The people of Ireland were sick and tired of waiting, he insisted. Deep down, they wanted to take matters into their own hands instead of hanging around while the politicians intrigued and argued.

'You heard what Michael Davitt said about the

Coercion Bill,' he said to his brother. '"Let them try to turn back the Shannon to its source – let them try to arrest in its flow the Celtic blood which nourishes in our Irish hearts an undying hatred of injustices and oppression and then, and not till then, will they succeed in making us abdicate our reason."'

'You seem to have it all off pat!' said Seamus, drily. 'But it's just *words*, Cathal. The ordinary man in the street doesn't want to be incited.'

'Davitt was speaking in front of twenty thousand people; you can't deny the extent of that audience,' Cathal said hotly.

'Well, you keep out of it,' Seamus advised. 'Leave it to Parnell and Gladstone to sort out between them and get on with farming.'

Seamus, at the age of twenty-seven, had recently announced his intention of entering the Jesuit order and Cathal reminded himself once again that the Fenians had found their most dangerous foe in the Catholic Church, which had condemned secret societies on moral and social grounds. The hostility of the church must have deterred masses from joining the organization.

He wondered what Seamus would say if he were to announce that he was setting up his own movement and forming the basis of a rebel army. That would wipe the sanctimonious look off his brother's face all right!

But he had no intention of confiding in Seamus, or discussing it with anyone who was not directly involved. Outside an immediate circle, secrecy was an imperative. Cousin John had trusted the wrong people and been ultimately betrayed.

He brooded on that, riding past St Munchin's Church and over Thomond Bridge, past King John's five-sided castle. On the tower nearest the bridge you could still see the shot-holes once made by the Williamite guns.

In contrast to the majesty of the castle the houses, which had grown up around it like fungi, were small and poor and decrepit. Barefoot children, their snow-white faces freckle-dotted, stopped playing as he rode by.

'Yes, mister,' shouted one of them. 'You going to see our Brigid?'

'What would a fine fella like him be wanting with the likes of her?' a small girl wanted to know.

Cathal rode on slowly, searching for a house, a number, conscious that the children were following him, reaching for excitement.

'Mister, where are you off to?'

He could see the house, as run-down as the rest of them, with a broken chimney from which sooty smoke poured undeterred.

'Will you keep an eye on my horse if I promise you a penny?' he asked the small girl.

She smiled at him eagerly, revealing the gap between her front teeth.

'I will so, mister. Are you going to see me da?'

'Is this your house?'

She nodded.

'So your name is Dinneen.'

'It's Moirin Dinneen,' she told him.

Her hair streeled untidily around her shoulders and her tattered dress was far from clean. But someone – some time – had lovingly embroidered a green shamrock on its bodice.

'Is your da at home?' he asked.

'He is so,' said the small girl.

She stood back from the door, waiting for Cathal to

knock on it. It was thrown open almost at once and he was confronted by an adult version of the girl – the pale face and dark untidy hair, the same questioning green eyes. Only the expressions were different. The child's was friendly, confiding – the woman's openly hostile.

'What do you want?' she demanded.

Her eyes took in his tweed breeches, the expensive cut of his coat. She did not like what she saw.

'Is himself at home?' Cathal asked her mildly.

'He is not,' said the woman, too quickly.

He had expected nothing better. It was always the women who stood in the way of what he was up to, frightened that risings would lead to bloodshed in their families and of losing their security, such as it was. We are going to be an army, prepared to do battle for our own land in our own land, he wanted to say to her. When we rise we will rise in strength and at an appropriate time, when our American support is fully secured and – hopefully – when the might of the British army is engaged elsewhere. We will gain independence and dignity for your children – for Moirin and all the others like her – and we will do so by *fighting as soldiers* – not by the use of dynamite bombs against innocent English people.

But it would be a waste of time talking to her. He stood his ground.

'I think he *is* in,' he said in a much louder voice.

His message reached its target.

'Let him come in, Mo,' a man's voice called out of the darkness of the room beyond.

Cathal peered into the gloom. At the back, near a broken window over which a piece of sacking had been

260

nailed, he could just make out the outline of a seated male figure.

'You'll have to come over here,' the man said, without rising from his position by the window.

'What is *wrong* with you?' cried the woman.

'Will you whist!'

In the murky light, Cathal could pick out a table, two chairs, an open fire with a three-legged cauldron on it, nestling into the ashes.

Dinneen's left leg was missing from the knee down and the leg of his breeches flopped sadly against the leg of the chair. But in the gloom the scars on his face were less repulsive than they had appeared at their first meeting, set up by Michael Lacey, a tenant on the Meelick farm and another embryo Fenian.

'I have a list here of the parties you should be seeing,' said Dinneen, coming straight to the point.

You had to admire him, a man who had been wounded in one of the abortive and impalpable risings that had followed the collapse of the Fenian movement in America. He still believed that they had been right to go ahead and fight, even without the promised American aid, and neither the loss of his leg, his inability to work, poverty nor the anger of his wife took from his patriotic spirit.

It was in Dinneen and his ilk, the lower and lower-middle classes, if you had to use the hated word class, that the hope of achieving independence lay. That had always been the Fenian belief – John O'Mahoney's belief.

'How many names?'

'Nine. Don't worry. We'll be adding to them in no time.'

Work in circles and add to them, that had been

John's method, and Stephens', with each circle presided over by its Centre. Fifty thousand John had recruited in America. In Ireland, Stephens was said to have had a force of seventy-five thousand, well-drilled and fairly well-armed. And *still* they had failed.

And here was Cathal, starting with nine. When you considered what he wanted to achieve it was a laughable number. For a moment he was plunged into gloom.

'. . . in no time,' said Dinneen, his eyes lighting up with fervour.

His enthusiasm was infectious. I am young, Cathal said to himself. I have my whole life ahead to dedicate to this mission. I can recruit hundreds – thousands – of Irishmen full of the purest patriotism, men who would sacrifice possessions, families, their own lives to obtain what we know is best for Ireland. *Believe that*.

'Dependable men?'

'The best you'll be able to find anywhere in the country,' said Dinneen, triumphantly.

'We have to find a safe place to meet,' Cathal said. 'We can't meet here.'

The woman was hovering by the door. There was no sign of the child.

'Lacey's cabin?'

'I don't think so. I don't want news getting back to the house.'

'One of the men will come up with some suggestion,' Dinneen insisted. 'Go and see this fellow. He's the best of the bunch. Dedicated . . .'

'Married?'

The man by the window laughed.

'He is not and never will be! Tierney – Tim-Pat Tierney. He's working as groom and coachman for

Dermot O'Brien the solicitor at Kincora House on the Ennis Road. When will you see him?'

'What's wrong with now?' Cathal said, decisively.

There was no farewell from Mrs Dinneen, only from Moirin, standing guard by the horse. When he dropped five pennies into her hand she gave him her toothy smile.

He made his way round the back of Kincora along a boreen overgrown with tangled blackberry hedges and a puzzle of thistles, nettles and clover. Once, his horse stumbled over a pothole funnelled out by rain. Coarse white angelica vied with cow parsnip, plantains and the faintly evil white 'fairy' candles, the wild flowers of his youth.

What would Tierney be like? Bitter, maybe – and aggressive. Ready to kill.

But unlikely to share that other aesthetic dream – the hope that one day the country would regain its love of Irish culture. If you said to a groom, look, there was a time when each great family in Ireland had a special book filled not only with records and genealogies but also with poetry – would he know that? In those times family libraries were well stocked with Gaelic books. Both Gaelic chief and Norman lord had his hereditary bard, historian and brehon whose function was to carry on the tradition of scholarship from generation to generation. Poets were patronized. There were schools to maintain the old, classical literature. Ireland was proud of being the Land of Saints and Scholars. What would it mean to a groom?

Pride in self. Pride in one's heritage. Of course it would mean *something*.

The boreen came to an abrupt end, opening on to a meadow. At the foot of it, winding away, was the

Shannon and nearby, the house he had been seeking, red-brick, with a wall around it. Branches of apple trees, pears and damsons peeked over the wall, showing off their delicate blossoms.

Cathal dismounted and tied up his horse, hooking the reins on to an old oak tree, and went in search of Tim-Pat Tierney.

This necessitated slipping through an unlocked door in the wall. On the other side, someone had been making tentative efforts to grow a wild garden. White climbing roses scrambled up the wall and under it was what looked like a beautiful accident: wild crimson peonies, subtly-scented violets, sundew, field poppy and yellow roserock in riotous disarray.

He looked around, concerned lest he run into a gardener, but all he could see in the way of life was a black cat intent on her own nefarious business, stalking what would doubtless prove to be a mouse.

The orchard itself was laid out very neatly in blocks with cobble-stoned pathways around them. At the far corner was another gate, which he discovered gave through to the yard.

About to explore further he stopped, listening. There was a carriage coming down the avenue bearing – perhaps – Mr Dermot O'Brien and driven – perhaps – by Tim-Pat Tierney.

Mr O'Brien he certainly did not want to meet. Before the carriage came into sight he had nipped back through the orchard and into the boreen. He would wait until Mr O'Brien was safely out of the way and track Tim-Pat Tierney down in the stables.

He sat down under the old oak and reached in the pocket of his jacket for his book.

* * *

264

The hatred Dermot felt when he saw Milliora again was so gargantuan that for a few minutes he wondered if he would be able to act his part in the *entente cordiale* with any kind of conviction. But he managed to instal her in the drawing-room with what he hoped passed for normality.

She sat bolt upright on a delicate, daintily painted chair that he knew to be most uncomfortable, and looked around her at the Persian rug that covered most of the cream and rose Wilton carpet, at the expensive hand-printed pale pink wallpaper, the upright grand piano, the strawberry design Belleek plates and Minton figurines. From where he sat, on an elegant rosewood armchair upholstered in dusty-pink sateen, Dermot could see her reflected in the ornate, garlanded and gilded mirror that hung over the fireplace and showed all the contents of the room and, in that sense, he was forced to confront dual images of his *bête noire*.

The slut, he thought, loathing her beauty and her elegance and the confident way she sat, like a smug little ginger cat perched on a sunny wall. If only he could shoo her off her perch instead of having to subtly persuade her to hand it over after her death!

He forced himself to say: 'Tell me, how have you been all these years?' leaning forward to receive her confidence in the way that invariably relaxed and charmed his clients at Dundon's.

In the long pause before she answered his question the grandfather clock in the hall boomed out its confirmation that it was eleven o'clock. At the same time – like a bird on a cuckoo clock – Bridie Flanagan thrust open the drawing-room door and came timorously in, bearing an enormous tray laden with tea and cakes and scones.

About to wave to the maid to tell her to place her burden on one of the small tables standing near the fireplace Dermot realized with horror that the oval silver milk-jug on the tray was one of the items he had purloined from Crag Liath and subsequently redeemed from Pashie Browne's after paying compound interest.

Then Milliora – when he was not expecting her answer – said, 'I'm very well, thank you, Dermot,' and Bridie, also caught by surprise, gave a convulsive start. Milk slopped out of the oval silver milk-jug and a dribble of hot tea landed on her rough, red hand. The tray wobbled perilously.

Don't you dare drop it, signalled Dermot's cold blue eyes.

Had Milliora recognized the jug? She gave no sign that she had done so. Surely she wouldn't – the likelihood was that she had never been near the dining-room sideboard during his mother's reign.

Bridie, her eyes wide with apprehension, laid the tray on the table and bolted from the room without pouring tea and passing cakes as Dermot had intended.

'*Very* well,' repeated Milliora, observing what was going on with – he thought – amusement. 'What a pretty milk-jug,' she added, bending forward to examine it more closely. 'The christening mugs I've brought for the babies are English silver, I'm afraid – not nearly as nice as I would have wished. I really like the country themes in Irish silver best, don't you? – the chickens and the sheep and the milkmaids, maybe because they make me think of Crag Liath.'

She did not sound as if she had identified the milk-jug, only as if she was making polite conversation, but Dermot still felt numb.

'I'm more interested in porcelain than silver,' he

266

heard himself say. 'I have – I must show you – a most interesting Royal Worcester dinner-service, created over a hundred years ago for the Earl of Coventry, who was blinded in a hunting accident. He asked the factory to design a pattern he could *feel*.'

'The Blind Earl pattern,' said Milliora, having the answer to almost everything.

No, she did not know of his part in the theft – he was sure of it. But it had been a bad moment.

As he poured tea and added milk and inquired as to the amount of sugar she wanted, he looked forward to this day being over and the groundwork laid that would ensure the return of Crag Liath to its rightful owners.

When Rosaleen heard Milliora's carriage coming along the avenue she had a childish impulse to leap out of bed and run downstairs to hug her old friend and welcome her to Kincora. What stopped her was less her own after-birth stiffness than the unease she felt over the whole business of Milliora acting as godmother to the twins.

She was apparently the only member of the family who had qualms about having invited her to take on this role with such an ulterior motive, Dermot's explanation to Mary and Carmel having been accepted, it seemed, without so much as a squeak of protest.

'You're all right, are you?' Mrs Galvin wanted to know, coming into the room.

'I'm fine. I'm going to get dressed today,' she answered, pushing back the bedclothes. 'I'm tired of being stuck up here in the bedroom waiting for people to come and see me. There's an old friend of mine downstairs whom I haven't seen for years and I'm going to go down and surprise her.'

'Do you mean Mrs O'Brien of Crag Liath?' Mrs Galvin asked, diverted. 'You and she were friends at school, I believe.'

'We were.'

'And then you had a big fall-out after Mr Tom O'Brien – God rest his soul – went and drowned himself in the Shannon. Oh, I'm glad you've brought the family together again, Mrs O'Brien – I am indeed. 'Twas a generous thought and no mistake, for all that Mr O'Brien and his sisters were against the lady being godmother to the twins.'

Looking in the wardrobe to see which of the costumes she had worn before her pregnancy would now fit Rosaleen paused with her hand on the door. Dermot and his sisters against the idea of Milliora being godmother – what on earth had Mrs Galvin got into her head?

'What are you talking about?'

'Didn't I overhear Mr O'Brien talking to his sisters downstairs the other night, explaining that 'twas you that asked Mrs O'Brien of Crag Liath to be godmother to the twins. "What about us?" says one of his sisters – the older one, I'd say – and Mr O'Brien said he had no option but to give in to your wishes in the matter, him wanting to be nice to you after you'd had the babies. "What got into her at all?" says the older sister and the other one says, "Mary, you don't know about it yet but you can get these ideas into your head after having a baby."'

More lies, thought Rosaleen furiously, sifting through his bombardment of words. And this time dragging me into it. How dare he? And how can I respect a man who isn't honest?

'Idealistic, your husband says you are, Mrs O'Brien

– idealistic and kind. You can see the same beautiful nature coming out in the twins.'

'I haven't got a beautiful nature,' said Rosaleen, shortly. 'I can assure you of that. I'm going to get dressed now, Mrs Galvin, and then I'll be in the nursery to help you get the twins into their christening robes.'

She felt irritable and jumpy, and all the more so because it would be hours before she and Dermot would be alone again and she could have the matter out.

'Rosaleen's *very* well,' Dermot was saying in reply to Milliora's question. 'She's probably fast asleep at this moment – '

Then the drawing-room door swung open, propelled by Bridie's invisible hand, and Rosaleen and two shrieking babies came into the room.

'Oh my God!' Dermot said involuntarily.

Milliora murmured, 'The babies,' and leapt up from her chair to go to them.

Both women's faces were reflected in the mirror and to Dermot's delight he saw that Milliora had undergone a metamorphosis. The soft hazel eyes were laden with happy tears, Milliora's bottom lip was trembling with emotion and she was already reaching out her arms to the two red-faced bundles of fury.

'Let me have one of them,' she mouthed to Rosaleen above the cacophony and took Daniel into her arms.

Miraculously, or so it appeared to his parents, Daniel ceased to cry, a change much less due to divine intervention then to the fact that the lace round the neck of his christening robe had been tickling his cheek and transference gave him relief.

How like Tom he is, thought Milliora, gazing down

at the baby. So tiny, and yet the resemblance is uncanny. She glossed over the fact that Tom had dark curly hair and that Daniel's seemed to be red, and that he had Rosaleen's eyes, not Tom's, and thought that he had the identical nose of his uncle, and the same mouth, and that his eyes were just as perfectly set.

This likeness – most of it a figment of her imagination because, at this stage, Daniel only looked like himself – seemed to her much more miraculous than the fact that the baby had stopped crying; a veritable gift from Heaven and an acknowledgement from God that she had suffered enough and was about to be forgiven.

Rosaleen was standing beside her. Looking up to tell her of the likeness she saw between Daniel and Tom, Milliora saw Eugene. He was still registering his anger but his godmother thought him an absolute charmer. And how incredible, she thought, that he, too, is like Tom – and maybe even more so. There is Tom in the deep blue eyes, and he has dark hair and the shape of the face is Tom's all right – you cannot mistake it.

'They are *wonderful*,' she said to Rosaleen, who in spite of Eugene's crying could now hear.

'Wonderful,' she agreed unreservedly.

All three adults lapsed into a contented silence, the women lost in mutual adoration of the twins, Dermot heartened that his plan was working so well already. He observed Milliora again in the gilded and garlanded mirror, and smiled.

'Heads I win,' he said to himself, and thought of Tom, who all too often had lost.

Today, Tom did not seem such a hero. How foolish he had been after all, to let Crag Liath slip through his gambling fingers. Let's see what I can do about it,

270

thought Dermot, and satisfaction and confidence began to seep into him in the most enjoyable way.

When Tim-Pat brought the carriage round – stopping to exclaim over the babies – Dermot installed Milliora and Mrs Galvin inside, each of them with a baby, and kissed Rosaleen on the cheek.

'Good-bye, darling. You go back to bed and rest.'

There was no reply but Dermot, for once, failed to notice his wife's reaction, being preoccupied with Milliora's.

The air was fresh and exhilarating and balmy and Rosaleen, watching the departing carriage, thought it was absurd to rest in bed. Instead, she would walk in the meadow behind Kincora, through the grasses and meadowsweet as she had done a few evenings before, feeling differently towards Dermot.

Cathal's view of the countryside behind the house was delightful – the river, serene and silver-grey, the meadow, brilliant green but speckled with the pink of meadow grass, and the hazy blue sky flaunting the yellow sun. He could see the city buildings, too, but he chose to ignore them. They were intrusive – the river and the sun were not.

He finished his book quite soon after his arrival, thinking it a coincidence that he should read *The Midnight Court*, Brian Merriman's vision poem about men being daft without women and women being worse without men, on a day that he was visiting an O'Brien household. Aoibheal, the heroine of the poem, was the fairy connected with the O'Briens of Clare, a lady who had ruled from her palace at Crag Liath from where she had foretold the outcome of the Battle of Clontarf and given the names of the men, including that of her lover – an attendant on Murchadh, King Brian's eldest son – who were fated to die that day.

Later on, Aoibheal became the heroine of other well-known poems written in Gaelic – Aislings, or dreams, the vision poems in which a beautiful woman appears to the poet telling him that she is Ireland, greatly troubled because her people are oppressed and deprived of their land and religion. But she also maintains that the bad times will pass. In an Aisling, the oppressor is defeated and the golden days come back.

Cathal yawned and stretched pleasurably. It was a lovely, lovely day. Any minute now, he would be sleeping . . .

And so he slept, quite heavily, until he woke with a start to find Aoibheal herself striding into his line of vision. She was small and dainty with a sweet, pale face and dark upswept hair and she was dressed in violet-blue which was the colour of her eyes.

Half-asleep still, and thinking that he might be dreaming, Cathal closed his eyes and shook his head from side to side before opening them again. Expecting Aoibheal to have vanished, he was enraptured to find her very much present. She was everything a fairy queen should be, he thought, except that – more in the manner of a witch than a fairy – she was carrying on her left shoulder the black cat he had seen earlier in the orchard.

A calm, gracious lady, the poets had called her. This Aoibheal, although she was undoubtedly gracious – and so very sweet – did not look calm at all. And, in spite of her pretty features and figure, she did not look unearthly.

'Good morning,' he said to her (or was it, by now, good day?).

She gasped, then recovered her composure and glared at him. 'And what are you doing here, may I ask?'

Not so gracious, after all, thought Cathal, struggling to his feet and realizing that she had probably come, not from fairyland, but from the house called Kincora.

He glanced at her left hand and noted, with regret, the gold band on the third finger. Mrs Dermot O'Brien? In which case, he had to do some talking.

'I'm sorry if I startled you,' he said. 'I'm waiting here for someone.'

'Who?' demanded Aoibheal, more annoyed than ever.

He was saved by the black cat, which spotted something of interest in the hedgerow and with a mighty leap took off in hot pursuit of it, knocking the book out of his hands and turning it cover upwards on to the roserocks.

'Oh!' exclaimed Aoibheal. Her expression changed from fury to interest. 'A book in *Irish* – you're reading a story in Irish!'

'Not just a story – an Aisling, a poem,' Cathal said, dazzled by her approbation.

'I know what an Aisling is,' said Aoibheal, complacently. 'I can read Irish, too.'

Intelligent and well-informed as well as beautiful, thought Cathal, mightily impressed. He met few Irish people who could read their own language, let alone a woman.

'How on earth did you get to learn Irish?' he asked.

'My father taught me. And then I was alone a lot

and had plenty of time on my hands, so it was easy to go on.'

'You put your time to good use,' said Cathal quietly.

Aoibheal had picked up the book and was turning over the pages.

> And as the court has recommended
> That all this nonsense must be ended,
> A judge was chosen without delay
> To hear what both sides have to say.

she read aloud. 'Say about what? May I read this book when you have finished it?'

'You cannot!' said Cathal decisively. 'It's a most unsuitable poem for any woman to read.'

'Is that so?' Aoibheal was intrigued. 'And what's so unsuitable about it, may I ask?'

Cathal's eyes twinkled. *The Midnight Court* was lusty, to put it mildly: the women who spoke to the bachelor poet did not mince their words, and the poet was outspoken in his.

'I'll strike a bargain with you,' he said, evading Aoibheal's question. 'I'll tell you the story and read you a bit of the verse if you promise to forgive me for frightening you just now.'

'That's a fair bargain.' She passed the book back to him and sat down on the grass beside him, more child now than fairy queen. 'Tell me the story.'

'The poet is sleeping by the shores of Loch Greine when he is awakened by a huge, strange-looking female,' Cathal began. 'She is seven yards tall and her face is terribly ugly, but she says she is the bailiff of the Midnight Court and that the poet has been summoned to appear before it.'

He had a magic-maker's voice, Rosaleen decided,

deep and enticing and steeped in warmth. She liked the way he looked as well, although he was not classically handsome like Tom had been. Beautiful Tom, who would never have read Irish poetry to her but, much more probably, what was on a race-card. We would never have got along together, Rosaleen thought. What I felt was nothing but childish infatuation, whereas Milly really loved him.

She did not compare Cathal to Dermot, and after a while she did not compare him to Tom either. She felt charged with joy again, alive and vital and happy. Time drifted by and she forgot that today was Daniel and Eugene's christening day and that, after their baptism at the church, a whole load of people were coming to the house for luncheon by which time, circumspectly, she should, like any new mother, be back in her bed.

If she had truly analysed her feelings she would have been shocked to discover that a mother of three-day-old babies, a good Catholic who believed implicitly in the indissolubility and sanctity of marriage, was wildly attracted to a man she had not known an hour before. But she did not indulge in introspection. She simply lay back on the grass and listened to magic words spoken by a magician.

Later, Cathal modified the poem for her, avoiding what he felt were the cruder phrases, concentrating more on the setting.

> And there, as I stood before my sight
> Was a massive mansion ablaze with light,
> Rich and radiantly draped
> Beautifully built and shaped.

A fine setting for the Queen of Fairies. But this Aoibheal, with her dark hair and her violet-blue eyes, was in need of nowhere as grand. Those eyes were deeper than clover and her mind was as bright as the sun. He was as enchanted by her as she was by him and every bit as attracted.

All the same, they both heard the sound of the returning carriage as it drove in at the avenue gate and realized that it spelt the end of their idyll.

Rosaleen got up, brushing grass-seed from her skirt.

'I'd better go,' she said reluctantly.

'Must you?'

With the carriage, he supposed, came the missing Tim-Pat Tierney, less important than he had been before Aoibheal came into his life.

'Of course,' the lady said, returning to her old severity, though this time she did not seem to be directing it at him.

At the gate she stopped and looked back. 'Thank you for the Aisling,' she said. 'Apart from my babies, I think it's the most wonderful present I've ever had,' and disappeared from view.

Babies! thought Cathal disgustedly. How many did she have? And what was the matter with him, getting attracted to married women – or to one married woman whom he would probably never lay eyes on again?

276

17

The week that the twins turned three Dermot bought them ponies and Tim-Pat fulfilled an ambition to teach them how to ride.

The morning of their birthday, Tim-Pat was up even earlier than usual, at four instead of five, to take another look at the two newcomers to the stables. They were Connemara ponies, with coats the colour of milk and heads like thoroughbred Arabs, and although their bodies were stocky and their legs short, their manes and tails were long and fine and silky. They were a good buy, he thought, noting the way they stood fairly on all four legs and how they turned in the stables, but then Dermot very rarely made a mistake when it came to buying horses.

He was looking forward to seeing the twins' faces when they were confronted with their surprise. Daniel, being the adventurous one, would be overjoyed, but surely reticent Eugene would be just as glad and just as likely to leap around with delight.

Fine-looking little fellows they were, the two of them, one with his mop of dark red hair and the other one with his brown-black curls – as sweet as two whistles, for all that they were so different; Daniel so cheeky and talkative he'd chat to a brass band and Eugene who wouldn't say boo to a goose if he could stay quiet in a corner. It was going to make Tim-Pat's day to see them on horseback, true O'Briens at last.

It was nine o'clock before they came to the stables and when they did, Tim-Pat was not particularly pleased to see that their mother was with them. He was no fonder of Rosaleen than he had been of Milliora when she was first brought out to Crag Liath, both women having got their hands on the O'Brien men and persuaded them to marry.

Still, even he had to admit that Dermot's wife was a marvellous horsewoman even if – as her husband had revealed – she had a weird reaction to hunting, loving the day out, revelling in the jumps and the chase, and then doing a fast about-turn and feeling sorry for the fox as if she was city bred like that liar and thief, the widow of Master Tom.

His irritation at seeing Rosaleen soon faded when the twins were shown their presents. He had been right, he thought, gratified – they *were* thrilled, just the way they should be, although, as you might have expected, it was Daniel who clamoured to mount while Eugene stood by his mother, watching what was going on.

'Come over here by the pony's left shoulder and take the reins in your left hand,' Tim-Pat told him. 'And lay ahold of the mane here, a bit in front of the withers.'

'I know, I know – I've seen daddy often,' Daniel said, eager to be up. 'And I take the stirrup in this hand . . .'

'Ah sure, you're great. We'll have you racing soon, standing up in the stirrups and winning all the point-to-points in Limerick and Clare.'

Daniel would get shaken into his saddle in no time, Tim-Pat decided. He was less sure how Eugene would take the inevitable falls that would follow his first lesson in equitation. When his turn came to get up on his pony he had nothing to say although he listened intently and followed Tim-Pat's instructions on how to hold the reins.

While Daniel had shouted out to his mother during his lesson, demanding and getting her praise and attention, Eugene made no similar demands. Yet every so often, Tim-Pat noticed, the boy cast a glance in her direction that was loaded, not only with longing for her approbation, but with adoration. He was a real mother's boy and no mistake. Master Dermot, who wanted his sons to grow up strong and independent, would not be pleased about that.

'You're only small. You can steady yourself when you're getting up by using the flap of the saddle. Do you see?'

Eugene nodded solemnly.

You'd think he hadn't a titter of wits, Tim-Pat thought, but his mind is working away. Isn't he just like his father! And the same compassion that ran through his love for Dermot seeped through him for Dermot's dark-haired son.

Having longed for this moment when he could be giving the children the benefit of his expertise, he was already in his element. There were happy days to come for all three of them.

'Be careful now not to touch the pony with your left toe when getting on to his back,' he said to Eugene.

The huge blue eyes grew larger still, gazing into his green ones. A sensitive boy – one who could be easily hurt. And one who badly needed protection.

'Don't worry,' Tim-Pat said to him. 'I'll always be here to help you.'

In the afternoon the twins, dressed in white sailor suits with their curls well brushed, went to Crag Liath for a birthday party and Tim-Pat breathed a sigh of relief.

For once he was glad that their mother was independent and had defied convention, insisting on driving the carriage to O'Brien's Bridge herself, although Master Dermot, who was planning to join them all later, would not be happy to hear it.

He wondered what Rosaleen would think if she knew that her groom and coachman would be following hot on her heels. Not to join the birthday party – the widow would never admit a member of staff to any one of *her* parties – but to go to a meeting arranged by Mr Cathal O'Mahoney on the widow's land.

He laughed aloud at the irony of that. She would go mad, Mrs Milliora O'Brien, a woman with a sharp point to her tongue these days according to Mrs Cash, if she knew that her own property was being used as a venue for Mr O'Mahoney's rebels.

Or, more accurately, for the leaders of a number of rebel groups which Mr O'Mahoney had set up, in the fashion of the Fenians, with each leader known as a Centre and each group as a Circle.

'Where shall we meet?' Mr O'Mahoney had asked long ago when the concept of many Circles was only a dream and the members numbered nine. 'Has anyone any ideas?'

'I know a place,' Tim-Pat had said, proudly, describing the place he had always thought of as his own, the hidden room, covered with grass and surrounded by reeds, which long-ago O'Briens had built on the triangular marshy strip of land bordering the river.

It had been built for a nefarious purpose – so smugglers could leave wine there for the family which would later be taken up to the house through a secret passage and relieve them of the necessity of paying excise duty – and it was intoxicating, in another way, to think that it could be used for a noble cause instead.

'But surely the O'Briens know about this place,' Mr

O'Mahoney had said dubiously. 'I can't imagine how it could have stayed unnoticed all these years.'

'They don't,' Tim-Pat said positively. 'I was the only one who ever found it. Master Tom and Master Dermot didn't go down there because of the marshy land and the people round believe 'tis a fairy place and don't dare go anywhere near it.'

'Why didn't you tell the O'Briens when you found it?' Mr O'Mahoney wanted to know.

And Tim-Pat said: 'It was *my* place – a place of my own, do you see?' and Mr O'Mahoney said he did.

All the same, Mr O'Mahoney said someone should stand guard during the meetings and was pleased when Tim-Pat volunteered for the job. He would do anything for Mr O'Mahoney, he thought – even giving his own life if that was required, although sometimes it was hard to understand his leader's mode of operations. Or even the man himself!

Mr O'Mahoney was very clever – anyone could see that – and since his father had died he was rich as well, with farming land in Meelick. He was a real patriot and full of fire when it came to getting the movement going yet on other occasions he could be as absent-minded as a man of a hundred whose memory was going.

Like the time he had come to a meeting late after forgetting that it was called. Tim-Pat had ridden all the way to Meelick on a freezing February evening to see what was wrong, only to find Mr O'Mahoney reading a book in front of a roaring fire.

And then another time he had turned up on foot, forgetting where he had left his horse. Sometimes, in the night, Tim-Pat woke up trembling, thinking what would happen if Mr O'Mahoney were to lose the records he kept about the organization.

Still, Tim-Pat was a fighting man, not a Centre, and

281

it was not up to him to tell Mr O'Mahoney what to do or where to keep the records. And he had better get going out to O'Brien's himself, or *he* would be late for the meeting.

By five o'clock Daniel looked an absolute sight. His white sailor suit was streaked with chocolate icing and blobs of raspberry blancmange and he had cake crumbs in his hair.

He was blissfully happy as he gulped down the last of his red lemonade.

The converted nursery in which the party had been held looked as if it had been hit by a hurricane, for the twins had swooped upon their presents – the twin rocking-horses, smart as real ones, with bridles and saddles and reins, the Noah's Ark with the carved wooden animals, the whips and tops and building blocks provided for them by Milliora – with whoops of joy, strewing coloured wrapping-paper all over the carpet. After that Eugene had dropped his plate of jelly into the very spot Daniel was putting his foot and a dish of sweets had been overturned and trodden into the debris. It seemed to the twins quite natural that Milliora should beam on them with utter approval throughout all this.

Their ability to concentrate on anything but ponies for more than a few minutes was limited, and now the novelty of the toys had somewhat worn off. Daniel, wearing a chocolate moustache, said they were going to explore.

'As long as it is in the house, mind, and not the garden,' Rosaleen said.

And Milliora added, 'No going out of the house.'

But these were unnecessary instructions since Daniel's plan for the next half-hour entailed remaining inside. He had opportunistically stuffed both his pockets with sweets before he set out and as he and Eugene went downstairs he transferred two into his mouth.

He was an innovative leader and he had already informed Eugene where they were going and what they were going to do. He had heard about the possibility of a secret passage at Crag Liath from Mrs Cash on an earlier visit and he remembered that it was supposed to run from the little room where the shoes and boots were kept. His mission was to find it.

With Eugene following him he reached the boot cupboard door and, having ensured that Mrs Markham was not snooping around, he opened it and they both went inside to be confronted by rows and rows of boots and shoes. Milliora had never been able to bring herself to throw away Tom's possessions and the other O'Briens, in their hasty departure from Crag Liath, had left old boots and shoes behind as well. The smell of old leather and of the feet that had once been encased in it was anything but pleasant and both boys wrinkled up their noses in disgust.

And then Eugene noticed that Daniel was stuffing himself with sweets and had not offered him any. Reticent he might be with outsiders but he was less inhibited with his twin. By then they were both over-tired and over-excited and one thing quickly led to another. Hot words were exchanged followed by angry punches. Seeking vengeance, Eugene pushed Daniel back against one of the walls.

He heard his twin's furious yelp of protest before both he and the wall vanished from sight and Eugene found himself alone, gazing open-mouthed at a black hole and terrified as he had never been before.

'Daniel!' he cried, but only his own voice echoed

back to him out of the awful blackness. Of Daniel, there was no sight or trace at all.

And it was all his fault. Shocked and guilty, he was too frightened at first to think of going for help. Instead, he threw himself on the floor and sobbed so quietly that Mary Markham, going past the cupboard to let Dermot into the house, did not know he was there.

'You're not the only one that has a poor opinion of Master Dermot, I'd say,' said Mrs Cash, looking under her black eyelashes at Mary Markham pounding the dough for bread.

'What do you mean by that?'

Mrs Cash leant forward on her chair, the better to confide her revolutionary viewpoint. 'Listen to me, there's not a sign of another baby, is there? Would you say Mrs Rosaleen hasn't time for Master Dermot or what?'

The concept of Rosaleen committing mortal sin by refusing her husband's advances shocked Mary Markham almost as rigid as the shock of Mrs Cash's nerve.

'It's not behind every ditch the like of *her* grows, Mrs Cash, and don't you forget it,' she said when she got her voice back.

'I'm neither running her up nor down. I have neither good nor bad to say about her,' Mrs Cash defended herself. 'She's like a black stranger to me, barring to know her face. If I was criticizing anyone, it would be Master Dermot I'd be after, not Mrs Rosaleen at all.'

'Oh?'

'There's a difference between the hearts and tongues of some people, Mary Markham,' said the washer-woman. 'And there are times when the body of a woman knows what her mind does not. 'Tis my opinion

284

that Mrs Dermot O'Brien's body is resisting the notion of a baby because it knows that man is bad!'

Imagine using the word body, Mary thought, shocked all over again. Nevertheless, what Mrs Cash was proposing was a fascinating notion and once Mary had ticked her off for her language they explored it for longer than either of them intended.

Mary was late going up to clear away the nursery. This time, as she went up the stairs, she noticed that the door to the boot cupboard was ajar. About to shut it she saw a small shoe sticking out. It did not need to be put on the shelf because there was a small foot inside it.

Its owner was fast asleep lying on the floor. And there was a large hole in what used to be a wall.

It took Mary some time to carry Eugene upstairs and even longer before she or anyone was able to piece together what had happened.

Cathal O'Mahoney was a leader of great vision who acted as an inspiration to them all, the Centres were unanimous about that. He was the theorist, the man of ideas with the courage to attempt to translate them into action.

They were also agreed that he was a man who would always require strong back-up, being less brilliant when it came to filling in the details of these ideas. As Ned Lynch, the south-east Limerick Centre said, the success Cathal had with the running of his farm was largely due to his having a first-rate overseer who got on with the more onerous business of carrying out his employer's wishes.

Still, everyone said that they would have given up months ago without their leader's encouragement and enthusiasm for the raising of an all-Ireland army. When they grumbled, saying that maybe he had seriously under-rated the apathy of the people and that, to many, to be styled a Fenian today simply meant being a crank, Cathal told them that their job was to break through the indifference and animate the men they were recruiting.

'It's hard to get their thoughts away from the question of the land,' John Roche, the inner-Limerick Centre said. 'The farmers' pleasure with what agrarian reform has been obtained has affected even the people in the cities. Time and time again men – even young men – say to me that we're winning the fight against landlordism so what do we want Home Rule for? You wouldn't believe the things I'm hearing.'

'It's a passing phase,' Cathal insisted. 'We all knew this was going to be a long drawn out process. What you have to do now is hold on to and encourage the men you've got for the time when public opinion will swing back again.'

'It's going to get worse before it gets better,' Ned Lynch said gloomily. 'What about the rumours that are going around about Parnell and the woman Kitty O'Shea? If it's true what Captain O'Shea alleges, that there's something between his wife and Parnell, the country will lose interest in the possibility of Home Rule altogether, the people will be that disillusioned in the men who are trying to obtain it.'

'That's nothing but idle gossip,' John Roche said uneasily. 'Parnell wouldn't be such a fool as to get himself involved with a married woman, let alone one who's married to a member of the Home Rule Party.'

'All that's beside the point,' Cathal said. 'Parnell's fight is with words, for all the good they're doing him. Ours will be a cleaner fight, with guns. And we're building the stores of ammunition well enough – ' he stopped, glancing at the guns lining the walls of the room, thinking of the arsenals they had set up in the attics of their homes around the country – 'without any fear of suspicion. You must – '

What he was going to say next none of them heard then for at that moment someone – or something – began to pound the wall against which he was leaning and in the horrified silence into which they all fell they heard, instead, what sounded like the scream of a child incarcerated behind it.

It seemed to be crying, and then they heard distinctly: 'Get me out!'

Only Cathal thought clearly. 'Be quick,' he said to the men. 'Get the guns out of here. Call Tim-Pat – he knows the place well. He'll find a temporary spot by the river where we can dump them for now. Whoever is behind this wall, someone is bound to be coming in search of him.'

'*Out!*' the aggrieved voice persisted.

Examining the wall, Cathal noted the cracks in it, some bigger than others. Kneeling down, he tried unsuccessfully to peer through. Only darkness. But the door of their own room was open, admitting reasonable light. It did not necessarily follow that whoever was behind the wall did not see more clearly what was going on.

'*Out!*'

The men were moving rapidly – the guns were being dispersed.

'Hold on for a minute,' Cathal said to the unknown entity hidden behind the wall. 'We'll have you out of there in no time. Are you all right for the moment?'

It was a foolish question, he thought himself, for how could a child be all right under those circumstances but, all the same, it seemed to have the effect of reassuring the prisoner.

'Yes,' he said, surprisingly, and then, 'Hurry!'

Whoever was in there did not sound as if he was easily bested.

'Mr O'Mahoney?'

'Yes, Tim-Pat, what is it? Have you found a safe spot?'

'Reasonably safe.'

'I thought he said this place was safe,' Ned Lynch said grously. 'A fine fellow he is to rely on and no mistake.'

Cathal gestured to him to be silent.

'Tim-Pat did warn us that there was probably a passage behind this wall. Move out of here, the rest of you. I'll be in touch with you within the week. Tim-Pat can stay back and help me break the wall.'

'So where are we going to meet?' Ned Lynch asked. '*I* can't risk your coming to the house . . .'

The others, intent on making good their escape, ignored him.

From inside the wall came another grumble. 'Quick!'

'I know that voice,' Tim-Pat said, startled. '"Tis Master Daniel that's inside the wall.'

'Then talk to him,' Cathal said. 'Reassure him that we're going to get him out. You're off then, Ned, are you? Keep your spirits up now. We'll make another plan.'

He should leave himself, he knew, but he stayed where he was, partly out of concern for the child and partly from curiosity. Young Master Daniel did not sound as if he was lacking courage.

And then Tim-Pat, with his hands, prised away part of the wall to the passage and a small red-haired boy, badly in need of a bath, stepped through the aperture and into his rescuer's arms.

'*Tim-Pat!*' he cried exultantly, rubbing his dirty nose with an even dirtier fist.

Looking at him, Cathal noticed next that the boy had the most extraordinary eyes – violet-blue, fringed with long dark lashes. He had seen eyes like that once before, he remembered, and in his mind's eye he could see a dark-haired girl in a violet-blue frock sitting under a tree. I know what an Aisling is, she had said – I can also read Irish.

And they had sat together for an enchanted hour, reading Brian Merriman's poetry.

'You're all right, are you?' he enquired, smiling at the small boy with the amazing eyes.

Daniel responded to the smile with a generous one of his own. He was certainly a charmer, Cathal thought, even if he had put the fear of God into the men.

'He's had a bump on the head but he seems well enough from what I can see,' Tim-Pat reported. 'I'll take him up to the house and make sure he's well looked after.'

'I thought Tom O'Brien's widow didn't have a child. I'm sure you told me he didn't.'

'She doesn't. This is Master Daniel from Kincora House – Master Dermot O'Brien's son.'

And one of Mrs O'Brien's babies . . .

Once again, Cathal was able to see the girl with violet-blue eyes, this time as she thanked him for the Aisling.

Apart from my babies, I think it's the most wonderful present I've ever had.

And now here was one of those babies, disturbing his meeting, coming through a wall!

'Wonders will never cease,' he said to Tim-Pat. 'Yes, take him up to the house. I'll see you later on.'

'. . . wandering in the garden,' Tim-Pat said glibly when Daniel had been reunited with his parents and brother and had been taken off for a bath by a clucking Mary Markham.

'He's very naughty,' Rosaleen said. 'We told him to stay in the house. Eugene thought he'd fallen into a secret passage at the back of the broom cupboard and he was in floods of tears.'

'That's boys for you so,' Tim-Pat said, mentally holding his thumbs that his explanation held. 'He must have got out of the cupboard again and gone out through the kitchen.'

'While Eugene was asleep. Mrs Markham found him sleeping. If it wasn't for the hole in the cupboard . . .'

'I'll close that up for you before I go if you like, Mrs O'Brien,' Tim-Pat said to Milliora. ''Tisn't a passage at all, as I recall, but an extension of the cupboard Mrs Fiona O'Brien stopped off, saying the wall in there was crumbly.'

'Would you?' Milliora said. 'It would be very helpful.' She stopped, considering, looking him up and down. 'It was lucky you found him, Tim-Pat, before he wandered any further. What brought you out here? Do you have a message for Mr O'Brien?'

'I came here to see Mrs Cash. I haven't seen her for a long time,' he said.

For the present, at least, his luck held and when Daniel came up with stories of men with guns the rest of the family laughed. By then, Rosaleen had forgiven her red-haired son for disobeying her wishes and was more

290

relieved that he had survived his fall than cross about his meanderings.

'To think I used to describe Eugene as the imaginative one,' she said to Milliora and Dermot as Daniel tried to enlarge upon his story. 'Now I've got two of them the same.'

Milliora laughed sympathetically.

'A right pair,' she said, taking Eugene on to her knee lest, with all the attention going to Daniel, he feel a bit deprived. 'But what would we do without you, may I ask? Oh, you don't have to leave so soon, Dermot, do you? Can't you stay for another little bit? Rosaleen and I were having a lovely chat and you know I can't see enough of the twins.'

'Then you must come to dinner with us,' Rosaleen said. 'Come next Saturday but come early in the day so you can have time with the boys and then stay overnight. I'll ask some friends to join us for dinner. It's time you met more people. You spend far too much time alone.'

'There's always so much to do at Crag Liath,' Milliora protested. 'We're digging the seed-drills and making the trenches now for potatoes and treating the turnip seeds with red lead before we sow them, as a guard against the birds. And that's only the quarter of it. There's the grain and – '

'And you need a break sometime, doesn't she, Dermot? No more arguing, Milly – you come in for the weekend. Yes, what is it, Daniel?'

'There *were* men with guns. I saw them through the wall.'

But Rosaleen was running her hand over the lump on his head, stroking back his hair.

'You don't think he's suffering from some kind of concussion, do you?' she said, anxiously. 'He's very persistent. I thought at the beginning that he was trying to distract me from ticking him off for going into the garden by coming up with a story, but now – '

'I'm afraid that's all he *is* doing,' his father said wryly. 'That's enough now, Daniel. We're going home.'

'No more stories about men with guns. None of us want to hear them,' Rosaleen said to Daniel when they were all ensconced in the carriage. 'No, Tim-Pat, you can ride behind with my husband. I'm perfectly capable of driving on my own.'

For once, Tim-Pat smiled at her words. No one was suspicious. The meetings in the room could safely be resumed.

18

Planning the dinner-party, Rosaleen thought how much she enjoyed being back in the old friendship with Milliora. In the three years since the twins' birth they had seen a lot of each other, united – apart from all they had shared in the past – by their conviction that Daniel and Eugene were the most perfect pair in the world, even if they did fight on occasions and, in the case of Daniel, throw furious red-faced tantrums whenever his will was thwarted.

Of course, Milliora tended to spoil the boys, which was not good for them, but Rosaleen had only to imagine how sad it must be to have lost a baby and her resentment promptly vanished. Poor Milly – pouring love all over the twins was the only way she could release her own frustrated store of maternal love.

When she thought of that she went on to envisage how nice it would be if her friend married again, and had children of her own, and she put out of her mind Dermot's plan for regaining Crag Liath for the boys.

Thinking about Milliora in relation to the boys, Rosaleen felt, not exactly superior to her friend, but at least just as good as her. It was as if the thing that was missing in Milliora's life balanced the scales between them, and compensated for the fact that, apart from the babies, there was nothing much on Rosaleen's side at all.

But in every other way, Rosaleen thought, Milliora was simply first. She had survived tragedy without going under and had made a wonderful success of Crag

Liath, turning herself from a city girl into a real countrywoman and gaining the respect of the men around her.

Whereas I – I am still second best, Rosaleen thought. I have a marriage that exists only because marriage itself is indissoluble, and although I have Daniel and Eugene I have failed to conceive another baby.

And what do I do with my life now? I act out a part as Dermot's wife, running his household, looking after his children, but what else do I do to justify my existence and find genuine satisfaction? I do no work for the poor anymore or for Ireland, since Dermot would object to my getting too involved outside the family circle and is horrified by my political views, and I go along with his wishes to maintain an equilibrium.

As I went along with his wishes over the christening so that there is an undercurrent in my friendship with Milliora that did not exist before . . .

It was pointless brooding on all this, she told herself sternly. It would be much more practical to go into Limerick and shop for the dinner-party.

It was a pleasant day and she decided that she would walk to town and have Tim-Pat pick her up later and help to take her purchases home. She strolled along the Ennis Road, glad to be out of the house, and over the Wellesley Bridge, modelled on the Pont Neuilly in Paris.

On the city side of the bridge she turned off to the right and went down towards the docks to buy from the open market. Tough, red-faced women peddled their wares, one from the battered remains of a baby's perambulator.

Someone shouted: 'Move the baby over, Katie, and let the woman see the fish!' and there was a raucous scream of laughter.

The market attracted Rosaleen more for its raw vivacity than for what there was to buy.

'How nice to see you!' said a voice.

She swung around, startled, then smiled delightedly.

'Father Matt Ryan! What are you doing, shopping in the market?'

'I have to eat, too, you know,' the priest said, cheerfully. 'I'm only a human being.'

'You've been behaving like a saint,' Rosaleen said. 'The last I heard, you had been arrested for campaigning against the evictions and the whole landlord system. It was all in the papers.'

A force of two hundred policemen, no less, had gone out to Hospital where the priest was living then, she remembered, and because they arrived early in the morning their advent had been announced by the ring of chapel bells. She laughed aloud, recalling what she had read in the *Weekly News* at the time.

'I was up too early for them,' Father Matt had said, grinning, when – much later – they got him all the same.

A brave man. And brave, too, the constable who, ordered to assist in the arrest, had said: 'Stop. I will throw off this jacket. I will never take part in the arrest of a priest.'

No wonder over two thousand people had assembled to give Father Matt a magnificent ovation just before he was taken off. And she thought: I should have been amongst them. *I* should have been there. And then she remembered that the arrest had been the best part of three years ago, the year the twins were born, and she thought: Where have I been since then?

'And what have you been up to since we last met?' Father Matt wanted to know.

'Not much,' she almost said, and then, shocked,

thought again of the twins. She was tempting Providence and God would take it out on her if she was not careful. 'I got married and I have twin sons,' she said instead, and looked up at him, frowning.

'And do you still read as much as ever? I remember you once told me you had a great interest in the old Gaelic literature.'

'I do. It's such a tragedy that we should lose our culture as well as our land. The irony is that we seem to be getting the land back while doing nothing ourselves in terms of writing!'

'I wouldn't say that,' said Father Matt. 'In fact, it's something of a coincidence that we should bump into each other because I was thinking about you only the other day when I got a letter from Dublin. I thought at the time – now there's something that's right up her street. Wait a minute now and I'll see if I don't have the letter in my pocket.'

Rosaleen waited as, fumbling, he produced a horde of bits and pieces – Rosary beads, several letters, keys – a piece of string.

'Here it is,' he said finally, waving a crumpled envelope with a Dublin postmark on it at her and extracting an equally creased letter which he thrust into her hands. 'Read it.'

'It's from John O'Leary,' Rosaleen said, excitedly. 'Didn't he write *Poems and Ballads of Young Ireland* and isn't he the editor of the *Gael*?'

'He is – and a former Fenian who was exiled for twenty years from Ireland. But read the letter. See what he has to say.'

She looked again at the letter, her curiosity aroused.

Dear Father Matt,
Thank you for writing to me to say how much you appreciate getting the *Gael*.

I meet regularly with a group of young writers in Dublin to discuss, amongst other subjects, the Young Ireland poet-revolutionaries of the forties whose aura still lives with us. You know my feeling – that our poets should be *Irish* poets, helping to develop the spirit of the nation.

Should you or any of your friends be interested in attending our meetings we would be pleased to have you join us. I attach a schedule of our activities for the next six months. . .

'I can't go to Dublin myself,' Father Matt said, 'but why don't you? That is, if your husband would allow you to do so.'

'Why don't I?' said Rosaleen thoughtfully. 'I can't see any reason against it at all.'

'Then don't look any further in case you stumble on one!' Father Matt said, smiling. 'It seems to me it would do you the world of good. And get in touch with me after you get back and let me know what O'Leary and his poets are up to in Dublin.'

Although she had no intention of allowing Dermot to stop her from going to Dublin, Rosaleen said nothing to him of her plans until the evening of the dinner-party.

It was not the first time Milliora had dined with them over the years since the breach between them was healed, but on other occasions there had just been the three of them and no attempt had been made to further extend the numbers.

This time, Rosaleen instructed Bridie to lay the table for eight. As well as the three of them, there would be Andy and Carmel, and Mary and her husband Noel, whose surname was also Leahy, and, as a foil to Milliora, a middle-aged barrister called Arthur Bennett whom Dermot often briefed.

When she had first mooted the idea of inviting

Arthur, Dermot had dug in his heels and said he could not see the necessity for including him in the party, but Rosaleen, tired of giving in to her husband, said it was too late and that she had already sent out a letter asking him to come. Privately, she thought that he would be more interesting company for Milliora than either of the Leahy men who, although kind, were both a little boring.

She only hoped that Mary and Carmel would be on their best behaviour and that they would not drag up the past with Milliora. They had all met twice for afternoon tea at Kincora since the day of the christening and, although Dermot's sisters had kept the peace on both occasions, the atmosphere had been strained. You could hardly blame them, she thought. They were bound to think emotionally where Tom's death was concerned, but at least they were not as obsessive as Dermot, who referred back to all that whenever he got the chance.

Now whenever Dermot raised the subject of Tom and the loss of Crag Liath with Rosaleen, she either changed the subject or went abruptly from the room.

But Dermot could be relied upon to behave superbly in Milliora's company. No one – least of all Milliora herself – would ever be able to guess from his demeanour that he detested her more than ever, or so he always purported. Sometimes Rosaleen found it difficult to accept that he nurtured such loathing and could act so perfect a part in front of his *bête noire*. Perhaps, deep down, he did not really hate her at all and his declaration of hatred was only a habit that he had not yet shaken off.

In that optimistic mood, Rosaleen prepared for the dinner-party, stuffing the goose herself and making a prune and apple sauce to go with it, and checking on the table setting before she went to change into a blue dress with a gored skirt and leg-of-mutton sleeves.

'You look beautiful,' Dermot said, coming up behind her as she sat in front of the mirror in their bedroom, putting up her hair.

He put his hands on her shoulders where the dress was cut away and began to caress her neck. Rosaleen tensed, watching his hand in the mirror, wishing he would remove it. The other hand proprietorially squeezed her other shoulder.

'Why don't you respond to me?' Dermot whispered. Bending, he kissed the nape of her neck.

She closed her eyes so as not to have to meet his in the mirror, her own hands automatically inserting the last hairpins, feeling for vagrant strands of hair.

'Tonight when they're all gone home we'll make love. I want another child, Rosaleen. You've been barren far too long.'

She was saved from having to reply by loud banging on the front door. The first guests had arrived.

Milliora had not grown out of her histrionic streak and she managed to make an entrance, arriving well after everyone else was sitting by the fire, and sweeping into the room in a vivid yellow dress with jet trimming on the bodice and jet earrings in her ears. By contrast, everyone else – even the men – looked faded and anaemic, Rosaleen thought.

Arthur Bennett was certainly impressed by the way Milliora looked and walked, even if Mary and Carmel probably wanted to kill her. Why do I feel protective about her, Rosaleen grumbled to herself – she's perfectly capable of looking after herself. But, all the same, she steered Milliora to the side of the fire away from the sisters, and settled her down in the Trafalgar chair with the pink seat and turned rope :notif that was her own favourite. A suitable throne for a queen – and sure enough Milliora was already behaving like one, even if, in her outfit, she looked more like a queen bee.

'I'm sorry I'm late,' she said to the room at large, 'but I was talking to Bishop O'Dwyer and that delayed me. A sensible man. I was glad to hear he is totally opposed to all this Land League nonsense. Apparently he has had threats on his life – can you imagine? – for daring to put forward his views.'

'He's always been opposed to Parnell,' Noel Leahy agreed. 'He fully supported the Roman Instruction prohibiting clerics from contributing to the Parnell Testimonial Fund for all he says he's a land reformer. Yes, Mary, what were you going to say?'

'There's some terrible scandal going round about Parnell,' Mary said. 'I heard it today from Kitty McCormac who heard it up in Dublin. She says Parnell is involved with Captain Willie O'Shea's wife.'

'Sure what's new about that?' Andy said irritably. 'We heard that months ago after O'Shea filed his divorce petition. Everyone knows 'tis only a rumour put out by those who oppose him to discredit Mr Parnell and Kitty McCormac's tongue has been bitter ever since Michael McInerney jilted her.'

'I don't know about that,' Mary said, enjoying the attention she was getting. 'Kitty knows the whole story. Oh, it would shock you, if you were to hear it, I can assure you of that.'

'Will you not tell it to us?' Arthur Bennett requested, mischievously. 'It can't be as bad as all that, surely!'

He was a gentle, well-spoken man, intelligent, and with a quiet sense of humour, thought Rosaleen, catching his eye and returning his smile. A nice man for Milly! How good it would be if no one had to worry about what would happen to Crag Liath and they could all look forward to its mistress marrying again.

'All right so, I'll tell you. Apparently – ' Mary leant forward and spoke in a hushed voice to indicate disillusion – 'Mrs O'Shea is not only involved with Parnell, *she's had a child by him already.*'

Much satisfied, she leant back and watched the shocked expressions. Milliora's cheeks were flushed and she looked particularly disapproving.

'How disgraceful to have a baby by a man who isn't your husband,' she said, forgetting to act the queen. 'What kind of a woman can this Mrs O'Shea be?'

No one was in a hurry to answer her question.

Then Rosaleen said quietly but quite distinctly, 'Maybe we should be considering what kind of a man is Captain Willie O'Shea?'

At dinner, Dermot was in good form, exchanging jokes about judges with Arthur Bennett and making everyone laugh.

'Justice Renihan has an eye for the women all right,' Arthur agreed after Dermot had had his turn. 'That last brief of yours, Dermot, the action brought by the two Halpin women: "Everything in this case is plain," says he, "except Mrs Halpin and her very charming daughter."'

Milliora joined in the laughter. Rosaleen had seated her next to Arthur and they seemed to be getting on well. Every so often Arthur turned to his companion, approving of what she was saying and smiling, gazing into her eyes a little longer than approbation required.

But Milly's not reciprocating as a *woman*, Rosaleen thought. She likes him – everybody likes Arthur – but only as a friend. There's no attraction from her side or, if there is, she will not allow it to be felt.

The talk around the table had moved away from the frivolous into a serious discussion about horses.

'Mount Royal is beginning to feel his age,' Dermot said, sadly. 'I'll have to replace him one of these days.'

'He's out to grass, is he?' Andy's interest was aroused by a subject nearer the land than law. 'The weather's good enough.'

'It is, but I find with Mount Royal if you turn him out too early and on good pasture he ends up too heavy for his legs. It's too much of a task getting rid of the fat before he can be got back into condition and he isn't up to a fast run any more. I could feel that last season. I should have taken Sprightly over from you, Milly. He's still in the stables, is he?'

'I gave him to Jamie Keegan a year or so back,' Milliora said, looking sad at the mention of Tom's old horse. 'Tom and he were so close, it seemed fitting. And if it wasn't for Jamie I don't know whether I'd have done as well as I have at Crag Liath over the last few years.'

'Well, I'm envious of you, Milly – I really am,' Dermot said. 'You're a clever girl. You've done a great job with Crag Liath and we all admire you.'

You could swear he meant it, Rosaleen thought, watching. Can *my* husband be as devious as this?

And Milliora was being deceived – was responding to his insincere songs of praises that were nothing but jibes at heart.

'You envious, Dermot?' she teased. 'Not you. You certainly don't live up to your name!'

'Do I have a name for being envious then?' Dermot enquired, more anxiously – Rosaleen thought – than he appeared.

302

And then Milliora took the wind out of both of their sails. 'I mean your Christian name – Dermot. It's the English version of Diarmuid – we all know that. You're the Irish speaker, Rosaleen. Didn't you know that Diarmuid means – literally – envy-free? It's such a good name for your husband. I always thought my brother-in-law the least envious of men.'

Rosaleen said: 'I should have thought of that a long time ago. So much for my proficiency in Irish!'

Watching the guests depart Rosaleen forgot, for a moment, that theirs was not a normal situation and that they could not converse like normal husband and wife.

'They all got on well together, didn't they? And Milly and Arthur seemed to hit it off. We must invite them together again one of these days.'

'Are you mad?' Dermot's fine face was pale with rage. 'What are you suggesting? Do you want to undermine my plan for regaining Crag Liath?'

'Of course I don't. I only suggested – '

'That we throw that woman into the company of an eligible man? *She mustn't marry*, Rosaleen – don't you understand that yet? She must be given no opportunity to produce children of her own!'

'Dermot, she's not interested that way in Arthur – you can see that. Milly is in love with the memory of Tom. She isn't looking for a husband.'

Dermot just glared at her. He swung away from the front door back into the hall, his nervous hands re-adjusting one of the fox's masks – moving a brass ornament a little to the right.

If only I could get away from him for a few days, Rosaleen thought – be on my own, without the surety that, tonight, he isn't coming back. I *have* to go to

Dublin, not only to attend John O'Leary's young writers' group but to rest from the tension that our marriage generates.

It was as good a time as any to raise the subject with Dermot, she decided – and it would distract him from endless reiteration of his hatred for Milly.

'I want to spend a few days in Dublin next week,' she said abruptly. 'I'll take the twins and Bridie with me and we can do some shopping and go to the sea and the zoo.'

Suddenly, she did not want to tell him of the meeting, aware that she wanted something in her life that was outside his intrusion. Envy-free! If only Milly knew what went on in Dermot's mind.

'Do you?' Dermot sounded dubious. 'Well, I suppose if you want to – '

'I do.'

He turned off the gaslight and with a candle in his hands went before her up the stairs, his shadow on the wall suddenly more ominous than the man himself.

He is the man I thought I knew – but his shadow is the dark reality, Rosaleen thought, following him reluctantly.

In the bedroom he undressed swiftly, returning his outer garments to the tallboy, placing them on hangers with his usual meticulous care. His shirt and under-clothes and socks he put in a white box with a tip-up lid intended for dirty clothes. He was naked, his body lithe and athletic and pale. Fully-clad, Rosaleen drew the curtains together and, turning, blew out the candle so he and the bed could no longer be seen.

'Hey!' Dermot protested, feeling around in the dark. He teased, as he sometimes did before making love to her: 'But I have supernatural powers, you know – fairy powers. I'm like the *Tuatha De Danann* – I can see in

304

the dark and make myself visible to human beings, if I wish to do so.'

There had been a time when she had been able to respond to this levity, in the days when she still believed in him and thought him a gentle and considerate lover. That faith had been irredeemably lost. There was no lightness, only the dark, in spite of Dermot's assertions of what he was able to do, and she had to force herself to accept him. Doing that was so dishonest, whatever the priests might say about the rules for marriage. Suddenly, she was angry, searching for an excuse to sabotage his atmosphere of love by picking an argument with him. And that, too, was dishonest and hateful and part of the thing she was trying to escape.

'Just for once I wish we could forget all about Crag Liath and the need for its restoration to your family and be content the way we are,' she said – and she realized that what she was saying was not dishonest but a final plea to Dermot to make their marriage work.

His voice came back: 'It's asking too much of you to try to understand. You were an O'Flynn. I am an O'Brien. I have the blood of kings running in my veins.'

In the darkness you could say things you would not say in the light.

She said, 'No, I am not an aristocrat, and no longhaired banshee tending her hair with a silver comb wails to say that I am dead.'

'What? Good God, Rosaleen, what did you have to drink?'

'Nothing,' she said, 'nothing to change the way I am.'

As she finally began to get out of her clothes she thought – for two, maybe three days next week I am going to be free.

19

Arriving in Dublin, Rosaleen booked her party into the Shelbourne Hotel, the red-brick and cream-stucco edifice gracing the ornamental landscape of trees and winding paths and artificial lakes of St Stephen's Green, to the delight of Daniel and Eugene and to Bridie's consternation.

They were not the only family up from the country staying there. The Shelbourne was an institution where mothers with marriageable daughters rented rooms for the two-month season. It was elegant and respectable, with a ladies' coffee-room and a hairdressing salon, illuminated by electricity and patronized both by the aristocracy and by leading lights from the nearby Gaiety Theatre.

'Oh, mam – 'tis terrible swanky.' Bridie – who had not been in Dublin before – was frightened by every aspect of the trip.

'Nonsense,' Rosaleen retorted. 'There's no need to be worried about anything. I have it all organized for you. Tomorrow, I want you to take the children to the zoo.'

'Lions,' Daniel said. 'And pigs and ducks and geese, the same as Crag Liath.'

'Tim-Pat is after telling me that the zoo is in the Phoenix Park, mam, where those terrible murders take place.'

'The Phoenix Park covers seventeen hundred acres of ground, Bridie,' Rosaleen said drily, 'and the zoo-logical gardens occupy thirty of them. You'll have

306

plenty of people all around you and you won't be anywhere near where those two men – only two – got murdered long ago. *And* they caught the killers after a year – a group called the Invincibles. It was a political murder – nothing to do with the likes of us. Children, do you know where the Phoenix Park gets its name from?'

'No,' said Daniel, bored.

Eugene, she could see, was equally disinterested. Persisting, despite their indifference, she said, 'It comes from *Fionn Uisge*. That means clear water.'

They looked at her blankly. Surveying them ruefully, she remembered her idealism when the twins were born. The greatest enemy of the Irish language sometimes seemed less adult apathy than the resistance of her own children who did not want to learn but far preferred to play.

Tomorrow, they could enjoy the zoo while she spent time in less-loved but – why deny it? – more stimulating adult company.

The twins, having breakfasted on broiled herrings, had been despatched with Bridie on their outing and Rosaleen walked down Grafton Street, looking in the shops. In Bewley's Coffee House, the ladies of the smart Dublin suburbs, in their silk dresses and coats from Barnado's the Italian furriers, ate sticky cherry buns and discussed last night's successful rendering of *La Traviata* at the Gaiety Theatre.

Further on, in College Green, she could glower at Trinity College, founded for the Protestant Anglo-Irish, its Palladian façade flanked by statues of Burke and Goldsmith. Opposite, above the pediments surrounding the Ionic portico of the Bank of Ireland, other statues represented Hibernia, Fidelity and Com-

307

merce, although the bank had originally been built to house the Irish Parliament.

Rosaleen strolled along in her red walking-dress with its white lace collar and cuffs, holding a red umbrella over her head to catch the slight rain, stimulated by the vibrancy of the city – the street-harper strumming away, the children whipping their tops, the revivalist preaching as the police stood by and the traffic – four-wheelers and side-cars, trams and ass-carts – adding to the din. The streets were filthy, lined with a patina of dust and mud, laced with horse-droppings, and the rain, falling softly but incessantly, at once reduced this exfoliation to a membrane of damp slush which ruined skirt hems and shoes.

The bridge where the quays flaunted second-hand bookstalls and the Liffey stank of old horrors, took her from the lifestyle of the privileged to that of the people of the slums, where one room housed a hungry family. On previous visits to Dublin, when she had been with Dermot, she had tended to shut thoughts of the hungry out of her head, to bury it instead in a book, or concentrate on looking at the good things Sackville Street offered – at the handsome General Post Office, the smart Gresham Hotel, Nelson's Pillar where everybody met.

Now, she was going to look at ugly things and take their memory with her. When she got back to Limerick, she decided, she would tell Dermot that she was going to work for the poor there, as the good Lady Aberdeen, wife of the Lord Lieutenant of Ireland, worked for the poor and dispossessed children of Dublin, although she was famed in the west, as well. A new hotel – a magnificent Norwegian building capable of holding any number of guests, had been built at Lahinch, the popular west-coast holiday resort, and had been named in her honour. Dermot wanted to stay there in the summer, saying that the holiday would do their marriage good.

Much later, Rosaleen found herself in Cork Street where the coffin-makers lived, having watched women waiting for the pawnbroker to open his premises so they could pawn their husbands' suits and shoes for money to feed their babies. There were other women too, with painted faces, who got money from men for selling, not their clothes but their bodies, and who jeered as she passed by, for she was the only well-dressed woman there and they had no way of knowing that it was compassion she felt for them, not scorn.

By the time she got back to the Shelbourne she was tired but – in spite of the sights she had seen – she was no longer depressed. A journey to the slums of Dublin might be a lot less pleasurable than shopping for clothes in Grafton Street – and she intended to do that, too – but like her visit to the market in Limerick, it transferred the focus of her attention from her own deadness to the problems of other people's lives.

Rosaleen lunched at the Shelbourne; Cathal O'Mahoney took his with the old Fenian James Stephens in another part of Dublin.

Stephens, diminished in power and almost forgotten by the authorities, had been allowed to live out his old age peacefully in Ireland. In the past, Cathal had been in two minds about the man who had requested John O'Mahoney's retirement from office. True, Cousin John had made an abortive attempt to possess Campobello Island, near Lubec in Maine, for a Fenian homeland and naval base, but then Stephens had gone ahead and filled his job himself.

But that was in the past and, apart from using the

old man's contacts to find possible recruits for the movement, Cathal had simply wanted to ask him what ultimate hope he could see for its success – a feeble enough question if you subtracted his own conviction of being, along with Stephens and Cousin John and all the others who had gone before them, a link in freedom's chain.

The outcome of their meeting was more heartening than Cathal had dared to hope. It was patience that was needed, Stephens reiterated. Soon, the wind of renaissance would blow through the country, sowing the seed of a new pride in self – in Irishness – and when that happened, Cathal's time would come. Look at the way the hearts of the young were being reached already, he said, through the inspired politicism of the Gaelic Athletic Association.

'All over the country, Cathal, young men playing a game of hurling are forced to remember their proud ancestors who did the same. You remember the legend: the young Setanta going along to Chulainn's house for a feast, amusing himself with his hurley and ball along the way, then being beset by a watchdog and having to drive the ball down the animal's throat? *Cu Chulainn* – Hound of Chulainn, they called Setanta after that. Of course, that wasn't the only reference to hurling in the Celtic sagas.

'The technical terms in hurling only exist in the Irish language, Cathal. As they play, the young are learning to speak it, and feel a pride in their race. Didn't the Greeks have the same idea, uniting the nation in the playing of ball-games, two and a half thousand years back? But only *we* have developed the concept. We have to make the young believe in their Irishness before we can persuade them to fight for it again. The time will come – it *is* coming – and you must have the patience to sit it out.'

'How long?' Cathal demanded.

The man opposite shrugged, his old, gnarled hands lying on the table, blue-veined and pearly white.

'Historically, there have been fifty years between rebellions. So in ten – maybe twenty years. A lifetime to you – now; a short time in terms of the years of our subjugation. You must learn to wait.'

That is the worst part, Cathal thought – the waiting. And never knowing how long you have to wait.

'What is the range of your movement outside the Limerick and Clare districts?' Stephens asked him.

'Coming along slowly. You know the apathy.'

'Only too well. Fight against it. I say it to you again – your time will come.'

Two hours later, they were still talking. Cathal almost forgot his other arrangement and when he did remember he thought he would leave it. Then he realized Stephens was tired.

Rosaleen underestimated the amount of time she needed to get to John O'Leary's house and she arrived to find herself the only woman in a gathering of men.

To make matters worse, most people seemed to know each other very well. Chairs and sofas were pulled up close together and everyone was preparing to listen to a young man with a pouting mouth and a shock of untidy hair who was standing up at the top of the room.

She found an empty chair in a dark corner near the door and shrank into it, hoping not to be noticed.

'Our poetry should have a local habitation when at all possible,' the young man began. 'We should make poems on the familiar landscapes we love, not the

311

strange and glittering ones we wonder at. There was a time when I preferred to all other countries Arcadia and the India of romance, but presently I convinced myself that I should never go for the scenery of a poem to any country but my own.'

At the back of the room there was a rustle as another late-comer slipped inside, murmuring apology. Chairs scraped as several people moved up to let the miscreant get through.

'*Ssh!*' said an exasperated listener, looking round, glaring.

'Sorry. Excuse me . . .'

Concentrating on the speaker's words, captivated by what he was saying, Rosaleen was not distracted herself until a tall figure loomed up beside her and with a relieved sigh sat down in an adjacent chair.

Instinctively, she glanced to her right, saw the profile of a long, pale face, a thick, dark moustache, light brown hair worn long at the nape of an elongated neck.

Her heart seemed to leap right into her mouth and stay there. She had one coherent thought – she was glad she was wearing her red walking-dress and looking – she hoped – rather good.

'. . . you can only attain through what is near you, your nation, or, if you be no traveller, your village and the cobwebs on your walls. You can no more have the greatest poetry without a nation than religion without symbols. One can only reach out to the universe with a gloved hand. That glove is one's nation, the only thing one knows even a little of . . .'

The young man with the untidy hairstyle was utterly enthralling. There was no excuse for not listening to him – unless you had in your mind's eye a three-year-old vision of two people under a tree, also talking of poetry. The magic-maker, she had thought of this other

312

young man in the interim since they had met, and the time they had spent together she had thought of as enchanted.

But she had no business thinking of young men at all – of young men other than her husband, and she must try to concentrate on the speaker's words.

'One should love best what is nearest and most interwoven with one's life. I'm working now on my play, *The Countess Kathleen*. It's Irish through and through, founded on a west of Ireland folk-tale. When that is done I mean to write a series of Irish ballads – folk-tales from Sligo set into rhyme . . .'

There is magic, Rosaleen told herself firmly, sticking her chin in the air, a poet speaking of his own work. The young man next to me, after all, only read from someone else's.

All the same, she was acutely conscious of the tall figure sitting in the chair beside her. *He* – annoyingly – was oblivious of her presence or, indeed, of anything but the fine words spoken by the man at the top of the room.

Mr W. B. Yeats – a young genius, Cathal thought, surveying the speaker. Fascinated, he did not look round until the meeting ended. Then he blinked in surprise and once more wondered if – like the last time they met – he had fallen into a dream.

'Aoibheal!' he said, spontaneously. 'What are you doing here?'

'Rosaleen O'Brien,' she corrected. 'What's your name? I never knew what it was.'

Mr Yeats and his friends had spilled over into the garden. John O'Leary, having seen them off, had gone indoors, and Rosaleen was standing against a bed of daffodils – a flower, Cathal thought, against flowers. Her lips were very red. And very, very soft.

Impelled by his need to hold on to the lady, lest she slip away and out of his life again, Cathal said, 'Would you care to join me for tea? Newly-iced cakes, do you think – and freshly-baked scones from a yet-to-be-discovered tea-room?'

'More than anything I would like tea,' Rosaleen said, and, without further ado, followed him over the lawn and down the avenue to the road, to catch a tram to town.

'Are you a friend of John O'Leary's?'

'You're wondering how I got to be the only woman in a room full of men. Father Matt Ryan – you've heard of Father Matt? – he had an invitation to come here and he passed it on to me.'

'And how do you know the admirable Father Matt?'

Rosaleen laughed. 'It's a long story. I may tell you over tea. What did you think of the meeting?'

'Who wouldn't enjoy listening to Mr Yeats?'

'Mr – ? You mean that was – '

'The poet and the editor. He's a grand writer – and will be more grand still. Do you know his poems?'

'A little. I sometimes read the *Gael*. His poems are – like looking at a painting.'

'He is the son of an artist,' Cathal said, 'and so he paints with words. You must read *The Wanderings of Oisin*. He's used the story of Oisin in Tir na nOg but interpreting it in his own way, stressing our struggle for independence.'

Only the poem under discussion was different. Otherwise, they might have been back at the end of the boreen, talking as they had talked three years earlier. Then too, the real world had been eclipsed by a poet's magic phrases. The tram rattled through wide streets sullen with excrement and neither of them noticed, any more than they noticed the simple grandeur of brick-fronted Georgian houses, the flower-stands outside them, or the equestrian statues that were also headed towards town, being too interested in what they had to say to each other.

'Where are you staying?' Cathal asked, finally.

Jerked back into the real world, Rosaleen was suddenly aware of her responsibilities towards Daniel and Eugene who, by now, might have returned from the zoo.

At the same time, she was beseiged by disquiet and foreboding. Should she – a married woman – be sitting in a tram-car with a man who was not her husband, planning to take tea with him, and loving every moment she was spending in his company? Of course, she should not. She should tell him, without explanation, that she had changed her mind . . .

'At the Shelbourne.'

'Then perhaps we should have our tea there.'

Now isn't that better? said Rosaleen to her conscience. The Shelbourne was so respectable. The twins, if they were back, could join Mr O'Mahoney and herself for tea.

'Yes, that would be best,' she said, relieved, yet disappointed that she knew what would happen at the end of the tram-ride.

There was no sign of Bridie and Daniel and Eugene. They took tea in Rosaleen's favourite room in the Shelbourne, the pillared drawing-room, where the ceiling was adorned with delicate plaster-work and fresco cameos, and the Adam-style fireplaces were inlaid with wood. In this familiarity the nudge of unease that had been plaguing her ceased its irritation.

As for her inhibition about being with a man who

315

was not her husband, she could tell herself that it was not as if Mr O'Mahoney was a flirtatious sort of man. He was very circumspect, interested only in discussing poetry with her, a most harmless occupation.

A hundred and twenty miles from Kincora she found it quite easy to fantasize about what she could achieve when she went back. She would invite Mr O'Mahoney to dinner and turn him into a family friend. He would be no good for Milliora, who was uninterested in poetry or any literature, but with his intellect and love of Irish he could have a good influence on the male members of her own family, persuading them that they could be interested in cultural matters without losing their own masculinity, as some men seemed to fear. This was a message that the twins – encouraged by their father to concentrate more on horses than on literature – needed to hear from the lips of a man.

She wondered guiltily where Daniel and Eugene were at this moment. Over tea, she had not thought of them at all.

'I'll just go and look for my children. They should be back from the zoo by now,' she told Cathal.

'Your children are *here*?'

He hoped he did not sound as alarmed as he felt. Tim-Pat had given him a reassuring description of how he had fobbed off the O'Briens with a story about finding Daniel wandering in the garden after his unexpected appearance in the secret room, and apparently they had believed it. What would Rosaleen think if Daniel came into the Shelbourne and greeted Cathal like a friend!

'You never told me your children were with you,' he said, keeping an eye out for a familiar red head and ready to spring to his feet and disappear if it came into sight.

316

'Oh, didn't I? Yes, I brought them with me, and our maid along with them. She took them out for the day but they should be back by now.'

Damnation, thought Cathal, knowing he should flee but reluctant to depart. The more time he spent in Aoibheal-Rosaleen's company, the longer he wanted to stay. Her intellect was only part of her attraction. Rosaleen might think him circumspect, and he was doing his best to appear so, but she would have been perturbed had she known that he was presently more interested in touching her body than her mind. Her red walking-dress camouflaged most of what he was after, but it made no attempt to conceal the shape of her breasts and the contrast between her tiny waist and the puff of her rounded hips. Neither the age in which he lived nor the dictates of the Church intimidated Cathal. He refused to listen to either of them and frown on his own natural urges, welcoming them instead.

Natural urges, however, could get a man into terrible trouble, especially in Ireland, where sex and guilt were intertwined. You only needed a breath of scandal to lose credibility with all and sundry, the men as well as the women, he knew well. Look at the rumours about Parnell and Mrs O'Shea. As for himself, his own men, with the ascetic outlooks of revolutionaries, would be far from happy if he were to get entangled with someone else's wife.

'So if you'll excuse me for a minute, I'll go and check,' said Aoibheal, disappearing in search of her sons.

Twins, Tim-Pat had said, adding that they were dissimilar. Three years old and one of them a threat.

What was he thinking of, to be sitting in the Shelbourne, risking confrontation with Daniel? He had to get away before the boy appeared.

Equally important was the need to keep contact with the child's mother, to see her again before she left Dublin, and maybe to plan to see her in Limerick as well, if she would allow him. The worst of it was, he did not even know when Aoibheal-Rosaleen planned to leave Dublin.

Rosaleen's red purse was lying near her empty cakeplate, ensuring that, even if Cathal was missing when she came back to the tea-room, she would be obliged to retrieve it from the table.

Glancing around again to make sure that Daniel was not coming, he took out of his pocket a copy of Yeats's *Oisin* and flipped quickly through the pages until he came to his favourite passage.

> See you where Oisin and young Niam ride
> Wrapt in each other's arms, and where the Finians
> Follow their hounds along the fields of tapestry . . .

Someday – soon – he would read all the lines to Rosaleen and maybe, then, she would be wrapped in his arms, after returning his kisses . . .

There was no time for sexual conjecture. Beckoning to a waiter to bring pen and ink to the table he encircled these lines and wrote above them in tiny letters:

Mrs O'Brien, I have been unexpectedly called away. I will return to the Shelbourne at eight and will enquire at the desk for you. Will you accept an invitation to lunch with me tomorrow?

By eight, the charming but intrusive Daniel should be in bed like every three-year-old and safely out of the way.

Propping the open book up against Rosaleen's teacup, he walked out of the drawing-room into the

318

hotel foyer. As luck would have it, the coach making the round trip to Bray and Greystones had returned, disgorging its passengers. There were people everywhere around him, talking about the beauty of the south Dublin coastline and their enjoyment of the day. Tall as Cathal was, they formed a human screen about him as he sidled through.

He had reached the reading-room when he spotted Rosaleen at the far end of the foyer, holding the hands of two small boys, one of whom was only too familiar, and talking to what was obviously the maid. His exit was effectively blocked off.

But the reading-room was well supplied with the latest newspapers and magazines. By the time Rosaleen and the twins, with Bridie in their wake, passed by, Cathal was sitting in there in a comfortable armchair, *The Times* in front of his face.

'Eugene is terrible fractious,' Bridie said, as soon as Rosaleen came up to her.

And Eugene did look cross and flushed and bothered, and not even pleased to see his mother.

'Did you not enjoy the zoo, darling?'

'No,' Eugene said, grumpily, just as Daniel said, 'I did.'

'Is he over-tired?'

'He says he's hot,' Bridie said, worried, 'and that his throat is sore.'

'I think he's probably over-tired. Maybe they're too young to take to Dublin.'

'*I'm* not too young,' Daniel said indignantly, scowling at his twin.

Eugene's bottom lip quivered and he put up his free hand to wipe away a tear.

319

'Take them upstairs,' Rosaleen said hastily to Bridie. 'I'll be with you in a couple of minutes.'

It was high time she attended to her duties and gave Bridie a rest, she thought. It was a pity she would have to leave such an interesting discussion but, after all, as a mother, she had to have more on her mind than poetry and philosophical thoughts. Mr O'Mahoney would have to understand.

But she owed it to him to say goodnight – and goodbye. Their farewell need only be for the moment. In due course, Mr O'Mahoney could come to dinner, as she had planned, and meet Dermot and the boys. One of whom was howling as he was propelled towards the stairs. Bridie was right – he *was* fractious and out of sorts. But maybe he just needed a good sleep. She would explain the situation to the waiting Mr O'Mahoney.

Only he was not waiting. Their table was empty. She felt strangely deprived, as if she had been given a long-coveted present by someone who had, just as unpredictably, taken it away.

About to sit down at the table and wait for Cathal to reappear she noticed the book propped up against her cup, saw that three lines had been encircled and that someone – he – had written a message in letters so small she could barely read them.

Unexpectedly called away. What inconsiderate person had prized Mr Cathal O'Mahoney away the minute her back was turned?

At several nearby tables sat mothers with daughters who had come to the Shelbourne for the express purpose of catching satisfactory husbands. Some were less attractive, one was plump and ugly, but several were lovely and very well turned-out. Dublin was noted all over the world for the beauty of its women. Had Mr O'Mahoney been summonsed by a lady?

She blushed at the thought. She felt stranded – cross with Cathal for having deserted his post. And then she was cross with herself for all the foolish thoughts she was having. Like the boys, she was tired, and should take herself to bed. Only she could not go to bed – or not until after eight, because Mr O'Mahoney was returning.

She tried not to ponder over how he could be spending the interim as she made her way up to the second-floor rooms taken for herself, Bridie and the twins. The door to the suite was ajar and from the landing Rosaleen could hear a continuing altercation between the boys.

'Will you be after leaving him alone!' Bridie wearily admonished one or the other.

'He has a nose like a *banh!*' Daniel or maybe Eugene said as their mother got to the door.

Bridie, she saw at once, was on the verge of tears.

'It's not nice to compare your brother to a piglet,' Rosaleen said severely. 'I'm going to put the two of you to bed. Come on now – stop this fighting.'

It took all her store of patience to get them there but, by eight, they were finally asleep.

Rosaleen patted her hair into place, pinched her cheeks for colour, and went downstairs to say good-night – and goodbye for the present – to the elusive Mr O'Mahoney.

20

Cathal had plans for Rosaleen that took little account of immediate farewells and when they met he began to explore the feasibility of putting them into action.

'When did you say you were leaving Dublin?' he asked, before she had a chance to say a word. 'On Thursday? What a coincidence. That's the day I'm off myself. *Are* you free for lunch tomorrow?'

Seeing her hesitate he rushed on: 'You see, I thought you might be interested in hearing more about John O'Leary and his aspirations. O'Leary himself would approve of my talking to you. He is anxious that as many people as possible share his ideas for using literature as a vehicle of nationality.'

Not so far from the truth after all, he thought. O'Leary would certainly approve of such a talk, although their ultimate intentions might be rather different.

The strategy worked.

'You're right. I *am* interested in Mr O'Leary's ideas. I had arranged for the children to be taken to the sea tomorrow so – '

'You *are* free!' said Cathal, happily. 'Which side of Dublin are they going to?'

'Bray and Greystones,' Rosaleen said. 'They're going with Bridie – that's our maid – on the *Hirondelle*. I thought they might enjoy a coach-trip. Why?'

'I just wondered,' said Cathal, nonchalantly.

Bray and Greystones were on the south side of

Dublin. The greater the distance between himself and the boys the safer he was.

'I've always loved the north coast myself,' he said, 'Malahide and Sutton and Howth Head. In fact, I had Howth in the mind as a venue for lunch. Would you like that? We could go to Sutton by train and on to Howth by tram.'

He sounded beyond suspicion. What harm could there possibly be in going on such an innocent excursion, Rosaleen asked herself, since they would be using public transport and remaining in public view? And, all the time, she would be learning more about her own literature and heritage.

Bridie, of course, might not understand the purity of her – of *their* – motives, being an unsophisticated countrygirl, and the boys might be jealous that she was opting for Mr O'Mahoney's company rather than for theirs. She had intended to shop for clothes the following day and had already told them of her intentions. Perhaps it would be better if they believed her plans unchanged.

'That sounds very pleasant,' she said to Cathal. 'I must see the boys off first – before I meet you . . .'

But he was a step ahead of her. 'The *Hirondelle* leaves here at ten o'clock. Shall we say I call for you here at ten-thirty, to allow for travelling time to Howth?'

'Ten-thirty. Good-night, Mr O'Mahoney.'

'Good-night, Mrs O'Brien.'

He nodded, and left.

Lying in bed, hardly sleeping, Rosaleen said to herself that her sense of excitement about the following days's excursion was entirely due to her interest in John O'Leary's work.

Cathal, on the other hand, had no need to practise

such self-deception. He wanted Rosaleen badly and although, in truth, he saw little prospect of getting her, he was driven by the oldest need to do his very best.

'Because our literature is not being translated into other languages, Europe has no knowledge of its richness,' Cathal said as the little train trundled past the spot where Brian Boru had broken the power of the Danes long ago. 'If we want to secure our proper place in the history of western culture we must do this job ourselves.'

'But first we have to ensure that we can speak our own language.'

'Of course.' He paused, thinking for a moment, then added, 'In a way, that sounds arrogant, intimating that there has been no previous attempts to highlight our cultural riches. That's not so. A hundred years ago, as you probably know, Dr Sylvester O'Halloran of Limerick played a notable part in the foundation of the Royal Irish Academy so that serious research could be done into the sources of our civilization. But all that was in the hands of scholars, and stayed there. We need to reach the *people*. As an old Fenian, O'Leary understands that well.'

'Have you been friends with Mr O'Leary for a long time?'

That put him on the spot. It had been part of his strategy to imply that he and O'Leary were close. Damn, he thought. He was not a natural liar and she was not a woman to whom anyone should lie since her own purity shone out from her lovely eyes and demanded truth in return. Yet he had been forced to lie to her already on a number of occasions, to get more of her company and to protect his work.

'I don't actually know him very well,' he said. 'I only know his work.'

To his surprise, she seemed content with that. It was he who was uneasy with himself. What kind of a fool was he, anyway, to think that he could have his way with her? She was obviously a good woman, and a perfect wife.

Lucky Mr Dermot O'Brien.

Yet Mr Dermot O'Brien – by all accounts a successful solicitor; by Tim-Pat Tierney's, a reincarnated saint – Mr O'Brien did not seem to have reached the essence of this woman. There was a loneliness in her, as well as a quest for knowledge, neither of which had been satisfied by her relationship with her husband, so that she was vulnerable and a challenge to him.

'Look,' she said. 'I can see the sea.'

'It's a pity we haven't more time to explore this side of Dublin,' said Cathal. 'It would have been grand to have taken you to Malahide to see the castle, or the round tower at Swords. Although, when it all boils down, I prefer the west coast myself. I suppose I'm basically a countryman.'

'You don't like Dublin?'

'It's a fine city but it's run by a professional aristocracy – doctors, lawyers, businessmen. If you've walked around the Grafton Street area, you will have seen the wealth.'

'Yes.'

'That's on the one hand. On the other, the majority of unskilled workers in the city are forced to feed and house their families on less than a pound a week. Rents go up to four shillings. The tenements are overcrowded and there are beggars in the streets.'

'Aren't the charities doing anything?'

'St Vincent de Paul is doing a lot. The other Catholic

charities are too preoccupied with keeping the orphans out of the clutches of the Protestant sects to take note of the needs of the slums.'

'Are you not a Catholic, Mr O'Mahoney?'

'I am, but that should not stop anyone from making critical judgements. I'm critical of the society, too. The city is divided on all sorts of deep-seated fronts: religious, social, political. Divided, the rich and talented are less disposed to dole out loyalty, commitment and energy to the poor. They're better over in England at doing that than we are. Maybe the trouble with oppressed people is that they feel they can't afford to grow a heart.'

Like Dermot, thought Rosaleen, involuntarily. But in the last hour her life with Dermot had receded and for a moment she was unable to conjure up his face. Daniel and Eugene, too – although in no sense abandoned – were tucked up and out of sight in a compartment of her mind to which, temporarily, she was not paying attention.

She reminded herself that Dermot was much more handsome than the man facing her in the compartment of the Sutton train. Dermot has a fine face, she told herself sternly. He has the deep blue eyes of the O'Briens, and thick, dark hair.

Whereas this man – his face was too long and his eyes, although nicely set, were too indeterminate a blue to be rated as attractive.

But there was nothing indeterminate about the man himself. He was not only intelligent, but sensitive, and she was sure that deep down he was truly good and absolutely honest.

As the little train pulled into Sutton Station the fire of her conversation with Cathal, which had already set light to the present, began to spread. The station, the beach, and the white-flecked, sun-mocked sea – photographs for her album of memory – were illuminated by this blaze. Cold as she had always been, it seemed entirely natural that she should be responding to this warmth.

The isthmus at Sutton led to Howth Head and village, once an island. The tram climbed south-east from the village to make a circle of the peninsula, affording panoramic views of Dublin Bay and the Wicklow Hills.

In the seat in front of Rosaleen and Cathal a child with long golden ringlets gazed at them with hostile blue eyes, her bottom lip stuck out petulantly.

Rosaleen laughed. 'Horrible child,' she said softly so the mother would not hear.

'Not like yours?'

'Sometimes like mine,' she admitted. 'Eugene was dreadful last evening and not much better this morning before they went off. I don't know what got into him. You must visit us and meet the boys when we all get back to Limerick. Dermot – my husband – would like to meet you.'

'I'll look forward to that,' said Cathal.

He was beginning to hate himself for his insincerity. But what can I do, he asked himself – tell her about our meetings – reveal everything? What choice do I have but to deceive?

He heard Rosaleen giggle beside him. Looking up, he saw that the child with the golden ringlets was pulling a hideous face.

He pulled another, for the satisfaction of hearing Rosaleen laugh aloud.

'I have a whole series of terrible faces,' he said. 'I used to practise on my brother.'

'A younger brother?'

'He's older than I am. He went off and joined the Jesuits. We went to Clongowes, the two of us – it gave Seamus the taste for the Jays.'

'But not you?'

'No. I had enough of them at school. My mother was bitten by the same bug as Seamus, though. After my father died she went off and joined the Poor Clares. She said she had always envied the lives of nuns. They had no responsibilities, she said, and she liked the thought of that.'

'And you – are you – married?'

She asked the question with trepidation, at the same time telling herself not to be silly.

'Of course I'm not!' Cathal said, startled at the notion and for no reason that she could fathom they both began to laugh.

The tram came to a halt.

'We're here.'

As she emerged into the village of steep streets she remembered something and challenged him: 'Did you know that the name Howth is derived from the Norse word *hoved*, meaning head?'

'No, I didn't,' he said. 'But I'll tell you what I *do* know . . .'

'What?'

'That I'm very hungry and I know a marvellous place for lunch.'

Over a meal of pink poached salmon and delicious new potatoes Rosaleen put on the blindfold worn by would-be lovers who are not free to go ahead, convincing herself that, because being with Cathal was so natural and pleasing, it was also fundamentally right, blessed by God and smiled upon by Heaven.

'Look out the window. You can see Ireland's Eye from here,' Cathal said, pointing to the island.

'There's a church on it.'

'There used to be an early Christian monastery. Sometime it would be pleasant to go over there by boat.'

'Sometime.'

'We would be taking our lives into our hands,' Cathal said, straight-faced. 'What if the sea fairies do not like us? Or what if they take us off to live in Tir fo Thiunn?'

Why did she laugh when this man talked of fairies and frowned when her husband did?

'Maybe it's pleasant living in the Land Beneath the Waves,' she smiled, and looked into the blue eyes that she had rated indeterminate. And could not look away.

Not for an instant did her mind make the admission that her eyes were making.

'I think I am beginning to love you,' the violet-blue eyes said to the man across the table.

'I want you,' all of Cathal shouted silently back.

'You really should see the view from further up the hill before we go back to Dublin,' Cathal said later that afternoon. 'It's still a little early. We have time.'

'Can we not see it from the tram?'

'It doesn't do it real justice. You need to be further up the hill again. I tell you what – we can take the tram part of the way, then get out and walk for a while and afterwards catch the next tram back to Sutton. What do you say?'

'Can you see the whole of Dublin Bay from the top?' asked Rosaleen, with her blindfold on again.

'And the Wicklow Hills. At the very top, on the Ben of Howth, there is a cairn over the remains of King Crimthan Niadhnair. But if you would prefer a look at the Bailey lighthouse to the grave of a king who lived around A.D. 90 we could walk along the cliff in that direction. Which would you prefer?'

'I think the Bailey lighthouse.'

'That's fine by me,' said Cathal.

Every so often, his conscience gave him a good nudge, reminding him that he was playing truant, that he had cancelled an appointment made for him by a contact of James Stephens', a clerk with a small house on the north side of the city where Cathal was sharing a room with a counterhand from Clery's Stores, in order to be here.

Tomorrow – he tried to appease conscience – tomorrow, I will work.

Which, in turn, necessitated making the most of what today might bring.

Despite this resolution, he was beset by a darker and more serious mood by the time he and Rosaleen left the tram and began to make their way further up the hill.

This walk, which he had taken twice before in company, remained an essentially solitary experience, forcing each participant into the awareness of being one with sky and cliff and sea, assuming their greyness. The path was narrow and Rosaleen walked behind him. The sea itself was a vast desolate expanse. There were no boats in sight, only the occasional gull swooping to plunder.

Rosaleen, avoiding potholes and loose stones with the expertise of the country walker, was happier than Cathal, lulled by false righteousness and numb to the premonition of danger.

The cliff path widened again, permitting her to catch up with him and she hurried to take her place at his side.

'Your book – *Oisin*. I gave it back to you on the tram, remember? I think you've left it in the restaurant.'

'I'm notoriously careless,' Cathal said.

He stopped, forcing her to do likewise, and swinging round, looked again into the violet-blue eyes that spoke of more than love beginning.

Giving her no chance to veer from this admission, he quickly pulled her into his arms, and pressed his lips on hers. She was encased in whalebone and inundated with petticoats, only her mouth and hands remaining free to feel and transmit passion. Her lips, urged by his, parted; her hands, tense and pleading, met at the nape of his neck. Tongues touching spoke the first, unhesitating, clear words of the lusty love language she had stumbled over with Dermot.

Their mutual desire, the intoxicating wild encouragement of sea and cliff and sky, should have led them on to making love. They were baulked by a schoolboys' expedition to the hill.

Tousled, she broke away from him.

'I can hear voices.'

'More than that,' Cathal said wryly as the first stocky figures came stumping into view.

His chance was gone and he knew it. No woman – let alone a woman with sons of her own – could be seduced after such an invasion.

The schoolboys were their chaperons at the lighthouse and followed in their footsteps back to the tramtracks. They were not alone again until they were back in the city.

In a hackney, on the way from Amiens Street, via the Custom House and quays, to the Shelbourne, he reached for her warm hand.

'Tomorrow – at the same time? Can you leave the children?'

She nodded.

The enchanted day had ended. Before he could offer to assist her down she had slipped out of the hackney and, with the same agility, had vanished inside the hotel.

She heard Eugene's sobs long before she reached the boys' room and, holding her dress and petticoats high above her ankles, she ran silently and swiftly along the corridor.

Before she could insert her key in the lock, the door was wrenched open and Bridie, holding the weeping child in her arms, was standing before her, tears of her own trickling freely down her cheeks.

'What's the matter?' whispered Rosaleen, fiercely. 'Has something happened to Daniel? Is that why Eugene's upset?'

But she could see her other son already, sitting up in his small bed, wide-eyed at the noise.

'What's the *matter*, Bridie?'

'Oh, mam,' said Bridie, weakly, 'I thought 'twas murdered you were when you didn't come back and Eugene is terrible sick.'

When Eugene had fallen into a restless, feverish sleep and Bridie and Daniel were sleeping soundly, Rosaleen saw the events of the day in her imagination as a series of pictures, all of them castigating her for having committed grievous sin.

As the hours went by, it became clearer and clearer how God had shown his disapproval for her behaviour by making Eugene sick.

She was no better than a harlot – a slut from Poole

Street or Faddle Alley, instead of the wife of Dermot O'Brien, a respectable solicitor, and the mother of two fine sons. Imagine letting Cathal O'Mahoney fondle and kiss her like that. No wonder God was wild!

The shameful picture kaleidoscoped over and over, and she blushed, watching herself respond to Cathal's kiss. She had been oblivious to everything else and had nearly been compromised before a party of schoolboys.

Obsessed with the vision of herself as – almost – a prostitute, she remembered only the physical details of this encounter: her open mouth, the touching tongues, and forgot the psychological affinity that she had known with Cathal.

Behind it all – and by four in the morning she understood this perfectly – was the Devil, luring her into mortal sin and at the same time weaving a web of false security, convincing her that being with Cathal was all right. More than that – was *good*.

It was frighteningly true what the priests told you of the easy way the Devil could get himself into your life. His adroitness and deviousness stunned her. He was as strong as fifty horses and she should have been on guard.

As for poor Cathal, she had been responsible for his mortal sin as well, allowing the kiss to happen so easily. *Not* Cathal – Mr O'Mahoney he would be from now on, if she ever saw him again.

This was unlikely. She had announced to Bridie that she was taking them all home on the eight o'clock train in the morning, after which she had every intention of being a good mother and wife, staying at home with the children instead of having a life outside the house.

She had already written a note to Cathal – Mr O'Mahoney – explaining that she could not see him again and she would leave it at the downstairs desk before they left in the morning. She hoped he would have the good sense and common decency not to try to contact her again.

Meanwhile, there was Eugene to consider. Scarlet fever was Bridie's diagnosis and she was inclined to agree with it. She must get them all back to Limerick first thing in the morning. If the hotel suspected that Eugene was infectious they could be placed under quarantine.

What if Eugene were to die from the disease? What if Daniel, too, got sick and suffered the same fate? Could God allow these things to happen?

She thought that He could. She had angered Him so greatly He must be sorely tempted to give her all that she deserved.

'Please, God, don't let the boys die – for Dermot's sake, if not for mine,' she pleaded, down on her knees in the night.

Poor Dermot, who had already been wronged – although he was unaware of it – and now stood in danger of being further punished because of his wife's behaviour.

'. . . faithful and chaste may she marry in Christ, and remain an imitator of holy women,' ran the words of the prayer from the Mass for bridegroom and bride.

From now on, she would be true to those words. She would never be alone with Mr O'Mahoney again.

Or even lay eyes on him.

'So please don't let Eugene die,' she whispered, and buried within herself the conviction that, in casting Cathal O'Mahoney out of her life she was meekly accepting another kind of death, against which she had rebelled before.

21

'Scarlet fever,' said Dr Walshe the following afternoon. 'See the spots behind the ears? He'll have them all over in no time.'

'Poor little boy – he's boiling hot, as well,' his mother said sadly. 'No, Eugene, don't move. You have to stay in bed and Daniel can't come in here.'

'Mind you, the other fellow is bound to get it as well,' Dr Walshe said lugubriously. 'With the two of them sharing a room the rest of the time, I'd say you were wasting your time trying to stave it off.'

'Daniel is always lucky,' Rosaleen insisted, clinging on to any vestige of hope. 'I'm going to send him out to my sister-in-law's – she'll have him to stay.'

'She won't if she hasn't had scarlet fever herself!' Dr Walshe seemed determined to be miserable. 'Keep Eugene in bed with the curtains drawn and give him plenty of water to sip. I hope you don't get it yourself.'

'I had it as a child,' Rosaleen said, 'and so did my sister-in-law – when we were at Laurel Hill. So at least I know I'll be free to look after Eugene all the time.'

He's so sweet, she thought – such a baby still. Panic lest she lose him began to well up inside her again. She hoped fervently that the pact she had made with God was acceptable to Him and that, where Eugene was concerned, her conduct would not be held against her forever.

'What about Daniel, mam?' Bridie asked. 'Are you going to send Tim-Pat out to Crag Liath with a note, to ask if the child can go out there tomorrow?'

'I'm not going to have him in the house for one minute more than is necessary,' Rosaleen said. 'Pack for him now, Bridie – pack all his clothes and whatever toys he wants to take. Tim-Pat can take a letter out to Crag Liath all right, but he can take Daniel with it. We won't have to wait for a reply – *I* know Mrs O'Brien will be delighted to have him.'

In spite of his high temperature, Eugene slept that night but his mother, standing guard over him, did not sleep at all. Nor did she sleep next morning, when Bridie came to relieve her, being much too worried to think of getting undressed and climbing into bed. She felt edgy as well as tired and, despite her contrition towards Dermot, she had a hard job controlling her irritation with him when she gave him his breakfast.

'It's cold,' Dermot complained, pushing his fried egg around on his plate with his fork as if it were an undesirable insect. 'I do like breakfast, in particular, perfectly served.'

Saying nothing to this – the better to appease the listeners in heaven – Rosaleen simply succeeded in stockpiling her anger. So when, long after Dermot's departure for town, Bridie announced that there was a pedlar at the back door, selling artificial jewellery and bits of ribbons, who insisted on talking to Mrs O'Brien, her immediate reaction was to explode into exasperation.

'But, mam, he won't *go* away,' Bridie said, bewildered. 'I told him you were busy but he says he has to see you himself, because he has a message to give you in person.'

'That's just an excuse to get me to go down and see his wares,' Rosaleen said crossly. 'Why are you so gullible, Bridie? Oh, never mind – *I'll* go down and get rid of the man, and I'll tell him what I think of his tricks.'

Ready to abuse the pedlar for the cheapness of his actions, she was knocked off balance when he produced, not samples of his wares, but a letter in tiny writing addressed to herself. Familiar writing. Her heart began to thump.

'I'm sorry to bother you, ma'am,' the pedlar said courteously. 'Herself told me there was a sick child in the house but I promised himself that I'd put this into your hands and no one else's.'

'Himself?'

'The tall man with the dark moustache I met on the Ennis Road.'

'He came *here*?' she asked before she could stop herself, and then – before the pedlar could answer, added: 'It was very good of you to deliver it. Did the man with the moustache give you some money for your trouble? He did? That's fine. Good-day.'

Closing the door behind the messenger, she leant weakly against it. What did Cathal – Mr O'Mahoney – think he was doing, taking risks like that? He was mad – or maybe not mad, only polite, sending her a note to wish her well, agreeing with her wishes. Polite and rather kind . . .

But when she ripped open the envelope and looked at the two-line letter she found that Mr Cathal O'Mahoney was being neither polite nor kind.

Rosaleen, I'm waiting by the boreen and shall remain there all night if necessary in order to see you. Can you come out and talk?

The nerve of it! Ready to wait there all night in the hope of seeing her! That was an over-heroic declaration

337

for a start in view of the fact that the weather had changed and the rain was pelting down. Mr O'Mahoney, waiting by the boreen, must already be soaking wet.

Flustered, angry with Cathal for his impudence, she felt angry with God too. Why had He not kept her visitor better under control, as He was capable of doing – used some device to keep him at home, where he should be – a bad cold or –

No, she thought – never scarlet fever!

'I'm *glad* You didn't make him ill,' she said to God, frightened in case, having put this idea into His head, He might take it up. 'You needn't worry about doing anything at all. It's all my responsibility. I'll deal with it myself.'

She was right only about one thing – Cathal was already soaking wet, and she was wet herself, by the time she reached the boreen.

He was standing under the old oak, sheltering too late, with his hair whipped close into his skull by the wind and raindrops on his face. The anger that she had carefully carried through the yard and orchard seemed to have slipped away.

'What happened to make you run away?'

He wasted no time on preliminaries, getting immediately to the point, and she found herself in two minds, vacillating between the need for defence and her impetus to be tender.

'I – my little boy got sick. Didn't I say that in my note? I'm sure I must have told you.'

'I thought that was an excuse,' Cathal said sternly, 'a way of getting out of our arrangement. I thought you were trying to get rid of me.'

'If you thought that, why are you here?'

338

Her aggression was an ineffective blanket over her tenderness, she was sure he noticed. Why did I think I could deal with *that* myself, she thought – I should have known much better.

'You get a better idea of people's feelings when you see them face to face. If she really wants to get rid of me, I said to myself, she can tell me so herself, instead of writing it in a roundabout kind of way in a letter. *Do* you want to get rid of me?'

I shouldn't have told God I could deal with it myself, she thought later – that was why He did not support me at that moment.

'I – can't see you again. I'm a married woman. Surely you can understand that?'

'But do you *want* to get rid of me?'

'I'm going,' Rosaleen said. 'I can't stand here and argue in the rain.'

'Go and look after your little boy,' Cathal called after her. 'I'll find out what's going on with him and when he's better I'll be in touch again.'

For most people at Kincora that was an awful summer. Eugene's illness was not fatal but it was prolonged, and he was still very ill when Bridie caught it and needed nursing too. Running from one to the other, coaxing the patients with special food, sleeping badly at night, Rosaleen was permanently exhausted.

And then, just as Eugene was gloriously on the mend, Dermot ran a temperature and Dr Walshe was back.

'Scarlet fever,' he said gloomily. 'I told you it was catching.'

'Daniel didn't get it,' Rosaleen said triumphantly.

Nor did he, neither then nor later on. That she could revel about, before immersing herself in what was now

339

a too familiar routine, rushing from bedroom to kitchen and back to bedroom again.

But there were two people, even if only one lived at Kincora, for whom that summer was good.

The first was Tim-Pat, recruited to act as surrogate mother and nanny to Eugene when the child was over the worst of his sickness.

It was a situation that suited Tim-Pat down to the ground. Doting on both the twins, he loved vulnerable Eugene more than independent Daniel. Looking after him gave the groom a small but necessary measure of power and when Eugene gazed up at him, telling him he was a marvel with a horse, Tim-Pat wondered how he had managed to live without it before.

Although Eugene thought that he had supernatural powers, at least in terms of horses, he, too, wanted something from the groom.

'You're going to make me a better rider 'n Daniel, aren't you?' he wheedled, when riding lessons were resumed.

'I might.'

Tim-Pat enjoyed holding back the goodies, doling them out one by one, watching the recipient fidget in expectation.

'Master Eugene, you're going to have to learn to be independent of the stirrups. Men rode horses before they had saddles. You must remember that. And the first saddles didn't have stirrups at all.'

He had picked that up from Dermot. As Eugene's eyes widened with interest, Tim-Pat searched around his memory for another element of magic that would add to his own reputation.

'Before the English came to take our land we Irish didn't use saddles nor boots nor spurs,' he said, and Eugene listened intently. 'All we required was a rod in

340

our hand, with a crook at the upper end of it, to urge our horses forward.'

'You know everything, don't you,' Eugene said.

It was a statement, not a question. Once Tim-Pat had ascertained that Dermot, too, was on the mend, he decided that the summer of 1890 was the best he could remember.

Milliora also benefited at that time by having Daniel to stay. Like Tim-Pat, she would have told you that she did not have a favourite but loved both the twins the same, but, deep down – buried much too deep for anyone to get at it, least of all herself – was a special love for Daniel.

This love was based on two factors, one rational and easy to explain if challenged – the other more fanciful, more private and yet extremely basic in its roots.

She loved Daniel because of his courage and honesty and cheek. Two of these qualities reminded her of Tom – she did not compare their veracity. Daniel was not a child who would let others walk all over him – he stood up for himself, and she admired that, being the same way herself.

She told Mary Markham that Daniel was a natural leader, a pioneer, and that he would be a lucky man when he grew up, since God helped those who reached out and helped themselves. But she did not tell Mary, or anyone else, the other reason why she loved him. Mary might have laughed at her, or told someone else who would, and Milliora still did not like being the object of amusement.

In the unlikely event of having the information bullied out of her she might have admitted that she loved Daniel on another level because of his auburn hair, and then gone further into explaining that, because his hair was similar to her own, it was easy to imagine that he was her son.

This was a dangerous fantasy and, not surprisingly, it led to complications, although there were positive aspects, too. Being bossy by nature, Milliora restructured Daniel's life from the moment of his arrival at Crag Liath. Although, of course, she took time off to play with him, and to read him stories, and his favourite food was served, she also introduced him properly to the way the estate was run, something that his relatively short visits had not permitted in the past. Although he was only three she took him round with her to see what went on in the dairy, and, as part of his education, he learnt to milk a cow. He helped feed the poultry and he watched the grass being mowed in the meadow, and got in the way of the men making haystacks, and he rode on the back of the floats when the hay was taken in.

At the end of the summer he was thoroughly involved with every aspect of life at Crag Liath and he was more interested in talk of harvest than in news of the rest of his family, who had retreated comfortably to the back of his mind, supplanted by day-to-day excitement at O'Brien's Bridge.

Milliora could not bear to think that, all too soon, she was going to lose him. Logically, she knew that she would have to accept the inevitability when Rosaleen, as she must, came to take him home but the more used to him she grew, the more it seemed that he had been at Crag Liath forever.

By autumn – always a difficult time for Milliora, bringing agonizing memories of Tom – she was plagued by other emotions, ones she had sincerely believed to be extinct within herself.

It was this simple: the longer Daniel stayed on at

Crag Liath, the more she dreamed of being his mother, the more she found herself pining for a mate with whom she could share the joy of surrogate parenthood.

Her initial response to this cry within herself had been to try to seek out Tom so that, even in memory, he could play Daniel's father for the duration of the visit. But Tom refused to be summonsed. When – bewildered – Milliora looked at a photograph of her dead husband, trying in that way to revive him, he stoutly resisted her efforts to make him come to life.

Milliora would not face it, but the impossible had happened. Tom O'Brien – responsible in death as he had never been in life – had finally released his widow from the manacles of her love. Try as she might to reach him, no matter how many photographs of him she might place around the house in order to keep him in mind, by the end of August one thing was perfectly clear: Tom had gone for good.

Freed from that love, Milliora found herself grounded in the real, raw world, dreaming of a handsome and unidentified man to act as Daniel's father, and she was utterly ashamed of her state. Superficial, she thought – I would not have believed it of myself. The way I feel is an insult to Tom and the happiness we knew.

The night before Rosaleen was due to come and collect Daniel, Milliora lay awake nurturing a blinding headache. Forcing herself to get up at the crack of dawn, she retreated back to her bedroom after a couple of hours to apply a compress of a fine linen handkerchief soaked with lavender and vinegar to her aching head.

Mary Markham, finding her there, bore down on her with a tray on which she had placed tea, tiny mustard and cress sandwiches, warm scones and a pile of fluffy chocolate cake. But when she entered the darkened bedroom Milliora, lying on top of her eiderdown, waved the tray away.

'You haven't had a thing to eat since yesterday morning – and what was that but a little slice of toast? You're going to make yourself sick,' Mary chided her.

'What time is it?'

'Just gone eleven.'

'And no sign yet of Mrs Rosaleen?'

'I think that's her now,' said Mary, cocking an ear to the window. 'Will you rest awhile here till you're better. A little bite of the dark chocolate cake? Isn't that your favourite?'

'I'm not hungry, thank you,' said a faint but inexorable voice. 'But if the carriage is here from Kincora, it's time that I got up.'

Rosaleen, too, dreamt of love. Cathal, true to his declaration, had not taken no for an answer. Having enlisted the pedlar once, he used him again and again, to deliver letters to Kincora. She was wasting her time resisting, he said – he would not go away.

Well, then, be my friend, she wrote back – be a friend of the family. I will say – quite truthfully – that I met you at John O'Leary's house. Come to us for dinner when Dermot is well.

But Cathal, perversely, did not want to be a friend of the family. It quite upset her, but he did not even want to meet the twins. That was a point against him – a big point – weighing against the enchantment of his letters, the stimulation and excitement and amusement (he could make her laugh and *that* was hard to resist) they brought into her life.

She told herself that she was honouring her bargain with God by refusing to see him and, as her patients recovered one by one, it seemed that God believed her.

The truth was – and she admitted it – that He should not place too much trust in her holding out. At the beginning of the summer, when Eugene was ill, it had been easy to desist from seeing Cathal but the intensity of her contrition was beginning to wear down under the strength of his onslaught.

His letters were so intriguing – that was the trouble – so seductive, and answering them – fending him off, in theory, at least – was an irresistible pleasure. And one which had carried her over the gloomy days of Dermot's illness, compensating for the fact that he was a bad and complaining patient. After listening to her husband's moans and groans all evening the stolen hour downstairs at the desk writing to Cathal restored her equilibrium.

What would Milly think about all this, Rosaleen wondered as the carriage approached Crag Liath? She would be horrified – would probably refuse to receive her. What had she said about Mr Parnell and his girlfriend: what kind of a woman can Mrs O'Shea be, to have a baby by a man who isn't your husband?

But all *I've* done is kiss, said Rosaleen to herself. A baby is far away from that, and now it's all platonic.

Is it? That's not how you really feel . . .

'Get on with you!' she said to Lair and lightly flicked the reins.

The mare turned in by the gates of Crag Liath and with a great effort she pushed Cathal out of her mind and refocused it on Daniel.

He, although pleased to see her, was obviously in no hurry to be taken home. Bending down to give him a hug, she was conscious of his arms, tender but undemanding, even before he said, 'Aunt Milly is coming, I think. Do I have to go?'

'Not yet,' said Rosaleen, slightly disconcerted. 'Is Milly upstairs?'

'She's not been well,' Mary Markham said, closing the front door and easing Rosaleen into the drawing-room. 'She's just now getting dressed.'

'Milly – getting up at eleven? That's not like her. She's not sickening for anything serious, is she?'

'Mrs O'Brien has a sick headache, nothing more, I assure you,' Mary said, cheerfully enough. 'Isn't that so, Master Daniel?'

'I think she's sick because you're here,' Daniel said with candour. 'She doesn't want me to go.'

It was a poor welcome for his mother, as Mary said when she went back in the kitchen.

'The poor thing,' said Mrs Cash. 'I knew it – it was bound to lead to trouble, having him here for so long. They'll be fighting next over him, wait and see, and we'll have herself with a face of thunder on her when Master Daniel is gone.'

'Why should they fight?' Mary demanded. 'They're the very best of friends.'

'Mark my words,' said Mrs Cash again, ''tis only a question of who will win, though I'd say, when it comes to fighting, Mrs Rosaleen would give as good as she got and settle all our hash.'

Sitting in the drawing-room, waiting for Milliora, Rosaleen felt anything but aggressive. Daniel was not a difficult child when it came to conversation and they were soon chatting away back on their old terms.

'We'll have to be getting you back to your lessons when you go home,' Rosaleen said.

'Mm,' Daniel grunted. Bored, his violet-blue eyes promptly clouded over.

'Do you remember your Irish?' his mother persisted. 'You've been out and about on the farm a lot, I hear. Tell me, what's the Irish word for cow?'

'Don't know.'

'It's *bo*,' said Rosaleen, patiently. 'And bull – I'm sure you remember that word.'

But Daniel only shrugged.

'*Tarbh*. Oh Daniel, surely you haven't forgotten all the words you learnt?'

'Irish is stupid,' Daniel said. 'It's a waste of time.'

'Who says so?' demanded his mother, indignantly. 'It's *not* a waste of time. Whoever put such an idea into your head?'

Daniel sighed. Life at Crag Liath had been very good until his mother had come and although he was pleased to see her again he was not enjoying the pressure she tried to apply. In an effort to put down his foot once and for all about lessons, he made a definite statement.

'Aunt Milly says so. She says Irish is for – ' he paused, searching for the word used by Milliora – 'for *pheasants*,' he concluded, triumphantly. 'For pheasants, not for us.'

His mother was enraged. 'She said that? How *dare* she say such a thing? How could she interfere?'

She was red with anger. Daniel shrugged again. He could hear Milliora coming down the stairs. It looked like trouble. Lest it have any repercussions for himself, he ran out of the room.

It was Bawnie Kinsella, balanced on a ladder, cleaning the staircase mural, who heard what went on between Rosaleen and Milliora, and gave a report of it to the kitchen.

Characteristically, Rosaleen took the bull by the horns at once, cutting into Milliora's not-over-effusive greeting and demanding to know what right she thought she had to dictate Daniel's education and prevent him from developing a true sense of national identity.

The speed of the attack caught Milliora off balance – that was obvious, said Bawnie. Traumatized herself, she had no way of knowing that Rosaleen was in a similar condition.

'A sense of national identity indeed,' she said, sharply. 'I have no time for that kind of nonsense, Rosaleen. You'll be joining the Ladies' Land League next, I shouldn't wonder.'

'And what's wrong with the League?'

'A lot of peasant rebels,' said Milliora with distaste, 'encouraged by people who ought to know better. It's one thing for Mr Parnell to involve himself in politics but that sister of his, Miss Anna Parnell, should keep her place instead of making disturbances in the land. I have no time for it, or her.'

'How stupid you are!' said Rosaleen crossly. 'And to think I used to look up to you. I'm not going to waste any more time talking to you, Milly. Anna Parnell is doing wonders as President of the League but you'll never understand the significance of her work. I won't stay to luncheon, thank you. I'd rather have it at Kincora. It's time Daniel went home.'

'Just as you like,' said Milliora haughtily, turning away so Rosaleen could not see her tears.

A silly row. And made all the sillier by the fact that Daniel, on being told he had to go, said he wanted to stay. An undignified row – so Dermot said when Rosaleen gave him the details. He was furious with her, saying that she had set back his plans for regaining Crag Liath.

A predictable row, Mrs Cash said in the kitchen after an analysis had been made by Bawnie and Mary Markham.

'So how is herself now it's over and done with?'

'Much good all that caterwauling has done her,' Mary said grimly. 'She's back in the bedroom, as green as a leek from the pain she has in her head.'

22

There were mushrooms galore growing in the meadow behind the boreen that month and Rosaleen thought as she found them that they were like troubles: when you had gathered all you could see, more grew up around you and demanded your attention.

As Dermot ranted on about reducing the chances of the twins' inheritance by indulging in foolish wrangling, Bridie got word that her father in Thomondgate had died of scarlet fever.

'So if you think I'm going out to Crag Liath to apologize to Milly you can think again,' said Rosaleen to Dermot. 'If our quarrel means that much to you maybe you can sort it out. I've enough on my mind as it is.'

'Will you behave yourself in Milliora's company if I put things right?' Dermot was uninterested in and unsympathetic about his wife's immediate problems. 'There's not much point in my going out there to see her if you can't maintain the peace after I get back.'

'I'll maintain it,' she said. 'Now leave me alone. I have to go to Thomondgate with Bridie to see her father's body. She can't face going there alone.'

Driving down the Shelbourne Road with Bridie sobbing beside her, past the City Home Workhouse, towards the crossroads with Sexton Street, Rosaleen narrowly missed Cathal, who had passed the same point minutes earlier on his way to a meeting at O'Brien's Bridge. But she was thinking of him, and his latest letter was concealed in a handkerchief in her bag.

She had not been able to bring herself to tear it up or throw it away but she had steadfastly refused his request for a rendezvous. The fate of Bridie's father might or might not be a sign that God was continuing to keep track of the situation and she was taking no further risks with the lives of her own family by agreeing to illicit meetings.

'Life is terrible cruel, mam,' Bridie sniffed as they turned into Sexton Street. 'I don't know how I'll be able to bear the sight of him laid out.'

'Ssh now.'

The guilt is mine to bear, Rosaleen thought, strengthening her resolve against seeing Cathal.

The cottage in which Bridie's family lived was awash with sorrow when the two of them got there. In the bedroom the body had been laid out and the three keening women who sat beside the bed, rocking backwards and forwards, were wailing over and over the name of the deceased.

Their howling was eery and wild and perfectly controlled for they were skilled at their craft and as the lamentation moved into a recital of the fine qualities of the dead man it became an exquisite piercing dirge, primitive and poetic.

'Oh, mam,' wailed Bridie. 'How is me ma going to feed the children without the money earned by me da?'

'*Och-Ochone!*' cried the keeners, leading the choral cry that concluded each verse of the recitative, and the other mourners, sisters and brothers and cousins, uncles and aunts, joined in so that the tiny cottage was transported into an heroic and epitaphic music box, the meaning of the lullaby contained not in words but only in the sound.

'I'm going to help her,' Rosaleen said.

In the end, you did not have to go out and find the

351

poor in order to appease your conscience – they presented themselves at your door, their hungry eyes daring you to close it.

If Bridie's mother was capable with a needle, Rosaleen decided, she would supply her with scraps of material from which she could produce patchwork quilts and shawls and cushions, which should go down well in Limerick. Apart from private orders, maybe the shops would be keen.

If the woman could sew . . . If she could not, she would have to be taught. It was a job that Milliora, she knew, could do much better than herself.

If only Milly wasn't so bossy and interfering, so sanctimonious and convinced that she was right.

As Bridie, too, joined in the keening, Rosaleen wondered if Dermot, presumably now in Crag Liath on his mission of peace, had managed to heal the breach.

Breach-healing, Dermot had reasoned, was best achieved by offering your opponent an irresistible gift, a bribe that coaxed them back into your camp for the time being. Telling Milliora that Rosaleen was sorry about what had happened was woefully inadequate. She would wonder why Rosaleen did not appear in person to say so and even if he were to explain about Bridie's father she would see his intervention as a watered-down affair.

On the way to Crag Liath he racked his brains for the additional bonus that could be proferred – a gift that would put Milliora in the position of being grateful to Rosaleen and himself.

And then, just ouside Parteen, he met with one of the Bloodsmiths, who was riding into Limerick.

'How are you, Dermot?' James Bloodsmith called out. 'Are we going to see Rosaleen and yourself at the ball this season? It's very early this year and I haven't had your reply.'

'I've been meaning to let you know,' Dermot said. 'Yes, of course, we'll be there. Wouldn't miss it for anything.'

The County Limerick Foxhounds' Hunt Ball was the most stylish social event of the year. How could he – who prided himself on his meticulousness – have failed to let the Hunt secretary know they would be coming?

This business with Milliora has distracted me badly, Dermot thought – and just like that he found he had his additional bonus in the palm of his pale hand. He would ask Milliora to accompany them to the ball, make up a large family party, say that Rosaleen had specifically asked him to do so. She seemed to want to be recognized as an O'Brien, and being included in such a party was one form of recognition.

The ball was not till the end of October but Milliora would appreciate all the more being asked so far in advance and, naturally, James Bloodsmith would want to know as soon as possible so he could reserve their tickets.

Pleased with his scheme, Dermot smiled. His party would certainly contain no attractive single men! There could be no risk in taking Milliora under those kind of circumstances.

And thank God Tom's memory was as charismatic as his presence had been – Milliora, in spite of his occasional fears, did seem blinded to the existence of desirable men.

He arrived at Crag Liath in an excellent mood, the best he had been in for ages. He was recuperating at long last from his illness – that was part of it, he knew;

he was positive and optimistic and ready to do battle on his sons' behalf.

'Dermot – what a nice surprise!' exclaimed Milliora, gratifyingly pleased to see him.

He kissed her cheek and, surprisingly, she blushed and lowered her eyelashes, almost as if he and she were would-be lovers rather than relations.

'Come in, come in,' she said, ushering him into the house with unnecessary speed. 'Come into the dining-room if you wouldn't mind. I'm just finishing hanging some new curtains in there and I'd be grateful if you would give me your opinion on the way they look.'

He followed her, his mood swinging back to the sombre as she opened the dining-room door. Whenever he was in this room the memory of his last night at Crag Liath flooded back to him with bitter acrimony. As Milliora fiddled with yards of brocade and smoothed down her handiwork, he thought he could see another figure in the room – a young man with a sheet in his hand creeping towards the sideboard, about to remove from it a silver milk-jug – a pair of candlesticks shaped like a lyre . . .

'Why are you here, Dermot? Are you making another will on behalf of a client in the district or have you just stopped in to pay a call?'

'To pay a call, of course,' he said, with forced gallantry, 'and also to tell you that we're making up a party for the County Limericks' Hunt Ball and – as Rosaleen said to me – we both feel it wouldn't be complete without yourself.' When Milliora did not reply he added quickly, 'Rosaleen feels so bad about the little tiff she had with you. I'm afraid she lost her temper, so she says. She's been under a lot of strain as you know and unfortunately you took the brunt of it.'

354

'Oh, that,' said Rosaleen vaguely, as if to her the tiff had been of little consequence.

And perhaps it had hardly registered. The portents were good. He must not permit memories to depress and disturb him.

'You will come to the ball, won't you, Milly?' he said. 'It will do you good to get out and meet more people. You spend too much time alone, and you work much too hard. We worry about you.'

Marvelling at his own ability to dissemble, he waited for her decision. To his surprise, she pushed the curtaining to one side and leant closer to the window, gazing thoughtfully out into the garden.

What was going on in her mind? Why didn't she speak? Her habit of allowing silences to fall between question and answer was one he found infuriating at the best of times.

'Speak, bitch, speak!' he willed her, but no one could have guessed from the amiability of his expression the malice in his heart.

Yet Milliora's thoughts would have been just as disturbing to him as his to her. His hatred for her was so intense that he was impervious to her beauty, and would never find her attractive. But suppose, thought Milliora, that Dermot were to know that when he kissed my cheek at the door I found myself responding to him not as his sister-in-law but simply as a woman? Or that, when he mentioned going to the ball just now, I saw myself there, dressed in a diaphanous gown, waltzing in the arms of yet another man, a handsome stranger whose face I have not seen before?

What is *wrong* with me to be having such thoughts, lamented Milliora, standing at the window – and where, oh, where is Tom? His photograph was in the dining-room, over on the sideboard. The garden, with the pale pink Sterling Silver and Bacchus roses, which were reminiscent of their first romantic meeting, called out for him as well, and to no further avail.

If Tom would not help her veer away from incipient madness she would have to rescue herself. She reminded herself sternly that her life was devoted to the efficient running of the estate and that there should be no room in it for lewd or romantic thoughts – quite apart from the fact that they were sinful and could pave the way to hell. Diaphanous gowns – hunt balls – dancing! From what she had heard recently, it was actually considered bad form in the best English circles to be able to dance very well!

'Well, Milly, what's your answer? Are you going to come with us to the ball?'

With every intention of politely declining Dermot's kind invitation, Milliora turned back from the window. Her refusal was on the tip of her tongue. But there it remained, drowned out by that deep, lonely, dissatisfied cry within herself that was stronger than resolution.

She heard herself say instead, 'Thank you, I would love to join your party,' and it seemed to her as if someone else was accepting on her behalf.

'That's wonderful,' Dermot said. 'Then I'll arrange the tickets.'

They both forgot about the curtains. When Dermot left, Milliora went upstairs to her bedroom, leaving them hanging, swaying like the sails of a boat in the breeze wafting through the windows that she had failed to shut.

That same day, Major Harry Fielding of the Sixth Inniskilling Dragoons, stationed at the Curragh, received by post a similar invitation from an old friend in Limerick although he had paid scant attention to it, pushing the letter into the right-hand top drawer of his desk, on top of another, much more disturbing in its contents.

While Rosaleen supported Bridie in her bereavement and Dermot beguiled Milliora at Crag Liath, Harry Fielding glared at Rogers, a young subaltern responsible for Mess catering, and told him for the second time that he had been grossly extravagant in his purchasing of late.

Ten minutes later, when the extravagant subaltern had been dismissed with a fine of a dozen of Champagne, the President of the Mess looked grimmer than ever. This time, however, his ire was directed at himself.

If only the boy knew what a predicament *I* am in, thought Harry, glumly. At the same time, he thanked his lucky stars that Rogers did not know. It was fortunate for regimental discipline and morale that he – who paid his debts promptly, had an incomparable seat on a horse, and was held up to all and sundry as a shining example of what an officer should be – was not suspected of an involvement with another officer's wife.

And why should they know, since it had begun far away in South Africa – in the Cape Colony where the Inniskillings had been posted during the eighties – land of sunshine and flowers and birds, and space enough for lovers to hide from disapproval.

Sarah Masters: ruthless and acquisitive, lacking in most of the qualities he admired in a woman, amongst them honesty and perfect self-control. But with a voluptuous and greedy body that matched well her lustrous, long, dark hair but not the deceptive, tiny, heart-shaped face that cried innocence, and the seemingly guileless eyes, green as the emeralds she would have liked, if she had not longed for diamonds.

357

Yet she had a life force so prodigious that you could not but marvel and laugh in her presence. That was what he had pursued – had craved after the death of a wife who, over three years, had seemed gradually to fade from life rather than die in that tiny Karroo village, refuge of others like herself suffering from tuberculosis, hoping that the desert air, as refreshing as dry Champagne, would act as a restorative upon their jaded lungs.

Lilian had never been able to enjoy the novelty of the Cape Province while he had revelled in the posting. She had been too ill, too tired from the beginning.

'What was she like, your wife?' Sarah had asked, and he had thought of the long, pale grey leaves of the silver tree which grows only on Table Mountain.

'You can write and paint on those,' Sarah had said, idly. 'Lots of people do. They sell them in the Cape Town shops – haven't you noticed?'

But Lilian had been without imprint, without colour, and after her death a strong affirmation of life was what he had been seeking.

And so Sarah. She was not the only woman to have pursued him in the months following Lilian's demise, only the most persistent. Harry was tall and well-built, with a handsome though rather heavy face, deep blue eyes and a full and generous mouth.

He was pleased when women pursued him, saving him the necessity of breaking down initial barriers, for there was a shyness in Harry, when it came to the female sex. He had been surrounded by males both in childhood and in adult life and he was usually more at ease with men than women. Under the veneer of the strict disciplinarian, there was in him something of the small boy who has been propelled too quickly into manhood, forced to take responsibility before his time.

Throughout his marriage to Lilian he had disciplined himself more sternly than he had ever disciplined others – only, at the age of thirty-five, to go off the rails with Sarah!

He groaned now, thinking of the madness of that affair – the easily-arranged meetings in the empty Cape homestead when Sarah's friends were away. That other trip, by train, all the way to Johannesburg, gold-fever city, brash and greedy like the lady he was with, where yellow dust blowing off the stamp batteries of the mines and their dumps of waste sand mingled with the red dust from the rough earthen streets being churned up by the wagons and horses and the feet of the avaricious. Another secret sojourn, this time in an absurd imitation Gothic house owned by another friend of Sarah's – one of the new aristocracy, an upstart grown rich who had fulfilled a vulgar fantasy, recruiting an English butler and a French maid and a cook who came from Ireland.

And a bed from God knows where. Once in it he had no qualms about being there with Sarah – she had seen to that.

Only later, when he was in the Mess, forced to dine with her dull and unsuspecting husband – to laugh at George's banal jokes.

When Harry received news that he was to be posted back to the Curragh he imagined that Sarah would have no conscience about replacing him within a couple of weeks, in spite of her protestations about having fallen deeply in love with him. He believed that when he saw her again – as he was bound to do – the affair would be forgotten by them both.

How could he have come to such a foolish conclusion – believed, quite erroneously, that he could so easily be safe?

From the right-hand drawer of his desk Sarah's letter seemed to sear up into his fundamentally ethical soul.

Darling Harry,
You'll know we are being posted back to the Curragh. Do you know that I still love, long for you . . . can't wait . . . arrive on 28th October . . .

How to dodge her? How (just as important) to avoid his considerable lust for a lady who was wrong for him, always had been (except, of course, in bed)?

He put his hand to his fair head and stared down at the desk, considering. He could not evade Sarah forever – that was perfectly obvious – but it would help, give her a hint of how he wanted things to be, if he were absent on her arrival.

And that was when Harry, too, remembered the invitation to the County Limericks' ball, sent on by Ted de Voy, an old friend who had inherited property in County Limerick and had married a local girl called Dottie. They hunted with the County Limericks, were eager for Harry to do the same, and had invited him down at the time of the ball.

The ball was to be held at the end of October – when the Masters were due to arrive. What could be more timely? He could travel to Limerick a couple of days before the ball and stay with the de Voys for two weeks, by which time even Sarah would have an inkling that his attitude had changed. She would be beginning to re-adapt to life at the Curragh – and, with luck, she might have replaced him by the time that he got back.

The idea of a successor gave him no jealous twinges. On the contrary, for the first time that day, Harry Fielding smiled.

23

Rain. It fell steadily and lethally throughout October. By the end of the month all the rivers in Ireland were in flood.

But it was not the weather that was troubling Harry the day he was due to leave the Curragh for his holiday with the de Voys, but the behaviour of young Rogers who, it transpired, had not only been extravagant in his purchasing for the Mess but had also juggled its funds.

The resultant court martial left a bad taste in Harry's mouth. There was no doubt of the subaltern's guilt, but it gave his commanding officer no pleasure to see such a large shadow cast on a young man's life.

And – *inter alia* – a small one cast on his own. The necessity to present at the court martial had delayed his getting away for two vital days. As a result, he got to the Curragh station on the day that George and Sarah were catching the same train down from Dublin that he would take on its later leg to Limerick.

In that sense, the weather was on his side, with visibility greatly reduced. He made his way furtively through the incessant mist as the train pulled into the station and, before it began to disgorge its passengers, slipped into the last compartment, praying that it was empty.

It was. He put his suitcase on to the luggage rack and, settling himself into the farthest corner, hid his head in a book.

A woman's voice sent a shiver of apprehension down

his spine, but she was plump and kindly-looking, and old enough to be Sarah's mother, at least. He stood up to assist her with her baggage, thanking his stars for a lucky escape.

'A soft day, thank God,' said the kindly lady.

'Perfect weather,' he agreed, thinking how perfect it was for him.

Relax, he said to himself. It's all right now. I've dodged her for the present.

And then, when he least expected it, a fracas blew up on the platform a few yards from where he sat. Harry did not see the elderly porter as he stood his ground in front of the angry dark-haired lady but he heard every word of their excited conversation.

'I don't care who lost it – find it!' the lady shouted. 'Do you think I've got all day to stand out in the rain, waiting for my bag?'

Harry cringed. Sarah – at her worst. The hand he put to the side of his face was intended to further conceal it, but it did not hide the perspiration on his brow.

'Are you feeling all right?' asked the kindly lady, concerned.

'Yes, I'm very well, thank you,' he managed to say.

'Been out in Africa?' His companion was on for a chat. 'I suppose you picked up malaria there – or would that be India? My cousin was there – in India – and he said it was strange how malaria affected a person. One minute you're right as rain, he said, and the next . . . My goodness, you're shivering, aren't you?'

Malaria didn't seem to be as serious as her cousin had insisted, she thought, as the train went on its journey. By the time it reached Limerick Junction her fellow traveller was looking quite perky and his shakes were a thing of the past.

* * *

362

Rosaleen and Dermot were arguing about arrangements for the ball.

'If you're so frightened of asking Arthur Bennett to partner Milly – though heaven knows why, since she has no interest in him whatsoever – why not Jamie Keegan? She's certainly not keen on him or they would have got together long ago.'

'I don't want her near any eligible men,' Dermot said, obstinately. 'You can never trust a woman like that.'

'That's ridiculous,' said Rosaleen derisively. 'The real truth is that you want to punish Milly. That's why you've asked old Mr Dundon to make up the party – so she's stuck with an old man all night who won't even want to dance.'

'So what if that's the reason?' said Dermot sulkily. 'It's no more than the woman deserves after what she did to myself. You haven't been out to see her, have you? It would help if the two of you were reconciled before the ball.'

'We'll be reconciled there,' Rosaleen told him. 'Oh, surely you can think of a younger single man who wouldn't be a threat?'

'I can't. I don't intend to.'

Well *I* can, Rosaleen was tempted to say, although she held her tongue. I know a man I'd love to invite to make up our party, a man who would be quite safe to ask to partner Milly. Perfectly safe, since his interest is in me . . .

But instead of saying anything even half as controversial she picked up the scrap pieces and the flannelette she had collected for Bridie's mother, and packed them into a basket to take to Thomondgate.

* * * *

Milliora put the finishing touches to the gown she planned to wear to the ball thinking that she liked the new shape of sleeves, peaked at the shoulders but otherwise fairly narrow, and the way the goring in skirts was carried up to the waist without a need for gathers. Sleeves and skirts were practical issues on which to focus the mind – a way of fending off the nervousness she felt about going to the ball.

It was not that she was frightened of being a wallflower once she got there. Milliora had no false modesty and – where her looks were concerned – no humility either. She knew that she was a beautiful woman who, at just twenty-eight, had lost none of her looks. The mirror confirmed that daily.

No, she was not frightened of being ignored by men. She thought she stood a very good chance of attracting admirers wherever she went and that there would be suitors at the ball, and – just possibly – someone she could love.

But hand in hand with the possibility of love came the possibility of loss. Although Tom had obstinately refused to come to mind of late she had not forgotten the pain of her bereavement.

So what did she think she was doing, she asked herself, about to embark on a search for a man that she might love? Dermot, of course, would probably laugh if he knew that she thought of the ball only in terms of possible romance. She was not a debutante but a widow, a matron, not a girl, a relation making up a friendly family party who did not have to step outside it to dance with other men.

That was what she would do – stay within the party, chat to Rosaleen and Carmel and Mary and their husbands and dear Dermot's elderly partner who was going along as well. There was no need for her to worry about the possibility of love.

She told herself all that and completed her gown and hung it up in her wardrobe, but her fear did not recede. By the time it came to prepare for the ball she thought she would not go.

What, after all, was the point of placing herself in a vulnerable position? In spite of her resolution to stay within the party, who knew what might happen at the ball?

She would put on an ordinary dress, she thought, and go downstairs and tell Bawnie Kinsella that, after all, they would not be driving all the way to Adare. He would be pleased about that. It was no fun for a coachman to drive out on a cold, wet night and wait until maybe five o'clock in the morning for the ball to come to an end for all that he stood the chance of being invited into the manor kitchen.

What excuse are you going to give him, demanded another part of her mind. Are you going to admit that you are actually frightened of going to a ball?

And then it's a waste of this gown – the time you've spent on that.

You can't *not* go to the ball. You've left it too late to back out. The die is cast already.

I suppose it is, agreed the timorous side of Milliora, the side only Tom had known. I suppose I have to go.

So get ready then, said her other side. Make a mighty effort. Put on your gown. Concede that you're pleased with what you see when you look in the mirror.

Mary Markham, seeing Milliora descend the stairs, thought that she had never looked more lovely. Mrs O'Brien, she noticed, had indulged her penchant for lace but the gown she wore was made entirely of black lace, not white, although, as she held up the long skirt

365

with one hand, the better to negotiate the stairs, Mary noticed that her petticoat had a white lace frill on it. The gown itself was cut low into a heart-shaped bodice, revealing the cleft of her breasts, the sleeves were unlined, and the full skirt was caught up on the left-hand side and tied with imitation black roses and falling black velvet ribbons. Her glorious red-gold hair was taken softly back from her face and arranged in a topknot, held in place by a spiky jet tiara, and her black glacé kid shoes had small ornaments on the toes.

'Will you not be cold, going out like that?' Mary wanted to know, casting a quick look at the low-cut bodice, a daring innovation for Mrs O'Brien and not far short of being described as positively indecent.

'I brought my black velvet cloak down earlier. Would you fetch it for me, please. It's in the drawing-room on the back of the rosewood chair.'

Hoity-toity, thought Mary, complying with this request. Knowing Milliora as well as she did she was wise to what might be underneath this veneer.

'How is she feeling, would you say?' Mrs Cash asked, when, from the hall window, they watched the carriage moving off.

'She's in a right nonplush, not knowing whether she's coming or going, that's the truth.'

'Ah sure,' said Mrs Cash. 'Would we be saying a *paidirin* for the poor child? There's nothing like the Rosary for making Them listen Up Above.'

And that was another cruel deed, Rosaleen said – letting Milliora drive all the way from O'Brien's Bridge to Adare when she could have broken her journey at Kincora and gone on from there with them.

'And stayed the night with us afterwards, instead of facing going home in this kind of weather.'

'I wouldn't be worrying too much about Milliora,' Dermot said. 'She can take care of herself.'

He was looking forward to the ball. When the hunting crowd met he was always in his element and he looked remarkably handsome in his pink coat, the same colour as the one he wore for hunting but made of lighter material, with his black trousers and white shirt and white bow-tie.

So Rosaleen thought, just as she thought that her husband's good looks simply left her cold.

'You're looking well,' Dermot said to her suddenly, appraising the pretty, deep blue gown and the dark upswept hair. 'Well, but pale. Don't tell me you're tired already. It's going to be a long night at Adare.'

And a good one, he thought, when they reached their destination and turned into the gateway of the Tudor-Gothic-style manor. It was, without doubt, the most wonderful setting for a ball and Adare, with its woods and the wide river, was unquestionably Ireland's most beautiful village.

A village of three friaries, with the ruins of one of them in the grounds of the Manor House itself, residence of the earls of Dunraven, descendants of the Gaelic sept of O Cuinn. A family that had held on to their land, Dermot thought bitterly, looking up at the parapet of the graceful, gabled house, reading the four-foot-high Gothic lettering of the text: 'Except the Lord build the House their Labour is lost that build it.'

All around them, carriages were drawing up, and out of them tumbled white-gowned debutantes, budding beauties still too plump for their dresses, and other girls and women in a multiplicity of colours, clutching embroidered bags. By a miracle the rain had stopped. The air was lush with excitement.

367

'Here we are,' Carmel said, coming up on Dermot's left.

Like Mary, who joined them seconds later, she was wearing an evening gown in an indecisive shade that was sadly out of date. He wished that the two of them would smarten up their appearance. Noel and Andy would probably not know the difference if their wives wore Paris gowns or dresses made from sackcloth, but that was not the point. As his sisters, they had standards to maintain. It did him no good with the hunting crowd to be seen with dowdy people.

'Dermot, I keep talking to you without getting an answer. I'm sure it's going to rain again in a minute. We should go inside.'

'I'd better wait for Milliora,' he said to Carmel. 'It wouldn't look good to have her arrive on her own. You go in with Rosaleen and the others. I'll wait here. She can't be very much longer.'

The rest of the party was hardly out of sight when the carriage from Crag Liath arrived. For a moment he hoped that the cloudful of rain that was hovering over their heads would break as Milliora appeared, ruining her hair and her ball-gown.

But what good would that do, apart from giving him a modicum of satisfaction? He needed the chic he knew she would have to counteract the dowdiness of his sisters.

'Dermot, how nice of you to wait for me. Is Rosaleen inside?'

'She is.'

Her black cloak showed up the red-gold of her hair and matched her saucy tiara but gave no clue to what she was wearing underneath. He took her arm and led her from the carriage into the manor, through a tangle of talkative revellers, towards the main rooms and the minstrels' gallery where the rest of the party waited.

'Just a moment. I must take off my cloak.'

'Of course. Let me assist you. We'll leave it for the cloakroom girl to mind.'

He stepped forward to help her and gasped, catching his first sight of the black lace gown and the cleft of her milky breasts.

At the same time he was conscious that other eyes – admiring, lustful, jealous eyes – were looking in her direction.

'Thank you, Dermot,' Milliora said and her husky voice seemed to him to emanate a quality – erotic and enticing – he had not connected with her before.

'You look – very nice,' he said.

Politeness and the necessity to keep on with Milliora demanded that he say it. But as he escorted her over to where the rest of the party waited he thought that, in spite of the need to keep up standards, he would have far preferred had she looked like Carmel or Mary.

The tall man in the blue uniform of the Inniskilling Dragoons thought simply that she was gorgeous and that she far outshone every other woman in the room.

Her hair – thought Harry, seated directly opposite the O'Brien table – that alone is amazing. But, unlike many redheads whose looks could not live up to her hair, she had the face to complement it. Add to that, her regal posture, her flamboyantly feminine gown, and you had absolute perfection.

He could not take his eyes off her although he felt he should, for having seen Milliora enter the room with Dermot, he thought at that stage that they were wed.

And haven't you had enough trouble on that score, Harry berated himself, without making eyes at this lovely woman.

369

'She's beautiful, isn't she?' Ted de Voy said with a grin, reading Harry's thoughts. 'Though I must say I've never seen her looking quite as beautiful as this.'

'You know her?'

'In Limerick everyone knows everyone else. Her name is Milliora O'Brien. The man she came in with happens to be my solicitor.'

'He's not her husband?'

'He's her brother-in-law. She's a widow. Her husband was drowned a few years back.'

'She's a widow?'

Harry looked again at the red-haired lady. A widow? But a widow out of mourning, in spite of the colour of her dress. But hardly likely to remain a widow for long . . .

'I'll introduce you to her if you like,' Ted offered, his eyes twinkling with mischief. 'What do you say, Dottie – shall we make a match between Harry and Milliora O'Brien?'

'Why not?' Dottie laughed back at her husband. 'Take him over to her table now and he can ask her to dance. Go on, Harry. Go with him.'

The music in this early part of the evening was romantic rather than boisterous as it would be later on, and several members of the party opposite were moving on to the floor. The red-haired beauty was seated now, sandwiched between an old man – her father? – and a small lady in a blue gown to whom she was talking.

'Hurry, you two,' Dottie de Voy urged. 'And mind you come back, Ted, and have a dance with me.'

She turned back to chat to her neighbour as Ted moved purposefully towards the red-haired lady's table. Divided between desire and inhibition, Harry half-reluctantly followed in his wake.

Closer up, his lady seemed less confident than her appearance would have you believe. He could swear that she was nervous. Her hands were restless – tapping on the edge of the table. As he watched she became conscious of them, putting them on her lap, out of view under the table. So the queenly façade disguised an uncertainty. The recognition that Milliora was less sure of herself than she looked acted on Harry as it had once affected Tom, bringing out his protective instincts, and – in Harry's case – breaking down the basic shyness he tended to have with women.

'Dermot – good to see you.'

'And you.'

A brief formality before the formal introductions. A smile from the ladies, acknowledging the newcomers. Nothing other than that – no second glance – no sign from the red-haired lady that he might be of particular interest.

At nearby tables other women were watching Harry, noting his fine physique, the gold lace girdle of his regiment that highlighted his deep blue tunic, wishing perhaps that he was looking at them.

'I think we're about to get into serious trouble, Dermot – our wives are wanting to dance.'

A ruse on the part of Ted to clear the way for himself. Take the plunge, said Ted's twinkling eyes as Dermot O'Brien said: 'Indeed. One should always have the first dance with one's wife,' and signalled to his to join him.

And then for one brief, unguarded moment the red-haired lady looked up at him directly and he knew she *had* noted him, *was* interested, would very much like to dance.

'Might I have the honour?'

The elderly man at her side beamed approvingly. He

probably felt nothing himself but relief at being relieved of the possibility of exertion. *Her* eyes, the eyes of a hunted deer, widened with what was unmistakably fear though her voice, deep and mellow, had no such intonation.

'You may.'

All the same, when he put his arm around her waist his suspicions of her uncertainty were confirmed. She might be a competent dancer – proved to be that and more – but she could not have been more tense.

Being the eldest of four children his fatherly instincts were well-developed. From the beginning he wanted not only to make love to her but to look after Milliora.

'You know the de Voys well?'

'Hardly at all,' she said, so softly that he had to bend his head to hear her words against the music and the talking. 'I've met them once or twice in Dermot's company out hunting.'

'You hunt with the County Limericks?'

'When I can spare the time.'

The time from what, he wondered. But that he could find out later. His immediate necessity was to secure her for another dance.

She did not smile when he asked her. Nevertheless, she said, 'Yes, you may,' and made no attempt to move out of his arms when the music died away.

When he finally got back to the table Ted – the worker of miracles – had contrived to join their two parties together, presumably for Harry's benefit. The musicians had paused but the noise was as uproarious as ever with hundreds of voices talking at once. Temporarily parted from Milliora, Harry found himself drawn into a cheerful argument about the use of whipcord on hounds.

'There was an English huntsman named Goodall who tried it with the pack – '

'It's all right for a whip – '

'You *can't* secure an obedient pack like that.'

His red-haired lady sat silently at the table. In contrast to her, the lumpy lady sitting next to the fat man never closed her mouth.

'What did you say?'

'. . . cubs have grown so bold they can no longer be held up . . .'

The musicians were about to play again. Obliged to dance his way around the extended party, Harry calculated. Fifteen waltzes and five lancers. Twenty in all and four of them gone already. Besides his beautiful lady there were seven women in all. He could still have nine more dances with the one that mattered to him. Starting immediately.

'Mrs O'Brien, will you dance?'

When they moved out on to the floor together, he made sure of the other eight.

'Will you take a look at the cut of Milliora? She hasn't as much on her as would keep flies off a sugar bowl!'

Dermot and Mary were dancing together. He frowned at his sister, wishing that she was less vulgar with her choice of words. Marriage to Noel Leahy had coarsened rather than cultivated her, more was the pity, though Heaven knew he was delighted to have her off his hands.

'Major Fielding is all over her. It's not surprising the way she's dressed.'

'Your own dress is nothing to write home about,' Dermot said. 'Where did you get that thing from anyway – out of the attic or where?'

There was no need to worry about what was happening on the dance floor. No need. In her mind, Milliora – as she had previously proven – would always be married to Tom . . .

Wouldn't she?

'You're horrible, Dermot – horrible. You always were.'

'Oh, be quiet, for God's sake,' he said to Mary. 'This isn't the time to cry.'

It's happening again, Rosaleen thought. We could be back in the garden at Laurel Hill on the afternoon of the fête, with Milly in a splendid gown, catching the handsomest man in the place.

While I am here with a man I do not love – to whom I happen to be wed . . .

Lucky Milly. Who has re-awoken to find love all over again.

And I, who have also discovered love, can explore the possibilities of it no further.

'You'd better chat to the old man,' Dermot said, his face pinched with anger. 'Milliora has completely failed in her duties as a partner.'

It was midnight. On a farm in Meelick, a man would be asleep.

'He seems quite content to me,' Rosaleen said. 'Unlike you, maybe he's glad to see somebody being happy.'

At two in the morning Harry was able to sweep Milliora quite literally off her feet in the third set of the lancers.

By then, tendrils of hair had escaped from chignons, a heavy foot had trodden the hem of a delicate dress, debutantes were flirting. The faces of the pink-coated men were flushed with drink and the ladies' cheeks were hot under their rouge.

In her black lace gown, Milliora looked unflustered with not a hair out of place. Andy and Carmel made up the set of dancers, changing partners with them in the fifth figure over and over again.

She was back in Harry's arms when the dance moved into the galop and he did not think she was tired.

'Hurray!'

A whoop, loud and getting louder, was reiterated as the men swooped their partners up. Holding her with both hands around her waist was an intoxicating sensation. Added to the alcohol he had consumed it urged him to join in.

'Hurrah!' he shouted.

She gasped, a faint enough sound but somehow he picked it up.

'Are you all right, my dear?'

'I'm just a little warm . . .'

Her feet were on the floor but she was leaning against his chest. He wanted to carry her away from the noise and the dancers, to the beautiful box garden, from where steps led to the cool River Maigue.

'I think the rain has stopped again. Would you like to come outside and walk awhile by the river?'

She shuddered, shocking him back into sobriety.

'Not by the river, no. Not tonight.'

Of course, he thought – her husband drowned. How could he have forgotten?

'I'm sorry. We'll do whatever you would like.'

He paused, looking down at her, his blue eyes filled with affection and compassion.

'You are a wonderful woman,' he said. 'I want you to be happy.'

24

Teaching the twins to ride was one of the most satisfying experiences of Tim-Pat's life and watching their progress was another.

When it came to riding there was little to choose between them. Daniel, as was his way, had made up for lost time and had acquired as much knowledge in the application of hands and legs for keeping a horse under control as his brother.

It was Daniel who was getting the most attention from Tim-Pat the morning after the hunt ball, while Eugene stood beside him, watching.

'Get down in the saddle as much as you can, Master Daniel. That's right,' Tim-Pat directed. 'It's all in the balance and in the way you grip your legs so your muscles won't get tired. And if they're not tired you'll stay in the saddle if the horse jerks forward suddenly. You won't be thrown like that.'

'Going over fences you must *sit* forward and *lean* back.' Eugene repeated what he had previously been told.

Before Tim-Pat could praise him for retaining this bit of knowledge he spotted Dermot with a grim face on him making his way across the yard.

Trouble – and, by the looks of things, bad trouble. Probably to do with the widow since no one or nothing else was capable of bringing that dark look to Master Dermot's face.

'We'll leave it there for the moment,' Tim-Pat told the boys. 'We'll go on with the lessons later.'

'What do we have to leave it for?' Daniel demanded. 'You said you were free for the morning.'

'Well, now I'm not,' Tim-Pat informed him. 'Down you get. Your father needs me.'

'And I!' said Daniel indignantly, but he dismounted and led his pony away, followed by his brother.

'Is it herself – the widow – that ails you?' Tim-Pat asked when Dermot reached him.

Sometimes, lately, he felt older than Dermot. Where once he had looked up to the other man now he felt as if, in a practical sense, he had grown beyond him. This shift of attitude was due in part to his involvement with the movement, which gave him a feeling of independence – a surety that he was fulfilling his own destiny, that, through it, he would ultimately avenge the wrong that had been done to his family.

In contrast, Dermot, by virtue of his position, was protected from life. It was exposure to life's dangers that made a man mature.

'Who else would it be?' Dermot said savagely, and proceeded to pour out the story of what had gone on at the ball the night before.

'You know what this can mean, don't you?' he concluded. 'That she could marry this blasted fellow and produce brats of her own who'll be heirs to Crag Liath.'

'I wouldn't say that,' Tim-Pat said, soothingly.

He might have been talking to one of the twins, picking him up from the ground after a tumble out of the saddle, dusting him down, offering comfort.

And hope.

'It's early days yet,' he said. 'What man is it, Master Dermot?'

'A fellow called Fielding – Major Harry Fielding. Inniskilling Dragoons.'

'An English soldier, is it?'

Tim-Pat spat viciously on to the ground, wiping the spittle from his mouth with the back of a venomous hand.

'English!' he said again, his green eyes, cat-like, dangerous as a tiger's.

'She has him just where she wants him, the bitch. You should have seen the performance.'

'I should not. And where does she want him?'

'At the altar, I'd say. And after – '

'Children. With their dirty hands round the throat of Crag Liath. It can't be allowed to happen, Master Dermot.'

'No.'

Once again, Tim-Pat had not failed him, Dermot thought, either in the offering of sympathy or in the recognition of the need to take action in a crisis. But what action?

Tim-Pat only said, 'We won't *let* it happen, Master Dermot.'

'That's easier said than done. How is Clasai getting along?'

'Great. Well-named. He's a trickster all right. But he'll be a great hunter yet. He has the courage and the shape and the speed. You did right to buy him.'

'You think so?'

'Come and see for yourself.'

The black horse, a chaser to look at, gazed thoughtfully out over the half-door of his loose box, gentle, this morning, as a satiated baby after sucking its mother's milk. It did not seem possible that, only yesterday, he had kicked himself out of his harness. A clever brute, snappy, with the brains to defeat his rider, as Dermot had already learnt, not once but several times.

'He's coming along, Master Dermot. Full of his tricks but he'll be a handy hunter yet.'

'He's too clever for hunting,' Dermot insisted. 'If I had the choice of two evils, I'd prefer a fool to a knave in horseflesh on the field. You don't want to be wasting time jockeying for power, when the hounds are tied to a fox.'

'It's early days,' Tim-Pat said for the second time. 'Still, you'd be surprised how the two of us are getting along. He has courage – isn't that the main thing? – and staying power – '

'And I have the bruises to prove it!'

'He'll go like a bird for you yet,' the groom grinned, rubbing the long black nose.

Clasai inclined his head in pleasure. Towards everyone else, his reddened eyes invariably burnt with latent anger. Dermot remained unimpressed.

'A handy hunter, is it? I'd be interested to see that.'

For answer, Tim-Pat opened the loose box and led Clasai out and into the yard. Nearer to Dermot, the animal quivered, swishing its black tail in a mixture of hatred and scorn.

'Stay there now, boy. Stay still in the yard.'

Obediently, Clasai halted, eyes riveted on the groom.

'Stay still. I'm getting your bridle. We'll go out to the back field. Come with us, Master Dermot. It will take your mind off the other.'

Following, Dermot kept a discreet distance, far from Clasai's reach. He would not put it past the black horse to kick out just for the hell of it, for all Tim-Pat's control.

Wending their way through the orchard, stepping on the sludgy remnants of old brown apples, they reached the boreen and the meadow that ran out from it.

Under the old oak tree Tim-Pat said: 'Hold on there would you and I'll show you how far we're progressing,' and leapt nimbly on to Clasai's bare black back.

Small and thin as he was, on horseback the groom had stature and a curious grace of his own. Clasai, docile as he never was with Dermot, stood still, awaiting his next instruction. A magician – a damned sorcerer, that was Tim-Pat with a horse.

'Come on, boy. Show your paces. Round in a circle. *That's* it. Stop. Good, good. Over now to the hedge . . .'

And so on. Child's stuff – except that a child would never ride Clasai – canter him down to the river, as Tim-Pat was doing, as if to control him was an effortless, natural thing.

Where the long boreen and the lush meadow coupled had always been to Dermot a fantastical place, where a man could believe in his legends. Here, one's spirit, lifted out of the taut conventional shell in which it was normally entrapped, was released, set free to contemplate the oldest Irish dreams. The magical tribe of the Tuatha De Danaan, defeated by the Milesians, his own forebears, had repaired to such places as this, to live within the elf mounds and the hills and the green plains of Ireland in palaces made of silver and pearl.

It was impossible to stand here on such a day, with horse and rider fusing into the silver-grey landscape, and not enter into the magic.

Urged by Tim-Pat, the black horse whirled into a gallop, wing-footed, graceful enough to bring tears into your eyes.

Impossible, too, not to conjure up an image of yourself on the black back, bare of a saddle, in just as fast a gallop, with a kill in the open at the end of your run, yourself the first man up. Independent. Free to be happy and wild. Free of the need to take revenge.

'So what do you think, Master Dermot?'

Rather like a heavy fall after a hunt breakfast, Dermot was back to earth with a thump.

'His performance with yourself in the saddle is one thing; he has me bested. The brute is a killer at heart, in my opinion. I'll never get the use out of him.'

Tim-Pat looked at him oddly.

'I wouldn't say that, Master Dermot. I wouldn't say it at all.'

'Ah, come on.'

But it seemed that Tim-Pat had lost interest in the discussion. As nimbly as he had mounted, he was off and on to the ground, sharing his secrets with Clasai. A wind was coming up from the river. Dermot shivered with cold.

'Shall we go in?'

'Wait a minute, Master Dermot. We have another trick to show you.'

'What's that then?'

Instead of answering, Tim-Pat tore off his heavy white shirt, one of Dermot's cast-offs, and threw it on to the grass so it lay, like half a body, with its arms thrown out from its sides. Exposed, his own thin body was that of a hungry boy.

'For God's sake, man – it's freezing!'

The groom ignored him, addressing, not Dermot, but Clasai. He spoke in a more agitated manner now, gesturing towards the shirt.

'Get him, boy – get him.'

He stepped back, away from the black horse, never ceasing to speak.

'Get him – get him,' mesmerizing with a couple of words, back under the old oak.

Then Dermot saw him make another gesture, circling his thin arms in the air. At once, Clasai reared to his full height, flaring his nostrils in rage.

'*Get him!*'

The tone of the voice was quite different. Where before it had coaxed the black horse into a trance, it now incited to turbulence and danger.

Clasai hesitated for barely a second, assimilating the inference of the new command, a huge god-horse poised on the brink of violence against the silver sky.

And then the outrage. The hooves flailing, pounding in fury on to the ground where half a body lay – dead, or so it seemed. Pounded into the ground, though that death still did not appease the assailant, the pulverizer, the giant miller mashing.

Transfixed, Dermot witnessed the detrition, powerless to stop himself until –

'Stop!'

The next enigma. The assailant halted, fragments of a garment like sick flowers sticking into the mud. The angry horse was still.

'Jesus Christ,' said Dermot weakly. 'How the hell did you train him like that?'

Tim-Pat's attention was on him now. He stared at Dermot with green opaque eyes.

'I can make Clasai do a lot of things, Master Dermot,' he said in a strange, faraway voice. 'Useful things. He'll be worth the money yet.'

On their way back to the house they both lapsed into their own silences, Dermot angry again at the concept of Harry and Milliora, Tim-Pat contemplative as a monk, as if he had reached a decision and was thinking about its finesse.

When they reached the yard it was the groom who spoke first and, though Dermot was unaware of it, there was a new, subtle, almost indiscernible authority in the few words he said.

'Don't be worrying yourself too much about the widow, Master Dermot. Yerra, there'll be no need for *you* to bother too much about her.'

383

25

In the time that was left to him before he returned to the Curragh, Harry was determined to see as much as possible of Milliora. She was in two minds about him, he could see that, interested on the one hand, and apprehensive on the other.

She resisted any suggestion that he visit her at Crag Liath at the beginning, although she did agree to meet him for lunch in the city on several occasions.

It was pointless rushing her, he decided. Like all animals she would run away if he moved too fast in her direction. So he made himself take it easy, making it clear that although he wanted to see her badly he would accept her terms. That seemed to reassure her. She lost a little, though not much, of her inner tension but her guard was still up.

He was therefore surprised when she invited him to a house party at Crag Liath the weekend before he left, along with the de Voys and the Dermot O'Briens. Remembering that he would soon have to deal with the problem of Sarah, Harry was tense himself when he got to O'Brien's Bridge and, perhaps because of the depression that was beginning to hang over him, he did not take kindly to Crag Liath House. It was too austere, flat-faced, sombre and dark – and probably draughty, as Irish houses were.

It did not please him either that, having been met at the front door by his regal and exquisite lady, he should be shown up to what the housekeeper announced was Mr Tom's old room.

'Her husband,' she said meaningfully, adding, when this had sunk in: 'Will there be anything else you need?'

'No, thank you,' he said, trying not to yawn.

The fresh air of County Clare was soporific enough on its own. When he thought of Sarah he became drowsy, too, wanting to drown his problems in sleep.

'I'll be leaving you then,' said the housekeeper, going away.

The room in which he found himself was barren enough, a place of sojourn, rather than of permanent habitation, but it had enough in it for his needs – a brass bedstead covered with a heavy rug, a tallboy and wardrobe for his clothes, and a small table on which he at once laid out his shaving mirror and hairbrushes. On another table beside the bed sat a functional brass candlestick and an ugly, fat alarm-clock with a loud tick that resounded all over the room. Unpacking, he considered the clock – then put it in the wardrobe underneath a coat.

He spotted a photograph reflected in the wardrobe's full-length mirror and turned round to confront it: a picture of a young man in his mid-twenties with a mop of black hair, a cheerful rounded face and an impudent expression. The husband who had been drowned? There was a likeness to Dermot O'Brien although his face, unlike Dermot's, was hedonistic and untamed.

He met the same young man in another silver frame when he went downstairs to the drawing-room. By then, Harry felt better about the house. It was much more attractive inside than out and Milliora – whom he held responsible for that – seemed to enhance it further.

Was it intentional or had she deliberately chosen to sit in the vicinity of the silver-framed picture, so that

385

she could refer back to it from time to time, as if asking her dead husband's views on the presence of a stranger in the house that they had shared? It was almost as if she had decided to bring the two men together to see how they got on.

Taking a quick glance at the photograph, he decided that he did not like the look of his predecessor. A clown, no doubt of that, in spite of his handsome face. According to the de Voys, Milliora had been widowed for about eight years. It was high time she forgot all about her former husband.

'Major Fielding, perhaps you would like to walk around the estate later on?'

'That sounds like a good idea,' he said, too heartily.

He did not relish the prospect. The estate had belonged to her husband. They did not need Tom to accompany them on a walk.

At dinner, the silver candelabrum set off to perfection the pale yellow Belleek porcelain, so thin that, if you held a plate up to the light, you could see your fingers through it. The same shade, repeated on the walls and in the curtains, relieved the heaviness of the mahogany furniture, the balloon-back chairs and the dominating sideboard, curved and bow-fronted like an *enceinte*.

Mary Markham, coming into the dining-room to refill the port decanter, did so anticipating the full brunt of Milliora's wrath. Why did you not check the port before, the hazel eyes were bound to demand, instead of now when the guests are present? In that mood, her coldness would freeze the blood as it went running through your veins.

Better late than never, said Mary, silently defensive – and wouldn't it have been a far worse thing if I had waited till the ladies had retired before I got round to it?

Do you think so? Mary could hear the sarcasm. Herself was that nervous this weekend, that she would lay it on.

All the while, as this conversation went through her mind, Mary was sneaking to the small cupboard with the marble top and brass gallery which stood alongside the sideboard, where the bottles of port, sherry, Madeira, whiskey and brandy were stored, wishing the visitors – and their hostess – could not see her.

'You hunt with the Kildares, I take it, Major Fielding,' Master Dermot said. 'They used to go out five days a fortnight in the old days, starting at crack of dawn. You've fine grass country up there with just enough woodland to be pleasant, and nicely sited coverts.'

'The fences are a bit stiffish, I find,' said Major Fielding. 'I must say, I'd like to hunt with the County Limericks.'

'Why not?' said Master Dermot. 'Come down. I can fix you up with a horse any time you like.'

'That's very good of you. I would like that very much.'

Not a word out of herself. Stealing a swift glance over at Milliora, Mary realized with relief that her own presence had actually gone unnoticed. She swiftly secreted the empty port bottle down on the floor on the right-hand side of the sideboard and slightly moved the silver coffee service, as if that had been her purpose all along.

And still Mrs O'Brien did not look over in that direction, to confer the glacial glance.

The weekend was a curious series of starts and stops: a moment when she spontaneously rested a hand on his arm and then, considering, withdrew it; her hesitation

387

when they found themselves alone at the foot of the stairs – the sudden, curt 'Good night!'

The conviction that while her body wanted him, her mind was still confused.

Well, they both had the legacy of past love to contend with, and sort out. In the meantime, Harry was a patient man, and would content himself with the concession that she would like to see him again soon, and a promise that she would write.

She saw him off at Limerick station, seemingly composed and hardly sorry to say goodbye.

Perhaps he was wasting his time and she wanted to live in the past, preferring a dead husband to a living lover. But that was an unbearable thought.

Nevertheless, it engrossed him all the way to the Curragh. He did not think of Sarah on the journey back. So he was totally unprepared, when he got back to his quarters, to find her waiting in his bed.

'Darling!' said Sarah, sitting up and holding out her arms. The eiderdown, which had covered her, fell away. Her breasts were taut, the nipples hard already.

'How the hell did you get in?' he said, shocked at his own excitement.

'Your batman let me in,' said Sarah, demurely. 'I told him we were old friends. I'm sure, if he's *your* batman, that he knows the value of discretion.'

'Which you do not. Where's your husband? Did anyone see you come in? How long have you been here?'

'Questions – questions!' Sarah said. 'Why bother about questions, Harry, when there are better things to do?'

'*No*, Sarah!'

'No, Sarah!' she mimicked. 'It's not like you to say

388

"No", Harry. I've been missing you. I gather you've been in Limerick?'

'You've been checking on my movements.'

'Yes. It was easy enough to find out when you were due to return. But not so simple to understand why you went away.'

'I went away because – '

He stopped there. Because I was trying to avoid you – he could hardly tell her that, or not now. He knew Sarah very well and was aware of the kind of scene she was capable of making.

'Why, Harry? Why did you go away when I was about to arrive?'

Her voice caressed, rather than demanded. He threw his suitcase into a corner, averting his eyes from her. It was months since he had been to bed with a woman, not since the Cape, and the necessity to proceed slowly with the one he was starting to love only intensified his need.

'Why?' A kitten's purr.

'It's very late,' he said, 'much too late for you to be here.'

'That never worried you in the past,' she said. 'Harry, did you – do you love me?'

'Yes, I loved you,' he said in a dead voice.

'*Loved?*' A different voice, bitter now and hard. That helped him.

'Sarah, it's – '

'Past my bedtime? Or past *our* bedtime? Which is it, Harry?'

He looked directly into her eyes.

'Past your bedtime. How are we going to get you out of here without your being seen?'

'If that's all that concerns you, don't worry – I know

389

how to avoid being seen,' said Sarah, getting out of bed.

She had a beautiful body, well-nurtured, the legs long for all that she was small, leading up to the triangle of dark hair that concealed that other mouth. He willed himself to stand still while she reached out for her clothes and quickly put them on. The inference that he no longer loved her was a blow to her ego that had saved him – but only for the timebeing.

'How chaste we are,' said Sarah, from the door.

Harry sighed. With Sarah, chaste equated chased – it was only a matter of when. He had not seen the last of Sarah Masters – not, he thought, by a long straw.

Within the week she was back, saying they should be friends.

'By all means.'

'I'll pop in and see you again.'

She was approaching on a different tack now, trying to soothe his anxiety and guilt before resuming normal relations. She came with a book to lend him – then came to take it back. He found her curled up in an armchair killing time until he should appear. He would have to put a stop to it.

But, in the meantime, he had to see Milliora and planned a weekend so they could be together in November.

'I hear you're off to Limerick,' said Sarah, paying one of her little visits. 'You seem to be spending a lot of time down there these days.'

'I go there to see an old schoolfriend,' Harry said. Later – he thought – I'll sort it out with Sarah later.

'You mean Ted de Voy?' said Sarah, airily.

How the hell did she find things out?

* * *

390

Harry was not staying with the de Voys. So that he could concentrate exclusively on Milliora that weekend he booked into the Royal George and did not let Ted and Dottie know he was in town.

He had written to Milliora to say he would arrive in Limerick late on Friday evening and would like to call on her on the Saturday, and she asked him to spend the day.

His coming advent had a dyadic effect on Milliora. She was on top of the world and longing to see him – and she wanted to run away. Her body and her mind told her that he was not only desirable but also, that rare being, a man of integrity and compassion, and with her body and her mind she was already three-quarters in love. But fear, that great destroyer, told her she should flee.

In the end, she compromised, standing her ground but, taking advantage of the truce with Rosaleen, asking Daniel and Eugene to spend Saturday at Crag Liath as well, to neutralize matters with Harry.

He was anything but pleased to arrive at the house and find the O'Brien twins there already. They were nice enough boys, he thought – attractive little devils to look at – but predictably they got in his way. He had said to himself that he had all the patience he required to deal with Milliora but it needed most of what he had to get through the day as first Daniel and then Eugene clamoured for her attention.

Finally, their mother, a pleasant, intelligent though rather quiet woman, came out to retrieve them and he was mercifully left alone with Milliora.

By then he was feeling edgy. The strain of resisting Sarah and not being able to have Milliora was beginning to tell.

'What a pity Daniel and Eugene couldn't stay for the

whole weekend,' said Milliora wistfully, coming back from seeing Rosaleen and the twins off. 'Rosaleen says the Leahy children are going to play with them tomorrow so they just had to go back.'

Thank God for the Leahy children, said Harry to himself.

The bruised, wounded look on Milliora's face prompted him to say, more daringly than usual, 'You're expending too much love on other people's children, Milly. You should have your own instead,' when she had poured a glass of whiskey for him and was putting it into his hand.

He might just as soon have shot her. She drew back from him in shock, bumping into a small gilded table, knocking a Worcester mug on to the floor and spilling most of his whiskey.

'Heavens!'

'It's all right. Nothing's broken,' she said, curiously breathless, and put the mug back in its place.

'I'm sorry,' Harry said. 'That was impudent and intrusive. It's just – Milly, I need to see you on your own.'

She said nothing. The hazel eyes were wary but at least she did not try to look away.

He was close to her now and he took both of her hands in his.

'Your hands are cold.'

'It's a cold day.'

'It's not really. And the fire in here makes this room as warm as toast. You're frightened, aren't you?'

'Perhaps.'

'There's no need to be frightened of me, Milly. I'm a very dependable person; I would never hurt you. Can't you make time for us?'

392

She half-turned from him looking, he realized, at the photograph of her dead husband in the silver frame.

'I don't know,' she said in a panicky voice. 'I don't know. Maybe – perhaps.'

Over her shoulder he could see into the garden. The blustery winds and heavy rains had wrought havoc on it, stripping the trees of leaves.

'Milly,' he said, and turned her round so she could see through the window. 'Look – look out there. See the nearest tree.'

'It's a plum tree,' she said. 'In autumn the leaves are usually purple-red . . .'

'The branches are virtually bare now, aren't they? The storms have seen to that. The tree has not attempted to fight against them at all. It understands the necessity of giving in when storms prove too strong – but you'll note it hasn't died.'

'Well, of course not . . .'

'It knows that in spring its leaves will grow again. Why are *you* fighting against that knowledge? The storm is over. You're young. You have all the time in the world to learn to live again.'

'What about you?' she said. 'Your wife died. What did *you* do then?'

It was his turn to be evasive. 'The action I took was even less commendable, I can assure you of that,' Harry said drily.

Ashamed of himself, he let go of her hands, just as Mary Markham banged the gong for dinner.

Harry returned to the Curragh determined on two counts. He was due leave. He would take some during December and still have several weeks in reserve, some of which he would take in New Year giving him plenty of time to pursue his courtship of Milliora.

Of which he was going to inform Sarah – that was his other decision. He owed her honesty, if nothing else.

Once in his quarters his first action was to attempt to clarify the amount of leave he was due. His records were filed in the third drawer of his desk, under Milliora's letters. But when he opened the drawer, he saw that her letters were not there. Was he becoming forgetful? Had he put them in another drawer instead?

Exasperated with himself, he looked into all the drawers. No letters, though nothing else appeared to be out of place or missing.

No, he was not becoming forgetful, he decided. The letters were not there because someone – a lady who came and went at her will – had taken them away.

So much for planning to tell Sarah of Milliora's existence. Sarah, being Sarah, had discovered it herself.

'Dear Mrs O'Brien . . .'

Who was about to hear that 'Dearest Harry' had a past!

Popping her own letter into its scented envelope, Sarah thought that, with luck, where Mrs O'Brien was concerned, he would not have a future.

That November, Captain Willie O'Shea brought a divorce suit against his wife, citing Charles Stewart Parnell.

Cathal winced, looking at the papers . . . 'The O'Shea Divorce Suit Today . . . Evidence of the Servants . . . Mrs O'Shea's Excuse to the Maid . . .'

The lovers were the laughing stock of the country. Particularly juicy was the account of how the Irish leader, under the absurd guise of 'Mr Fox', had fled down a fire-escape at Brighton to evade Captain O'Shea. In Britain, newspapers, cartoonists, music-hall comedians, even toy-manufacturers had a field day at Parnell's expense, with models of the Brighton fire-escape and a miniature of Parnell going on sale in the shops.

It was less sympathy for Parnell that Cathal felt – although he was sympathetic towards him as well – as acute awareness of the censoriousness of his own men where adultery was concerned.

'No man in the public eye can afford to lust after an immoral woman,' Ned Lynch had announced.

'A common prostitute. Having spent her husband's money, she made an eejit out of Parnell.'

'Her sister was in it as well, by all accounts, going after the husband. A base bunch. 'Twill be the ruin of Parnell. A man of that character is not fit to be Chairman of his party.'

'Did you see what was in the English papers?' John Roche had asked. '"The uncrowned king is crowned with everlasting infamy . . ." Oh, great good he's done the people who trusted him, consorting with Kitty O'Shea.'

It was pointless talking to them, telling them that there could be another side to the story, that the couple seemed to be in love – that O'Shea was a rotten husband who had neglected his wife for years. They could not see it. In the matter of men and women their thinking had already been done for them by the celibate rulers of Ireland – men like his brother Seamus – and they retained or wanted no rights to independent thoughts.

It was left to Cathal to consider his own position or what it would be if he went ahead with his pursuit of

Rosaleen O'Brien. If he doggedly persisted, he thought he could succeed in that pursuit. She was starved of what she wanted and he thought she wanted him.

And if he succeeded would she end up disgraced, derided, reviled as a prostitute and a base, base woman like the unfortunate Kitty O'Shea? Was that what he wanted to happen?

No, it is not, Cathal decided – for all that I want her.

Nor – most importantly – was he seeking disgrace for himself. He could not risk being the target for stones and neither could the movement. It was that simple, however much he disliked it as an axiom: if he did not want to jeopardize the movement he should get out of Rosaleen's life. The future of the cause could be Ireland's future – wasn't that what they all believed?

He looked again at the papers: 'Parnell under a moral cloud . . . Parnell's clear duty to send in his resignation to his constituents . . . He should resign – that much is due to public morality . . .'

I won't see you – I cannot see you, Rosaleen had written.

Nor I you, Cathal thought.

Bundling the papers up, he hurled them into the grate, and grimly watched them burn.

26

'*You are not the only woman in Major Fielding's life. I thought you ought to know.*'

Milliora looked at the letter with distaste, trying to convince herself that she was not upset at receiving it and that it made no difference to what she felt for Harry.

'. . . *his love for another lady. He doesn't stay faithful for long* . . .'

Disgusting, she thought. And probably invalid.

But was it? What did she really know of Harry Fielding, beyond what he made sure she knew?

Can't you make time for us, he had pleaded, implying that their relationship was important, and she had believed that it could be that, in time. He had appeared to be totally sincere but maybe the truth was that he asked such questions of several women, or certainly more than one?

But why should she be affected by an anonymous letter since the sender himself – or herself? – must be a person of lowly worth whose purpose in writing it was to mischief-make, not to inform?

But I *am* bothered, Milliora confessed to herself. Whether I like it or not the letter has shaken my confidence in Harry, and made me aware of the fact that I know so little about him. He is an Englishman, a Protestant, something which, in any case, would give rise to serious problems if we were to become involved. If only I knew the de Voys well enough to ask them what kind of person he is.

But then she thought – maybe Dermot knows. Maybe *he* heard from Ted de Voy. I'll ask Dermot. I'll see him in his office, discreetly, and show him the letter and ask him what he thinks.

'Milly – what a terrible thing to receive.' Dermot found it almost impossible to keep the exultation out of his voice. 'You must be very distressed.'

'It's not pleasant. But what I really want to know is what you think of – '

The insinuations about Major Fielding's character, she had intended to add, and then suddenly found she could not. Having gone to Dermot's office with the express intention of discussing Harry with her brother-in-law she was disgusted at the thought of doing anything of the sort.

It was so louche, so shifty to talk about him behind his back, even with a member of her own family, and probe for information passed on by a friend. The thing to do was not to beat about the bush, but to take her courage in both hands and confront Harry – send him the letter and ask him for his comments on the accusations it contained.

'Milly?'

'Dermot, on second thoughts, give me back the letter, I know now what to do about it. Naturally you won't tell anyone that I have received such a thing. I know I can trust you on that.'

'Naturally,' said Dermot, keeping a straight face with difficulty.

He could hardly wait to get home and tell Tim-Pat that, in the hostilities in which they were engaged, a mortal blow had been struck.

Being devious by nature, it was always difficult for Dermot to understand others taking a direct approach to a problem. Sooner or later Harry would have told Milliora all about Sarah though he had thought it prudent to establish himself in her affections before making confessions that, at the beginning, might weaken his case.

Faced with Sarah's letter and Milliora's he knew he had no alternative but to put his cards on the table. A letter would not suffice. He secured the leave he wanted in order to return to Limerick.

But, first, there was the unavoidable heart-to-heart with Sarah which would leave her in no doubt that her tactics had not worked.

It was worse than he had expected – Sarah wild with jealousy and thwarted desire but not, he thought, when it all boiled down, with unrequited love. Hate rather. Why was it, he wondered, that when a woman believed you loved her she rated you superior to other men yet if you rejected her she insisted you were the lowest of the low? Logically it made no sense, but he did not say so to Sarah.

With Milliora things proved very much more simple. He had written back to her saying only that he was coming to Limerick and when, and that he would explain everything when they met.

She received him in the library and he thought that in that environment it might somehow be easier to tell her of Sarah and himself and of how the letter came to be written.

She seated herself on one of the wholesome library chairs and gestured to Harry to do likewise. All around him was evidence of that other life, the one she led on occasions with Daniel and Eugene: backgammon pieces which the twins had at some stage taken out of the games box; stray playing cards; books out of alignment.

'Pour yourself a drink,' she said, very much the grande dame, and therefore self-protective. A slender hand waved him towards a cupboard in the corner.

'A whiskey would go down rather well,' he admitted, doing as the hand commanded and helping himself to a stiff one.

And then, at last, he talked to her, conjuring up a more specific image of Lilian, first – one that for two years he had not permitted himself to recapture, in that way evading some of the guilt that lay like rejected lumber in the attic of his mind.

'We were cousins,' Harry said. 'We played together as children. I say played but even then she was remote. Not so much aloof – she was never disdainful or contemptuous – as detached, living in a world of her own from which the rest of us were totally excluded. In a way, that inaccessibility was part of her attraction. It offered a challenge and, at the same time, it intrigued. One wanted to break into that world, force her to share it and then, I suppose, carry her out of it into the real one. That was the effect she had on me when we were young. And she was a pretty woman – pale, lustreless, but with very beautiful, very fine hair, skin that was almost translucent. I always felt that I should grasp her before she disappeared.

'Our families took it for granted that we would ultimately marry. It isn't something a young officer is encouraged to do – marry, I mean. You are expected to have your evenings free so you can spend them in the Mess with your fellow officers, but in that sense Lilian was an ideal wife. She made no demands, never objected to my comings and goings. I could not criticize her for that, or for anything . . . It was my fault from the start for indulging in a fantasy, a young man's misconception of what I believed her to be. It's just that sometimes you can set out to enter and conquer an unexplored world and find to your surprise and disappointment that there's little or nothing there to possess. The truth is that I was bored. And then she became ill. I felt guilty about that – as if her sickness had been brought on by my disillusionment with the relationship. I told myself that was another foolishness but guilt seldom responds to the rational. It's too deeply entrenched for that.'

'Were you faithful to her?'

'While she lived, yes. Afterwards – '

And then he told her of Sarah.

'More guilt. I can't justify it. I can only say that I was consciously grabbing at life. Can you understand at all?'

'About guilt?' Her hands were crossed on her lap. The right one caressed the rings she wore on her third finger. 'I live with it myself, although it springs from another source. If I had not been grabbing at life eight years ago my husband might be alive. You know about that?'

'Yes. I heard about it from Ted. His death was an *accident*, Milly – you can't blame yourself for that.'

'For the quarrel we had before he died – ' she began.

But he interrupted: 'I know about the quarrel. Limerick is small enough for people to remember the details. It's you who should forget them. It's much easier for me to say this to you than to say it to myself, but the truth is that life is a gift we should accept with pleasure instead of turning it down in an attempt to expiate real or imagined sins. I daresay that I shall always feel guilty about Lilian but it does not mean that I am going to punish myself forever – certainly not now, when I've found you. I love you, Milly. You are a beautiful, brave, strong woman and you have no business living on your own.'

'My husband is dead,' she said, startled. 'I have no alternative but to live alone.'

'Perhaps in the past. Not in the future. I want to marry you, Milly. Does that surprise you so much? No, of course it doesn't. You knew this was going to happen. That was why you were so afraid.'

'Marriage,' she said, all the same, as if she was experimenting with a new word she had not pronounced before. 'I – '

She looked up at him almost as if to seek clarification of the word's meaning and then it was there – the honest and unashamed mutual recognition of each other's attraction. He reached for her hands and pulled her to her feet, and she did not resist, neither then nor when he bent forward and pressed his lips on hers.

She quivered, but not with fear, and her soft lips, responsive and yielding at the same time, told him what he wanted to know. He began to kiss her more purposefully, caressing with one hand the hair at the nape of her neck, tightening his grip on her waist with the other, releasing with mounting excitement the passion that was in her, that had been repressed for so long and was now willing to be expressed.

'Aunt Mil*ora!*'

With lips still pressed against Milliora's, Harry looked over her shoulder towards the window from where this unwelcome greeting came. Outside, looking in with interest, were two familiar figures – Daniel and Eugene, small vicarious novelty-seekers, fascinated by the scenario unfolding in front of their eyes.

Drat them, Harry thought furiously. What the hell are *they* doing here?

'Aunt Milora,' called Daniel, or maybe Eugene.

402

Although they were quite different to look at, he could not remember which was which.

This time, Milliora heard the cry and, shocked, pulled away, patting her hair into place.

'Children! Oh my goodness! I'd forgotten you were here.'

'They're staying here?'

'They have been. They're going home today.'

'Thank God for that,' he said as Daniel or possibly Eugene shouted, 'We're bored. We want to come into the house.'

Oh no, you don't, thought Harry with determination. He liked children, as long as they stayed in their place – and that was not in the library when grown-ups wanted to kiss!

He strode to the window and pushed it open. The impudent faces drew back.

'I don't think you want to come in for a moment,' he said. 'I think you would like to go out and watch the cows being milked.'

'We've done that,' one of the twins said, but less cocksurely than before.

'Then do it again,' said Harry, willing them to depart.

Four large eyes gazed at him, nonplussed – uncertain.

Then: 'All right,' said one of them, and both the faces were gone.

Intrusion had temporarily stifled passion.

'Come,' Harry said, gently. 'Sit down here beside me and let me tell you something else. I've watched and studied you ever since we met and it seems to me that your concentration on Crag Liath and all that goes with it is an unhealthy thing, born out of your guilt, although you may have genuine love for the land. Am I wrong?'

'I suppose not,' said a much more humble voice.

'You must break away from your memories – and break away from those twins. Let me put another thought into your head. I am not a poor man. I have land and a very pleasant house in Dorset. When I was in the Cape I used to think how pleasant it would be to farm it. I often thought at one stage that I should resign my commission.'

'You'd do that?'

'Quite happily, and all the more so now I've found you. Marry me and farm with me in Dorset – and make Crag Liath over in trust to the O'Brien twins. Marry me – I know we can be happy.'

'You're a Protestant,' she said. 'Mixed marriages are difficult . . .'

'What if I were to convert? I'm not against that. What do you say – about Crag Liath, as well as us?'

'But, you see, I had always intended to leave Crag Liath to Daniel and Eugene,' Milliora explained, 'though that was in the future. I suppose – '

'Yes?'

'I suppose I could put it in trust for them until they are twenty-one. I must talk to my solicitor about it. Perhaps Dermot could run it on their behalf until they're old enough to take over. Let me look into it, Harry, but – '

'But what? But you don't like the thought of marrying me – or of farming in England, either!'

'But nothing at all,' she said. 'I think farming in England would suit me very well.'

They were still in the library when Dermot arrived to take Daniel and Eugene home. Now that he had

Milliora where he wanted her Harry was not too disgruntled at being interrupted again.

And he wanted to talk to Dermot O'Brien about the possibility of getting in some hunting during his stay in Limerick. People maintained that February was the best month for the sport but he had always favoured December for memorable runs.

The weather of late had been fairly open. There should be a fair holding scent with alert foxes on the lookout for huntsmen and hounds.

It struck him initially that Dermot O'Brien was not in the best of moods and was not particularly pleased to see that Harry was down again from the Curragh. But then he decided that he had been imagining things – that the dark look he had thought he had seen on Dermot's face was only a trick of shadow and light. As soon as the subject of hunting was raised Dermot was the self that he remembered.

'Of course, it rains a lot in Ireland. But this October, for instance, being particularly wet the foxes could not shelter in drains. We had a lot of very good hunting.'

'I look forward to joining you, then,' said Harry, thinking – I must ask him again for the loan of a horse.

'You'll find a fair sprinkling of the military from the Limerick garrison out when you come, not to mention men from Cork. They come from all over the place to hunt with the County Limericks.'

'Indeed. And from all backgrounds. Here, you can ride alongside a groom, or even a priest! You can't do that in England.'

'Harry, how can you run England down – especially after talking me into marrying an Englishman!'

Milliora was sparkling with a new and heady excitement. It was something he loved to see.

'What?' An abrupt intervention from Dermot.

Strange, Harry thought, it almost sounds like anger.

But Milliora was running on, bubbling in her delight. 'Harry and I are getting married, Dermot,' she said, happily. 'Isn't that good news? You are the first to know.'

There was a moment's silence. It seemed to Harry that the library light was playing tricks again, casting another shadow on Dermot's narrow face. Or had Milliora been tactless, announcing their engagement in this room? One had to remember that she had once been married to Dermot's brother. Who knew what memories of Tom O'Brien lingered in this house?

Dermot was standing near the bookcases where three glass paperweights – two of the millefiori type and one depicting a Christmas greeting – were indiscriminately laid out. He moved them so they lay equidistant from each other. Then, relinquishing these, his hand shifted to a chessboard, re-arranging the chessman.

He said, 'I see. When will the wedding take place?'

'We haven't even discussed it!' said Milliora.

She sounded playful – almost flirtatious, no longer sombre and sad.

'Can I offer you a drink, Dermot,' she said, 'by way of celebration?'

Instead of replying, Dermot picked up a book by the controversial Mr Charles Dickens and idly flicked over the pages.

'Have you read any of his books?' Milliora asked, brightly. 'From what I hear, he is saying some terrible things. Making a big fuss about the wickedness of poverty when we all know that it is God's will that the poor be as they are.'

'Is he really?' said Dermot.

He closed the book, wiped a fleck of non-existent dust from its cover and found a place for it on a shelf.

'I must find the children,' he said. 'Then I have to be off.'

He probably *was* a little upset by the news, Harry thought. Still, he would get over it in time.

The back door was ajar. Dermot kicked it open and a nervous Dubhfoilean, roused from a doze in the clothes basket in the scullery, fled from his advance.

'Rosaleen! Jesus Christ, where are you?'

'Coming.'

But when she emerged from the dining-room, where she had been setting the table for dinner, she said, 'Why are you blaspheming like that? The children will hear you,' gesturing towards the stairs.

'Don't criticize me,' Dermot virtually hissed. 'There's bad news. Those two are getting married.'

'We were expecting that, weren't we?' Rosaleen said, reasonably. 'All the signs were there.'

'It's different now it's happened.'

And that was true. It was – quite different and very much worse. The difference between thinking you were going to fall from a horse and the moment when you did. Rosaleen's calm reaction infuriated him. There was no point in talking to her, he thought – she never understood.

There was only one person who did, who sympathized with his feelings – Tim-Pat, who had always stood by him in his hour of need and who, unlike Rosaleen, would not fail him now.

He heard Tim-Pat before he saw him, singing the song that had been composed as a tribute to the two policemen who, ordered to arrest Father Matt Ryan, the campaigner against evictions, had steadfastly refused.

'Where are you?' Dermot shouted, as the refrain ended.

'In here, Master Dermot.'

The groom's carroty head appeared over the half-door of Clasai's loose box.

There was no need for words. Tim-Pat took one look at Dermot and understood at once.

And there was the comfort.

'I told you before, there's a way around these things, Master Dermot,' Tim-Pat said soothingly. 'Come in to the harness-room where it's private. I'll tell you the plan I have.'

27

It did not make sense, Rosaleen thought on St Stephen's Day – Dermot assuring her that Clasai was cured of his tricks yet announcing that he was going to buy another hunter.

'With Grian that will be three,' she said. 'You can't put Mount Royal out to grass at this time of year. Where are you going to stable him?'

'You can leave that to me to arrange,' Dermot said, loftily. 'We managed when we thought Cu Chulainn was beyond it.'

'By taking him out to Crag Liath,' Rosaleen said. 'Is that what you're going to do this time? Milliora's stables will have nothing but old horses in them. Her horse, Bealtaine, must be getting on.'

'Why do you call the new horse Fear Gorta, Mama?' Daniel, sitting at the breakfast-table, stopped eating his oatmeal porridge in order to ask.

'I told you but you don't listen. That's the Irish for hungry grass – and Fear Gorta's always hungry!'

'That's what happens to you if you step on that kind of grass,' Eugene warned. 'You'd be craving for food in no time unless you had a bit of it on you at the time – a piece of bread or even a crumb maybe.'

'Do you resent my buying another hunter then?' Dermot challenged his wife. 'Should I feel guilty about spending my own money or what?'

'Not at all. It's your money. Do what you like with it. I was only wondering.'

And she had little enough time for even that, she

thought, between the house and the children and the way the needlework project she had set up with Bridie's mother had blossomed, with so many orders coming in from McBirney's alone that the Flanagan family were well on their way to becoming self-sufficient.

If only tiring yourself out ensured that you would sleep at night, Rosaleen thought, but the truth was, it did not. More often than not, she stayed awake into the small hours, thinking about Cathal and what a pity it was he had seen her point of view, while Dermot snored gently beside her. And there was contrariness for you!

Bang! went the knocker on the front door and children's voices promptly chanted:

> The wren, the wren,
> The king of all birds,
> St Stephen's Day was caught in the furze;
> Up with the kettle, and down with the pan,
> Give me a penny to bury the wran.

'The Wren Boys!' Daniel and Eugene whooped in delight. 'Mama, we want money.'

'I'll give you money,' Dermot said. 'Here you are – take it out and get rid of them.'

'I hate the Wren Boys,' Rosaleen said. 'It's a horrible custom, catching a harmless little bird and killing it and tying it on to a bush. It's barbaric.'

'You had those sort of inhibitions about hunting at one stage,' Dermot said. 'Now you seem to enjoy it.'

'I like the chase . . . Wasn't Harry Fielding going to hunt this month or has that been forgotten?'

'He is,' Dermot said, pushing his napkin to one side and getting up from the table. 'He was tied up with Milliora until now but he'll be out with us next week. Let's hope we don't have frost. I must be off to have a look at this horse I'm thinking of buying. Do you want to come?'

'Dermot, I'm too busy – '

'That's all right,' he said. 'I'll take Daniel and Eugene instead.'

'Who's the seller?'

'A fellow called O'Mahoney. Lives in Meelick. He had an advertisement for a half-breed hunter in the *Limerick Leader*.'

With his labourers off for Christmas, Cathal had been grip-making himself, using his hands to excavate the wide deep trenches that ran around each field to prevent the land from flooding, lest the cold of January ice up the soil and make the work more difficult.

All the fields except for the water-meadow, which was in low-lying land closer to the river, had been drained by St Stephen's Day. He wanted the water-meadow to become flooded and lodged, so that, when the country was beset by frost and maybe even snow, it would maintain a higher temperature. When it was drained in the Spring it would be well ahead of the other fields, in terms of early pasture.

He was extremely dirty, his hands and clothes filthy with mud, as he walked back to his house, and yet exhilarated by the job he had completed.

He walked up to the well and, turning the handle, lowered a pail to fetch up some water. He must have an elementary wash before going into the house. That was how Dermot found him.

'Good morning!' he called out, an immaculately turned-out figure peering out of a carriage. 'You had an advertisement in the *Leader* for a half-bred hunter.'

'So I did!' said Cathal, hands still encrusted with grime rubbing water off his face.

He had almost forgotten about his decision to sell the chestnut half-bred. He looked at the trim man who had leaped out of the carriage and was surprised. Men of light frame with the money to spare – and this fellow's clothes and carriage said he had that – usually went for a thoroughbred, unless, of course, he was planning to hunt in cramped country where the thoroughbred, with his hind legs not so well under him, was inclined to do less well. Maybe he was buying on behalf of someone else.

But then the stranger went on to explain: 'Thirty pounds is the price I want to pay at the moment – and I gather he's seven-eighths pure-bred.'

'That's right,' Cathal said – and got the shock of his life.

Out of the carriage tumbled two small boys, one with a mop of dark hair – the other distinctly red, and horribly familiar.

Young Daniel O'Brien! he shouted out, fortunately only in his mind. In reality, he could not say a word, waiting for the child to recognize him and publicly denounce him.

But Daniel did nothing of the kind. He and his brother glanced without interest at the figure by the pump, doubtless categorizing him as another boring adult, and, whispering to each other, began to potter round the yard, bothering the hens.

Daniel had forgotten him completely. Eight – nine months added up to a long time in the life of a very small boy.

'I imagine you want to have a wash before we take a look at the horse,' Dermot said in the kind of patronizing tone that grated on Cathal's nerves.

So this was Rosaleen's husband – the kind of Irishman who attempted to demonstrate superiority by

412

aping the snobbier English ways. He had a strong desire to land a good kick on the seat of Dermot's well-ironed trousers with the sole of his muddy hob-nailed boot. It was amazing that such a good, intelligent, beautiful woman could ever have been attracted by such a pretentious man!

'I won't bother,' he said shortly. 'Come into the stables and I'll let you take a look.'

The chestnut half-bred was just under sixteen hands, with a neat, well-formed head, narrow across the forehead but full between the ears, a well-composed and high-couraged animal whom Cathal would be sorry to lose. The combination of running the farm and the movement had left little time for hunting now.

'A hardy constitution. Jumps well, I'd say,' said Dermot, taking in the sloping shoulders, the wide and powerful hips, the muscular loins well united to the back.

'He does.'

'Hunted him, have you?'

'Once or twice,' said Cathal, coldly.

'Legs and feet are clean and sound.'

Stepping back from the chestnut Dermot's eyes dropped to Cathal's own mud-encrusted legs and the feet in the muddy hob-nailed boots as if trying to reconcile their owner's grubby condition with the gentility of his voice.

Fool, thought Cathal, forgetting what Tim-Pat had told him about Dermot O'Brien – here is an Irishman who has had nothing to do with the land and would never be likely to soil his soft hands with an honest piece of mud. Not a fool, though, when it came to horses. He knew what to look for there.

'Was it thirty pounds you said? I'll take him.' And then, unexpectedly, he added, 'Good land you've got here, I can see. Fine grazing. I notice you've gone in for Dexters. Good milkers – and they fatten quickly. Fine, sturdy little breed, I always thought, though we didn't stock them ourselves.'

'You know a lot about cattle.'

'I'm a farmer at heart,' Dermot said. 'It's the only life.'

He walked back into the yard and stopped, gazing beyond Cathal, beyond the house, to the Clare hills, bare and barren, where the land was spongey under the feet and cattle did not graze.

A lonely sort of man, Cathal decided. In that moment, he felt sorry for Dermot.

'There are many who would disagree with you,' he said, to lighten the moment. 'Farming in Ireland is a tough and often unrewarding business.'

'It can be profitable, if you go about it the right way,' said Dermot, and the arrogance was back. 'Well, I suppose we'd better be off. Come on, boys – get back into the carriage.'

About to step into it himself he called over his shoulder to Cathal, 'If you're passing that way of an evening drop in and have a look at the half-bred and stop for a drink. We live on the Ennis Road.'

With this coincidence to mull over, Rosaleen only gave passing thought to Dermot's decision to lend Clasai, rather than Grian or the new Chestnut, to Harry Fielding for the next meet of the County Limerick Foxhounds.

'Are you sure he'll be able to handle Clasai?' she asked.

Dermot said with a laugh, 'He's in the Dragoons, for Heaven's sake! He's a cavalry officer. If Harry Fielding can't handle a difficult horse, I'd like to see who can.'

'But I've seen Clasai with you even – throwing his head, kicking. He's a real brute, Dermot.'

'Harry knows full well how to shake him up if he kicks,' Dermot said. 'But he won't. Not now. As I told you, only you don't listen, Tim-Pat has him broken.'

After which she returned to forbidden thoughts of Cathal, trying to imagine the meeting between Dermot and the twins and himself.

'I asked that fellow O'Mahoney to come in for a drink sometime. You know, the fellow who sold me the horse,' Dermot had said after the chestnut had been put into the loose box, and Rosaleen's heart had missed a beat.

So maybe Cathal would call in? She remembered the time when she had believed that he could be a family friend. Maybe that was what he was cut out to be, and she should be content with that, seeing him now and again at Kincora.

What woman in love could be content with such an arrangement, she thought a few days later as she and Dermot and Tim-Pat went to the Four Elms, where the foxhounds were due to meet. There was a great covert at nearby Ballinagarde House where the hounds almost always drew and Dermot and Tim-Pat, whose role was to ride from covert to covert, ready to swop horses with Dermot when the first hunter got tired, were talking non-stop about the day ahead.

She felt like an animal herself, only a caged one whose energies have been curtailed but who is yet raging against its imprisonment, beating at the bars. If only she could talk to someone about her feelings for Cathal, it might be easier to contain them. Maybe she should talk to Milly, as she had been able to do at school. But Milly would be shocked if she were to divulge her story, Rosaleen thought, and who could blame her for that? Even to be harbouring thoughts of a man who wasn't your husband was a mortal sin, as Milly would doubtless point out.

Master and hounds were already at the Four Elms by the time they got there, and a big number of followers, mounted, and a crowd of local people on foot milling on the perimeter, who were only there to watch on.

And the excitement was there. You could almost smell it: the overt elation of the laughing followers, just as you could witness the scrabbling of the hounds as they sniffed the grass on the side of the road, eager for the scent of a fox to follow.

In the background were the hunt servants, dressed smartly in black or dark grey, contrasting, like the women, in their sobriety with the pink jackets of the men who were ready to hunt. Over their white breeches the pink-coated men wore leather aprons, and some were drinking hot toddies while their servants polished their boots.

Swank! There was a lot of it at the County Limericks' meets, with money coming in from Adare and Bruff and Ballyneety itself. But there was courage along with it – and a genuine love of the chase.

She smiled, thinking of the Crokers of Ballinagarde House, who were devoted to hunting. Dermot had told her that when old John Croker was seriously ill he watched the hounds from his window with a hunting-horn.

'His clergyman son came in and said, "You're going to a better place, Father," and Croker senior said, "I doubt it," so now, "I doubt it, says Croker!" is an expression commonly used in town.'

'What are you smiling at?' Milliora said, drawing up beside her in the carriage with Bawnie Kinsella at the reins and Harry Fielding beside her. All dressed in green again and radiating happiness, gazing at Harry Fielding as if he was the most wonderful man on earth.

So maybe he was. He was certainly a nice man – and a handsome one, as well.

'You're not hunting today?'

'I'll follow on from the road,' Milliora said. 'I must replace Bealtaine. Though sometimes I wonder if it's worth it with the way the Land League is bringing pressure on decent people, making them give up hunting. The Curraghmores had to give up altogether, Harry. Now isn't that the end?'

'The Muskerrys gave up too, for a while, but they have restarted. I don't think the League is that vindictive,' Rosaleen said pertly.

'They're dreadful people!' Milliora said. 'If I find any of them on my land in the future – '

She stopped, looking at Harry, and inexplicably, they both laughed at some private joke. Conversations with Milly were so frustrating, Rosaleen thought. She had preconceived notions about virtually everything and she would never alter her views, no matter what light was subsequently shed on the matter under discussion. So much for thinking you could tell her of your indiscretions! She would throw the whole Catechism at you and make you feel even more guilty than you were at the start.

Still, Harry Fielding seemed to adore her, making a great show out of kissing her cheek and patting her hand before he got out of the carriage to join Dermot and Tim-Pat and the horses.

'Isn't it nice to see how well Harry and Dermot get on?' said Milliora. 'I see Dermot has a new hunter. Who did he buy him from?'

'A fellow called O'Mahoney,' Roseleen said – and

417

suddenly she was back in the classroom at Laurel Hill, more nervous than happy, desperately wanting to giggle at something that was less funny than sad.

Coverts had already been marked out by the huntsmen and whippers-in – the hunt was showing signs that it was ready to move off.

On Fear Gorta's back, Rosaleen edged over to Dermot and Harry.

'I hear we're going to try first at Ballinagarde,' she said, intending to be friendly to Harry.

Hardly a controversial or an aggressive remark – or one likely to cause jealousy in your husband. Yet Dermot gave her a chilling look, ignored her words and, pointedly turning from her, began to talk to Harry about the County Limericks as if she did not exist.

Now that she came to think about it, he had been in a queer mood all morning, edgy and nervous, and happy in fits and starts. Whatever was up with him one thing was clear – he did not want his wife to be near him. If that was how he was feeling she would stay out of his way. By the time the hunt had reached the impressive stone entrance to Ballinagarde House, Rosaleen had dropped back, letting Harry and Dermot ride ahead.

'Wind's died down,' someone observed beside her. 'I think we'll have some rain.'

Surprisingly, they did not draw – or not then. The next covert was some three miles on, necessitating a long trot. Exchanging jokes, taking the odd nip from their hip-flasks, the hunt moved on, acknowledging the people in the carriages as they went.

A young brown horse, upset by a bird which flew out of the hedge beside him, jumped off all fours and began to buck with vigour, throwing his head between his forelegs and arching up his head. As his clever rider leant well back, accommodating his seat to the erratic movements of his mount, Fear Gorta moved disapprovingly out of his path.

By the time they reached the second covert the rain, which had been predicted, was spilling lightly but persistently, the web of a giant spider falling over horses and riders, and getting into your eyes.

And then they were into the covert, plunging one after the other into the tangled overgrowth and they had drawn, and the red predator had streaked away, and the hounds were in full cry. For a short while Rosaleen too was caught up in the mad magic of the hunt, hurtling on Fear Gorta's solid back across the first field, over a loose stone wall without much effort, and downhill to a bank.

A horse baulked, and another rider shouted, 'Beat him – beat him, sir! He'll come again!' and horse and rider were over, though a hat was left behind to be trampled by flying feet. She was part of a wild, vivid forward drive and she liked it and was able to laugh to herself at Miss Walshe, a well-known coward, dodging the obstacles and sneaking by on the road, and she had no thought yet of the time when the gallant fox would be caught.

The hounds did not slacken, racing along up the middle of each field, veering neither to left nor right for the best part of an hour. Field after field, until, leaping an apology for a gate – two stone pillars with a gap between filled with an iron bedstead and thorns – a young horse landed with his fore feet on a piece of stray timber and fell on to his head and knees, throwing his rider off.

It was the moment of sobriety, when the wildness went out of you and concern took its place. She pulled

419

up out of the way of more frantic riders, going to the young man who was lying on the grass.

'Are you hurt?'

But it was his dignity that was most impaired, and all the more so by her asking.

'I'll be fine. I'm only winded. Get out of the way of the hunt.'

'Are you sure now?'

'*Yes!*' he said, impatiently, although he was curled up into a foetus position with his head protected by the curve of his arm, lest he be kicked by an oncoming horse. Afterwards, she glanced back and saw him stagger uneasily to his feet in the direction of his horse.

After that the fox, up to old tricks, ran through a drain and they checked while the hounds went into the water. The misty rain was turning to heavy sleet. Put off by the heavy going, a couple of riders dropped out, amongst them, Rosaleen realized, amused, the faint-hearted Miss Walshe.

It was only then that she noticed that Dermot and Harry were missing and that it was a very long time since she had laid eyes on them. Not since the three of them were together on the Ballyneety road, but that was ages back.

The hounds were out of the drain, on the other side, and the riders were going after them, splashing in the mud and the dirty water, the need to preserve a tidy image diminished in importance. The young man who had fallen was back in the saddle, his horse apparently none the worse for a heavy fall.

But still no Dermot and Harry.

She wiped the rain away from her face with her gloved hand, wondering. Across the drain, the hounds had picked up the scent and were going nearly as fast as ever under the direction of the Master. Maybe they would kill.

Or maybe not. It was no longer any concern of hers, Rosaleen thought, for she was going back, retracing her path from Ballinagarde, to look for Dermot and Harry.

'Don't tell me you're turning back. The day is still young.'

The last man up. She waved at him, but her face was solemn. Going back over the fields and the stone walls and the hedges, all the way to Croker's covert, she ran into no one else, and her unease grew with the miles. Alone, she rode out of Ballinagarde, back on to the Ballyneety road, heading for the Four Elms. By then she was soaking wet, and worried out of her mind.

She saw the four elm trees a fraction of a second before she saw Dermot on the chestnut half-bred riding up ahead, and she urged Fear Gorta into a canter, knowing all the time that something was wrong.

Although by then Dermot should have heard those other hooves on the road behind him, he did not look back, cantering fast on the chestnut so she had to gallop in order to catch him up, with the sleet tearing at her face and a horrible fear in her heart.

The two horses were level. Dermot did not react.

She screamed, 'Dermot. Slow down! Slow down!' and he did not look to the side.

He was soaked to the skin but there was not a dirty mark on him, not like the rest of the hunt, and her mind demanded – Where *were* you all this time? Why are you riding so fast?

'Slow down, for God's sake!' she shouted at him again, swallowing rain and gulping and gasping for breath.

This time, her words registered, or so it appeared.

He obeyed, cantering more slowly, trotting. Finally stopping still.

His face was haggard. She knew then, without any doubt, that something had happened to Harry.

All the same, she asked him, 'What's the matter?'

And he said, quite simply in a high, cold and seemingly unemotional voice, 'Rosie – Harry's dead.'

He said:

'We took a short cut – easier for Harry, who isn't used to the drains and banks. We went over to the left.'

He said:

'Then Clasai went beserk. He trampled Harry to death.'

He said:

'Tim-Pat is with the body. I was going for a doctor – and a minister of the Church.'

She was inside the Four Elms public house and the landlord was calling to his wife to put the kettle on for a hot toddy and to bring a rug to put over Milly's shoulders and to stoke up the fire.

And Milly was trembling and saying, over and over, 'Rosaleen, I am cursed.'

Dermot's voice said, 'We took a short cut – over to the left.'

And a voice inside Rosaleen was saying – But why take a short cut? A *hare* tries to confuse its pursuers by running around in circles, but a fox, despising such tricks, keeps in a straight line – always.

So why move to the left?

'Are you feeling better, Mrs O'Brien?' the landlord's wife asked, looking sadly at her husband.

'Would you have another toddy, ladies?'

And maybe that was the answer. Maybe another toddy would drive foxes out of her head.

28

'Show me the pictures, Mama – show me the pictures,' a child's voice would plead, much later, when her own life was changed.

'I can show you *some* of the pictures,' she would say.

And she would fetch the papier-mâché box with the mother-of-pearl inlay in which her treasures were kept, and tip its contents on to the table, and suddenly there they were: Milliora, in a yellow walking-dress with enormous balloon sleeves, looking as haughty as ever; Daniel and Eugene, sailor-suited in white; Milliora and the twins together, pictured at Crag Liath.

There were also the pictures only she could see, since they existed in memory, not on paper. A poignant image of Milliora, dressed in black silk, on a bleak day, talking sadly of Harry.

'I knew him for so short a time,' she said, 'and yet he taught me so much.'

But just what Harry had taught Milliora, Rosaleen did not learn, or not then, because Mary Markham came into the room.

'Beg pardon, Mrs O'Brien, but you'll not be forgetting that tomorrow is St Brigid's Day. Out the back they want to know if you're going to be there for the turning of the sod.'

The first of February – the beginning of the year on the farm when the annual ritual that preceded the first ploughing was accompanied by the recital of prayers.

'Yes, I'll be there,' Milliora said, wearily. 'We have a new multi-furrowed plough, Rosaleen. I don't know what to make of it yet. My own opinion is that it needs too many horses to pull it.'

How strange life was, after all, Rosaleen thought – here is this city girl turned into a countrywoman while I have been moved to the town, and forced to get used to its habits.

But that was a superficial thought, bearing in mind the way Milliora must be feeling. It was easy enough to guess at that, but far more difficult to actually reach her and offer a form of comfort since, in spite of what she had to say about Harry's qualities, she seemed to be only partly present, the rest of her mind sealed off as if, by obturating it, she could protect herself from pain.

'Should Liam Lenihan go on with fencing?' Mary Markham wanted to know. 'He says he needs a new slasher, but he wants the money to buy one.'

'Give it to him then and tell him I hope he does a better job than he's done in the past, or the cows will get down to the river!'

In one sense, Milly had not changed one whit.

'It will soon be spring,' Milliora said suddenly. 'There will be new leaves on the plum tree. Are *you* well, Rosaleen – and Dermot? I don't seem to have seen him for ages.'

'He's well enough.'

The conventional answer but not, in this case, the honest one, although she was not prepared to inflict her worries on Milliora by telling her the truth. 'Dermot is odd – he had been, since Harry's death,' was hardly reassuring.

'All the same, you seem – well, not your usual self. Are you worried about something? Are the twins all right?'

'The twins are grand,' said Rosaleen to the old Milly,

424

maternal, offering comfort when she was in need of it herself.

And Rosaleen felt like her old self, desperately wanting to respond to Mother Milly, and confide in her as she had been able to do when the two of them were young.

Outside, clouds more black than grey raced over the cheerless sky. In the rose drawing-room, a turf fire blazed – their chairs were drawn up alongside it. The warmth she needed was there.

In that moment Rosaleen very nearly told Milliora of the love she carried for Cathal. She started to do so, unapologetically changing the subject, saying, 'Milly, did I ever tell you about the person Dermot bought the chestnut half-breed from – a Mr Cathal O'Mahoney? He's farming in Meelick. By sheer coincidence he turns out to be someone I met before. He was at a writer's meeting I went to in Dublin last year – at the house of John O'Leary, the editor of the *Gael*.'

Milliora was completely with her now – Rosaleen realized that.

And Milliora did register the fact that Rosaleen wanted to tell her something of importance for her voice shook as she mentioned Cathal's name. And yet she could not stop herself – the words she spoke were out of her mouth almost before she thought them.

'John O'Leary – the former Fenian who was exiled from Ireland? Oh, Rosaleen, how can you be mixing with people like that?'

And the moment was gone forever. Under the circumstances, Rosaleen felt that she could not be angry with Milliora, but she asked herself what more had she been expecting from her but comments like these.

As for telling her about Cathal, that was out of the

question. Milliora, with her entrenched views about life and love and politics, would not accommodate such a confession, she was sure, and would never understand.

'It's difficult to explain,' she said. 'Never mind. Is there any more tea in the pot, Milly? If there is, I'll have another cup.'

But for all that Milliora was tactless and against the nationalistic cause, where love was concerned, Rosaleen misjudged her. She had always been a romantic; she had learnt from Harry a little of the complexities of men and women and love, and was unlikely to make a judgement, and she would have understood only too well about sleepless nights spent longing for a man who was not there.

But she missed the opportunity to say anything of the sort and Rosaleen went on to talk of other things.

'Before you know where you are the ploughing will be done, and the harrowing, and you'll be sowing the seeds and planting the potatoes,' she said as she was leaving. 'It's a good thing you've always been busy. You won't have time to think.'

Milliora sighed and grimaced. 'I thought this would be the last spring I'd have at Crag Liath,' she said, opening the big front door. 'Of course, I never told you – I hadn't completed my arrangements – but Harry had persuaded me to give up Crag Liath so we could farm in England.'

'Give up Crag Liath! But what would happen to it, Milly? Surely you'd never sell it?'

'Rosaleen – naturally not! It seems strange that I didn't tell you – I was making it over to Daniel and Eugene for when they are twenty-one. That was what Harry wanted. As he said, he had money of his own.

I'd rather hoped – Dermot might keep it going till the boys were old enough. As it is . . .'

But she did not complete the sentence.

Rosaleen said, 'Harry must have had a lot of money to be able to shrug off an estate like Crag Liath. It's a curious thing to do.'

'But he had. There is an estate in Dorset and he was the eldest son. I shall be meeting his brothers later this year when I go over to England. And you see, Rosaleen, he felt very strongly that I should break my ties with the past – with Tom – and make a new life with him. At first, I was uncertain but I thought about it and I could see he was perfectly right. We cannot live in the past.'

'No. So you're going to England?'

'Only for a short stay,' Milliora said quickly. 'It won't be the same without Harry. But I have to go. There's a lot to see to – papers to sign. But there's another thing I haven't told you – the estate in Dorset is mine, Rosaleen. Harry made a new will after we became engaged, and left everything to me.'

Rosaleen had been feeling desperately sorry for Milliora. She had only to look at the dark circles under her friend's eyes, to note how thin she was, to know she was grieving for Harry. She could acknowledge, with one part of her mind, that life had been hideously cruel to Milliora, giving her the gift of love for so brief a span before permitting death – for the second time – to snatch it out of her hands. In contrast to that anguish, her own unhappiness paled, for although Cathal O'Mahoney could not be hers, at least he was not dead.

Yet another part of her mind asked coldly: Why is it that Milly always ultimately wins? That, no matter what tragedy befalls her, forces conspire to put her on top? She has always been powerful. With Harry's estate added to Tom's – more land – more riches – what will she become?

'But it's so cold on the doorstep – I mustn't keep you talking!' Milliora said, suddenly full of concern. 'It's been lovely to see you, Rosaleen. Please come again soon – and give my love to Dermot.'

'And Daniel and Eugene!' she called from the steps, but Rosaleen had taken the reins into her hands, and the carriage pulled away.

It was partly the envy of the hypochondriac who believes that he or she is suffering from the malaise of being second best – partly the worry of the perfectly well who has detected a sickness in the family.

Dermot was suffering from his nerves. Ever since Harry Fielding's death, Rosaleen knew, he had not been himself.

And old Mr Dundon knew it. Snap! went the camera in her mind and there was Dermot's partner talking to her. Was it that day or another?

'His mind is not on his work,' old Mr Dundon said. 'His clients are dropping off. Word of mouth – it's not a big city where things can go under the carpet.'

'It was Harry Fielding's death – he feels responsible. We'd had trouble with the horse to begin with, but then we thought he was right.'

'Hunting!' old Mr Dundon said. 'I remember the time Lord Waterford bought a hunter from the Master of the Meath Hounds. *He* had what you'd think was a harmless fall over a two-foot wall, but he never got up again. Dermot is a clever man, but he could fall himself if he doesn't watch out – and then where will the two of you be?'

Out in the cold, Rosaleen thought, as I was, when

428

Father died. Back in the bad old days, hopelessly insecure, at the mercy of other people.

'I'm sure he'll be fine in a month or so,' she said.

'Will he?' the old solicitor replied. 'I wish *I* was so certain.'

But I'm not certain at all, Rosaleen wanted to say, thinking of Dermot at home, standing at the window, gazing into space, when he should have been at work; of the remarks that were addressed to him, which he did not seem to hear; of his growing obsession with order, so that he fussed over what clothes hung next to each other in the tallboy and checked the buttons on his shirt every morning before he got dressed, convinced they had fallen off.

All because he had been deceived by a horse, and had lent it to a friend.

'It's not your fault, Dermot,' she said to him, wanting to take his guilt away. 'You thought Tim-Pat had Clasai cured – how were you to know he had not broken the brute? He always succeeded before.'

He did not answer – did not seem to hear.

Yet there were other times when he was – not exactly his old self, but tantamount to normal. On those occasions, she *believed* a month would put him right.

In the next picture he was perfectly sane, sitting in front of the drawing-room fire when she returned from Crag Liath, and his face lit up with pleasure when she came into the room, rubbing her hands to warm them.

'Are the children having their supper?'

'Bridie's giving it to them now.'

Everyday question and answer yet holding out the promise of a normal family evening, an insistence that Dermot was in his right mind and always would be, that Cathal O'Mahoney did not exist, that Clasai had not killed Harry and had not been destroyed as a result, on the insistence of the hunt, while Tim-Pat cried like a baby.

Oh, surely, she could restrain her own imagination, cease dreaming of Cathal, rein in those dreams and break them, offer her husband compassion if not love, on which to build a future.

All the objects in the room – chosen, purchased and, in some cases, made by herself to give pleasure to Dermot – seemed to be calling to her to find the strength to do that, to pull her husband out of the depression into which he had sunk through no fault of his own. The Minton figurines, the grand piano, the horse and rider on the tapestry screen calling softly: We are part of the structure of the edifice you have erected with this man, and should live with unto death. And why not, since he is rational, intelligent, sound-minded – with faults, as all men have – who is over-sensitive and tortured and much in need of love?

'Did you go to the office today?' she heard herself saying, as if, by asking that question, she was seeking confirmation that he had retained his balance and was his old self.

On several occasions lately, during the week, he had stayed home all day, but now he said, 'I did. I had a lot to get done. A lot to catch up with. I've only just got back.'

After all, what need was there for her to worry about ever being insecure again and at the mercy of others? What need to be envious of Milly's riches and power since Dermot was all right?

'You must be tired,' she said. 'I'll go and see to dinner.'

She told him the news from Crag Liath at dinner when the twins had gone to bed, mentioning Milliora's

430

inheritance first, pushing the jealous thoughts away and trying to keep it light.

'She got the lot?' The hatred of Milliora was back in Dermot's voice. He slammed his hand on the table.

'So it seems. I wonder if there will be opposition to that from Harry's English family?'

But Dermot was not interested in idle conjecture. He said bitterly, 'Have you any idea of what she's laid hands on this time? I thought not. Well, I have. After the ball I made a point of talking to Ted de Voy about Major Harry Fielding. He owned a fifteenth-century manor-house at a place called Wimborne in Dorset and several thousand acres of land. Did you glean *that* when you talked to Milliora?'

Out of the corner of her eye she could see his pale hand on the white lace tablecloth, the nails perfectly cut. His recent depression had not affected the way he was groomed or the perfection of his dress.

'We didn't go into that much detail but – '

'Yes?'

'Milly's not greedy, Dermot,' she said, ashamed of her previous jealous thoughts. 'Nor was Harry Fielding. And you were going to get what you wanted for the twins as a result of their getting married.'

The hand twitched, knocking a tiny spoon out of the silver salt-cellar, spilling some grains.

'*What do you mean?*'

His voice was high and cold – the same voice that had said, 'Rosie – Harry's dead . . .'

'She was making Crag Liath over to Daniel and Eugene for when they were twenty-one. Harry wanted her to break her ties with the past and make a life with hm.'

The hand was moving, brushing the grains of salt

431

through the white lace on to the table. Using his napkin as a dustpan, Dermot gathered them up.

'How – funny,' he said in a high voice. 'How very – amusing. To make her break her ties with the past.'

Outside, a furious wind joined the heavy rain in an attack on roof and windows and trees. Inside, a door slammed, but it was the other sound that caught and held her attention and made a mockery of her passing belief that life was back to normal.

Dermot's laughter was shrill and wild and utterly without humour – hysterical, pixilated laughter to which there seemed no end. It rose high like the wind, and when she looked at her husband she saw that, like the rain falling outside, his tears were streaming down.

'Dermot?'

But there was no stopping the laughter. Just as there was no point in ever telling herself again that Dermot could be normal. That picture of her husband would be always in her mind.

And with it a moving picture. Waking in the night, she saw him climb from the bed and walk naked to the door, fumbling for the handle.

'Harry,' he said, 'Harry – are you there?'

'It's Rosaleen,' she said softly, pitying him, getting out of bed to take him by the arm and ease him back into the room. 'There's no need to worry about Harry. You're talking in your sleep.'

He emitted a curious sound, more animal than human, slumping on the bed, with her sitting beside him.

'Ssh now. It will be all right when you've slept.'

He was in her arms, nestling into her breasts, a baby, not a husband, reaching out for suck.

'Ssh.'

432

And still a man, fumbling under her night-dress, searching for love where even pity failed.

He was still asleep but his eyes were open – she could see that in the gloom.

'Harry,' he said again. 'Harry . . .'

And then, quite clearly: *'You need not have died.'*

29

By moving a few inches to his right, Tim-Pat could just see into the drawing-room, as well as being able to hear what the man and woman inside it were saying to each other.

The audibility and view of their earnest profiles was a bonus to which he felt himself fully entitled – a small compensation for the menial work in the garden, which had been added to his duties in the stables over the last two and a half years, ever since Master Dermot's resignation from Dundon's had led to shortages in the house.

In the past, casual labour had coped with the garden. But Mrs Rosaleen had explained that they were no longer in a position to pay out for casual labour – or for help in the kitchen, either.

'I'll be running the house myself,' she had said, 'and you'll have to cope with the outside just as best you can.'

At that stage, he had not blamed her for what had happened to Master Dermot. He had not liked her – had never cared for any woman – barring old Mrs O'Brien, who had taken him into her house and saved him from starving to death on the road – but he had acknowledged then that she had been fair to Bridie Flanagan, instead of casting her on to the street, setting her up in a sewing business with her mother, which, by all accounts, had turned into a gold-mine.

But that was before she had sold the chestnut half-bred back to Mr O'Mahoney and admitted him into her life.

'We need the money, Tim-Pat,' she had said at the time. 'I know Master Dermot only paid thirty pounds for the horse but thirty pounds is thirty pounds needed now. And it isn't as if we'll be needing a second horse for the Master – he won't be hunting this season, I'd say, or maybe never again.'

At the time, he had seen her viewpoint, or thought that he had, believing it was the money that she was after, and he had offered to take the chestnut half-bred out to Meelick and bring the money back.

'There's no need for that,' she had said. 'I've written to Mr O'Mahoney asking him if he would consider the deal and he's replied this morning, saying he'll call in at the house.'

When he had called – as soon as the words were out of her mouth, no less – Mr O'Mahoney had worn an innocent face, as if he had never, in a month of Sundays, laid eyes on Tim-Pat Tierney, which was the sensible way to behave, and that was the way they had carried on, until Mr O'Mahoney had come to the house several times and it was the natural thing to issue each other a greeting.

Several times . . . Oh, Tim-Pat knew what was going on when Master Dermot's back was turned. You couldn't but know, the way Mr O'Mahoney and Mrs Rosaleen looked at each other, with their eyes glazed over with lust.

What he did not know was when the thing had begun, or whether it had been going on all the time, with Master Dermot knowing nothing about it. For it seemed from the odd remark he picked up now and again when the two of them were unaware he was listening, that Mr O'Mahoney and Mrs Rosaleen had known each other before the original sale of the horse – up in Dublin, you would conclude from what they said, although, to the best of his own knowledge, she had only been up there the once.

Still, there was no accounting for women. You could not point a finger at Mr O'Mahoney, that fine nationalist, with the sorrow of Ireland on his shoulders. Never at him. Only at her, Mary Magdalene herself, the arch-adultress, the temptress, luring men into sin.

She had unbalanced Master Dermot with her unnatural craving, her insatiable need for men, destroying him in the process, just as that other hussy, Mrs Milliora O'Brien, had sent Master Tom to his death.

'I wish I *could* have gone to Dublin with you, Cathal,' she was saying now to Mr O'Mahoney, her voice all honeyed and sweet. 'It must have been very exciting.'

'It was – with all that there were only nine of us present,' Mr O'Mahoney said, 'and none of us possessed of public influence. The idea came from Eoin MacNeill, a civil servant from Antrim, and the Reverend Eugene O'Growney, Professor of Irish in Maynooth College, who's editing the *Gaelic Journal*, has taken it up. The Gaelic League, the organization is to be called, and its object is to keep the Irish language spoken in Ireland. Dr Douglas Hyde, a Trinity man, will be president and weekly meetings are to be held in Dublin to discuss ways of arousing the public mind to the importance of the issue and to see what can be done to improve the position of the language in education.'

'They'll have an uphill battle there,' the temptress said. 'The people are ashamed of the language – and some of them are even hostile towards it.'

'That could change,' said Mr O'Mahoney with his

436

customary optimism towards all things Irish. 'It *has* to change. The men in Dublin are adamant that it can – and will.'

'I was reading the other day that Irish is only taught in fifty national schools now,' the temptress said, trying, no doubt, to impress Mr O'Mahoney with the knowledge she had about Ireland, 'but it's taught as a dead language, the way Latin is, and with far less interest or enthusiasm. It's an admission that we as a people are dead.'

'It is not!' Mr O'Mahoney said energetically. 'We'll not be so apathetic – you shouldn't be so apathetic yourself! What we need are strong, vigorous campaigners to get out there and do something about the language – restore our pride in it, instead of dwelling on the shame.'

'Wasn't that what we hoped would happen with the Gaelic Athletic Association – getting young people to use the technical terms for hurling and so get back to the Irish?'

'And it worked! Still works! But we need to go beyond technical terms for hurling. If the Gaelic League gets going it won't only encourage people to speak Irish, but to wear Irish clothes and take part in Irish dancing, and poetry and song – anything that will distinguish Irishness from Englishness and remind us that we were the scholars of Europe before falling under the English throne.'

'It does sound exciting,' the temptress said. 'I wish I could be part of it.'

'But you can! You could go out this very day and start a branch of the Gaelic League in Limerick. All you need is a handful of people to start with. All over the country, in every town and village we want people setting up branches, liaising with the men in Dublin – waking up the national conscience.'

'Me?' said the temptress. 'You want me to do that?'

But what else she had to say about her ability or lack of it to form a branch of the Gaelic League in Limerick, Tim-Pat never found out.

'*Got you!*' shouted two triumphant voices – and they were on him, Daniel and Eugene armed with makeshift guns made out of sticks, attacking him from behind.

'Arrest him!' Daniel directed his brother, adding as an after-thought, 'The Fenians are here, to liberate Ireland – and you are Mr Gladstone, and we're taking you hostage until we get what we want.'

'Indeed you're not!' Tim-Pat yelled back, pulling his leg free.

Wrestling – only a quarter in earnest – he wondered how the child Fenians would react, if they knew of his real involvement.

'I don't know if I would be capable of such a thing,' Rosaleen said, getting up and closing the window on the children's noise. 'Long ago maybe, but these days – '

'That's rubbish,' Cathal said, 'and what's more you know it is. The Gaelic League has enormous power potential, Rosaleen. Douglas Hyde speaks of it now as an apolitical movement but of course it has separatist implications – how could it not? You're a nationalist who's looking for an opportunity to contribute to nationalism. Here is that opportunity. Take it. At the very least it's a good alternative to the low-level politicking we've had thrust upon us since the death of Parnell. Parnellism equates adultery, and so on. The people are sick of that, and looking for a more noble mythology to latch onto. This is the chance to strike while the iron is hot. You must know a few people in Limerick who share your political views; I certainly do. Get them together – call them to a meeting and let it snowball from there.'

'You'd come yourself?'

'Yes,' he said. 'But I haven't the time to run it. That would be your job.'

But I *could* do it, Rosaleen thought, with mounting excitement, after Cathal had gone. There are a couple of people who would be keen to join in and they could lead to more. Meetings would have to be held in one of their houses – not here, not with Dermot the way he is, so peculiar and sad.

She smiled. As usual, she had been infected by Cathal's optimism and insistence that she was a capable, innovative person, instead of second-best. There was no rivalry in their relationship, the way there seemed to be when Milly and herself were together and envy reared its head.

Had Rosaleen known what Tim-Pat thought about her relationship with Cathal, she would have been shocked out of her mind – and justly so, since the reality was very different from the fantasy envisaged by the groom. They were not lovers – in spite of the times that he came to the house and the talks they had together, and the love they would have liked to have made . . . But did not. That was implicit in their understanding, and Rosaleen could even convince herself on occasions that their emotions were perfectly tethered and unlikely to break loose.

Writing to Cathal, asking him if he would consider buying back the chestnut half-bred, she had not deceived herself, knowing that she was reaching out for comfort, the adjunct to love that can be used as an excuse for meeting until the time has come for love.

That time had not come – or had not been permitted to arrive by either of them.

Dermot, vague and often bufuddled, acted as her conscience, but the curious thing was that so far from fending off the possibility of offending God, he seemed, simply by existing, to provide another occasion of sin.

It was a very grievous thing to hate your husband, Rosaleen thought, to resent the stranglehold he had on your life, to shudder when he was near you and secretly wish that he would die.

But she did hate Dermot, did resent the stranglehold, did sometimes wish that his life was at an end, and although she revealed all of this in Confession and was absolved of her sins, the feeling came back again and confused her even more. For she was caught in the whirlwind of that hatred, she thought, and did not know where to turn for release. By hating you committed a mortal sin. By suppressing your hatred you lied to yourself and then you were sinning again!

As usual, when these thoughts were upon her she tried to lose herself in work, going into the scullery and, rolling up her sleeves, throwing a pile of dirty clothes into the tub to wash.

'Rosaleen?'

Dermot was there, as immaculately dressed as ever and ready to go out.

'Are you going into town?'

'I'm going to the office,' he said, sounding surprised. 'I have a pile of work to do and another will to make.'

'And will you be back for dinner?' she said, humouring him, since it was well over two and a half years since he had darkened Dundon's door.

Acting out the necessary charade, she wondered what Dermot was thinking. He looked so normal; he remained a handsome man. But the medical diagnosis was that part of his mind was shut off and probably always would be, due to that terrible shock he had experienced at the hunt.

'I may be late,' he said. 'Maybe you'll keep it hot for me if I am.'

Only he was never late – never stayed out for more than minutes at a time. He was always at home – always under her feet, worse than any child.

'It will be hot, whatever time you come home,' she said, immersing a shirt in the suds.

Outside in the yard, she could hear the children's laughter. What effect did their father's behaviour have on them? At six they were at the age of reason and could see what he was like.

And at six they were ready to learn – it was time they went to school. It was already the beginning of August, and time arrangements were made.

But she had been putting off making plans – delaying facing the truth that the twins must go to boarding-school, away from their father, to lead a normal life. Now something had to be done.

When the washing was done she would write to Clongowes College in Naas, asking the Jesuits if they would find places for the twins. Maybe – if she stated her case well enough – they would consider reducing the fees.

'Mama?'

Daniel, peering round the door.

'What is it?'

'When will Aunt Milly be home from Dorset? We want to go out to see her.'

At Wimborne Manor in Dorset Milliora was sitting in the library, thinking of the twins.

She did not enjoy staying at Wimborne Manor, although as a house it was very fine – ivied, flanked by battlemented towers, known for its mullioned windows, and filled with interesting furniture, pictures, ironwork and tapestries, with an Italian frieze in the drawing-room and a tithe-barn out at the back.

In the great hall a painting of a beautiful lady wearing a pedimental head-dress and a gown with ornamented girdle dependent from three rosettes reminded those who entered the house of the long and noble line from which Harry Fielding came.

Yet Wimborne Manor was also undeniably one of those old manor-houses which, over the centuries, had descended in the social scale to the status of a farm. Pigs had been kept and subsequently slaughtered in outbuildings designed for a purer purpose and the tithe-barn, although originally built to store the plentiful products of a rich land, lost must of its dignity when used to shed the cows.

And still the house succeeded in intimidating Milliora in a way that Crag Liath had never attempted to do. It did not welcome her, she was certain of that, any more than the domestic chapel adjoining it on the south side beckoned her to come inside and pray – although that was of little consequence since, as a Catholic, she could not risk committing mortal sin by doing anything of the kind.

She had not enjoyed any of her visits to Wimborne Manor, certainly not the first one when she had been met at Dorchester by Harry's youngest brother, Anthony, and provided with the obligatory refreshment at the King's Arms before being taken to Wimborne.

Perhaps if Anthony had been more forthcoming, less cold . . . But Anthony, while not exactly hostile towards her, as she gathered from him that his other brothers were, was not friendly either towards the woman whom the Fieldings felt had usurped Harry's wealth.

And she was left with no illusions about Anthony's near cordiality. As the youngest son, he could have harboured the least expectations after Harry's death; he had lost the least to herself. Richard and Edward, further up the ladder, had made their attitude plain from the start, saying they had no wish to meet her, then or at any time.

Was it her imagination or did their inimical feelings spread to the house, creep into the beautifully proportioned parlour, divided by a transom – up the oak staircase to the long gallery – into the bedroom in which she would sleep?

On that first occasion, Anthony had conveyed her to Wimborne, introduced her to the staff at the house, and had then proceeded to more or less dump her, saying he had to get home. There had been no offer to entertain her at a later date – to invite her to meet his wife. No hint that he would return, and, in fact, he had not done so. She had not heard from him again.

It was not at all what she had been expecting and, still raw from the wound of losing Harry, she had cried herself to sleep.

Later on, of course, she had discovered the positive things about Wimborne. Dorset was truly delightful, a county of wild moorland, firwoods, downs and majestic coastline, with a surfeit of castles and abbeys – and Wimborne Manor, nestling behind lichen-covered walls, a pleasurable sight to behold.

The house was expertly run by a lugubrious butler and a kind, if distant, housekeeper who between them had the domestic staff right under their thumbs. And it had been pleasant to discover that Harry's workers on the estate made up a well-drilled and highly disciplined army. The estate, divided equally between cattle-rearing and dairy-farming, seemed to operate with consummate ease.

The evidence that it did so had not stopped her from investigating exactly how it was run, in spite of initial hints from a suspicious manager that he did not need her help. Ignoring him, she had penetrated into the heart of the estate at Wimborne, learning much and winning grudging respect.

The difference between farming methods in England and Ireland fascinated her. In Dorset, teams of oxen – three to a plough – were led by one man while another, in a frock-coat, came to hold the plough; there were giant corn-ricks placed high on saddle-stones, and the milking pans were made of maple because it was easy to keep clean.

And the neatness of Dorset villages intrigued her – the bonnets worn by the women, with little frills at the back, the smocks worn by the pipe-smoking men and the Venetian red waggons designed to cope with the long, steep hills of the county.

But for all that, Milliora was in an alien land, where she felt perpetually uneasy. Wimborne Manor would never be home. She was quite incapable of staying away and permitting the estate to continue to be perfectly run by Harry's efficient workers – her nature demanded that she interfere and command. But on each visit to Wimborne she thought constantly of Ireland and Crag Liath and could hardly wait to go back.

More than ever now, Crag Liath needed her. The idea that Dermot could run it until the twins were of age had died with the onset of her brother-in-law's madness.

'Crag Liath will be still Daniel and Eugene's one day,' Milliora said aloud to the walls that were filled with books. '*That* has not been changed.'

And it was only right that the twins should inherit. The attitude of Harry's brothers had made that even more plain.

It was impossible not to compare their attitude with that taken earlier by Dermot, who had been in a similiar position in terms of a lost estate. Unlike the Fieldings, Dermot had shown generosity towards her – generosity and brotherly love. It was tragic that he might never understand that she wanted to pay him back for everything he had done.

But Daniel and Eugene will understand, she thought – there is that, at least.

The twins – the twins! She felt enormous love as she had done in the days before Harry came into her life and tried to chase them out. Now she knew that she would never marry, never have children of her own to adore, she loved them all the more.

My babies! she thought – Soon I'll see you again.

And then it occurred to her that Daniel and Eugene were no longer babies – or toddlers, either, but boys – boys of six who were ready to go to school.

And it's *August,* thought Milliora, appalled – they should be at school next month! What arrangements had Rosaleen made about their education?

Hand to head, she realized that the possibility of schools for the boys had never been discussed, had, as it were, fallen between two stools in the traumas of the years. But surely Rosaleen must have considered it – must have laid some plans. Unless . . .

Was she worried about money, Milliora wondered.

And suddenly she was stricken by conscience that Rosaleen should be dreading the prospect of sending the boys to school.

How selfish I am, Milliora berated herself, not to have thought of money in this connection before. With Dermot out of the practice, there may be a desperate shortage of funds.

Rosaleen might even have shelved the idea of a private school education for Daniel and Eugene – toyed with the alternative of sending them to a national school, as if they were ordinary boys and not the sons of O'Briens!

The sheer horror of this made her gasp for breath.

'It won't be necessary!' she said. 'You won't have to do that!'

For the first time since she had arrived in Wimborne she was glad to be in England, for although she was due to leave in a matter of days she could initiate a plan, and put it into effect on her homeward journey.

Lost in thought, she failed to hear the first knock on the library door – and started at the second.

'Excuse me, madam,' the butler said with a tragic air, 'but dinner has been served.'

Milliora turned to face him.

'Thank you, Burton,' she said in her regal voice. 'But it will have to wait. I must send a letter to Stratton-on-the-Fosse.'

30

Milliora's compulsion to spend part of every year in England was less incomprehensible to Mary Markham as unsympathetically received. There was an element of disloyalty in her departures that struck a jarring note at Crag Liath; her annual disappearances into foreign parts were not entirely offset by the gifts she always brought back.

'Still, there's no one more *coomoragh* than herself – that I will say,' Mary remarked to Mrs Cash the day after Milliora returned from Dorset. 'Have you seen the hat she's after bringing me this time, with birds and feathers on top?'

'Kind and thoughtful she may be, and I'm not denying she is,' the housekeeper said, 'but it isn't natural, in my opinion, having two homes and not being able to settle in either.'

'That's money so for you.'

'Her having so much to throw about must be a tough nut for Mrs Rosaleen O'Brien to swallow, with Master Dermot by all accounts not having as much as would jingle on a gravestone. And I'd say it would take the biscuit the way some people would try to avail themselves of her money, and still show her a cranky face!'

Mary Markham hesitated, torn between an urge to surprise Mrs Cash by repeating what she had heard when she had taken the tea-tray upstairs, and the prudent requirement to hold on to her tongue and desist from involvement in gossip.

447

'I'd say you'd be right about the cranky face,' she said finally. 'I've seen signs of that myself.'

'There you are!' said Mrs Cash triumphantly. 'Just the way I said. And I suppose money came into it earlier on – or didn't you hear what happened?'

The look on the washerwoman's pudgy face proved Mary Markham's undoing. That and the inference that she did not know or did not hear precisely what went on in the house.

'Indeed I did hear!' she said with dignity. 'I hear much that I don't repeat to you, Mrs Cash or anyone else, either. But it so happens that I can confirm this particular matter down to the last iota. Money was mentioned all right but herself knew what to do.'

The reply from Clongowes College came within a couple of days. It was friendly, brief and to-the-point on the two questions that mattered: yes, there were places for the twins; no, there could not be a reduction in fees.

Rosaleen stood in the hall with the Jesuits' letter in her hand unaware that Dubhfoilean, needing to be fed, was rubbing her sinuous black body against the hem of her dress. Along with the letter the college had enclosed details of their fees. Not unreasonable – not unless you multiplied them by two and added in the extras. And multiplied that sum by the number of years the boys would be at school . . .

Such a commitment was out of the question for the household at Kincora. She remembered that she did not even know for certain what Dermot had in the Bank of Ireland although the agent there was friendly and sent her monthly cheques. She could go and see him and –

But what was the point? She knew from what old Mr

Dundon had said that there was a bottom to the pit. What remained in the bank must be conserved for day-to-day expenses.

I have to make money myself, she thought desperately, and raise the first year's fees. Surely there was a way? Having got the Flanagans' sewing business off the ground she should be able to help herself.

Starting a business takes time, Rosaleen thought, and I need the money now. When the twins are settled at Clongowes I can direct my efforts towards a business of my own.

So sell something, said her more practical side. Not the house – that's in Dermot's name and so is what is in it. But who's to know if you sell, for instance, some of the Minton plates? Or one or two of the hunting prints she'd bought for him? Or a rug – or maybe some of the silver?

No, not the silver, she corrected herself, for most of that is O'Brien silver and must be left for the twins when they grow up, whereas the Minton plates . . .

Stumbling over the cat she went into the drawing-room and took two of them off the wall. Later on, she would remove their brackets too, so no one could tell the difference. And perhaps the Belleek plates could also go – and some of the china and glass? Now that she came to think of it, there were lots of things to sell.

She carried the articles selected from the drawing-room through the hall and placed them carefully on the dining-room table. Dubhfoilean was at her heels and she picked the black cat up and put her outside the door, shutting it behind her lest she knock anything down from the table.

That hunting print could go, she decided – and the other print of the two carriages heading for a crash. She took them down, grimacing, aware of the fact that the wallpaper where they had hung looked new in comparison to the faded area that had remained uncovered. The room was in need of repapering and repainting after all these years, as was the whole of the house, though this could not be done.

The fact that she had found a way to raise immediate money and deal with the problem of fees was a boost, large enough to dispel any feelings of gloom she might have about the deterioration of the house. After lunch, when the household chores had been done, she would take all the things she had to sell into Limerick to Sexton's auction rooms and ask if, as a special favour, they would give her cash. She itemized the articles on the table on paper, and put a rough estimate on what each was likely to fetch, adding up the total.

The problem was more than solved: there would be money left over after the sale to go towards the second year's fees. She looked up and saw her own reflection in the mirror above the sideboard. Her eyes were shining bright and this unusual view of herself, sparkling and almost happy, took her aback, so that just for a moment she thought another woman had entered the room.

Less happy-making, more sobering, was the thought of parting from the twins at the beginning of term. Apart from the fact that she would miss them, there was the question of how the boys themselves would adjust to life at boarding-school at the age of six and a half. Daniel, the extrovert, was bound to come through the experience better than introverted Eugene. It was typical of the two of them that this morning, Daniel should already be outside riding, or helping in the stables, while Eugene was up in his room, probably trying to draw.

This was a new development in Eugene. He was

450

showing the first signs of having artistic talent, something she was eager to see developed although Daniel, who was not artistic at all, tended to mock his twin on this account and tell him that drawing was only for girls.

Once more, she ran her eyes over the articles on the table, then, closing the door behind her, she went through to the scullery, fed Dubhfoilean and picked up the pile of clothes that she had washed yesterday when it had been too wet to hang them out, and put them into a basket. Today was different: the sky was actually blue, the sun was shining already, the washing would get dried – and her problems with money would be solved – anyway for the moment. Carrying the basket, she went out to hang the clothes. By the door into the stables Tim-Pat Tierney was conducting an animated conversation with Daniel. The groom, hearing her footsteps, looked up and his eyes, green as Dubhfoilean's, met her own. In spite of the warmth of the morning, Rosaleen shivered, conscious, not for the first time lately, that Tim-Pat disliked her – more than that, seemed almost to hate . . .

But that was fanciful nonsense.

'Good morning, Tim-Pat,' she said cheerfully. 'Do you think you could do a clean-up in the orchard later on today? A lot of apples have fallen.'

'I'll do that,' said Tim-Pat in a strangely unemotional voice. 'We should be pitting the apples, I think, and potatoes as well, to be prepared for the winter.'

'*I* can do that,' Daniel volunteered, ready for involvement. 'We need earth – and straw. They'll be reaping at Crag Liath. We can go and get some there.'

'It's too early for straw – you'll get that after the threshing,' Rosaleen explained.

Dermot's illness made her see strangeness in all

things, she decided. How could Tim-Pat be nurturing hate, and least of all for herself? The sooner she occupied herself with practical matters – the setting up of some little business and organizing a branch of the Gaelic League – the less time she would have over for fancies. Soon, the twins would be at Clongowes and with only Dermot to cook and wash for there would be plenty of time for what she needed to do.

Sunshine and freshly-laundered shirts hanging on the line. Her back was warm from the sun and she was wrestling with a clothes-peg, pinning up a sock . . .

'*Mama!*' Screaming, Eugene was running over the grass.

'Darling – what is it? Have you been hurt?'

Or Daniel?

And then she could hear the rest of his words.

'Mama – come quickly! *Papa's going mad!*'

He was in the dining-room, sitting on the floor, surrounded by the fragments of their treasures, which were smashed to smithereens.

And yet there was a pattern to the unrecognizable pieces of porcelain, the torn shreds of paper, which had been ripped from the broken frames of the prints: the disunited scraps had been positioned in neat piles, five fragments to each, lying equidistant from each other in an almost perfect circle around the seated man.

He did not look up.

In the odd, high voice he had affected for the first time on the day of Harry Fielding's death, Dermot said, 'The room was not tidy. You were not here. I was obliged to put it in order myself.'

Under the crook of Rosaleen's arm Eugene was nestling, still shaking with fear. That alone eliminated

452

any reservation she might have felt about calling out for help.

I will have to borrow the money for the fees, Rosaleen thought, and in spite of the shocked state of her mind it began to calculate coolly who was best to approach.

It was a swift calculation, dismissing at once the possibility of borrowing from Cathal and thus finally emasculating her sick husband in the eyes of the man she loved, and depicting him as inept.

And Carmel and Andy – Noel and Mary could not be asked since it was a difficult year for many farmers and they were not doing well.

'*Mama?*'

'Fetch Daniel,' she said to Eugene. 'You boys said you wanted to see Aunt Milly. I'm packing you a suitcase and we're going to Crag Liath.'

She was standing in the middle of the cornfield wearing a frilly, vivid yellow dress that was quite at variance with the apparel worn by her men and women workers, and telling them what to do, and her red-gold hair was glinting in the sun. In one hand she was holding a sickle and she was instructing a thin man with a heavier toothed reaper how to reap the corn; bending over it, taking a grip on the straw, inserting her hook and pulling it into her body as if she was going to saw.

'You'll lose the grain unless you are gentle,' Rosaleen heard her say. 'Cut low and clean to the living earth – *that's* the way to reap!'

'Aunt Milly!' Daniel called out. ''Gene and I are here.'

The welcome was there the way it had always been. Milliora's expression, her open arms – the sickle had fallen to the ground unheeded – assured them all of that.

'*Children!*' she said – and Daniel and Eugene were in her arms and she was holding them tight.

It was almost possible for Rosaleen to believe that she herself was a child as well, coming to Milliora for love and security, as she used to do at school. It will be all right – I'm sure of it, Milliora used to say, fifteen or sixteen years back, and somehow, then, it was.

'How I've missed you,' Milliora said, over one red and one dark head. 'It's never the same in England. You're not there – the children aren't there. I miss you all the time.'

Standing in the cornfield, surrounded by the ripe golden yellow corn, Rosaleen felt as if she had come home after a brutal and lengthy journey to be welcomed into the fold.

Heightening this sensation, Milliora said, 'Come up to the house. We have so much to catch up on,' adding to the workers, 'You with the loghters – you should be working more quickly after the reapers, binding the corn into sheaves.'

She caught up her dress, showing a flash of white stockings, and, holding a twin by each hand, began to head for the house, striding over the stubble in spite of her incongruous high-heeled shoes, while Rosaleen stumbled behind.

They were almost at the front door when Milliora said, 'Can't the boys come to stay – it's ages since they've been here?'

And Daniel said, 'We've brought our things already.'

'You see – '

'I think I do see, Rosaleen,' Milliora said. 'Boys, go down to the kitchen and get Mary Markham to give you some cake. Your mother and I want to talk.'

It all seemed so simple.

'I need to talk to you, Milly – about the twins,' Rosaleen began. 'They must – they have to be sent away to school.'

'My feelings exactly,' Milliora said briskly.

'We can't afford the fees, Milly. I'm not sure what Dermot has left in the bank and I'm afraid he's getting worse.'

'The twins must not grow up in an environment like that,' Milliora said firmly. 'That must not happen and, of course, you're right – it's time they went to school. You can't begin young enough with the right kind of training. The Benedictines are so skilled at educating young gentlemen. Tom and Dermot were perfect examples of that in their day. Now, you're going to be delighted when you hear what I did for you in England. I went to Somerset, to Downside College, and booked the children in. The fees, of course, will be my responsibility – for the whole of their school careers.'

'You did *what?*'

The sun, shining into the room, glancing on gleaming walls and sparkling procelain, drew attention to the fact that Crag Liath, unlike Kincora, had been redecorated while Milliora had been away.

'Yes – and we're so lucky that Downside could find places for the twins so late in the day. They're very young, of course, but they have each other and I was thinking – I will take them over myself. I'll make the time. After all, you can't leave Dermot for long.'

A voice that did not seem to have anything to do with herself was making a protest on her behalf. It said bravely, 'But, Milly, I don't want the boys to be educated in England. Clongowes will have them. I've been in contact with the school. It's just a question of fees for a year.'

'Clongowes?' Milliora was scornful. 'Oh, I know some people think it's a good school but England, after all, offers the best education and if Dermot was normal he would want his children to go to Downside, as he did. The Benedictines, in any case, have far more style about them than the Jesuits and style is important when you're bringing up a child.'

Mary Markham brought in tea. Plates of chocolate cake and buttered bread, wafer thin, were being handed round.

'No, thank you . . .'

'You really must get this silly notion about the validity of Irish education out of your head. I don't want to hear another word about Clongowes. I'm offering the boys a *real* opportunity.'

And a deliverance.

('*Papa's going mad.*')

Out of the past, Rosaleen thought she could hear a nun's voice making a passing remark. Mother Mary Gonzaga saying, 'When Milliora Fitzgibbon digs in her heels there's nothing a person can do.'

Milliora was set on Downside. Her mind had been made up.

But there was Cathal's voice, too, saying, 'Anything that will distinguish Irishness from Englishness and remind us that we were the scholars of Europe before falling under the English throne.'

The Gaelic League wanted people to be proud of being Irish – to speak the language, to wear Irish clothes, to take part in Irish song and dance – to be proud of being the sons of Ireland, who went to school at home.

Wanting to rage at Milliora – shout that she was being forced to compromise her principles – Rosaleen realized, loathing herself more than her friend, that the twins might suffer if she did such a thing. She could not even afford to lose her temper. She, who believed in honesty, was, by her silence, telling a lie that she despised.

'So that's all settled then,' said Milliora, mistaking quiescence for compliance. 'Mary, tell the boys to come up here, will you? Shall we break the news?'

She took her anger with her, carrying it carefully in the carriage, down through the avenue of birch trees, through the tunnel made from the hedgerows, all the way to Kincora, and it matched Tim-Pat's anger, when he saw her, coming through the gate.

He, too, could not afford to lose his temper; fought to control his voice, not to sound accusing as he said, 'Master Dermot is asleep in his room, Mrs O'Brien. I found him wandering round the grounds, wondering where you'd gone.'

But her own anger was too great a weight to carry and she had too much on her mind to suspect him of hatred again.

Without the twins, the house was lonely – a foretaste of what was to come. And in it, in the dining-room, was – literally – the ruination of her hopes awaiting clearance. Her anger was inside her now, swelling in its ugliness, like a drowned and bloated cow. It sustained her as she swept the pathetic piles assembled by Dermot into a corner and carried them, bucket after bucket, out to the back, unaware of Tim-Pat's curious and constant surveillance.

When she sat alone in the drawing-room, that anger ripened, like cream that has been skimmed from the top of the milk and is ready to change with the churning.

Yet Cathal, calling to the house within the hour, did

not at first sense the precondition for change that would be to his advantage.

'Dermot not around?' he asked, more out of politeness than anything else. Still, he had grown to pity rather than to dislike or despise Dermot over the last few years. The presence or absence in a room of her husband made little difference to what went on inside it between Rosaleen and himself.

'He's been in bed this long while,' she said, the anger agitating inside her, a staff turning into a cross.

'Have you altered this room in some way – taken some pictures down?' Cathal said, looking at the walls from which the plates had been removed.

Rosaleen did not answer and when he looked at her, wondering why she did not, he saw that the difference that was of importance to both of them was actually in her.

It was as if all sound had been cut off in the world. Outside, quarrelling crows had been silenced, and a mother shouting for a child. What he could hear Rosaleen transmitted to him without speaking – the potent agreement, made from the power of anger, that she was willing to make love.

He was shocked. He had thought about making love to her a hundred – a thousand times, and his initial reaction was to distrust his luck, to doubt if he had really walked through a doorway into another place where all the rules had changed.

Schoolboy shock – and a dizziness, and a fantastical feeling that, in spite of his disbelief, she was about to be his.

And then, and only then, the excitement.

She was sitting in a low chair by the side of the fireplace and violet-blue eyes, clamant, curious, invited him to kneel, hold, fondle, kiss. She attempted no stratagem – her lips opened, received his tongue, gasped as it started to probe, responding with her own, warm and wet and wild and maddening to a man who had waited too long.

'Take off your clothes,' he said, thwarted by the shackling, maddening killjoy of women's clothing – garments that rustled in a coy and stealthy frou-frou.

'Not here.'

'Oh my God, I suppose the children – '

'They're at Crag Liath,' Rosaleen said. 'And Dermot is asleep. But not here. Not inside this house.'

'Then *where?*'

She pushed him away and stood up, ignoring her crumpled dress.

'It's warm outside,' she said, taking his hand, holding it low against his hip, leading him out of the house, towards the gate that led from the yard into the orchard. Her anger now had metamorphosed completely into desire and she was in that state of euphoric anticipation that made her float rather than walk on the cobble-stoned pathway that led towards the door in the wall.

'Does no one ever come along that boreen?'

'I never see anyone out there and if it was children they'd be put to bed by now.'

'Other lovers maybe?'

They were by the wild garden, more overgrown than when he had first seen it riotous with roserock and poppy and sundew and the flowers of the spring.

Seeing that, but having eyes only for the woman beside him, Cathal did not look around, not to his right, to the other side of the orchard where Tim-Pat Tierney stood still as an apple tree, watching the two of them as they opened the door in the wall and escaped out of his sight.

'No lovers,' she said.

'Only us. Come here.'

Holding her only with his mouth he began to undo the multiplicity of tiny buttons that ran down the front of her gown until after what seemed like an age the garment finally fell to the ground, revealing another layer to remove.

And then he was lying her on a bed of scattered garments, under the old oak tree, too eager to look for long at her neat, delicate, slender body, cupping one white, rounded breast in his hand, waiting for her reaction as he bent over the shell-pink nipple and licked it into life.

When she closed her eyes there was green water all around her – pale green trees on a distant shore, dark green reeds nearby, the whiteness of water-lilies. And she herself the water – a pool with the green reeds changing into one reed and over it a huge pale moon, suddenly very near.

Black flowing in on the moon from the left, at the bottom. Light from the right, at the top.

'I love you,' Cathal said. 'I love you.'

She was only partly lost. Part of her was detached, watching the landscape change.

He was inside her, thrusting, and she could hear herself cry because of the joy and relief of love.

Still watching the landscape.

There was a dam now, across the water. It was a knife and she could feel its sharpness, seeing the water flow beneath.

'I've got to come,' he said.

The dam was breaking and the moon was swooping down, pink, opaque-pink, flooding the water – swelling into the pool so all the green was pink.

'Why are you crying?' Cathal asked.

And she said, 'I cry with love.'

31

Remembering, she lay beside Dermot under the white lace bedspread which he had not removed from their bed before getting into it several hours before, and the still vivid recollection of making love with Cathal sustained her against his not being there.

Beyond recall was the green water flooded, the opaque pink of the moon. She could see now what she had not seen then. Cathal's head bent over her breast, the arches of their craving bodies were golden sections of a masterpiece executed by and for herself.

'*Get him!*' Dermot mumbled in his sleep, the way he often did.

Her husband, her jailer, over whom she continually had to stand guard. But she was feeling now as if the bars of her cage had been prised open by the love she had shared with Cathal, as if she was free as a golden plover to form a flock and fly.

She could not sleep for excitement. Dermot slept nine or ten hours at a stretch without waking, in spite of the torments that seemed to beset him throughout the night. Without fear that he might wake, she got out of bed and, groping around in the dark, found a cape to put over her night-dress to keep her warm downstairs.

The kitchen fire had gone out. Seized by old energy, she rekindled it, poured water into the hob-kettle and put it on to boil.

Sitting by the kitchen table she realized the other

aspect of the metamorphosis she had undergone through love.

For the first time in my life, Rosaleen thought, I do not feel second best.

Not to Milly. Not anymore.

Rich Milly. Poor Milly – who had no man to love.

Whereas she was a woman taken by fairy power from her husband – Aine, lover of Manannan Mac Lir, to whom she was dearer than all of the human tribe.

Cathal, she thought, feeling his lips and his tongue on her breast, and slipping her hand beneath her cape she felt her nipple respond.

Cathal rode back to Meelick in that melancholy state that, for him, sometimes followed the act of love, plagued by the purely practical realities of having a long-term affair with Rosaleen.

Starting with the premise that he had to have her again, and soon, he was faced with the problem of where. They could hardly continue to make love in a meadow behind her house, for all that the dangers inherent in doing so had added a spicy element to the intensity of the act.

And he could not invite her to his own bed, not with a housekeeper living in the house and his workers in and out of it all hours of the day and night.

The need for subterfuge depressed him even more. He had always rebelled against what he condemned as the hypocritical nature of the society and the age in which he lived. The country was too dominated by austere and disapproving moralizers, soul-snatchers who befuddled the minds of men, forcing them to imbibe a potent brew devised more by themselves than by Jesus Christ, and all the while holding the rod of excommunication over their heads, lest they hesitate over the drinking; priests cast in the mould of his brother Seamus, held up to him in childhood as an example to emulate and ever since resented.

Oh, there were fine priests, too, in Ireland – many of them. Men who cast no stones. But there was too much power in the hands of those who demanded from their parishioners fear as well as respect. Like the preacher who, once the crisis over the affair with Mrs O'Shea had erupted, had categorized Parnellism as a simple love of adultery.

How could you argue with, or – more important – defeat a mind as narrow as that?

How, in such a climate, ask if a husband was as insane as Dermot O'Brien, Rosaleen could be said to be married?

Or maintain that, while she acted only as a nurse-maid to a madman, to yourself she was not whore but wife?

In Ireland? In Limerick, in 1893? You would not stand the shadow of a chance. You would do better by far to conserve your energy and redirect it towards solving the problem of where two lovers could meet, away from censorious eyes.

That problem remained unsolved in the morning when – to compound his irritation – Tim-Pat Tierney arrived unexpectedly in Meelick, to sanctimoniously remind him that he had altered the date of the movement's weekly meeting to tonight.

'I thought, like, that you might have forgotten, Mr O'Mahoney,' Tierney said glibly, 'having a lot on your mind at the present time.'

What did that mean, Cathal thought, looking sharply at the groom – looking for signs that he was suspicious of his relationship with the woman who employed Tim-

Pat. But Tierney's face was bland. There was no clue to his thoughts in the curious cat-like eyes.

'I hadn't forgotten, in fact,' Cathal said coolly, although the change had slipped his mind.

Despite the fact that in every possible way Tierney had lived up to the expectations of Dinneen, the fellow gave him the creeps. But maybe that was only his own guilt talking – the knowledge that Tierney, by being based at Kincora, was too close for his own comfort – wielded his own rod, the threat that he could leak information about the affair to members of the movement.

'I hear there's a bailiff been murdered at Patrickswell, and cattle injured, and two hay ricks burned,' Tierney said with satisfaction. 'It's more of that kind of show we need, to counteract eviction.'

'We don't want to have the authorities on the rampage at all,' Cathal said irritably. 'The next thing you know you'll have more soldiers drafted in round the Limerick area, and the police numbers stepped up, and picking up on our trail. Much good that will do the movement.'

'The authorities are a pack of eejits,' Tierney said derisively. 'And at the head of them all is the old fool Gladstone with his abortive Home Rule Bills that he tried to impress and subdue us with, and couldn't get through the House of Lords!'

'He might have swung it, along with Parnell, had the circumstances been different,' said Cathal, filled with an absurd urge to argue with Tim-Pat. 'As it is, we've seen the last of the old man's attempts in that connection.'

'Had Parnell not been ruined by the adultress, Mr O'Mahoney, everything might have been different.'

Like Rosaleen, Cathal was not freed by love. At

every turn of the narrow road, his escape route seemed to be blocked.

That evening, riding close to the Clare hills, on the back road to O'Brien's Bridge, Cathal remembered the haunted cottage. It stood some distance from the road on his right, behind a field wall, a seemingly artless construction of rough boulders with a phantom gate in the middle portion of its wall, which could be knocked down and built up again as needed, to act as a bulwark against the wind in the way a wood or an iron gate would be unable to do.

He had never been inside the cottage, knowing it only by reputation. Unlike the secret room at O'Brien's Bridge, this would-be hideout had nothing at all to do with the fairies. What had driven the locals away from it was an all-too-human crime – the memory of a man, driven mad with the drink, who had battered his wife to death. All in the long-ago past now – fifty years at least – but she was still there, the aggrieved woman, or so it was said, waiting her chance for revenge.

He doubted if Rosaleen, not having come from the area, was acquainted with the tale. If not, he had no intention of enlightening her, lest she be put off by his suggestion that here was a place they could meet, unless it was well beyond redemption as a tryst and had become the habitat of cows and pigs and rats.

He would be late for the meeting – a bit – but it was worth stopping to check the cottage out. The wall that surrounded it was low enough – an easy jump – and on the other side of it was the decaying cabin with its door and two small windows boarded up.

Touching one of the boards criss-crossing the door, Cathal grinned, feeling it loose and ready to crumble. In a couple of minutes he had removed the facile barrier and was inside the long room. There was a small shelf built out by the fireplace, presumably for the purpose of taking a bed, and a crane, supporting a griddle in which bread had once been baked, was a pathetic reminder of the domesticity that had ended in tragedy. The remains of an old hand-turned bellows lay breathless on a floor reinforced with dung.

Hardly the Shelbourne Hotel, he thought ruefully. In the far corner the dusty remnants of a three-tier wooden hen-coop bore testimony to the fact that hens, carefully tended lest they plot amongst themselves in the night to take flight and leave Ireland for Norway, had been free to roam and lay their eggs in nesting boxes made of woven straw.

And beyond that nothing. Curiously – or perhaps because of expert thatching long ago – the cottage was not damp. Cleaned up – a job that would take some time – it would be perfect for their needs.

Leaving the cottage, attempting to reposition the boards, Cathal had another thought. They would be safe enough from intrusion once they were inside the cabin – its reputation would ensure that – but their tethered horses, seen from the road, would be bound to lead to comment.

There was a solution to that: Rosaleen was going to have to ride a bicycle, which could be carried into the cottage. He would buy her one as a present, and one for himself as well.

Preoccupied with his plans for the cottage, Cathal arrived at the meeting even later than he had antici-pated, to find Tim-Pat Tierney hanging around outside the secret room in obvious search for him. Cathal wrenched his thoughts reluctantly away from the sub-ject of future love to the present state of Ireland.

He had hardly settled inside the room when Ned Lynch challenged him.

'You've been talking for some time of going to America, Cathal, to take up your cousin's contacts, and rebuild our support from there. Have you made any plans to go?'

'I haven't, but I intend to do so. Stephens has been a great help in that connection though it's the sons of the men he knew that we need to be after for money.'

'It's only right that those who left and got rich should plough back into our land,' Ned Lynch said in his usual morose way. 'A quarter of the population of Ireland we lost to emigration in a ten-year stretch – two million people – and most of them in the United States, filling up their pockets.'

'Those that didn't die of hunger first,' Cathal said, and managed to change the subject.

But his own dilemma stayed with him. A matter of days ago he would have been wildly enthusiastic about planning his trip to raise material resources for the movement. Now, with the fruition of his affair with Rosaleen, he knew he did not want to go. On top of that, having no intention of telling her about his military involvement, he would have to invent a credible excuse for her, for being away for so long.

In one evening, the worm of love had eaten into his soul, debilitating his true virility, diverting him from the movement, and for the first time, in the presence of his Centres, he began to feel ashamed.

'. . . build up of further ammunition,' John Roche was saying.

Parnell, Cathal thought – you poor fool. *Now* I know how you felt.

* * *

And still he could not stay away from her, not even when, at the beginning of September, Daniel and Eugene came back to Kincora for four days before being sent to school. There had been much preliminary debate about that, their mother, on the one hand, wanting to have them with her for a short while, and on the other, worrying about the way Dermot was going to behave.

And then Carmel stepped in, and carted Dermot off to her own place, safely out of the way for the sake, she said, of the twins.

On the second evening, Cathal yielded to temptation and dropped in to Kincora at a time when he surmised the children would be in bed.

They were, but only one of them was asleep. Eugene, wide awake and troubled at the prospect of going to school, lay rigidly in his narrow bed, looking over at his brother. Nothing worried Daniel, he thought – nothing ever would! The thought of going to school in a foreign country seemed to him an adventure instead of an ordeal.

The puzzling thing was that Daniel did not appear to mind that he would be leaving Mama – would not be seeing her for several months at a stretch, during which time he would be forced to spend days and nights in the company of strangers.

Leaving Mama to spend time at Crag Liath was another story altogether. When you stayed for any length of time at O'Brien's Bridge Mama came to call.

That would not happen when they went to school in England, Aunt Milly had told them, explaining that they would have to be brave and strong the way boys should be, and even if they did not feel courageous, they must never resort to tears.

That was easier said than done. He had only to think about leaving Mama and the tears began to come.

'Boys – especially *O'Brien* boys – never, ever cry . . .'

But his cheeks were wet already and his nose had started to run.

Perhaps, Eugene reasoned, if he were to get up and go downstairs, he and Mama could have one of their chats and see if, between them, they could find a way to fend off the tears. At least if he got out of bed he would be taking action instead of moping under the sheet.

It was still quite light – light enough, anyway, to see his jumper lying on the chair where he had laid it with the rest of his clothes before putting his nightshirt on. He got quietly out of bed and reached for it, adding his trousers and shoes without socks before making his way downstairs. Mama would be in the drawing-room – she was always there at night, sewing or reading a book.

But when he reached the drawing-room door he stopped. There were unexpected voices coming from inside the room. After all, his father must have come back from Aunt Carmel's earlier than they had planned. Most assuredly, he did not want to see his father – not after what he had seen happen to the prints and precious plates, but, just as certainly, he did not want to return uncomforted to his bed.

Tim-Pat, Eugene thought – I'll go and find Tim-Pat, and talk to him till Papa goes to bed. Then I'll go and see Mama.

As quietly as he had left the bedroom, he crept out of the house, making for the stables and the harness-room where Tim-Pat should be sitting by his fire, for the weather was turning colder.

'Are you there?' he called loudly before he actually got to the harness-room door, to reinforce his courage.

It was strange how much darker it seemed now that he was actually outside the house, and stranger still how familiar things – stable doors, the outline of the coach-house, even the horses in their loose boxes – seemd to metamorphose at night, assuming more sinister aspects. The shovel leaning against the farthest wall cast a shadow of a very different shape – a banshee maybe, the fairy woman who comes to the house when people are going to die, a small woman in a red dress down to her toes and a red cape on her shoulders. And a handkerchief in her hand, for wiping the tears she has to shed . . .

'*Tim-Pat!*'

Eugene threw himself against the harness-room door, hoping in that way to frighten the banshee lady, and it swung open, so he nearly fell.

'Tim – '

Except that Tim-Pat was not there.

O'Brien boys don't cry, or show fear, either. Most banshee ladies were not big, according to Bridie Flannagan – only the size of a doll, for all that the one standing by the shovel had seemed to him to be large enough.

But crying. Remember that. A lady lacking in courage despite her fairy powers.

With a gargantuan effort, Eugene forced himself out of the corridor that ran between harness-room and stables, back into the yard, where the shovel was, and the crying fairy lady, to find that –

She was gone! There was no sign at all of anyone, let alone a small banshee.

Pleased with himself for having driven her off, but nevertheless apprehensive, he went round the house, between the orchard and the drawing-room window, in search of the missing Tim-Pat. He found him, half-hidden by a tree, lost in contemplation of some peculiar adult thing, so engrossed that you could get right up alongside him before he knew that you were there.

'It's me – Eugene!'

'It is and all,' Tim-Pat said softly. 'And what are you doing out of bed? It will put the caibosh on things if your mother finds you out.'

'I've come down to talk to her,' Eugene said, with dignity because, for all that Tim-Pat was a special person and his friend, he was also only a worker who should stay in his rightful place.

'Oh, you have, have you?' Tim-Pat said, but not in his normal cheerful voice. 'Well, I don't know if that's a thing I'd be doing myself, not at this hour of night.'

So what did that mean? And why was Tim-Pat looking away from him – looking again at the peculiar adult thing in which he had been engrossed before?

Even as part of Eugene's mind formulated this question, he found the answer.

Because from where he and Tim-Pat were standing it was possible to see through the window with the undrawn curtains into the drawing-room where Mama and Papa had been having that lengthy talk.

Except that, now he could see directly into the room, he realized that the man in there was not Papa after all, but Mr O'Mahoney who often came to the house.

And that he and Mama were not having a conversation but were locked in each other's arms. Kissing. As if they never intended to stop.

No one had ever told him that such behaviour was wrong but Eugene knew at once that it was. Terribly wrong. Bad enough to make you forget the necessity for courage and for tears to come into your eyes.

'Tim-Pat?'

It was only a whisper but Tim-Pat caught it and he was on his knees so you could rest your head on his shoulder and have him stroke your head.

And tell you the things you had to know, about all that was going on: that it was Mama's fault that Papa was not normal; that Mama was a wicked woman who had power over men; *that you were going to school to let her be with him.*

All the time, as Tim-Pat talked, there was a bubble of pain inside you, with a knife in its centre, and you were sure that it would burst so the knife would cut into your body and then you would be dead.

'Her fault. Remember that now – *her* fault. Not his at all. The man has been bewitched.'

'Yes,' he said. 'Yes . . .' with his head on Tim-Pat's shoulder, until the story had been told.

Afterwards, he had no need to talk to his mother for she was a woman he did not know, who had power over men. It was Tim-Pat who took him into the house and put him back to bed. Ruffling his hair, touching his cheek. Telling him not to forget.

As if he could forget.

'Are you all right now?'

'Yes.'

You had to be brave. Even when, in the night, as Daniel slept in the adjoining bed, the bubble burst – the knife cut into his heart.

'I don't know what's the matter with Eugene, Milly. He's as miserable as sin.'

'Oh, that's natural under the circumstances,' Milliora said. 'He's more sensitive than Daniel and he's worrying about school. But it will all be different when he settles down over there and begins to make friends.

472

And don't forget he's got Daniel to pave the way for him. In a couple of weeks he'll be fine and we'll have difficulty persuading him to come home for the holidays, there'll be so much going on.'

'Do you think so?'

'Of course I do. Please don't worry. I have everything under control. As soon as we get to London we'll have the boys fitted for their uniforms and they'll have the experience of staying at the Savoy Hotel where all sorts of famous people can be seen.'

'What an exciting life you lead, Milly,' Rosaleen said, without envy.

For who would want to stay at a smart hotel when you could make love in a humble cottage?

'One of these days you must come to London with me,' Milliora said. 'It would do you good, Rosaleen. You need a break from Dermot and it would be an interesting experience to visit a sophisticated city and look at the shops and enjoy really good theatre, instead of bothering with all this outmoded nonsense about reviving peasant Irish culture.'

'Milly, how can you make such outrageous statements? Our heritage is so rich. We are the people with the deep cultural traditions whereas the English – '

'Of course, I know there are *some* Irish writers who are not peasants,' Milliora swept on. 'There's a playwright called Oscar Wilde who has absolutely taken London by storm with his amusing comedies, and he writes poetry and books, it seems, as well. Apparently, he's the son of a doctor from Dublin, Dr William Wilde, who became a court physician, so the family is well-connected.'

'Of course!'

But it was pointless using sarcasm or irony against Milliora since both went over her red-gold head. And it was too sad a time, with the children going, to instigate a fight.

'One last hug,' Rosaleen said to the twins, trying to make light of their departure, forcing a smile on her face, holding Daniel tight, since he had rushed into her arms.

'Hug?'

It was Eugene's turn. But his blue eyes were cold and unforgiving. They focused on her briefly, without love, before their owner turned away.

Behind his back, Milliora mouthed, 'Don't worry. He'll be fine – you'll see.'

And they were gone, driven away to Limerick station and out of her life for months. She went back inside the house, conscious of the void – conscious of its unnatural tidiness, now the twins had left.

To counteract the emptiness she went upstairs to the nursery and sat down on Eugene's bed, encouraged by the presence of toys and books to believe that she still had sons. The wooden animals Milly had bought – a broken Jack-in-the-box.

And Eugene's drawing-book, lying by his bed. He must be encouraged to draw and paint at Downside, she thought, picking up the book. When she wrote to him she would tell him how the monks who had illustrated the famous Book of Kells had used the fine hairs of foxes and badgers in place of an artist's brush.

She opened the drawing-book, to see how Eugene's skill had progressed. A drawing of Dubhfoilean, depicted from the rear. Another of the horses – of a lady in a hat. She was excited now, instead of sad, for – beyond doubt – there was embryonic talent in the immature sketches – a natural feeling for line.

She turned the pages, noting that the more recent drawings were – recognizably – of events at Crag Liath, recorded these last few weeks. Better and better. Here was Milly, out in the fields, and Mrs Markham inside the house.

And Daniel, with a loghter-hook, and a man that, by a stretch of imagination, could be Bawnie Kinsella.

And – She gasped, looking at another image recorded by her son – a fearful image, hardly credible as having come from Eugene's hand. So terrible that she closed her eyes to obliterate its horror: the image of a woman with a knife. A boy being stabbed to death.

Drawn by *Eugene*? But unmistakably by Eugene – the line, the form was his.

But the content? From what abyss had this image been sucked? It must have been implanted. No six-year-old was capable of such morbidity as this, not without adult intrusion. Someone at Crag Liath? One of the workers perhaps, with a sick, disordered mind?

She would mention the incident to Milliora and between them they would ensure that Eugene, and Daniel, too, could not be exposed to such sickness again.

Meanwhile, it was as well that they were going away, out of such enemy's clutches. For all that she hated the concept of an English education, at Downside Eugene would be safe.

32

It seemed to Milliora that there would be no end to the rain. All through the winter there had been no let up from it and now it was spring, early April, and it was still coming down in buckets, turning the estate into a soggy mud bog and threatening to play havoc with the newly-planted crops.

'The potatoes are going to be late going in,' she said, accosting Liam Lenihan in the cart-track that led from the haggard to the yard. 'I'd laid great store on the Red Elephants but as it is there's no point in even putting down Aran Banners for the pigs.'

As if the weather was all *my* fault, thought Liam, instead of the Almighty's.

'It'll ease off in a couple of days – you'll see,' he said, only to placate her. 'We have the lazy-beds all ready. There's no need for you to be fretting at all.'

A right flutter-guts she was and no mistake, with woeful steam coming out of her.

'. . . and I see that there are more crows around than ever this year, ready to gobble my grain.'

'They'll not be there for long, Mrs O'Brien. Bernie's going down to the fields with the clapper-boards now and we're going to build a *taibhse*.'

'Yes. Well maybe a scarecrow will achieve more than you have done, over the last few weeks,' Milliora told him crossly. 'If I've told you once, I've told you a thousand times that Crag Liath needs workers, not idlers and parasites living off the land. I just hope that none of the workers on this estate are slowing down in their duties because they've fallen prey to those political agitators who would try to take Crag Liath away.'

'Not a bit of it, Mrs O'Brien,' Liam said, marvelling at how she pitched her voice so even he could hear every word she said.

'*Agitators!*' he heard her say again as she walked towards the stables. 'Balloting again in Parliament for another date for another wretched land bill!'

But even as she said this, Milliora's practical mind had returned to the damage wrought at Crag Liath by the incessant rain . . .

'Mrs O'Brien, there's no drying and there's damp sheets all over the place and I can't change the bedding.'

'Then we'll sleep under blankets, Mrs Cash,' she called as she swung Samhrain, Bealtaine's successor, out of the yard, in the direction of the fields.

She was surrounded by inadequate people, she thought intolerantly – who were too incompetent to take decisions of their own. Men like Liam Lenihan, hangers-on, who did not justify their keep, and would never hold down a decent job with any other employer.

She was in that snipey state, activated by loneliness, that motivated her to seek out a target for her frustrations and when she discovered that the rain damage was less serious than she had feared she was only partly mollified. At the far end of the turnip-field she paused, unaware that she was only seeking another direction in which to train her sights.

And then it came to her that she should check the fencing carried out by Liam Lenihan during the winter months. Crag Liath fences, generally, were disgracefully untidy, lacking the precision of those at Wimborne. It was time she introduced all who worked at

Crag Liath to the concept of organized thinking in relation to the estate.

Riding on, her eyes roved over the ditches, searching for possible gaps. At the same time memories of Wimborne reminded her of the happy Christmas she had spent there with Rosaleen and the twins. It had been good of the Leahys to take on Dermot so Rosaleen was able to go, and it had given her enormous pleasure to offer the trip to her friend as a gift.

Yet, all the time, while she was obviously trying to appear cheerful for the benefit of the twins, Rosaleen had been, not exactly miserable, but detached, as if her mind was someplace else.

And Eugene, who had been so out of sorts before he started school, had been odd with his mother during the holidays – polite, beyond reproach in terms of his manners, but certainly lacking in love.

Maybe that was what was distracting Rosaleen during those few weeks. And so she had remained for at least two weeks afterwards, and then sprung into life . . .

It was as if – but, no, that was quite impossible, in spite of what that nasty gossip, Kitty McCormac, insisted the day they met in McBirney's.

'Your friend, Rosaleen O'Brien, that was in your class at school, is having a great time for herself these days, being seen at her Gaelic League meetings with a certain gentleman friend . . .'

Salacious nonsense, a fact that she had observed to Kitty the minute the comment was made. Mischief-making nonsense of the worst kind.

And yet – Rosaleen was distracted, the way women were with love . . .

All the time the rain was falling, so having set out on her tour of inspection in a spring dress with balloon sleeves – quite improper for riding – Milliora now felt and probably looked a sorry mess. In her indignation with Liam Lenihan she had not even thought to put on a hat and her hair was soaking wet.

'We'll go down to the field nearest the river,' she said to Samhrain, speaking aloud the way she often did when she was more or less alone. 'We'll check the fencing he's done down there and then we'll head for home.'

The grey mare plodded on through the sodden fields, retracing a path taken more than twelve years earlier by Dermot marvelling at the power God had put into his hands, until the marshy strip of grassland with the hump in the middle was in Milliora's sights, and before it, a gap in the hedged ditch where – by the looks of things – an animal had got through.

She swore in a way that would have shocked the daylights out of Liam Lenihan had he happened to hear, and coaxed Samhrain into a trot so that she was in a position to see beyond the gap.

She spotted the creature at once – one of her prized heifers, stuck fast in the mud by the side of the river and, in the manner of cattle, docilely accepting her fate.

'Over!' she commanded Samhrain, scorning the gap in the hedge-ditch, jumping it instead. 'Go *on* – before she sinks . . .'

'Get out of it!' she shouted at the heifer a couple of minutes later, hoping that the anger in her voice would frighten the creature and make her try to move, and when she did not – only opening her great brown eyes wider in fear – Milliora reached for the nearest stone and threw it at her, hitting her on the rump.

She twitched but did not try to move her legs.

'You damn' fool!' she said to her furiously. 'Do you

479

realize that unless you try to get out of there you're going to die and the good money I paid for you will be lost in a puddle of mud!'

For all the good that did her . . .

And then it came to her what she must do. A remedy used to rescue horses caught in this situation but one worth trying, nevertheless, on the heifer which, if she went to fetch help, might die before it came. The part of the bank on which she was standing was still intact and only inches from where the trapped animal stood. She could touch the heifer – did so – put one arm over the muddy back and pulled herself astride her, throwing herself forward on to the animal's neck.

And, as she had intended, she reacted spontaneously with the back of her body, kicking up her back legs – spattering mud all over them both – and finding that she could move.

Doing so – making for the bank, her desire to get rid of the rider overcame the terror of the mud.

And they were on the bank and Milliora was sliding off the filthy back, laughing in relief.

And then laughing at herself as she had never done in her life for her dress and all of herself that was visible was caked in stinking mud.

She was still laughing when she saw the decaying wooden doorway cut into the hillock from which an overgrowth of grass at some stage or other had been firmly pulled away. A doorway leading to – what?

Open-mouthed, with mud all over her face, she stood gazing at the doorway while the heifer ambled off through the gap in the fence.

So investigate then, she told herself – stop standing around like a gombeen, startled because there's a doorway – a room – on your land you never suspected was there.

A room? And a small boy's voice – Daniel's voice talking of men with guns . . . (*'I saw them through the wall.'*)

'Stay there,' she said severely to Samhrain, although the grey mare was doing just that, and she strode towards the door.

And pushed it open. On the other side was a good-sized room and one which – since there were few cobwebs and the floor was relatively clean – looked as if it had been used recently.

By men with guns?

Fenians, she thought furiously, and Land Leaguers – for they were all the same in her mind. Men who planned to do away with the big estates, dissipate good land amongst peasant farmers who could not cope on their own. Revolutionaries, daring to meet – to plot – on her own land, under her very nose.

Who were these men? Surely not her own people? Pondering on that, she looked around the room again and, this time, spotted the boarded-up portion of the wall through which Daniel had tumbled, a few years before.

If you accepted his story – and there was no reason now to doubt it – you were left with the reality of a small boy who had fallen from a broom cupboard into a secret passage, to emerge at the other side.

'Wandering in the garden,' according to Tim-Pat Tierney. 'He must have got out of the cupboard again and gone out through the kitchen.'

And Tim-Pat it was who had closed the hole in the cupboard so nobody would know that it was not, as he had said, an extension of the boot-room closed off by Fiona O'Brien, but part of a secret passage.

It was Tim-Pat who had lied. And Tim-Pat Tierney who hated the English for the way his family had died.

481

A man born, out of his bitter hatred, to be part of a rebel group, whose impudent members, by the looks of things, continued to hold meetings on her land.

Milliora's cheeks flamed with fury under their layers of mud. She would put a stop to their nonsense immediately – this very day no less. She would write to the police about the incident – about Tim-Pat Tierney in particular, and see he was put in goal.

Her pleasure in having saved the life of the heifer ebbed away in her rage, but when she reached the gap in the fence again she stopped and blocked it up. Then, wet, shivering and extremely dirty, she galloped back to the house.

But when – bathed and changed, with her hair bound in a towel – she sat down to write to the police she began to have second thoughts about implicating Crag Liath in their investigations.

What if Liam Lenihan and the rest of them were to hear that rebels had been meeting on her land all this time without her taking action? They would conclude that she was weak and foolish and, worse, they might decide that a revolutionary movement that operated so successfully under the eyes of the enemy was exciting and attractive.

But there was no way Tim-Pat Tierney was getting away unpunished for what he had done – no way either that she would condone the behaviour of men with guns.

One alternative to presenting the police with the whole story was to send them an anonymous letter suggesting that they keep an eye on Tierney, who presumably had contact with his associates other than on her land. That way, there was at least an even chance that the gang could be located outside Crag Liath.

But an anonymous letter was a cowardly thing, reminiscent of the dreadful Sarah Masters. Milliora O'Brien of Crag Liath was a better woman than that!

So she would tell the police in an authoritative manner that Tierney was involved with a secret society and that they should follow him over the next few weeks and round all the criminals up. And she would sign her name at the end.

'Men with guns!' she muttered aloud, picking up her pen.

'She's talking to herself in the library,' Mrs Cash reported. 'I was going past the door with a pile of sheets when I heard her ranting and raving and mentioning men with guns!'

'And were the sheets aired, may I ask? Or were you proposing to put them back on the beds wringing wet, the way they were this morning?'

'I've *ironed* them dry, Mrs Markham. Some of us use our heads in our work and some of us do not.'

'And some of us never did a tap of work in the whole of their lives,' Mary added darkly.

But she was intrigued by what Mrs Cash had said about men with guns.

'What else did Mrs O'Brien say?' she asked, casually, pretending to be examining the salt in the wooden box that hung beside the fire.

'Not much else,' said Mrs Cash airily. 'But enough for me to be able to form the impression that she's distracted in her head. The poor thing! Wasn't she cursed from the day of her wedding, it coinciding with the murders that were done in the Phoenix Park.'

'Political murders,' Mary said coldly, 'done by three men that were caught the following year. There's no curse on Mrs O'Brien, whatever you might be thinking, and where her head is concerned she's as hardy as a snipe. It's over-tired she is, going here, there and everywhere in a hurry, running two estates.'

'And what for, may I ask? Doesn't she know she can't take the money with her, there being no pockets in a shroud. Ah sure why doesn't she enjoy herself – go off on another holiday with Mrs Rosaleen O'Brien?'

'Isn't she busy as well, making cakes to sell in the town and running this Gaelic League.'

'A quare kind of an institution,' Mrs Cash observed, knowing that, in expressing this opinion, she was on common ground with Mary Markham. 'What would we be wanting to speak Irish for, instead of civilized English?'

'I can't imagine,' Mary said.

But to Mrs Cash's disappointment she did not pursue this subject further. She went to the dresser and reached for a wooden noggin, filling it with milk.

Men with guns? What did that have to do with writing letters? What had Mrs Cash really heard? What was going on?

What could be going on in Cathal's mind, Rosaleen wondered, that he was talking of travelling to America for the second time inside six months?

He had been hazy enough about the reason for his first visit at the end of last year, only explaining that it was in some way connected with relations there – saying that he would be away during the Christmas holidays and well into the New Year. Since he had not volunteered any more information on the subject than that she had not intruded by pressing him any further.

She had tried to compensate for his absence by accepting Milliora's invitation to join her, with the twins, at Wimborne Manor. Apart from the inevitable pain of missing Cathal, there had been a distressing ambiguity in that holiday for – although it was splendid being reunited with Daniel and Eugene, Milliora was her usual generous self and Wimborne itself was delightful – she had been acutely conscious of her hypocritical role, taking hospitality from Milliora while, at the same time, counting the days when she would have enough money saved with her cooking to transfer the children from Downside over to Clongowes.

From Eugene's point of view the sooner that happened the better, she thought, for he was withdrawn and uncommunicative, unlike his bouncy brother, and she had been hurt by his attitude towards her – the way he had turned from her when she bent to kiss or hug him – the way he never smiled.

All that would change – *had* to change when he was back again at school in Ireland and closer to herself, she thought, creaming the butter and sugar together for the cherry cake she was making for the teashop owned by Kitty McCormac, Carmel's friend, who was one of her culinary clients. Thank goodness the cooking venture had got off to a flying start, with decent demand for her macaroons and rice biscuits and cakes. Having started off on her own she was now in a position to employ two assistants on a regular basis.

And things were going well at the Gaelic League, for all that they had so few members. It was more of an uphill struggle there than she had anticipated, arousing people's interest in the heritage they had very nearly lost. The effort in setting up a branch had been all hers, and she was proud of it, but Cathal had diligently escorted her to every single meeting, and given her valiant support.

So really there was nothing to worry about except

perhaps – But, no – surely *she* did not have to consider that . . .

Cracking three eggs into a bowl she began to beat them, grittng her teeth when her arms began to ache. Cooking was hard work and she was dead tired at the end of a day when all her orders were done. She was about to put the cake into the oven when she heard a knock at the front door.

'I'm here – I'll be with you now!' she shouted, although the caller probably could not hear her voice echoing through the house.

Still wearing her apron she went through to the hall and tugged at the heavy door, which was swollen by the rain. Whoever was on the other side simply stood there, not assisting with a push.

'Father Moloney,' she said, when the door was finally open. 'Come in. Did you come by foot?'

'I did,' said the parish priest. 'The exercise is good for one so I thought that I would walk.'

A friendly enough beginning but there was a coldness in his voice.

'I'm afraid that my hands are rather floury – I've been baking cakes,' she said, trying to act naturally, trying to behave as if she did not suspect the reason for his visit.

'What can I offer you? I suppose it's a little early for a drink?'

'I'll have nothing at all, thank you,' he said, following her into the drawing-room and waiting for her to be seated before perching above her on the pink sateen chair. Looking at her with cold grey eyes. Searching for admission?

He attacked at once.

'You are a member of my parish,' he said. 'You come to Mass on Sunday but it has come to my

486

attention that you refrain from the sacraments. Why is that the case?'

Direct. Permitting no evasion, even if she had been prepared to lie or try to fend him off.

'I can't answer that question,' Rosaleen said.

'You are risking your immortal soul by not going to Confession and Holy Communion. You surely realize that?'

'Yes,' she said wearily. 'I realize that is so.'

'Then why are you taking this risk? You are the mother of two sons. I understand that you are involved in the activities of the Gaelic League, a moral cultural organization set up to elevate our people not only in their own eyes but also in the eyes of the world. The meetings of the Gaelic League are not hideouts for sinners, Mrs O'Brien, nor should they become such.'

'I understand that.'

'You will give the League a bad name if it is known that you abstain from the sacraments. Will I see you at Holy Communion on Sunday?'

'I don't know,' she said. 'I don't think so . . .'

He got up, towering above her, and his voice was colder than before.

'In that case, I would suggest that you resign from your position at the League, Mrs O'Brien – resign from the League altogether. This is a Catholic country, not a heathen one, and there is no place in its societies for those who give over their faith. The Gaelic League is a spiritual as well as a cultural body – it has and will have influence over generations of Irish children. It is no place for the likes of you.'

When he had gone she returned to the kitchen. Her assistants – cousins of Bridie Flannagan's – were not due in for more than an hour. There was plenty of work to get on with before the two of them arrived.

She did not do it. In her mind she was having a conversation, not with Father Moloney, but with God Himself, asking if He could equate her love with sin.

Surely not. No matter what the priests – what the Church might say. Celibate men spoke with disdain of lust, having no understanding of the spirituality attached to the act of love. But You understand that, she said in her mind – for You invented love.

Such thinking was heresy. Father Moloney would excommunicate her from the Church if she openly questioned his interpretation of God's will where lovers were concerned.

Thy handmaid . . . joined in matrimony . . . may she fly all unlawful connections . . . Remaining prudent – faithful – constant to her faith. The requests made on her behalf to God by Father Moloney, when Dermot and she were wed.

But how could you remain faithful to an impotent man who had long since lost his mind?

And how – when you had been longer dead yourself and the gift of life had been put into your hands – could you give that bonus up?

It was not raining now and from where she sat at the kitchen table Rosaleen could see Dermot with a broom in his hand, sweeping imaginary dirt from the path that ran around the house. He was a ghost who drifted through her life, who had to be regularly fed but made no other demands. A ghost who had accepted death.

While she wanted to live – *was* living to her full capacity now, every day of her life.

Do You want to take that life from me, she asked – will You tell me what You feel?

And still she did not have the answer.

'*You will give the Gaelic League a bad name . . . a*

488

*spiritual as well as a cultural body . . . no place for the
likes of you . . .'*

Lost in her thoughts, Rosaleen lost track of time
completely. In the oven the cherry cake intended for
Kitty McCormac's teashop baked, reached perfection
and ultimately burned without her knowledge. Or
maybe her stomach noticed what her mind and eyes
and nose had failed to observe, for it reacted against
the stench from the oven, heaving.

She was just in time to get to the kitchen sink.
Bending over it, holding on to her sides with shaking
hands, she was horribly, painfully sick.

33

A matter has come to my attention which I feel is of much interest to the authorities . . . a man called Tim-Pat Tierney who used to work at this house as a groom and a coachman some twelve years back . . .

Captain Bill Pollard wrinkled his nose, surveying Milliora's indignant letter.

'What would *you* make of it?'

'She calls him a dangerous agitator,' his deputy said, shrugging. 'A member of a secret society that's well armed with guns. It sounds a bit of a story to me. The close of the Parnell era seems to have put paid to the power of the agitators. After all, the full weight of the Church has been against them. Though there are those who say they're working in a different way, initiating an educative movement designed to breed revolutionaries in the coming generation.'

'The Gaelic League? There's nothing there – just a collection of high-minded intellectuals thinking they can restore a dead language. There's no politics in that and by all accounts it isn't that popular either.'

'Otherwise I'd say that the days of political societies in this country are well over. Their arms' supplies have dried up and grown obsolete and so has the supply of sympathy money that used to come over from America.'

'Exactly. As for this letter, if you went into it, you'd doubtless discover that the personalities involved had it in for each other. He probably pinched from the house.'

'All the same, if you like, I could have him followed by one of our young recruits. 'Twould do no harm.'

Captain Pollard yawned widely. 'None at all,' he said. 'Take the letter and compose a polite reply to her while you're at it. Isn't it amazing the tricks women resort to, when they want to get back at a man?'

All of a sudden the weather had changed, had become more summery than spring-like, and Cathal was inspired by it to surprise Rosaleen with an outing, not to the haunted cottage but further afield and, he thought, very much more romantic.

The proposed expedition entailed the purchasing of food and with a picnic in mind he went into Limerick to look for a suitable hamper.

The surprise was not entirely altruistic, he admitted to himself. Along with the gratuitous element went the more ulterior motive of making atonement to her for the fact that, this time, he would be going to America for a minimum of two months and possibly even for three.

On his previous visit, the descendants of the former Fenians had embraced him with an enthusiasm he had not anticipated in his wildest dreams, pressing money and support on him wherever he went, and giving him valuable lists of contacts and assurances of further aid.

The time he had allotted for that assignment had been too short, so he had arranged to return as soon as possible afterwards and to stay for several months.

Planning his second trip, he had drawn up a detailed itinerary, which – along with the record of his first – he now carried with him on his person in a notebook wherever he went lest those at home should come across it and be tempted to peruse its contents.

He found the picnic basket he was after at Todd's –

the right size for two people and yet big enough to take a generous amount of goodies – and he walked up George Street holding it in one hand thinking what else he needed to buy.

Bread and butter. And cold ham and a cooked chicken. But what else did you take on a picnic? His imagination, lacking only in domestic matters, sagged under the strain of having to plan a menu.

He was passing the teashop run by someone called Kitty McCormac and he decided to go inside and ask for some advice. In order to get it he would have to buy some of the cakes that were on offer although he could hardly take those on an expedition with Rosaleen since she would have baked them herself and might be sick of the sight of them.

He pushed open the teashop door and sniffed with pleasure at the deliciousness of the smells: fresh macaroon biscuits, Madeira cake, and, best of all, a cake that was threatening to burst asunder with red cherries. It was more than a man could withstand. The teashop itself was attractive, with small tables covered with clean white cloths and waitresses in trim black dresses with white frilly aprons and caps.

So what was he waiting for but a pot of tea and a generous helping of cake?

He sat down at one of the tables and beckoned to a waitress to take his order, and a young girl, who looked vaguely familiar, came across the room.

'Mr O'Mahoney, 'tis good to see you again.'

He peered at her more closely: dark hair, green questioning eyes – she looked about fourteen . . .

'Moirin Dinneen!' he said, recognizing the young woman who had grown from the gap-toothed friendly child. 'Are you working here long?'

'Six months on Friday,' she said, pleased with herself

about that. 'I'm making good money and I got the job meself.'

'Well, isn't that nice! And your father – is he well?'

'He's well enough,' she said. 'As well as you could be, in his state. Were you going to order some tea?'

'I was. And some of that cherry cake with it. And maybe a macaroon . . .'

'All right so,' she said, and went off towards the kitchen, moving like a woman, now, inside the sombre dress.

Thinking of her father made him remember that he had to speak to the movement tomorrow night about his plans to go to America.

He reached into his pocket and took out his note-book, thumbing through it in search of relevant facts. Most important was the need to set up a central council in the United States to dispense with the need for such frequent visits by himself after the present year. There were enough trustworthy supporters, but they lived too far from each other and needed to be coalesced by a leader living centrally who would be prepared to travel between the towns. On his next visit, a suitable man had to be appointed to undertake this task.

Having set up the movement and gathered the guns with a young man's enthusiasm, he had realized over the years how embryo his initial efforts had been. It had been naïve to think that he could take Ireland by storm without massive overseas support. He should have started by creating a strong American branch of the movement before extending its work – recruiting its Centres at home.

Still, better late than never. Deep in thought, he did not notice that Moirin Dinneen had returned to his table bearing a laden tray.

'Here's your tea so.'

'Thank you. Would you say it's as good as it smells?'

'It is indeed!' she said proudly. 'There's a woman Miss McCormac uses that's a wonderful cook. Taste them macaroons for yourself – now, have you ever eaten the like?'

'I have not!' said Cathal. 'You can tell Miss McCormac from me that she's a clever lady to have located a woman who cooks in such a superior way. Do I pay you?'

'You can if you like. I'll write down the amount for you.'

Over-tipping her, he closed his notebook and pushed it to one side, concentrating on his solitary feast. Self-indulgence on a grand scale, and more of it planned for tomorrow when Rosaleen and he took off. She deserved it, even if he did not. She was working too hard at her cooking, trying to put money aside he supposed, although she refused to discuss finances with him, or anything relating to the life she shared with her husband, and he had learnt over the years not to attempt to bring the subject up.

Still, with her star.dard of cooking she was probably doing fairly well! He finished his slice of cherry-cake and gulped down a second cup of tea, feeling suddenly guilty for being in town at all.

There was enough to do on the land at this time of year without his taking time off, today as well as tomorrow. And soon for several months . . . It was one thing to leave during the winter months, but being absent when the grasses were in flower could instigate a whole set of serious problems for the farm.

Absently, he got up from the table and made for the door having quite forgotten that he had intended to ask for advice about food from Kitty McCormac's staff. He strode long-legged down the street towards the stables where his horse was waiting, swinging his hamper with the food he had bought inside it.

A lovely man, Moirin Dinneen thought, moving to clear his surrendered table. And generous – and clever, just as Da had said.

Only he had forgotten –

She was out the door and down the street in search of him, as quick as her legs would go, waving his notebook in her hand.

'Mr O'Mahoney?'

Several people turned around but none of them were him. Ah well, Moirin thought resignedly – I'll give the notebook to me da. He can give it back.

'Take the carriage to the village of Mount Shannon and stable the mare at Stritche's,' Cathal had said. 'Then walk down through the trees on the little road that leads to the edge of the lake, and I'll be waiting there.'

Obeying this direction, Rosaleen felt unseen eyes boring into her back, demanding, in the manner of Father Moloney, the details of their secret. The conviction that she was being watched was so strong she swung around on the little road ready to confront the vigilantes. But only the trees – hazel and ash, willow and alder, birch and buckthorn – and the turf-brown sky that was tinged with pink were there to watch her progress.

He was standing by the lake shore, just as he had promised, and when he saw her the seriousness went out of his beautiful face.

'Hurry up! What's keeping you, woman?'

'Nothing's keeping me!' she called, not caring now whether the vigilantes heard or did not hear. 'Have you been waiting long?'

'Much too long!' he said. 'Ready to sail you over the

ocean to Hy-Brasil . . . Do you remember the day we went to Howth for lunch?'

'Pink salmon and new potatoes,' said Rosaleen. 'I remember very well.'

'You're greedy. When we were in the restaurant I pointed out Ireland's Eye to you – yes? I said there was a monastery on the island and that it would be pleasant to go out there by boat.'

'That was when I began to fall in love with you.'

Behind them, the lake sparkled and rippled, as if it had been overlaid with a myriad of silver fish scales. By the shore, pondweeds, bogbean and loosestrife tangled with germander. There was a pungent smell of mint.

His arms were round her now and she could see that his eyes were sparkling with mischief. Suddenly he swung her round to face the water.

'Look,' he said. 'There is another island, every bit as holy as Ireland's Eye, possibly even more so! It's called Holy Island, no less, and there are monastic ruins on it *and* a fine tower into which you won't be able to climb because the entrance is too high up. See – there it is.'

'But we haven't a boat to get out there.'

'We have! That's my surprise. I've borrowed one from someone I know in Mount Shannon, I've equipped it with food and we're about to set sail. No more dalliance. In you get and for goodness' sake sit still.'

All the way to the island he thought that when they got there they would make marvellous love. Even the water lapping against the side of the rowing boat, caressing, insistent, seemed to speak of seduction, and he could hear the whisper of love in the singing wings of the white plumed mute swans that flew gracefully over their heads. His desire was intensified by facing

Rosaleen in the little boat; he could gaze into the violet-blue eyes, interpreting their promise.

'I want you.'

'And I you,' she said, and he thought that it was her honesty that he loved most in her, the way she did not attempt to hide her own desire from him, lowering her eyes or resorting to coy commonplace devices, the way other women did.

And that made him feel ashamed of his own deviousness, of the secret life he had apart from her – the smokescreen he set up to disguise the reason for his visits to the United States.

Maybe I can tell her after all, he thought. By nature she is loyal, in spite of the predicament she is in through her marriage to Dermot O'Brien. At heart she is a nationalist. She would sympathize with the aims of the movement – relate to what we do. Perhaps I will tell her today, when the moment is right for talk, instead of love.

They were nearly at their destination. It was still possible to see the high, round tower but straggling trees at the water's edge cut off the view of the old church, the graveyard and the monastic ruins that he remembered from the past.

Once ashore, Cathal found the short walk led to what he remembered: the ruins of five ancient churches; the tower with the entrance twelve feet up from the ground, belfry and sanctuary from which saintly men, having fled with the monastery's precious vessels, could pour boiling water down on the heads of the heathen, looting Danes.

'Come and see the well.'

'A holy well? One that will cure?'

'I doubt it! They used to hold festivals here in the bad old pre-Christian days – Bacchanalian revelries.

The local squireens would turn up and steal the prettiest local girls. It got out of hand after a while and they had to put a stop to it. Isn't that a terrible pity!'

'For the squireens maybe.'

'The Celts were an erotic people before guilt stifled us and we became ashamed of being men and women.'

His eyes were dark. Does my face change, too, when I want to make love, she wondered, so that it is as if another personality – more beautiful, hardly comprehensible yet still familiar – entices him? In my eyes is there also that quality, akin to cruelty, that is more necessary than tenderness now if we are to open passion's dam?

Because of the tedious necessity of removing clothing, there was that moment in which Rosaleen felt both angry and humiliated, obstinately refusing to resort to banter and angrier still because she felt she should.

The grass under her naked body was thick and studded with white and yellow daisies. He parted her legs and knelt before her, bending his head.

'Is this nice, my darling?' The whisper of compassionate love, though she did not want him to speak.

When she half-opened her eyes she could see, as well as the tower, cattle, island-born and bred and bound, grazing in the rich pasture, the trees – her own white body – the top of the bowed and busy head.

Then it was not the island at all she could see, or Cathal, either, but the huge ivy-covered house, with the green lawns around it on which white swans incongruously nested, watching the stranger approach.

She could watch and yet cry out when he entered her, knowing how he would look as he did so – his long, lean body arching with the thrust. She could suck him into her, honouring him, and at the same time see herself move around the exterior of the vast and intimidating house, seeking a way to get in for it had been built without a door – had only windows for access, heavily curtained, through which you could not see.

'I can't bear it . . .' Her own voice, using silly, inadequate words.

'You can,' he said inexorably. '*Take it*. Love me.'

She could see then what she had previously failed to see – that the curtains in one of the windows had been parted, or had never been drawn at all. Through the window, very dimly she could make out the outline of a face.

'Love me.'

A woman's face – desperate. The face of a prisoner, pleading for release.

'I love you. I will always love you. Please . . .'

Half-speaking to Cathal – otherwise to the people – the men and women, arriving on horseback, moving in on the house.

Granting mercy. The woman who had been imprisoned was delivered from her pain.

The house was deserted – the people had gone – the swans had left their nests, and only love remained. Love or would-be lovers, lying on straw, dressed in silver mesh.

'Food!' Cathal said. 'After love you have to eat. Let's go down to the little church that's nearest the shore.'

'What's inside?'

'An early altar-piece and a much later plaque in the wall – seventeenth century as far as I remember. Oh – and you won't like this very much – some more recent O'Brien graves.'

'Relations of my husband's?'

'I don't know,' he said. 'By the way, is William

O'Brien, the former editor of *United Ireland*, any relation of Dermot's?'

'Michael Davitt's friend? Not that I know of. But then Dermot would never had admitted having cousins who supported the Land League, or any other nationalist cause. It was a difficulty between us when he was normal – the difference between his political views and my own. Let's not go inside the church. We can have our picnic here. Are you hungry?'

'Ravenous,' said Cathal, yawning happily. 'And tired. I could go to sleep but the company and the smell of good food emanating from that hamper is too strong an argument against dozing off!'

If it was not for the responsibility she feels for her husband, I could take her to America with me, he thought. After all, her children are safely at school. At least, she could come for a while.

'Have you ever thought of having Dermot committed?' he asked suddenly, risking offending her and secretly holding thumbs that he would not be snubbed for this intrusion.

'Put away in a mental home – an asylum?' Predictably, she was shocked at the suggestion.

He decided to brave it further. 'That's exactly what I do mean. He's off his head, Rosaleen. He could even be dangerous. Have you never considered that?'

'If I thought there was any harm in him it might be different,' she said, reaching out for the bread and a piece of ham, 'but Dermot is as gentle as a lamb – he really is, Cathal. He wouldn't say boo to a goose, neither long ago when he was normal nor today when he is not, the poor man. No, I'd never have him committed.'

So that's that, thought Cathal, abandoning that line of procedure and accepting the sandwich she had made for him. He bit into it thoughtfully, wondering how best to introduce his revelations about the true reason for his visits to the United States. It was important that Rosaleen understand from the onset lest she be put off, how he felt about the formation of a rebel army that would concentrate on military targets, scorning the use of violence against innocent civilians.

'Had Dermot been normal I would never have been able to attend the Gaelic League,' Rosaleen said, 'let alone form a branch of it on my own.'

'We know all the arguments against the Gaelic League by heart, don't we?' Cathal said, searching in his jacket pocket for the notebook outlining his American progress and plans. When Rosaleen realized what he was about to set in motion there, when he told her how much good she could do him just by being there with him, she might even be able to make some arrangements to have Dermot looked after while she was away. 'No nation wants to live in the past as much as Ireland does. The League teaches a false and reactionary doctrine of racial superiority. Worst of all, Ireland's ceaseless cry for freedom only masks her whispered admission of subjugation.'

Where the hell is it, he wondered – I always keep it with me. I couldn't have left it at home . . .

'That wouldn't really be Dermot's attitude,' Rosaleen was saying. 'He lived in the past himself . . .'

My God, Cathal thought – the teashop! I left that damn' notebook in there. Anyone could have picked it up after I had gone. Anyone could have thumbed through it, made only too obvious deductions, and handed it to the police.

'Don't you agree?' Rosaleen asked guilelessly.

He stared at her blankly.

'Oh, yes – you're right,' he said, his mind several miles away in Limerick.

Maybe Moirin Dinneen had picked the notebook up? But that was asking too much.

Watching Cathal, Rosaleen thought that something had gone horribly wrong with the day. Had she said something to upset him – something about Dermot? But how could that be? If anything, *Cathal* was the one who, by his suggestions, could have antagonized her. As if she could consider committing poor innocent sensitive Dermot to a mental home, even if there were times, too many times, when he drove her to distraction and she – But she would not think of hate.

Not when there was love to talk of, and the penalties that went with it.

I wanted so badly to talk quietly to you now, she thought. There's so much I want to say.

But the mood of the day has changed. The time for love has gone and – inexplicably – the time for conversation.

Even the weather was beginning to change. On the hills, in the distance, white misty rain was hovering.

'I'm cold,' she said, just as Cathal was saying, 'We should go home soon.'

Just like that. But *why*?

In his anxiety over the missing notebook, Cathal did not notice his own coldness, or what passed for it. If that notebook has fallen into the hands of the police, he thought, the movement – the possibility of freedom for Ireland – is ruined once again.

Rowing back, they found that the surface of the water was silver and tranquil no longer. It rippled in an ashen anger, presaging a storm.

Soon, Rosaleen thought, I will be alone again, a

prisoner at Kincora with Dermot – and Cathal will be gone.

When they parted at Mount Shannon she did not follow his example and head for home. Instead, she headed the carriage for the Clare hills and rested there looking down at the outline of Limerick city, wondering what she should do.

34

The young constable designated to follow Tim-Pat had been bored for most of the week. He hung around the boreen that ran at the back of Kincora, or in the orchard, for hours at a time trying to sight his quarry and ensure that the groom did not slip away to attend a rebel meeting.

Instead, he was forced to conclude that Tierney led a completely blameless life, not to mention a dull one, spending most of his time either in the stables or talking to the gormless man he presumed was Mr Dermot O'Brien, who seemed to say little back to him.

It was much the same at the weekend when other men got together for a drink, or went to watch a game of hurling or handball. Tierney appeared to have no friends, which was the one thing about him that was in any way remarkable.

Earlier in the day he had watched Mr O'Brien's wife taking off in the carriage. She had not returned by the time Mr O'Brien, who had been meandering around the garden talking to himself, went back to the house with Tierney beside him.

'Are you going to have a rest, Master Dermot?' he heard the groom say. 'A sleep would do you good.'

The two of them disappeared. But then, after about a quarter of an hour, the groom came out of the house alone and, much to the relief of the young constable, took one of the horses out of the stables and made off.

The constable's own horse was tied up to the old oak tree out on the boreen, and he ran to her, excited that, after a week of tedium, something seemed to be happening.

Tim-Pat turned off down Shelbourne Road and then to the left towards Redgate, where he began to canter, scattering a gaggle of geese trailing over the road.

So he was in a bit of a hurry. The constable grinned, and patted his gun affectionately, feeling the languor induced in him by the week's waiting beginning to drain away.

And then – rather disappointingly – in Meelick the groom turned in at a gateway to a respectable-looking house near the road, bordering a large farm. Even worse, as the grounds were treeless and deprived of camouflage, he had no alternative but to hover near the gateway, hoping to catch a glimpse of whoever opened the door to the visitor.

The elderly woman, even more respectable in appearance than the house in which she lived, did not look as if she spent her spare time convening rebel meetings and the groom did not seem to have much interest in her either, for after a brief conversation he tipped his cap to her and took his leave, after which he returned to the Ennis Road, simply going home. As a quarry he was about as useful as a lighthouse in a bog.

Still, the policeman had no alternative but to keep tabs on the man. Once more, he took up his watchful position in the orchard, anticipating another boring evening.

Although . . . He frowned, reconsidering. Perhaps he had been wrong in dismissing the elderly and respectable-looking woman who had opened the door to Tierney as an innocent. A large proportion of the Irish were racially disposed to crime – so Captain Pollard said. Just because the woman was old, looked like a housekeeper, did not mean that she was incapable of being Tierney's rebel contact. Or maybe her employer was; maybe Tierney was looking for him, or her?

By failing to confront and interrogate the woman he could have missed a vital clue.

It was a short enough ride to Meelick. The young constable decided to go back on his former tracks.

Just in case he had been mistaken about leaving the notebook in the teashop Cathal, returning home before going to the meeting, took the house apart – unsuccessfully.

Upset about that, the news that Tim-Pat Tierney had been on his doorstep, presumably to jog his memory about tonight's arrangements, irritated him all the more.

As if he was likely to forget the occasion on which he had intended to reveal the details of his American plans to his Centres and recapitulate on what he had achieved on his earlier visit to the United States, to keep their interest heightened.

He was in his drawing-room when, to his horror, he saw the young constable ride round to the front of the house. It was fortunate that he was downstairs and could intervene before Mrs Lavelle got a chance to go to the door for, good woman as she was, she was a stranger to discretion and would be offering information to the constable before he even opened his mouth.

Like telling him of Tierney's recent visit. There was no reason to implicate Tierney. The notebook, which had obviously been picked up and handed over to the police who were about to conduct their enquiries, did not mention the groom, or the Centres, either, only his own name and that of his American contacts and their relevance to a rebel movement based in the Golden Vale.

'I'll answer it!' he called out to Mrs Lavelle when the knock came on the door.

The fellow who was standing there looked very young and very junior to be carrying out enquiries, but he was authoritarian enough and came directly to the point.

'There's a man named Tim-Pat Tierney about whom I've been authorized to make enquiries,' he said. 'He was at your house earlier on. Do you know why he was here?'

They know more about us than I had feared, thought Cathal, and with what he hoped was a residue of aplomb he gestured to the young constable to step inside the house.

'That would be Mr Dermot O'Brien's groom and coachman,' he said, managing to keep a steady voice. 'He was here to deliver a message to me, I should imagine, about the Gaelic League. I always give Mrs O'Brien a lift to our meetings. Her husband isn't very well and it isn't a good thing in this day and age for a woman to be driving alone at night.'

'It is not,' agreed the young constable. 'A lawless nation we have, sir, and lawless people in it. This man Tierney now – we've had our eyes on him for some time.'

He looked hard at Cathal as he said this and Cathal returned his steady glance.

'Is that so?' he said. 'The O'Briens' groom? Well, now – *there's* a turnabout for the books.' Ready to bluff it out to the last – for all the good that was going to do him with the notebook where it was.

But perhaps the young constable did not know of the existence of the notebook. Perhaps he was making elementary enquiries intended to throw the suspect off balance so he would make a false move that would lead the police to his fellow rebels later on?

'So that's all you know about Tierney, sir, is it?'

'I'm afraid so. It's the O'Briens who are my friends.'

'Then there'll be no need for me to question your housekeeper, I think,' the young constable said. 'I'll be going. Sorry to have troubled you.'

'Not at all,' said Cathal, seeing him out.

The movement would have to close – for the moment, at least. That – instead of his American plans – he would have to announce to his Centres tonight.

If he ever reached the meeting. He was bound to be followed. Other policemen could already be stationed on the farm, ready to pursue him the minute he moved from the house. Yet he had to get to the secret room – had to warn the others of what was going on. There was no one else he could send in his stead.

Before heading for O'Brien's Bridge, he fine-combed the area round the house, looking for would-be followers. No one – or no one that he could see.

Continually looking over his shoulder, Cathal rode under the Clare hills, taking the back route towards his destination, holding his thumbs that he had been lucky tonight, and had managed to gain a reprieve.

Tim-Pat made a far later start in setting out for the meeting. Dermot was still asleep when he got back from Cathal's house, but there was no sign of Rosaleen whom he had expected to be back at Kincora by then, ready to take over from him and look after her husband for the rest of the night.

No wonder Mr O'Mahoney was missing, he thought bitterly. It was *her* – *she* was distracting him and leading him astray. And she was going to make himself late for the meeting – the frst time he had been tardy in all the years since the movement had been formed.

Anxious to be on his way, Tim-Pat waited for Rosaleen for over an hour, by which time the young constable was back at his post in the orchard, half-asleep with tedium and convinced that Captain Pollard had got it wrong and there *was* no secret society to which rebel grooms belonged.

When Tim-Pat, having exchanged a few curt words with the newly-returned Rosaleen, finally managed to set out on his travels again, the young constable was agreeably surprised but not particularly excited. Experience had taught him that Tierney's rides turned inevitably into irrelevant red herrings and although he automatically patted his gun as he went after the groom he felt no emotion other than relief that he could actually leave the orchard for the second time that day.

True, this time, Tierney took off at a great pace, cantering down Shelbourne Road and breaking into a gallop the minute he was on the country road that led to the Sweep's Cross. The young constable was hard put to it to keep up with his quarry, who, like no rider he had seen before, seemed grafted on to his horse.

There was only one small similarity between pursuer and pursued: Tim-Pat also carried a gun which he had purloined from the gun hoard of the rebels years before and carried with him at all times, hidden under his jacket. As he galloped along he could feel it thud against his ribs, a virile metal hand pressing against his body, offering power and support.

He was riding – as he always did – the half-bred hunter, which Cathal had long since given back to Rosaleen for use at Kincora, and, his body in unison with the horse, he felt not bitter but ecstatic, transported, by virtue of being in the saddle, into another, more glorious world.

He was quite oblivious to the fact that a less accomplished rider plodded on behind him as he rode through Parteen on the last leg of his journey to O'Brien's Bridge or even as he passed the gateway to Crag Liath and galloped the half-bred hunter on to the river bank.

In his ecstasy he forgot, for one vital minute, the erosion caused to the bank by the recent rains, and by the time he remembered his horse had slithered on the marshy ground so he had to pull to a halt.

At once he heard other hooves coming up behind him. Though he thought that it was someone from the movement approaching, his right hand went to his gun, pulling it out from under his jacket, pointing it as he swivelled the half-bred hunter round in a semi-circle, to face the rider at his rear.

It was *not* one of the Centres arriving as late as himself, nor a countryman out for a ride, but a member of the police. Following him. About to learn of the existence of the movement and Mr O'Mahoney's involvement in a rebel cause. Unless . . .

He aimed at the man's head, shooting at the precise moment the enemy shot at him. Both of them missed their targets.

Retreat. Into the grass on the Crag Liath side. Hope, in that way, that you will draw your enemy away from the secret room – save the men who are inside it.

Tim-Pat shot again. This time the bullet struck the belly of the policeman's horse, not, as he had intended, the head of the pursuer.

'Jesus!'

Pity for the animal, rearing in its agony, though he had no compassion for the policeman hurled to the ground.

He prepared to take aim again, but the enemy had recovered – was on his feet, out of the way of his injured horse, and his gun was still in his steady hand.

The confrontation had brought out the cooler, more calculating reactions of the professional hunter. Unlike Tim-Pat, the young constable knew that the body was a more certain target for a trained marksman than the head. Tim-Pat's right arm was still raised, leaving his body unguarded and at a three-quarter angle towards where the policeman stood. His trunk was the perfect target. The policeman took aim.

When the bullet penetrated his side, exactly where his assailant had intended, Tim-Pat felt no pain. His mind was numb to all else but the necessity to prohibit his enemy from finding the secret room. He did not know that a bullet had lodged in his abdomen although, if he had put his hand to the gaping hole, it would have been soaked with his blood.

Like the young policeman on the river bank, he prepared to shoot again.

Most of the men were already assembled in the room by the river when Cathal got to the meeting. He looked around at their faces, hating himself for having let them down by so foolish an act as allowing a notebook left in a teashop to fall into the hands of the police. A fine leader he had turned out to be – a worthy successor to his cousin John!

'Good to see you, Cathal,' John Roche said. 'You didn't see Tierney in the course of your travels, by any chance?'

'No – isn't he here yet?'

That was surprising and alarming: Tierney was always in time. Unless, of course, the young constable who had called at the farm had decided to pick him up.

'Not a sign of him. Odd.'

'It is,' Cathal said slowly.

Any minute now he would have to enlighten John Roche and all the rest of them about what had been going on. The door opened and two other men came in and sat at the back of the room. They were all present now – all except Tierney – waiting for him to talk, to give them inspiration to go on, to reinforce their hopes of freedom.

He took up a position facing them, steeling himself against what he had to say.

'Look,' he said, 'I'm not going to mince words with you. Something has happened which you are entitled to know about at once. It's my doing, but – '

They never heard the details of what he had done, hearing instead the first of several shots from somewhere near at hand.

Shock immobilized all of them. No one looked at the door – or at each other. For several moments, no one dared to speak.

Then Ned Lynch jumped to his feet.

'We must get out!'

'*No!*' Cathal hissed. 'Be still – every one of you. Don't let one man of you move an inch!'

'It's the police – of course it is,' Ned Lynch said querulously. 'They'll be in here shooting at us before – '

'Not necessarily,' said Cathal, cursing himself for having led them into danger out of his own stupidity. 'They're not going to burst in here shooting unless we draw attention to ourselves.'

'Then what do you want us to do?'

Ned Lynch was the only one who looked at him accusingly – the only one who was accurate in his views.

'I don't want you to do anything for the next half hour,' Cathal told them. 'I'm going to slip out myself. If I have not returned in that time – if there appears to be no further trouble, disperse one by one. All right? Give me a gun.'

Someone obliged.

'Is it loaded?'

'It is.'

Holding it ready to fire, Cathal prised the door open, peering round it. From that angle, he could not see down the bank. He squeezed out, closing the door behind him, frantically looking around.

He saw the wounded horse first, lying in its own blood upon the grass, but he did not spot Tim-Pat further off in the hollow, on the Crag Liath side of the bank. Then he noticed the policeman who had called to his farm a few hours earliers, but too late, for the constable had seen *him* seconds before – had already aimed, fired, struck him in the chest, narrowly missing his heart and dropping him to the ground . . .

Pain – excruciating pain. And yet –

Knowing that, from some other vantage point, another shot had been fired at the man who had aimed at him.

Pain – the worst he had ever known. And yet –

Knowing the man who had shot at him had been killed by someone else . . .

Dutifully, he attempted to crawl away from the river bank towards the fields in order to divert attention away from the secret room and not leave a trail of blood that would lead to the men who were there in case *his* constable had been accompanied by others who had not yet appeared on the scene . . .

His thoughts were getting fuzzy and his head was starting to swim as the pain in his chest redoubled. Yet he managed to half-turn his body so his head faced towards Crag Liath. Then, slowly and tortuously, biting his bottom lip to stop himself screaming with pain, he forced himself to crawl.

Tim-Pat's instinct was also to move away from the vicinity of the meeting for the same reason as Cathal, but he did not leave at once, for his pity-filled eyes were focused, not on the dead policeman but on the half-dead horse lying on the ground beside him writhing in agony from his wound. He moved in closer to the animal, raised his gun for the last time and shot it through the head.

Then, satisfied that the creature was out of its misery, he spoke to the half-bred hunter, telling it that they should head for home, cutting away through the marshy fields, avoiding the river bank, lest anyone see them go.

Mark Markham and Mrs Cash had spent a pleasant evening discussing the endless subject of Milliora's husbandless state, until Bawnie Kinsella came into the kitchen and began to express his opinions.

'If she was a poor woman, 'twould be easier for her,' Mrs Cash opined. 'We'd have had the matchmaker round here long ago, with one party giving his son maybe a slip of a pig, and the other his daughter a pair of blankets, to make a go of it, and set them up for life.'

'I thought Mrs O'Brien's father was dead,' said Bawnie, innocently. 'Mind you, 'tis not only the impoverished that do be making marriages. Will you contemplate the way Mr Andy Leahy married Miss Mary off to his uncle, after all those years she spent as a spinster. Didn't I hear he put a hand into his own pocket to make a dowry for her, after Miss Carmel set it up. Can you imagine a man bribing his own uncle to wed?'

It was too much for Mary Markham to take.

'*You* seem to listen to lots of rumours,' she said tartly. 'And half of them doorshey daurshey and not reliable one bit. I don't know what you're doing in my kitchen at all, it being so late at night.'

Bawnie could not resist it.

'Don't tell me you still have work to do,' he said impudently, getting up from his chair.

Mrs Markham visibly bristled.

'I've said it before and I'll say it again,' she said. 'There's a donkey in every job. And I'll say as well that 'twould suit me better if the two of you were gone.'

Criticizing the family – introducing the subject of matchmakers in relation to Mrs O'Brien! Another overworked woman, sitting upstairs on her own, sewing for all her worth at a time when others would be in their beds.

I'll just pop up and ask her if there's anything else she requires for the night, Mary thought, skirting around the two bicycles Milliora had recently purchased in anticipation of Daniel and Eugene's summer holidays.

Trundling up the stairs to the hall she thought, for a passing moment, that she heard a funny scrabbling sound coming from outside the front door.

Cats, she thought – or one of the farmyard dogs, settling down for the night at the front, the nerve of him, instead of at the back.

She was about to tap on the drawing-room door when the scrabbling started again.

Only it was not exactly scrabbling but more of a knocking sound, coming from the lower part of the door, as if someone very small indeed was asking to be admitted into the house.

Fairies! Mrs Markham thought, scared to death at the thought. The Good People – though they're not good at all, from everything I have heard. Oh, I knew we should have protected ourselves against them this very week when the Black-Poll heifer calved, by singeing the hair under her udder with the flame of a blessed candle, and passing it under her belly and across her back. And the first milk of the heifer should have been taken and poured out on the ground beneath a fairy tree, the way it always was until that new parish priest spoke to the milkers and told them that was not Christian belief, and fairies did not exist . . .

Another knock.

'*Mrs O'Brien!*' Mary called out, opening the drawing-room door without stopping to knock herself. 'Mrs O'Brien – quickly! Come!'

'What is it, Mrs Markham?' Milliora asked, looking at her with much disapproval. 'I'm surprised at you to be bursting into a room like that, without giving prior warning.'

'It's fairies!' Mary said, almost in tears at the thought. '*Fairies*, Mrs O'Brien, knocking at the front door, wanting to take the milk.'

'If that's all they're after they're welcome to come in and help themselves from the jug,' Milliora said coldly. 'Please control yourself, Mrs Markham. There are no such things as fairies, I can assure you. Didn't Father – '

'Maybe not, Mrs O'Brien, but there's one outside the door this minute, screeching to come in.'

'What nonsense!'

Milliora put her sewing down and cast a withering look at Mary before striding into the hall.

'*Fairies!*' Mary heard her say as she wrenched open the front door. 'Have you ever heard anything as foolish as – *Oh!*'

Fairies, thought Mary complacently, forgetting her terror in the light of being right. She peered into the hall and the light from the china lamp fell on the figure of a strange man, lying on top of the steps, bleeding . . .

'He's wounded,' Milliora said unnecessarily. 'Shot, by the looks of things. We'll have to get a doctor. Here – help me drag him in.'

'He's scarcely conscious. How did he manage to knock? And who do you think he could be?'

'A Fenian!' said Milliora crossly. 'Oh, you have no idea of what has been going on, Mary Markham, on my land with all this rebel nonsense. Still, we can't let the man die. The bullet must be removed and the wound dressed before he's handed over to the police and dealt with in the appropriate manner. I've got his shoulders. Can you take his legs?'

'Shall I get Bawnie Kinsella to go for the doctor now?' Mary asked when Cathal was in the hall.

'I suppose so.'

This is exactly what I wanted to avoid, Milliora thought – people being shot at Crag Liath, news getting round the estate that I have harboured rebels on the land for years without being aware of the fact. I'll be the laughing-stock of the country before tomorrow is out.

'First fetch some water and some rags so we can clean the wound and try to stop the bleeding,' she said to Mary. 'And blankets – we'll make a bed up here.'

'Yes, Mrs O'Brien.'

I must be mad to be looking after a rebel, Milliora

thought, sitting on the floor beside Cathal, cradling his head in the crook of her arm.

For what else could he be, to be getting himself shot and having to beg for help. Along with others of his men? Had they been in the secret room by the river and been surprised by the police?

'How many more of you were down there?' she asked the inert figure. 'How many more have been shot?'

To her surprise, Cathal opened his eyes and blinked, trying unsuccessfully to focus.

'Well?' she said in a gentler voice. 'What have you got to say?'

His lips moved, murmuring.

'*Rosaleen*,' she heard him whisper and then, as if to make quite sure she understood what he was trying to say he added a fraction more loudly, 'Rosaleen O'Brien . . .'

Then Mary Markham was back in the hall with the water and the rags. At least *she* had not heard what the wounded rebel said.

35

The half-bred hunter was cantering up to the Sweep's Cross when Tim-Pat felt the first pain.

Up till then he had been suffering from delayed reaction and he was surprised by the reminder that he had been shot in the side of the stomach, and piqued, wanting to protest that, in spite of what the young constable had tried to do to him, he had managed to get off free.

Then another wave of pain hit him, harder this time, so he winced and had to will himself to sit straight and retain his seat. He was beginning to suffer from loss of blood by then and with the pain came a dizzy attack as well.

By the time the half-bred hunter had reached the City Home workhouse, going into the last straight, Tim-Pat knew that he was swaying in the saddle.

'Will you look at him – he's going to fall off his horse!' The jeering and half-hopeful words of a grubby child.

But Tim-Pat did not fall off on the journey home. In his horsemanship lay much of his dignity, and his skill sustained him all the way. Or maybe part of the apparent ingenuity he showed in staying in the saddle was due too his strange rapport with animals, and the horse looked after him.

Rosaleen checked that Dermot was sound asleep before going into the garden to admire the fine sight the Judas tree made in full flower with each twig carrying its quota of purple-pink pea flowers. Unlike the house, the garden improved as the years went by although there was plenty to do in it still, and she saw that her attempt to grow a viburnum had failed because of heavy rains.

She wandered along the avenue towards the road, anxious to be out of the house for as long as possible, to keep her thoughts at bay.

On either side of the avenue gate she had once planted two Maythorn bushes, now fifteen feet in height, their heads growing together to form a pretty crimson-flowered arch. They, at least, looked after themselves, she thought.

'Good evening to you, Mrs O'Brien.'

'Oh – good evening, Father Moloney. Are you out on one of your walks?'

'I am,' said the parish priest in a more kindly voice than he had used during their previous conversation.

He looked slightly sheepish, too. Maybe he felt that he had been too hard on her on that occasion and would like to make amends.

'Is your husband well?' he wanted to know.

'As well as he can be. You know how things are with him.'

'Yes . . . Having a look round the garden, are you? I'm a keen gardener myself. I see you have a good specimen of syringa in the far bed. I have one of those myself.'

'It's nice, isn't it?' Rosaleen said, 'though I think I should do a better job thinning out the old stems after the flowers have gone this year . . .'

What a hypocrite I am, she thought, chatting away about gardening when all the time – But perhaps priests were hard to shock, when you came down to it, even if they could not understand.

'The syringa is one shrub that looks good for most of the year,' Father Moloney was saying, almost as if, through the subject of gardening, he was trying to find another way to reach her soul, as the chestnut half-bred clattered down the Ennis Road and turned in at the gate behind them.

Glancing round, Rosaleen thought that Tim-Pat must be drunk to be swaying like that in the saddle – not to acknowledge Father Moloney or herself as the chestnut cantered past.

Very drunk, which was unusual for Tim-Pat did not drink. And very pale. His eyes . . .

'Is that your groom?' Father Moloney asked. 'He looked under the weather to me. Is he the only person you have here at the house with you other than your husband?'

'Yes. But usually he's all right.'

'He doesn't look all right to me tonight. I think I'd better take a look at him to make sure you don't have any trouble with the fellow after I have gone.'

'Thank you,' she said. 'That would be kind of you. I can't imagine what has happened.'

'I see enough of that, I can assure you,' the priest said wryly, following her down the avenue. 'It's a terrible country for drink, Mrs O'Brien. I don't know what we can do to cure it.'

But she knew Tim-Pat's ailment had nothing to do with drink the minute they reached the yard and saw him, lying on the groud in a foetus position, holding his stomach, groaning in pain.

Father Moloney saw that, too – just as they both knew that Tim-Pat was very close to death.

Father Moloney reached him first and knelt on the ground beside him, surveying the open wound.

'Gunshot. Go and fetch what you think he needs to

make him comfortable. There's no point in trying to dress the wound. You'll be all right, my son. You needn't have any fear. God is with you.'

'Should I not go for a doctor?'

The priest shook his head, mouthing, 'It's too late,' before turning back to the groom.

But Tim-Pat, too, seemed to have accepted that life was running out of him by the time Rosaleen had fetched water and a blanket and a pillow for his head. As she ran back into the yard she heard him say, 'Father, I want to confess.'

'Yes. Would you take a sip of water?'

Rosaleen held the glass to his lips and although he drank from it he seemed oblivious of her presence then and when she slipped the pillow under his head.

'Stay there with the water, Mrs O'Brien, in case he needs it again. Bless me, Father . . .'

'. . . for I have sinned.'

I should not be here, Rosaleen thought fiercely – I should not be present when Tim-Pat speaks of the things that he has done. That is, if he is able to speak again.

Tim-Pat's face was ashen and what energy he had left he seemed to be using to tense against the pain.

He will die before he has the time to confess, she thought, oddly relieved, and just before he does Father Moloney will touch him five times, touching the contact points of the five senses, as if he had oil of chrism with him and was offering Extreme Unction. And what is the matter with me to be worrying about hearing what he has done in his life, for it's bound to be nothing at all in comparison to my sins.

'Father, I have killed a man – myself and Master Dermot . . .'

'Yes, my son – go on.'

Go on and describe the plot to murder Harry Fielding – to train Clasai to trample him to death. In spite of his condition, Tim-Pat managed to tell the story in detail, leaving nothing out.

'It was *my* idea, Father. *I* thought of it. Master Dermot only came along with what I planned.'

As if that was not enough.

Instead of the yard and the dying man and the priest, Rosaleen could see herself riding on to the Ballyneety road, looking for Dermot and Harry. Seeing the four elm trees that fraction of a second before she saw Dermot, riding the half-bred hunter up ahead.

And she was urging Fear Gorta into a canter, going after Dermot, knowing that something was wrong . . .

('Where *were* you all this time? Why are you riding so fast?')

'A short cut,' Dermot had said. 'Easier for Harry – we went over to the left . . .' Speaking in the high, cold and seemingly unemotional voice that had startled her at the time.

Now, as then, the thought inside her: why take a short cut? A hare runs round in circles – a fox runs straight ahead. Why move to the left? Why did I not use my head instead of becoming confused? Why did I not realize that the anger Dermot carried inside him was dangerous enough to make him kill?

'In the name of the Father and of the Son and of the Holy Ghost. Amen. It's all right, my son – all right.'

'You must say nothing of this to anyone, Mrs O'Brien. Say to yourself that if you did, you would be breaking the Confessional seal. It is better like that. He's dead now and in God's hands and there's no point in speaking of the thing that was done.'

'But we'll have to tell the police.'

'Oh we'll have to do that all right. He died of internal bleeding, of loss of blood caused by a bullet wound. That's a matter for the authorities. But it has nothing to do with the killing of Harry Fielding. You had no suspicion of any of this? You never thought that it might have been guilt that caused your husband to lose his mind?'

'I should have done. The evidence was right in front of me only I failed to see it, fool that I am. I was married to a murderer, Father, and I didn't even know.'

'You must not attempt to judge your husband, Mrs O'Brien. That is for God to do,' he said. 'Your duty is to look after him in this life and God will look after him in the next. Stay here now with him and I'll go and get the police.'

'God would still want me to stay with my husband after what he has done?'

'You *must* look after him,' he said. 'He's a *duine-le-Dia* and God will forgive him, even if you cannot.'

Duine-le-Dia – child of God. The charitable way of describing the mentally ill, no matter what they had done.

And the gentleness in Father Moloney's voice as he spoke of Dermot – the love he had shown towards Tim-Pat Tierney just before he died, in comparison to the coldness in his grey eyes when he had suggested that she resign from her position at the League.

For, of course, he suspected that she and Cathal were lovers. Others did, she knew, in spite of their efforts to be discreet. There was love in their eyes at all times when they were together, and you could not blot that out to smother the gossips of Limerick.

A duine-le-Dia – God's child.

524

'The Gaelic League . . . has no place for the likes of you.'

Only in Ireland, she thought, could the sin of murder rate lower than the awful sin of love.

'A surprising business altogther,' Captain Pollard said. 'Mind you, I'm glad you called me out of bed, Father. This was something I had to attend to myself.'

'It struck me as important,' Father Moloney agreed. 'I must say Mrs O'Brien and I were surprised enough when the poor man came riding in wounded.'

'You had no idea that Tierney could be involved in any kind of revolutionary movement, Mrs O'Brien?'

'We knew he hated the English,' she said. 'That was all.'

'I'm surprised that your sister-in-law – that's how you're related – to Mrs O'Brien of Crag Liath, isn't it? – I'm surprised *she* never mentioned her suspicions about him to you. After all, she wrote to us about them.'

'Milly did? Milly wrote to you saying she suspected Tim-Pat Tierney of being involved in a rebel movement?'

'She did. And we put a man on to him to keep track of his movements. You saw no sign of *him*? No. Well, if he hasn't reported by the morning we'll have to instigate a search for him. Perhaps Mrs O'Brien of Crag Liath could give us some further information. Tell me, by the look of his horse, did it seem as if your man had ridden far?'

'It was in a bit of a lather. I'd say he had, now I come to think of it. But I can't imagine from where.'

Captain Pollard smiled at her benevolently. 'Thank you for being so helpful, Mrs O'Brien. It's been a bad night for you and I gather you have your own troubles.

We'll have the body removed at once and taken to the mortuary. There will be a post-mortem in due course and we will have to ask you to give evidence, I'm afraid, but I'll be in touch with you about that. Goodnight to you. I hope you manage to get some sleep after all that's happened tonight.'

Vain hope. When the officers and priest had dispersed Rosaleen sat in the drawing-room thinking about Milliora and the friendship that they shared, on and off, for so long, knowing that for too long she had envied and later disliked her old schoolfriend. Had hated her, deep down, for having had the power to take the twins away and put them to school in England. Although I have tried to suppress that thought, she admitted silently – tried to bury it in smug pity for Milly, saying to myself how lucky I was by comparison, in being properly loved.

I've tried to tell myself that it did not really matter that Daniel and Eugene are being temporarily educated at her expense in a foreign land because I will soon be able to get on top of that situation by saving the money to reverse it, bringing them back to be schooled by the Jesuits in Naas.

Making use of her while fearing her power. And all the time not knowing that it was *my* husband who took love and life from her, and had them trampled to death at a hunt.

'Rosaleen?'

'Yes, Dermot,' she said, looking at the lithe figure standing in the doorway.

In the dim light it was perfectly possible to believe that he was a normal, handsome man.

'Why are you out of bed?'

'I'm looking for you,' he said pitably. 'I came to look for you.'

'Then go back to bed,' Rosaleen said without compassion, 'for you have found me and you may as well get used to sleeping on your own this night since I will never sleep beside you again.'

'Go back to bed?' he said vaguely, unsure of what she meant.

But *I* am sure, where *you* are concerned, she thought, watching him turn and obey. I owe you nothing – no more wifely loyalty and compassion and care – not after what you have done to my friend.

'You must look after him,' Father Moloney had urged. 'He's a *duine-le-Dia* and God will forgive him, even if you cannot.'

Maybe one day I will be able to forgive him, she thought, even if that seems impossible tonight, but I will not look after him. No matter what you say to me of duty, I'm going to have him committed to a mental home.

For the sake of the twins, who should be able to return in the holidays to a normal home.

For my sake, that I can live.

For why should the three of us be punished for the sin committed by a man who has escaped the consequences and is now protected by his madness and labelled child of God?

Rosaleen was still awake when a cock began to crow.

Tim-Pat's death presented practical problems – extra work to be done, horses to be fed and exercised and groomed, water to be drawn, weeds to be taken out of the garden, the yard and stables swept.

She had only succeeded in feeding and watering Fear Gorta and the half-bred hunter when she heard a carriage draw up in front of the house.

It was barely six o'clock in the morning. No one in

their sane senses would pay a call so early, she thought,
shutting Fear Gorta's stable door and hurrying round
the side of the house to find who the eccentric visitor
was.

'Mrs O'Brien?'

'Bawnie Kinsella!' she said. 'What are you doing
here? Is it Daniel and Eugene? Is there something the
matter with them?'

'No. Only herself wants you to come out.' In his
innocence, Bawnie added, ''Tis nothing to do with
yourself at all. But I must tell you now, Mrs O'Brien,
that there are quare things that do be going on at Crag
Liath.'

36

Queer things – like the presence of Jamie Keegan at Crag Liath so early in the morning, opening the door to her and welcoming her in as if (but surely that could not be the case?) he was Milly's lover?

Like the fact that Milly was not neat and tidy, and her hair was in a mess.

Like the furtive way both of them looked around the grounds before leading her into the house.

'Milly, what's happened here that you sent for me so early in the morning?'

'Rebels!' Milliora said darkly. 'Can you believe that there was a shoot-out on my land last night? One of the Fenians – or whatever it is they're called these days – got himself shot and crawled all the way up to the front door from the river so we had to have him tended.'

So that was it, Rosaleen concluded weakly, following Milliora into the drawing-room and collapsing into a chair. She knows of a connection between these rebels and Tim-Pat. That's why she sent for me.

'He's dead,' she said flatly. 'Tim-Pat Tierney's dead. He managed to make it home. Father Moloney was with him at the end to hear his Confession and afterwards we had to call the police.'

'Tierney?' Milliora surprisingly asked. 'So he got killed, did he? Well, that's no great loss. Far more important – what did you say to the police?'

'There was nothing much I could tell them, except about his death and the fact that he had been shot.

They knew all about him, Milly. You know that. You were the one who wrote to them saying you suspected him of being involved in a rebel movement.'

'So I did!' said Milliora. 'So I did. What else did the police have to say?'

'They said one of their men was missing and if he hadn't turned up by the morning they'd have to instigate a search. They thought maybe you might be able to give them further information so I suppose that they'll come out.'

'We were frightened of that, weren't we, Milly?' Jamie Keegan said inexplicably.

A conspiratorial glance passed between Jamie and Milly, and Milly said, 'Jamie, you'd better leave us for a while. We need to talk alone.'

'I'll be downstairs when you need me,' Jamie said, tender-eyed, looking at Milliora.

As the old photograph of Tom O'Brien looked out at her from the silver frame.

'What a night this had been, for both of us, I imagine,' Milliora said. 'Rosaleen, I must come to the point at once about the man who has been shot. His name is Cathal O'Mahoney and I know about his relationship with you.'

'Where is he? Is he going to die?'

'He's not going to die,' Milliora said. 'Wait. I'll tell you the whole story.'

'When I first saw Mr O'Mahoney I was going to send for the doctor. But a doctor would be honour bound to report a matter like that to the police and the next thing we would have them all over the place, asking questions and going down to the secret room. So after Mary Markham and I cleaned Mr O'Mahoney's wound and settled him down, I rode out to look for Jamie.

He's as good as any doctor in terms of his qualifications and he has the added advantages of being both unscrupulous, discreet and dependable.

'He rode back with me and had the bullet out of Mr O'Mahoney in no time, telling me that he had a lucky escape with it missing his lungs and only succeeding in crushing one of his ribs. Painful, and he's lost a lot of blood, but he'll mend in time.

'Mind you, Mr O'Mahoney did not know that when he started to talk about you. I suppose he thought he might be dying and he wanted to make sure I got a message to you, saying how much he loved you and was there any hope that I would bring the two of you together before –

'I'm putting up with no nonsense, I said to him. I know that you're an agitator and that you have been holding secret meetings on my land and I told him exactly what I thought of those kinds of carryings-on. You needn't think you made a complete fool of me, I said, down in the secret room.

'There will be no more of those meetings, for the police are on to them and until he was foolish enough to get himself shot he was intending to go to America to stop out of the way until the commotion had died down. Quite right, too, I said to him. There's no place in Ireland for your kind of organization, perpetrating outrages and trying to take the land out of the hands of decent people.

'Shooting indiscriminately, I said to him – which was when I managed to extract another piece of information out of him. There was a dead policeman, he told me, or a badly wounded one, down on the river bank.

'Something must be done about that, I said to Jamie. We can't have the poor creature suffering if he's alive,

531

and if he's dead we can't have his body discovered on my land.

'Indeed we can't, Jamie said.

'So what are you going to do about it, I asked him. He may be heavy to carry, I said. If it's dead he is you'll have to think of somewhere else to put him – somewhere the police will find him before his body is decomposed and his poor mother made more distressed than she has to be. We need two trusted men to help us, I said. So I went out and got a hold of Bawnie Kinsella and Liam Lenihan and I swore the two of them to silence. It's more than your jobs are worth, I said, if you talk about tonight. And then the four of us went down together to the river bank to see what was going on, leaving Mary Markham alone with the patient.

'Soon enough we found a dead horse – and its rider lying dead, too, beside it on the ground. Poor boy, he was only nineteen or twenty. Oh, I was mad then, I can tell you, with Mr O'Mahoney and his lot, to be causing innocent deaths.

'But we had to deal with the bodies. The horse was more of a problem to us than the dead policeman, it being so heavy to move.

'We could try to shove it into the river, said Liam Lenihan.

'But that would leave the problem of the blood – everywhere – so much of it. Even if we tried to wash it away – a futile thing to attempt at night – there would always be some stains on the grass, and how could I explain those away to the police if, after all, they were to come out this way on the trail of the young constable, and start to search the land?

'But I found a solution. You can come back here with a sharp knife, I told Liam Lenihan, and cut the dead horse up into sizeable pieces, the way it can be given for fodder to the County Limerick Hounds. It's too late in the season to be feeding them on horsemeat the way you do when they're hunting – you and I know full well that their blood would get over-heated if you did that during the summer and they'd fight. But what do the police in this country know about hunting, I said to myself, keeping my fingers crossed. We'll tell them one of my horses died of natural causes and they'll never question that. And as soon as the light came up and it was possible to see the trail of blood left by Mr O'Mahoney the meat could be taken up across it so the police could be deceived. And in the meantime Mary Markham would have washed the steps and the hall of blood.

'There was no blood coming anymore out of the dead policeman, so we didn't have to worry about leaving a trail from him. Bawnie and Liam carried him up to the house. Get the carriage, I said to Jamie, and take him in towards Limerick and leave him as close to the city as you can without anyone seeing you, the way he'll be found before tomorrow is out.

'We were hard at it all night, I can tell you – Bawnie Kinsella, too, for I had other work for him. There was always the possibility – a certainty from what you've been telling me – that the police might be on our doorstep early in the morning. We couldn't do anything else . . .'

'But, Milly, you were the one who initially called the police,' Rosaleen said.

'I wanted them to deal with the rebels who were meeting on my lands,' Milliora replied. 'Then I realized that I did not want word getting out about that and spreading around the estate. But that was before I knew about you and Mr O'Mahoney. As soon as he told me he loved you I understood that I had to look after him above all else and protect him from the police. But that should be obvious to you, Rosaleen – aren't you my greatest friend?'

'No matter what he has done? After all you have said – all you think about nationalism and the Gaelic League and the stupidity of speaking Irish? In spite of the way you feel about revolutionary movements?'

Milliora said impatiently, 'Of course – although I still think all those things. I haven't changed my mind one whit. Don't you want to see him?'

'Cathal? You mean – he's still here – in the house?'

'Where else would he be? And why did you think I sent for you so early in the morning? Oh, don't worry – the police won't find him. He's not only well looked after but well hidden. Come.'

'But where is he?'

'You'll see,' said Milliora mysteriously, leading Rosaleen down the stairs towards the kitchen, stopping at the boot cupboard door.

'In *here* – but there's only boots and shoes.'

'That's what you think – and that's what the police will think if Bawnie has done his work well enough. See this wall – the one Daniel fell through on his third birthday? Bawnie's replaced the partition so it can open like a door. *And* I've had him go down through the tunnel – it exists all right – Daniel was quite correct in all he said – and reinforce the wall into the secret room so if the police do find it they won't think there's a passage leading out of it to the house.'

'You've thought of everything.'

But Milliora had opened the new partition door and Rosaleen was able to see a tunnel veering away behind it and, by the light of the candle on a small table, the figure of a man lying on a bed . . .

534

'Cathal!'

'He may be still asleep.'

. . . lying on his back, with his eyes closed, and his long thin hands stretched across the blanket.

'Milly, are you *sure* he's all right? He looks so sick and pale and – '

'I told you – he'll be fine. Now you're here *you* can look after him. Mary Markham and I have quite enough to do without nursing men who are foolish enough to get shot!'

'Yes,' Rosaleen whispered. 'Milly – I suppose someone should look after Dermot for the time being. I've made up my mind. I'm going to have him committed to a mental home.'

'I see,' Milliora said and even in her lowered voice the disapproval was strong. 'Poor Dermot – '

'You don't know – ' Rosaleen began.

And must not know, said a voice in her mind. It's better like that, Father Moloney had said. There's no point in speaking of the thing that was done – and it will not bring Harry back – only destroy the image of Dermot, brother of Tom, descendant of Brian Boru, High King of Ireland, in Milliora's eyes, prepetrating hate. And there has been enough hate. The cycle has got to stop.

'I'm sorry, Milly,' she said, 'but that's the way I feel now. It's just not possible for me to look after Dermot anymore.'

'Then I will send Liam Lenihan in to stay with him until you have made suitable arrangements,' Milliora said, stepping through the partition door and out of the door beyond, and it seemed to Rosaleen that the ghost of a servant girl and a man who had killed for love on those stairs made way and let her go.

* * *

'Rosaleen,' he said, half-bemused, 'I can't believe you're here.'

'I'll stay until you're well.'

'Even so, I must talk to you at once,' Cathal said, waking up properly and reaching out for her hand. 'You must have been told by now what happened last night. You must have some idea of my involvement with a post-Fenian movement, a rebel army that was set up with the object of taking our freedom by force.'

'Was that why you went to America at Christmas – to raise money for this army and why, before all this happened, you were planning to go again?'

'Of course. I felt I couldn't tell you. Are you angry with me?'

'Not at all. Only concerned that you have been hurt.'

'That's nothing,' he said. 'But when I can leave here – that's what matters to us. I'm going to have to go to America, at least for a year or two, to get out of the way of the police. My fault – I did something stupid, but that's neither here nor there now. There are so many things going round in my mind. It's difficult to concentrate. Tell me, before I go on, did someone die because of me? There was a policeman – I remember that. Somebody shot him, I think.'

'Tim-Pat Tierney,' she said. 'But the policeman must have already shot him. He died last night at our house.'

'Tierney's dead . . . And the others? Do you know if the others got out of the room?'

'Nobody else has been shot, at least I don't think that they have. Down at the river it was only the policeman and his horse and Milly has dealt with that.'

'She would, wouldn't she?' He smiled at that and then, frowning, added, 'It's bad about Tierney. He was a particularly loyal man.'

'Yes,' she said, 'Tim-Pat Tierney was loyal. To Dermot, as well as to your movement. Too loyal –'

'If it was not for Dermot you could come to America with me,' Cathal said. 'If you could only see sense about having your husband committed to a home . . .'

'I have seen sense,' said Rosaleen. 'I've thought about what you said in that connection and I think you're right.'

'Then come with me. It's a golden opportunity to start again and make a new life. We could never do that in Ireland. As long as Dermot lives we would be at the mercy of gossip and surmise in this society. In America, no one will know what we are unless we choose to tell them.'

'God will know.'

'Then let God be our judge instead of the Catholic Church. It's only in name that you have a husband – the mind of the man is gone. God is not that harsh.'

'We'll talk about it again. I have something else to tell you. Something I nearly told you on Holy Island –'

'Rosaleen, come to America with me,' Cathal said. 'We'll live there – happily – as man and wife. You know full well I love you.'

How can I refuse to go to America with you, Rosaleen thought. As long as we are together I will not face the void.

'I do not understand why the knives are not kept sharpened,' Milliora said at lunch-time, when Cathal was asleep. 'You have a perfectly good knife-grinder in the kitchen, Mrs Markham. Therefore why can you not use it?'

'I'm sorry, Mrs O'Brien. It won't happen again.'

'And where is the calves' feet jelly?'

We are women in our thirties, Rosaleen thought, and yet at the back of my mind, whenever I am with Milly, I nurture a childish fear of her maternal disapproval. With Cathal, I am free. I can say exactly what I wish knowing that I will encounter no fences in his mind, and yet, with Milly, after all these years and in spite of her incredible kindness towards me, I worry lest the palisades will prove to be too high.

'I have something to tell you, Milly,' she said when Mary Markham had gone out of the room in search of the calves' feet jelly, 'something you may not like. I'm afraid it's going to shock you.'

'Good heavens, what on earth is it?' Milliora said, startled.

'Milly, I'm going to have another child,' said Rosaleen. 'Cathal is the father.'

In the infinitesimal pause that followed this statement, Rosaleen held her breath.

For Milly – the very woman who had said of Katharine O'Shea that her behaviour was disgraceful – of course, she is going to be shocked. Condoning an illegitimate baby was far from the airy-fairy acceptance that two people were lovers . . .

'But Rosaleen, it's wonderful news. I hope it is a girl. What made you think I'd be shocked?'

No palisades. None at all. Not even the smallest twig. All she could see on Milly's face was delight at her unexpected news.

'But there was a time when you would have been shocked,' persisted Rosaleen perversely. 'After all, you're Dermot's sister-in-law. You're such a good Catholic, Milly – much better than myself, as we know. Why are you not prepared to condemn me for being pregnant by another man?'

'Good heavens!' Milliora said again. 'You're *looking*

for condemnation! But you're right. I used to be self-righteous. I thought that was the way to be until I met Harry and he taught me to be better than that, not to make judgements about love or its consequences – to leave all that to God. So, you see, all I can think of is that I wish I was in your position, that I was going to have a child. You've always been so lucky, Rosaleen. I've always envied you.'

From where she was sitting Rosaleen could see the green land of Crag Liath stretching away to the blue-black hills. Two thousand acres of some of Ireland's richest land. The sideboard was laden with silver. They were eating from Belleek plates.

And there was also Wimborne Manor – more gracious than Crag Liath, if not as deeply loved.

Money. Power.

'I've always envied you.'

While I lost myself in the nonsense of being – feeling second best.

'I can't imagine why you envied me, Milly,' Rosaleen said, luxuriating in the new freedom of being able to speak her mind. 'Did it never strike you that you could be envying a selfish, introspective fool who was incapable of seeing the good solid wood amongst the trees?'

Liam Lenihan was not sure which prospect was the more daunting: standing watch over Dermot or telling Mrs O'Brien that he was too frightened to look after a mad man.

Having concluded that no one could be as formidable as Milliora when vexed, he was delighted to find, on arrival at Kincora, that Dermot was sound asleep in his bed, and not a peep out of him even when, backing away, Liam fell over a black cat that had followed him mewling into the bedroom.

Liam went downstairs, made himself a strong pot of tea and sat down for a rest. It was not until he was awoken by his own snores that he realized he must have dozed off.

It was getting on for five o'clock. The day was nearly over. With a guilty start he remembered that he was supposed to be keeping an eye on Master Dermot, who might well be awake and even now out of the house without a by your leave to his keeper.

'Master Dermot,' Liam called out, fearful of what Mrs O'Brien might say if such a thing had happened.

There was no reply, and no sign of Dermot downstairs either when Liam went to look, so he trudged upstairs again to the door of the master bedroom.

'Are you there, Master Dermot?'

His knock sounded louder than he had intended. It reverberated through the silent house. But there was no answer.

Or maybe there was and, as usual, he had failed to hear it.

Going unbidden into the room, he smiled. It was all right – Dermot was there fast asleep in the same position he had been in earlier on. There was no need for alarm.

And no need for fear either. Wasn't the poor fellow only as harmless as a fly crawling on the wall.

The only strange thing was his stillness, the way he did not seem to have moved.

Or to breathe . . .

'Master Dermot!' Liam was shouting now, he knew it, but the man in the bed did not react.

And then Liam knew. Knew for certain that if he were to touch Master Dermot's body it would be icy cold and stiff.

Knew that Dermot would never speak again.

What could have happened to him? The empty bottle of laudanum on the table beside the bed surely could not have had anything to do with his death. For wasn't that only a medicine that made you feel better when you were sick.

'Mother of God, help us,' Liam whispered. And then: 'But what am I going to do?'

Two bodies in two days. How could anyone cope with that?

Except, of course, Mrs O'Brien, who could cope with any kind of contingency.

Liam had never moved so fast. Before five minutes were over he was on the road for Crag Liath.

And still Cathal slept.

'I suppose you're trying to make up your mind what is the sensible thing to do,' Milliora said, in the afternoon. 'Whether you should go to America with Mr O'Mahoney, the way he's suggested, or whether you should stay here in Ireland.'

'Something like that.'

'To my way of thinking you can't possibly drag Daniel and Eugene out of school and take them over there without having a settled home. And after all, to be completely practical, we don't know that Mr O'Mahoney would want to have Dermot's children over in America with him. You haven't discussed that aspect of things with him yet. If you're set on committing Dermot to a mental home – '

'I am.'

Rosaleen rose and went to the window. Liam Lenihan was galloping down the avenue and coming into her line of vision, but she hardly noticed.

'Then you should let Kincora,' Milliora said. 'It isn't as if you're entitled to sell the house, it being in

Dermot's name, and you'll get a good price for it every month and the money can go into the bank. That gives you two clear alternatives. You either go to America with Mr O'Mahoney while I keep watch over the twins – bringing them back here for the holidays and so on. Or you move in here with me and let people in Limerick think that the new baby is Dermot's. If I were you – '

'But you're not me, are you, Milly,' Rosaleen broke in. 'And I've already made up my mind what I'm going to do.'

Milliora blinked. She was blushing. She looked confused, confronted with a new thought so foreign to her nature, so breathtaking in its complexity that she could not cope with the ideas it conjured up.

'Well – maybe you *do* want to work it out on your own,' said Milliora slowly. 'Maybe I shouldn't – ? Could it be that I have interfered enough in your life as it is, Rosaleen O'Brien?'